Midnight at Sea

MIDNIGHT AT SEA

a novel in reverse

by

Hoyt Rogers

with

Artemisia Vento
and
Frank Báez

SPUYTEN DUYVIL
NEW YORK CITY

ACKNOWLEDGMENTS

Midnight at Sea is the second volume of *The Caribbean Trilogy*. In different versions, passages of the trilogy have appeared in *The New England Review*, *AGNI*, *Eunoia Review*, *The Summerset Review*, *The Writing Disorder*, *Axon*, *The Bitter Oleander Review*, *Offcourse*, *The Dillydoun Review*, *The Courtship of Winds*, *The Fortnightly Review*, *Isla Abierta*, *The Raven's Perch*, *spoKe*, *The Light Ekphrastic*, and *The Literary Review*. My sincere thanks to the editors of these publications for supporting my work over the years. I also owe a debt of gratitude to Jonathan Galassi, Siri Hustvedt, Edmund White, Paul Auster, Marco Genovesi, Robin Saikia, Frank Báez, Nicholas Callaway, Ricardo Bernardo, Anne Davenport, Nellie Barletta, Pablo Báez, Amy Bernstein, Michele Casagrande, Lena Papadaki, Peter Bernstein, Annalyn Swan, Esther Allen, Bishan Samaddar, Marc Vincenz, and Anthony Seidman, who encouraged me along the way. For information about my other books, please visit hoytrogers.com.

© 2025 Hoyt Rogers
ALL RIGHTS RESERVED
ISBN 978-1-963908-79-4

Library of Congress Control Number: 2025944618

No part of this book may be reproduced in any written, electronic, recorded, or photocopied form without the written permission of the publisher and the author, except for the use of brief quotations in a book review.

This is a work of fiction. All names, characters, places, and incidents are figments of the imagination. Any resemblance to actual persons, living or dead—or to entities, events, or locales—is entirely fortuitous.

Published by Spuyten Duyvil; maps and cover images by Mary Heebner; book and jacket design by John Balkwill, Isa Benedetti, and T Thilleman; supplemental editing for volume one by Joan Tapper.

Midnight at Sea, first edition, ISBN 978-1-963908-79-4, printed in the United States. Available directly from the publisher, or through Ingram, Amazon, and bookshop.org.

For R, E, and all the voyagers
who seek their 'untold want' on the open sea

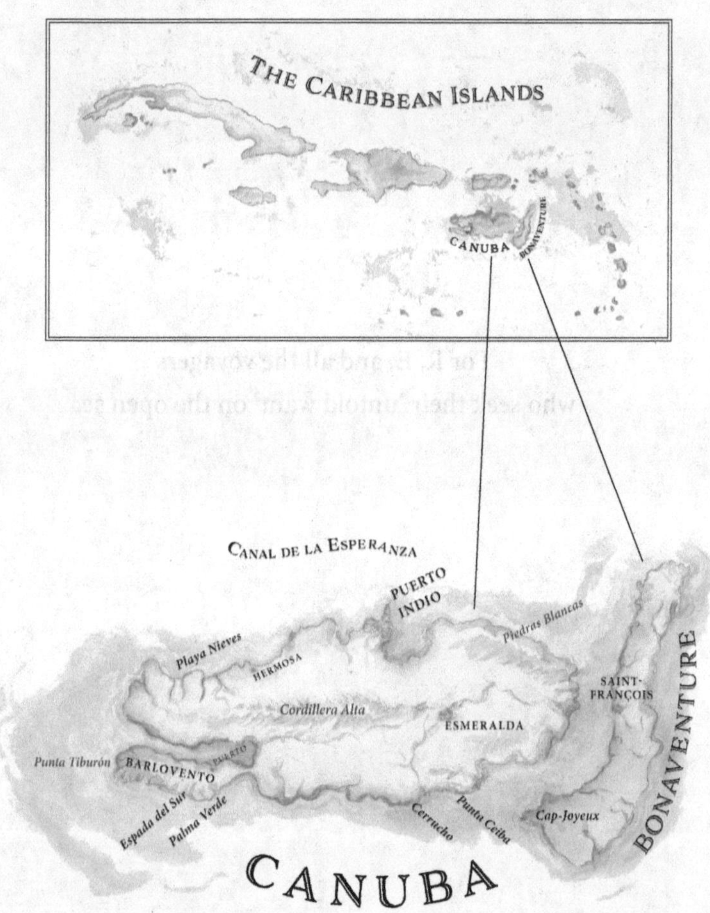

THE CARIBBEAN ISLANDS
CANUBA
BONAVENTURE
CANAL DE LA ESPERANZA
PUERTO INDIO
Piedras Blancas
Playa Nieves
HERMOSA
SAINT-FRANÇOIS
Cordillera Alta
ESMERALDA
Punta Tiburón
BARLOVENTO
PUERTO
BONAVENTURE
Espada del Sur
Palma Verde
Cerrucho
Punta Ceiba
Cap-Joyeux
CANUBA

Though it stands fully on its own, Midnight at Sea *is the second volume of* The Caribbean Trilogy. *Like its predecessor,* Midnight at Sea *draws on notebooks I received from a Sicilian journalist, Artemisia Vento, on the eve of her departure for an unnamed country in Asia. She was determined to live out the rest of her days in a cloistered retreat—whether Buddhist, Christian, Vedic, interfaith, or secular, she wouldn't reveal. Discrepantly, she also spoke of an 'environmental hermitage,' far from any contact with mankind. 'You're a translator and editor,' she said. 'These scribbles are a farewell gift to you. Make of them what you will.'*

Among her jottings, I found a lengthy narration. When pressed, she claimed it wasn't autobiographical, merely a record of 'wayward fantasies' she now disowned. In the pages that follow, various voices recount their story in reverse chronological order—which she identified as the natural flow of recollection. 'Tragedies and comedies take place in the course of time,' she explained; 'at some point, they happen to us all. But they're never the final chord: we constantly revise and transform the past. Our dead survive within us in the present. Memory is the surest form of resurrection.'

If readers choose to adopt a linear chronology, they could start with the last of the monologues in each section, and thread their way back to the first. Or they could skip from episode to episode, as in the randomness of passing thoughts. In that sense, this foreword might be an afterword—or simply an 'interword.' Where germane, I have reprised certain portions of the prologue and the epilogue from the previous volume of the trilogy—though in large part, the texts in Midnight at Sea *are entirely new.*

Artemisia replaces quotation marks with periods, colons, or em dashes framed by blanks. Dialogues hover between the said and the unsaid. Her ambiguity was deliberate. 'Half our message is conveyed by our gestures and our faces,' she remarked. Because of her checkered background, her prose mixes British usage with American. Many of her notes are in other languages, ancient and modern, or in multilingual creoles and dialects. In translating those passages, I've kept a few key terms from the originals, as brushstrokes of linguistic coloring; but I've surrounded them with Anglo equivalents, so readers needn't worry they're missing a link.

The characters splice their mother tongues with English at will—just as occurs throughout the modern world, from Chile to China. I agree with Artemisia that hybrids like Spanglish and Germglish are idioms in their own right. Wherever they come up, I've slanted them heavily towards '-glish,' for smoother reading. To avoid other road bumps, I've limited the capitals and exclamation marks of 'emphatic' speakers to a minimum. Most importantly, I've ensured the authenticity of the island voices—under-represented much too often—by working closely with the noted Caribbean author, Frank Báez. When the satire flirts with stereotypes, it's self-parody: the cast making light of their own personae. Above all, we should bear in mind that—regrettably— ethnic, appearance, and gender sensitivity had not even reached today's low standard back in the nineties, three decades ago.

Artemisia urged me to emend her writings as I saw fit, or throw them away; in any case, she asked me to destroy them in the end. If I recycled them as fiction, she told me to use my own 'byline'—an allusion to her former career. She also wanted me to retain the copyright; she sincerely wished to 'vanish from the world once and for all.' I've preferred to acknowledge her by a pseudonym, 'Artemisia Vento.' Vento, or 'Wind,' is a traditional Sicilian surname. The painter she most admired was Gentileschi; the wind was what she wanted to become.

—HR

MIDNIGHT AT SEA

Better to sink in boundless deeps, than float on vulgar shoals; and give me, ye gods, an utter wreck, if wreck I do.
—Melville

LAMIA

2001-1991

There's nothing left but memories. I keep going backwards in time, Chiara, to when we first paired up—ten years before my breakdown ruined my career. All right, all right, I can 'face the music.' There's no future for me now, but at least I have the past. They say your life unreels before your eyes when you're about to die. Since all my hopes are gone, that must be what's happening. Thank God I have you. People always think I'm a dragon lady; but they should know that even dragons have a heart, and mine is yours. If I blast you with flames, if I bite off your head, it's because I've always been afraid to say those three simple words: the ones that start with I, L, and Y.

At least the LESSER musicians can't blame me for hurting them—much as they try, the two-bit bitches, bastards, and skunks. Calderón and the orchestra get vetted by a Latino version of Sol Hurok from Miami, who's in the audience the night of my fiasco. From September through October, they do their Millennium Tour with a stand-in, a Venezuelan cellist who's like a noodle on drugs. She can't play Horacio's concerto half as well as me—who COULD? Anyway, the piece is too demanding for most listeners. Let's face it, most of them are DUMB.

To wow the crowds, our wannabe Patton and his troops fall back on a bubbly suite, the *Carnaval Canubano* by Lorenzo Prats. That pendejo Prats: what a bozo! In island syncopation, he jazzes up the brass with percussion and cutesy folk-tunes. He's been trying to promote the cambuca, our answer to the salsa and merengue. He says he wants to give our Afro-Spanish beat 'classical crossover rank'—like what Piazzolla did for the tango in Argentina, or what Villa-Lobos did for the sertanejo in Brazil. GOOD LUCK on that! It's all a crock of mierda to me. I'll stick to the three B's: Bach, Beethoven, and Brahms.

When it's over I'm angry with myself, angry with the WORLD, and what's left for me now but to hang around bars and tell my sorry tale to anybody who'll humor me: yeah, while we knock back a liter or two of Ron Real. I have to admit, our Canuban rum beats Bacardi hands down. Here you are, Chiara, with your sad little pony-face, letting me jabber for hours.

Chiara's not a Sicilian name, you keep reminding me: it was your godmother's name, and she's from Padova. But it fits you to a tee, since you're always 'clear' and calm. You're so good to me, better than I deserve! I have to thank you for forgiving me, for letting bygones be bygones. When I think of the horrible things I did to you, I feel ashamed. But you're such a masochist, maybe YOU should thank ME.

Anybody but you, I can't scare up much sympathy, not even when I pay for the drinks. My catty remarks about my colleagues have caught up with me. Karma chameleon— isn't that a pop song by some 'ducky' Brit? They want to walk all over me, and kick me now that I'm down. It's not just the musicians, it's the wives and girlfriends of my jilted lovers. Those guys resent me too, especially since they've lost their looks. What PORKIES! They've aged a lot more than me. There's hundreds of em I've drained to the last, sticky drop, then tossed aside like a soda-pop can. They despise me and themselves, because they longed for MORE of me, back then.

They're like an army of the walking wounded, and they join forces with the usual chismosos, the idle gossips: in Puerto Indio, our harebrained capital, who ISN'T a gossip? Everybody likes to rehash the details of my downfall. She got what was coming to her, they say. In public, I hold my head high. I give them a piece of my mind, if they cross the line. They still fear a whipping from my tongue. But in private, when I'm with you, Chiara, I have to fess up that the years have taken their toll.

Let's get drunk again tonight. I'll go on and on, and you'll repeat our standard phrase, how 'the videos are broken and the mirrors are cracked.' I wanna say something like that, and you put the words into my mouth. Now I'm just a PARROT, squawking about the old days, when I used to go to love-motels with all the hunks, and we watched the hottest porn and made new flicks on the spot, flashing from the mirrors on the ceilings and walls. Sure, Chiara, my stories are always the same. Like music, I have my leitmotivs, my secondary themes, my ritornellos and da capos. The silver screen, 'lippo-suction,' bowing techniques, athletic teams, and ethnic aesthetics—what you call 'racist claptrap.' When it comes to that, you just don't get it: you're a typical GRINGA.

Even that jerk Filiberto, my so-called husband, has left me for his mistress, a slut he's been screwing for years. Trust him to go for a SKANK. He bought himself a crummy house not far from hers, financed by his bonuses from Grupo Metaxa: my father's company, to top it all off! His hold on the business is tighter now since Papa's heart attack. Cowed by the doctors' orders, he's practically given the firm to that dorky accountant he made me wed. When was it, five or six years ago? It's always been a marriage made in HELL, a fig-leaf to hush up the talk about my 'loose shenanigans' with you, Chiara. Yeah, and with packs of chest-beating cavemen, too. So what? I was only following Papa's example. When he was a sailor, he kept the proverbial whore in every port—and maybe a hustler or two, for all I know.

It's the Greek captain's eleventh hour: time to buy a ticket to heaven. That means he's wasting his dough on the Orthodox Church, gonzo as it is in Puerto Indio—just a HIDEOUS chapel called St. Nicholas, painted blue and white. My mother looked after him for several years, but now she's come down with Alzheimer's herself: no way she can take care of him or her catatonic brother, my Tío Severino. He's still the way he's been for decades, deaf and dumb as a scarecrow. To make ends meet, I've had to sell my flat on Ocean Drive, and move back to this concrete barn where I grew up. My Aunt Claribel and I deal with the three dotty shut-ins, without much help from a lazy, shiftless nurse.

'It's all bedpans now!' That's what I tell people when they ask me about my cello. After what happened at the concert, I'm TERRIFIED to pick it up again.

How do I kill time? Oh, once in a blue moon, I go to a party. I've gained weight, but I try to primp and wear fancy clothes in my new size. It's not much fun because I know everybody's laughing at my 'clown makeup,' and my silk dresses as wide as sacks. I used to pooh-pooh your BS about 'lookism,' but now I know how much it hurts when people run you down. I mostly stay at home, like the other women in our neighborhood—one more matron noshing on snacks, watching the telenovelas, and bossing the only maid we can still afford. She's a brain-dead girl from Bonaventura, the island east of ours. But what can we do? Bonos come cheap.

I've had ONE satisfaction, at least. That decrepit Calderón doesn't enjoy his victory for long, the arrogant toad. Right when he thinks he might be named the Chief Conductor here again, Horacio Miranda issues a veto from that monastery where he lives, way out in the sticks. He tells his society friends, Carolina and Frederica, to appoint Pablo Morales, the first violinist.

Of course, those rich old hens will do anything Maestro Miranda wants. They're the ones who got Calderón replaced by Horacio as Chief Conductor, seven or eight years ago. The whole situation is déjà vu because our tricky-dicky Horacio conducted in Milwaukee for a season, and Calderón came back from Medellín to stand in for him. Then WHOOPS, to the old man's disappointment, Horacio reclaimed his post.

All to end up droning Gregorian chants on some God-forsaken hill, buried in the mountains. You snicker at the way Horacio talks, Chiara, but we're used to it. When he was a boy he seemed like that cartoon character, Poindexter, in the reruns on TV, except he was always playing sick. And using highfalutin words like his father, Ambassador Miranda—President Espinosa's hoity-toity diplomat.

Calderón is DISGUSTED when his rival returns from the wilds of Wisconsin. 'The cryonic tempests, the wuthering boreals almost euthanized my flagellated corpus,' Horacio gripes about the snowy Far North. But then it isn't long till the sicko's two brothers kick the bucket, and he neuters himself by becoming a monk—nothing new, since he was born that way. He joins the Trappists, probably the only suckers who'd take him in. Calderón is even MORE DISGUSTED this time, when he loses his job to Pablo Morales. Fagged out by his concert tour of the Americas, he's pensioned off by the Countess Fund, for good.

I've performed impeccably in the first two movements. Before the third one starts, I lean forward and stare at the audience demurely. Yes, I'm very proud of myself. I'm preening, and I know they hate me for it, but that's exactly why I do it: I like to get their goat. After fiddling with my cello's tuning pegs, I caress her curved shoulders—LOVINGLY. Oh, she's the love of my life, even more than you, Chiara! How could she ever betray me? I take my own sweet time. When I nod to Calderón, the orchestra launches into Horacio's finale, like an eighteen-wheeler driving downhill, putting on the brakes so it won't lose control.

There's something STRANGE going on, because the music seems so physical I can almost touch it. In a milder way, I noticed this in the earlier movements, the allegro and the presto. Harmony has always bored me: it's as dull and dry as math—flats, sharps, thirds, augmented sevenths, the circle of fifths. But I never thought it could be visual. This adagio is based on a passacaglia, a swelling bass theme that repeats and repeats. Right from the outset, it rises up in front of me, a palace I'm exploring, not knowing what comes next.

I'm climbing a massive staircase, with picture windows instead of walls. In the interlude Calderón labels section B, I pop out of a side-door in treble staccato, just as the steps are spanning a vista of ocean waves. I'm watching them through your eyes, Chiara, since you tell me you can SEE music when you hear it, almost hold it in your arms. Synesthesia, you call it.

After that first frantic flourish when I enter, the adagio subsides into an infinite peace, like the middle movement of the G major piano by Ravel. All I need for Horacio's finale is the musicality I've got in spades, even when I never practice—on PRINCIPLE—or when I fudge a note in a pointless arpeggio or silly run. This is my last chance to show the impresarios what I can do, and I'm staying on course.

Yes, I whisper to you, YES. I'm sorry I ever wronged you, Chiara; but there should only be smooth sailing from now on. Over the tide of the full-voiced ensemble, an orchestra huge enough for Bruckner, I unreel the seamless legato that will carry me straight through. From hearing you jaw about history, I remember Columbus on his Second Voyage to Canuba, when serene blue skies and steady breezes urged him on. That's how I feel, at the top of my game and triumphant, with all my dreams on the verge of coming true.

I barely pay attention to the conductor anymore, much less to the orchestra. I'm twining LOOPS that lead me from terrace to terrace, panorama to panorama, continent to continent. The sea becomes a desert that snaps and crackles under a blazing sun... then a canyon that slashes like a machete through giant red rocks. I watch a band of horsemen race down the tundra, on endless steppes far to the north. They head for a ring of mountains that shiver in cold blue light, somewhere at the summit of the globe. You told me once about glaciers, how they calve with a crash, and I see them giving birth to icebergs… where no human being has dared to go…

You weren't invited to our wedding, but you probably heard how Filiberto and I went to Hawaii for our honeymoon. What a cliché! I'm back inside a memory from that trip. But thank God, I've ditched him. I'm all ALONE, walking along a barren lava-bed, in high heels that melt into flip-flops. A lumpy stream of fire crawls toward a wooden shack, just fifty feet away. Inside, a fight breaks out: sharp questions that don't have answers… a chorus of voices ranting in bitterness and fear. I'm listening to people for the first time in my life, and I can't tell what they're saying; I only hear the tone, the HATE. We've reached section J, and I'm standing on the porch of the cabin. The walls, flimsy as paper, burn away.

What's HAPPENING? Chiara, I can't explain it, but my cello is morphing into a weird, fleshy tube. It rears up uncontrollably, bucking and shaking. A soft dome like a dickhead pokes out of the brownish, saggy skin. The pleats lose their creases as the giant penis gets stiffer and stiffer, flexing colored spots of rusty green, piss-yellow, and snotty white. The crazy PINGA towers and mushrooms, standing in full erection. It sways back and forth until I'm hypnotized.

You've invaded me with all your talk from long ago, so I'm thinking like YOU. The enormous cock rears up like a whale, jumping from the waves in slow-mo—'breaching,' you prompt me from off-stage. Only the tail is hidden, but the 'flukes,' as you say, are getting rounder and rounder. They bulge like balls behind a zipper that spreads across the floor, opening up with a ZZZZZZZ—a noise from a comic strip. Right below me the pelotas full of semen start to churn, mauled by the musicians with their chair-legs digging in, so the fat cojones swirl and grind in a whirlpool of sweat and blood.

I'm bracing for the explosion I hope to GOD will drown out every voice but yours—all those voices in the house on fire I'm walking toward, deep inside the whale. The spout geysers through a blowhole, you used to tell me. Yeah, you're right, it's spewing out a hundred gallons of cum, the gobs of semen I've absorbed with every hole in my body, year after year, trying to escape this day. It's a scalding downpour of milk, what Latinos call LECHE, but it's spurting from men in Europe, too—wherever I've had sex. Boiling below the white-hot sky, I hear myself admit a simple fact: I'll never be loved, because I've never loved.

You've tried to HELP me, Chiara, so it's not your fault. I'm like a castaway, shipwrecked in the letters you used to write, begging me to change. I stare through an equal sign and all I see is my face, hardening on a desert island. I'm marooned with nobody but myself. Cracking and shrinking, I fight with ghost-crabs for a jellyfish or dried-up oyster. With my eight spindly legs and my eyes on little stalks, I'm spooked by every shadow. A foot's about to crush me… another foot. The last words from the burned-down cabin are flat and DEAD, like the house itself is talking. It tells me again and again that I'll never be loved, because I've never loved.

Later I find out that Calderón, the orchestra, the impresarios, the assembled Ministers, President Espinosa, his henchman Ángel María, and the rest of the audience don't have a clue about what I'm going through. They only know that I, LAMIA—Canuba's premier musician, the stuck-up virtuoso, the media hog—I've broken off my playing in mid-phrase. They see me gripping my Scarampella as if she's pulling away, and muttering something to her shiny, polished scroll. I'm slumping forward, clinging to her maple-wood waist, and my pernambuco bow has clattered to the floor. The concerto has finished without me.

Nobody cares as long as the conductor, the brass, the woodwinds, the percussion, the xylophones, and the ORDINARY strings reap the public's applause as their due. I've been forgotten in the thunderous ovation. I wander off the stage like a sleepwalker, leaving my cello propped against a chair. Rushing from the wings, my eight-year-old cousin Oswaldo hands me a spray of birds-of-paradise, as my Tía Florinda ordered him to do. But the tall, fleshy flowers slip from my arms, and I stumble past him without a backward glance.

Teatro Espinosa, October 1999: the prelude

When he writes this work, my mealy-mouth frenemy says he's modeling it on ME: MY special talents, MY God-given gifts. Horacio prefers to conduct symphonic music, so he can emote like Lenny B on the podium. But when he composes, it's stuff that sounds like madrigals, plainchant, and all that baloney. Music for tired queens, I call it—worse than Broadway, and even duller. This time, the joke's on him. The Ministry of Culture commissions a 'full-bodied concerto' for the Gala, and Sister Horacio has to obey. Ditto for his abbot, who gives him a few months off from 'labor as prayer'—peeling the yuccas, weeding the cilantro, scrubbing the loo. The vengeful monk screws the bigwigs by making the adagio almost endless. It's a JINX, it's so simple: a Sancerre you knock back, till it knocks YOU down with a left-hand hook.

Horacio pulls some other loony tricks to thumb his nose at the politicos. He arranges the movements in an ass-backward tempo scheme, allegro-presto-adagio, and loads them down with THREE xylophones. They jangle right behind me, not at the back where they belong, with the gongs and kettledrums. 'My Occidental homage to the supernal gamelan,' he calls them. I call em SABOTAGE, Chiara. I would've stuck the F-word in front, but you've gotten under my skin. I'm more ladylike now, and I don't cuss as much. I'm 'proper,' the way the nuns brought you up. You'd think I might feel rattled by a premiere like this, especially after the liquor and drugs and 'extract of teens' I've vacuumed up in the weeks before the concert. All right, I've been having too many orgies, but that's nothing new— and now that I'm pushing fifty, I have to take WHATEVER comes along.

In fact, the drink and grass and sex seem to make me stronger. At the rehearsals, my bow whizzes back and forth like a shuttlecock, and I skip through the fingering with ease, hardly aware I'm touching the strings. Yeah, I know a lot of musicians in the orchestra are jealous. They never made the grade, whereas I'm a famous soloist—famous on the island, anyway. They're praying I'll trip up so they can take me down a notch. But as always, my superb technique wins out. No matter how much they bitch, they can't deny I'm AMAZING. Besides, they've got a vested interest, since their concert tour depends on my success. I'm inspiring them to do their best. Calderón says he's never heard such 'crisp phrasing' and 'luscious expressivity' as in the build-up to the Gran Gala: Canuba Canuba Canuba.

When the historic evening arrives, the 'comeback

conductor' marches into the hall with a simper on his face, like a wily Cheshire cat. Thanks to free plane tickets, meals, and hotels, top-drawer agents from Europe and the States have gathered for the event. As he always predicted, the buzz surrounding me, the NOTORIOUS cellist, has packed the auditorium to the gills. And I can see you, Chiara, sitting up there in Countess Frederica's loge, along with her, Carolina, and Leandra—the three richest women on the island. The other boxes are filled by high officials in the government, from the President on down. The Mayor of Puerto Indio is wearing his 'CAPITAL CITY' ribbon draped across his chest. Normally, all these boneheads avoid classical music like the clap—but caramba, this is for the homeland, the Patria!

A jumbo Canuban flag, that CHINTZY ring of blue and yellow stars on an apple-green field, flutters from the central chandelier. Bursting their buttons with pride, everybody leaps to their feet as the Maestro raises his baton, and strikes up the national anthem. I've always disliked that bouncy hymn: it sounds like something from a Rossini opera. Believe it or not, it won a prize in a contest way back when, defeating even the 'Marseillaise.' I can't stand songs like that—they're too bombastic. And the lyrics of this one are SOOO TYPICAL of the period. Here's how the Brits translated the ditty, when they ruled our country for a while: 'Hail Canuba, our homeland in the sapphire sea! / To Thee, our love; from Thee, our felicity!'

Humph! Gimme a break!

Compared to those blaring strains, the *Serail* overture seems like a Mozartkugel to the benighted public, a lightweight bonbon. As for the next piece on the program, the cambuca suite by Lorenzo Prats, our local Gershwin, they've heard it a hundred times on the radio. Though the orchestra belts it out with gusto, everybody's focused on the main event: the concerto by Horacio Miranda. It's been hyped by his allies in the press; above all, it features the famous cellist, LAMIA METAXA! Here on the island, everybody treats me like a world-class icon already, as they should. God knows my publicist and I have been working overtime for months. If I'm going to have a future, this is my last chance, and I want mega-perks to go with my mega-fame.

After the intermission, I grandly sweep in from the wings. When Calderón salutes me, backed by his troops, the audience lets out yells and whistles they'd usually reserve for a cambuca star. A DIVA has to please her fans—but she keeps them in their place. I acknowledge the cheers with a curt nod and a tight-lipped, condescending smile.

I look like a nuclear bombshell tonight: I'm almost radioactive in my ultra-tight, ankle-length dress, covered with thousands of purple sequins. A padded brassiere cantilevers my bust, and my jet-black hair is shellacked in a 'Venetian twist,' as my nellie stylist calls it. A lyre-shaped barrette of 24-carat gold, a good-luck gift from my father, clamps the flaring curves at their base. But maybe that's not such a great idea. At the dress rehearsal, I catch sight of myself, reflected on a tuba. From the SIDE, when I turn to sit down, the two black folds seem like a cobra's hood.

A hush of AWE overtakes the crowd when I begin the first movement, the allegro non troppo. I play solo for the first twenty bars, and already I should guess that something's about to change. I develop the lacy leitmotiv, no problem; but I'm almost in a trance, and I'm visualizing the notes as I've never done before. I feel like I'm turning into you, Chiara, like you've cast a spell on me—even if I don't believe in junk like that. However you wanna slice it, I'm in ecstasy. My sul tasto bowing paints reddish-orange streaks, and they gleam through the orchestra's muted pines. The bassoons and oboes seem like TREES that sigh and hum, stirred by a shining breeze.

Even the frequent double stops, and my sudden switches to da gamba underhand, never make a hitch in the smoothness of my strokes. For all the critics and impresarios in the audience, I'm proving what a MONUMENTAL ARTIST I am. My left fingers massage the glissandi into swoops and understated whoops, and I apply a tear-jerk vibrato to every minim and whole-note. It's like I've gone on a hike with you, Chiara—and you know I wouldn't do that in a million years: nature's too dirty, too boring. But it's morning and we're climbing through the sierra, and my execution has NEVER been so flawless. I'm scaling unparalleled heights…

In the caffeinated presto that follows, the woodwinds bloom like flowers, one by one. My whirring gigue sul ponticello zips around them. Chiara, I'm one of those hummingbirds you love. Pizzicato, col legno, spiccato: I flip through my fingertip gymnastics, astonishing even myself. The whole composition wraps around me, a chateau I survey in every detail. My technique has always been outstanding—when I paid it any mind—but now I'm spinning out my lines like a silkworm stitching her cocoon. Yeah, I bragged about my PIZZAZZ in those same words on a late-night talk show; it's one of the phrases I write on my hand, to trot out when I need them.

But now that trite malarkey seems true, TRUE as can be: the concerto feels like it's growing out of my womb, a warm, enclosing shelter—the stable over a manger, the cradle of my fulfillment, with a star dangling in the sky. The crisscrossing threads I weave offer me up to my admirers. The limelight I'm destined for will never blind me: it's there to speed my miraculous change. More lame platitudes like those come ALIVE as I play. I'm ready to emerge from my chrysalis, to fly away from this petty Toyland, on the daring wings of art. I'm high on my own spiel about how glorious I am! At the end of the presto, I toss my head in triumph… I lean forward, basking in the sun of universal praise.

Fish-belly foreigners think I'm 'black,' just because my skin is a shade darker than theirs. I call it 'avellana,' hazelnut. In Latin America we're a rainbow of hues, twenty at least, from ebony, to tamarind, to russet, to fawn, to beige, to golden, to ivory. They used to be listed on our official Canuban IDs, along with the color of our eyes. We're not racist, we're realistic. We're TECHNICOLOR, not black and white. We personify the ethnic diversity Americans like to preach about.

Who's 'white' anyway, Chiara, except for rice-powder geishas and ghosts? You Europeans are olive, tan, pink, and peach, anything but white. Instead of judging us, you should mind your own business. All right, maybe we do have an obsession with hair. On the island, people call me 'light Indian,' after our Taino blood. We're proud to be African, but we're proud to be Native American, too. How's that for PC? I've got 'pelo bueno,' as we say, long straight hair—and it's not just 'good hair,' it used to be BLOND, platinum like Marilyn's.

For me, the months leading up to the Gala are a shot in the arm! All the fanfare produces an unexpected spin-off: men are after me again. Over time, my sex-appeal has waned, along with my physique—and my acid tongue doesn't add to my charms. By daylight, anybody can see my boobs are drooping, my skin has shriveled up, and cellulite has thickened my hips. Frequent dye-jobs have frayed my shellacked coiffure, and 'laugh lines' make me look like a marionette. But filtered through a camera, video or still, my defects melt into a haze. I'm Blanche Dubois, in that movie I love: what a three-way, Vivien and Tennessee, both drooling over Marlon! YESSSSS, I feel like I'm REBORN. As an image in magazines or on the screen, I can still make the macho lions roar.

All their lives, the young cubs around town have heard I'm 'available'—a word men like to drawl with a wink or a leer. They've lapped up gossip about me ever since they played horse on their fathers' knees. I'm GLAD my name has been a sleazy byword, the punchline of locker-room jokes. It's good advertising to get more lays. Of course, these rich-kid brats imagined me as an iguana, only worthy of contempt. But once I molt my wrinkled skin under the media lights, their beepers start to ring in their jackets, gym bags, and jeans, right next to their CROTCH. Their car-phones and bedroom extensions go into overdrive. 'Hey, dude: there was this chick on TV last night, the same one our dads always screwed. Guess what—she's a knock-out! A mujerón, a woman and a half! My old man says she's hotter now than back in the Stone Age, when he used to fuck her.'

That's how I end up getting oodles of fan mail, addressed to the Puerto Indio Orchestra—mostly from boys in their late teens, 'jevitos' from good families. They tell me I'm 'super-cool,' that they 'get off on MILFs.' Sometimes they add 'I don't mean you're old,' in case they've offended me. They're just colts feeling their oats, awkward and shy. They send me their phone numbers, so I can get in touch—or as one of them jokes, '*really* in touch.' They also include their high-school pictures. For a middle-aged NYMPHO, as the peanut gallery calls me, this is just what the doctor ordered. I multiply my TV interviews, to widen my net. And I'm well informed! I've always swooned over the Marschallin in *Rosenkavalier*, and Geraldine Page in *Sweet Bird of Youth*. I don't like books, but I've read a couple to fluff up my remarks. Now, on the talk shows, I can bring up Collette's *Chéri*.

A month before the gala, I've totally mastered the concerto: no more challenges there. Sure, it mixes diatonic and atonal, kooky zigzags, breakneck tempi, and wobbly signatures, but I've learned it by heart. I don't suffer from stage-fright, and my photographic memory never lets me down. My retro-Fortuny dress, designed by Caramela Sosa, is hanging in the closet; I've tried it on a dozen times, and it fits me like a glove. I'm idling morosely, in a standby mode. I've kept my pact with that old coot Calderón, fair and square. I haven't missed a single rehearsal, and I've BEHAVED. No more Everest to conquer. But I'm lonely. Filiberto sleeps in a separate bedroom, crammed with computers and diskettes. I lie on my custom-made, cello-shaped bed, staring at the putti who hold up the velvet canopy. I'm bored to DEATH…

Even a dog or cat would be more exciting than my husband, I grump to myself, if they didn't shed hair and beg for food. But children would be even worse. How do their mothers put up with them? Crying, peeing, and shitting—or when they're older, whining all the time. And for starters, giving birth, with that bone-ball tearing up your uterus. A NIGHTMARE fuck, but in reverse—something out of *Alien*. Nine months of nausea, no booze, and buckets of belly fat. Clothes like coconut sacks.

What a torture! Thank God I had my tubes tied in Miami when I was twenty-two, behind my parents' back. Not that I'd ever question other women's choices: to each her own… Ángel María has fathered eight children with Leandra, Carolina's daughter, and she's as happy as a clam… Anyway, I'm bored, bored—bored out of my mind. On the night-table, my vintage Princess phone is as pink as a condom. Beside it, I keep a pile of boyish faces: they grin from their pictures, stacked in order of cuteness. I've copied their phone numbers on each one… Oh, to HELL with Calderón. I promised him rave reviews, not a chastity-belt.

Filiberto's internet searches are slow. He keeps telling me he hopes the technology will improve. Whatever! I don't know if it's business or porno loops he's doing, but he doesn't seem to register that I'm never home, in the weeks before the Gala. This time I've really fooled him. He swallows my story that rehearsals and solo drills take up my every waking moment. Deudys, the chauffeur, is my husband's SPY. He hauls my cello case downstairs, first thing in the morning, then drives me straight to Teatro Espinosa. He picks me up there at nine PM, and then he reports to Filiberto, who fills my father in on every trivial detail. They've been watching me like this for years. Sure, I have a practice session every day with the orchestra, but that only lasts till noon. After that, I take a taxi to the Hotel Carlos Quinto, where I pay for a palatial suite in cash, under the name Paloma Casals. I've told the staff I'm giving MUSIC LESSONS.

The first teen on the menu has lunch with me in my sitting room—hamburgers and fries, the 'pubescent plat du jour,' as I like to tease. I'm not a nutjob, though, and I DO check ID cards. I don't want to mess with underage boys. My reputation's bad enough, without getting sued or going to jail; and then there's always blackmail, in case some kid is a budding 'entrepreneur.'

I only drink booze, because food ruins my figure. After the meal, we have a SUCCULENT siesta on the king-size bed, whipped into cream by hardcore cable. The second student comes at three, and the third shows up at six. Whoever's game can stay till my next pupil knocks on the door, and then there might be a threesome—or even a 'moresome.' With that spark igniting their hormones, some guys bring a friend or two along.

The numbers mount up, and so do the combos. I've always been a VIRTUOSO. I know how to play these rookies like a one-woman band. To stimulate my 'puppies,' as I call them, I've laid on a stockpile of alcohol and weed. For myself, I've got bottles of Royal Rum, our supreme Ron Real. I suck them down by the case. Passively, I'm also inhaling the marijuana smoke, I guess. None of that keeps me from performing like Schoenfeld at the rehearsals, so why should I stop?

I close the curtains and light the rooms with dim, sputtering candles. If the kids get too CLEAR a look at me, it might spoil their appetites. After a few hellos, I discourage small-talk as un-erotic. Before long, my little pets—drunk, or high, or both—don't know WHAT they're doing. Or WHO they're doing. It's my duty to help them conquer new frontiers. I've never liked teaching before, but I'm enjoying this. Many of them are having their first sex with a female—and with a male as well.

I don't mean just with the other boys. My HUNGER is so outrageous, my gender is wavering, too—leaving the set menu, going à la carte. In that film, am I Bowie, Sarandon, or both? Some of the teens are as pretty and graceful as girls. I pinch their tender flesh in the flickering glow, and feel their silkiness glide down my crinkled skin. I lick their hairless chests, backs, and buttocks. I crave their tasty scrotums, their balls that quickly recharge, their members that reinflate in a minute or two. If they're game, I strap on a dildo, lube them up, and impale them with aplomb. I'm gentle and respectful: I want them to learn and have fun.

Streams of ENERGY rush through my frame, and my body seems to shed a year with each scrumptious coupling, each delicious tripling or quadrupling. In the week before the concert, I try some of the heavy-duty drugs my students bring along, mostly ecstasy, meth, and coke. Yeah, they give me a kick. I'm a teenager myself again; but this time, I'm even more stylish than before. I feel like a frigging vampire, not just a vamp. My diet is white-and-lite: only pure, fresh milk, squirting down my vagina, rectum, or throat. If I'm lucky, I glug a sweet, liquid feast with all three of my mouths at once.

Puerto Indio, summer and spring, 1999

When Calderón invites me to his office in the spring of 1999, I've already heard the buzz about the Gala. Who else would he want but me? People think I'm conceited, but I'm not. You're not vain if you KNOW you're the best: it's just a fact. Playing is no problem. To tell the truth, I don't care about music as much as all these 'melomanes,' who split hairs over every semitone. Whether Starker's more gifted than Rostropovich. Whether Li-Wei Qin should've won the Tchaikovsky instead of Shapovalov. Blah, blah, blah.

Call me superficial, but I'm mainly interested in wearing my latest wardrobe on the 'Americas Millennial Tour' Calderón keeps yacking about.

He makes me pledge that I'll give the concert my all. — This will be a milestone, Lamia—you'll see.

I plant a kiss on the ancient frog's bluish lips. I don't mind. I got used to cadavers in my Last Tango days: I put out a HELLUVA lot more than smooches for Don Belisario, the homely owner of your house. Why do you think he's evicting you? MEA culpa! That's how I fixed your wagon, Chiara! For Calderón, on top of the besito, I throw in some blowfish sounds. Mmwwah, mmwwah, mmwwah.

He blusters at me, the ungrateful creep. — Let's stick to business, please. I'm counting on you, Lamia. This is the Battle of the Bulge, your final chance to shine. You might win the agents' attention, and become a major artist. Better late than never—and that goes for both of us.

I have to swallow my pride. The nerve of that shriveled-up rodent! At seventy-seven, he's my senior by thirty years. But he does have a point. Conductors can reach their prime when they're geezers, but soloists mature much earlier. Many of us start as child prodigies, like Mozart or Ludwig van B. With my usual MODESTY, I've often compared myself to them. When I was only ten, I cranked out Chopin on a local talent show. Eons ago, I should've won an important competition, given recitals at Carnegie Hall, and appeared with a big-name orchestra. I've been too lazy, too indifferent. It's now or never, if I want to make an international splash. As the Maestro puts it, this is my last shot to 'jump from our island pond into the Seven Seas.'

Right away, Filiberto notices the difference. He says he can hardly believe his ears! I'm practicing six hours a day in the music room of our Ocean Drive apartment. Normally, I'd be stealing off in a taxi to 'play a duet with my colleague Olena'—my serial fib for bedding down with men. Instead of the seedy love-motels I went to when you I and first met, now I go to upscale hotels. My standby is the Carlos Quinto. I love the airy courtyards, and the classy decor by Caramela Sosa: that dyke's trademark pops up on EVERYTHING these days, from chess sets to underwear.

Canuba's like Sicily, Chiara, where you grew up. There's more freedom for wives than for single girls. No virginity to preserve: that's the THEORY, anyway! Papa still keeps tabs on me, but not like when I lived at home. I can troll for lays in my red convertible, upgraded from the Corvette to a Porsche. My pick-ups have to clomp through a ritzy lobby, even if they're wearing ragged T-shirts, drawstring shorts, and beat-up plastic shoes. They couldn't care less: Canubans always think they're the bee's knees, no matter what.

I used to be the dump-fuck for upper-class men, and they treated me like royalty. With the guys who tool me now, I have to foot the bills, and shell out juicy tips for expert servicing. Wham, bam, thank you man! I throw them wads of cash from an ATM, as soon as they've strutted their stuff. I'm careful to use my private MasterCard, instead of my joint accounts with Filiberto. A lady has to be DISCREET. He can save face for himself, at least—though I can't rein in the tittle-tattle of this town.

There's plenty of dough for my indulgences, since I don't have to share it with Filiberto anymore. My Papa has upped his salary through the roof. He says the pimply little nerd has saved the Metaxa Company MILLIONS in taxes; and he's diversified the operations, too, from shipping and restaurants to finance and pharma. But he's never developed any social skills. He can't close deals: he doesn't have the gift of gab. My father takes care of that with his cronies. All they do is drink, jabber, and slosh their money around.

Papa's glad Filiberto stays home, glued to his desktop, rigged with all the bells and whistles. That way, he can keep an eye on me—or so Papa likes to fantasize. Filiberto values his cushy job too much to rock the boat, no matter what I do. Besides, he has a sideline of his own: a WHORE he screws twice a week at her condo, doling out the escudos to pay her rent. In the months before the concert, the bean-pusher comes in handy for more than just camouflage. He feeds my mother the line that I'm slaving for Calderón. Her grapevine of dowdy matrons takes care of the rest: I've dubbed them my 'PR Department'.

Sure, I've got my work cut out for me. I don't know if Miss Trappist wanted to trip me up, but the landmines in his concerto would blow any other cellist to bits. Thank God I'm a GENIUS! To execute some of the off-beat tones in the allegro non troppo, I'm forced to use an underhand bowing stroke. It's a relic of the viola da gamba, and went out of fashion centuries ago. Through the whole movement, my part is barely linked to the orchestral staves. Calderón describes it to the press as a 'throbbing soundscape, densely textured like a piece by Steve Reich.' I'm left suspended in space, in danger of missing my cues.

The presto erupts out of nowhere, smack in the middle of the work. My sixteenth notes FIZZ like champagne, as heady as a Bach toccata. The score splices pizzicato and spiccato with percussive tricks: tapping or knocking the wood, even softly scratching it. The atonal sequence grants me no melody, no mnemonic device; all the tunes are in the orchestra. Like a scuba diver, I could easily lose my bearings. But 'la noblesse musicale oblige,' as Professeur Poulet-Malassis used to cluck, at the École Normale de Musique. And no gawky music stand for me, thank you: a consummate ARTIST doesn't need a crutch like that. Besides, I want the audience to admire my figure with an unimpeded view.

Oddly, the composition ends with a serene adagio, as minimalist as Górecki's *Third Symphony*. Horacio has always been a cannibal, and he flagrantly lifts several passages from that work, moshing them into his stew. That's what he calls 'conflationary transubstantiation.' I call it plagiarism. In his version, my cello parts replace Górecki's settings for voice. In an interview for a high-tone glossy, *Cultura Canubana*, he claims that 'the violoncello depersonalizes the vox humana, and ineffably elevates us to an Ultima Thule of ethereal disconnection.' Yada-yada-yada. All I know is that the final passacaglia sticks to the conventions, *abacadaeafaga*, and the ostinato *a* is as quiet as a prayer. It suits Horacio's title, *In Memory of an Angel*: he filched it from Alban Berg. Like the *Symphonie Fantastique* by Berlioz, the movement highlights every instrument in turn.

I can see why the concerto fits in with Calderón's aims. It not only flatters the soloist, it showcases the entire symphony—and above all, the CONDUCTOR, who's marshaling his troops. To keep the wavy contours clean, he has to display both rhythmic rigor and coloristic tact. People believe I'm just a Dummkopf, but when it comes to stuff like this, I'm not. All those years in music schools rubbed off on me. In the rehearsals, Maestro General Patton pushes hard, punching the orchestra into shape: building on its strengths, and patching up its weaknesses. In his office, he croons about saving his career, 'in retrospect.' He's going to be 'crowned by triumph.' He already sees himself extolled in *Grammophone* as a 'twilight superstar.'

As for me, he's started naming me his 'late-blooming

rose.' Humph! I may be a Venus-flytrap or a tiger-lily, but a sappy rose I'm not. He's extremely content I'm working so hard; he even forgives a few of my foibles that surface in the media. He brushes them off, because the public is BLOWN AWAY by our patriotic teamwork: the Puerto Indio Orchestra, with a Canuban conductor and a Canuban soloist, performing music by Canuban composers. Even the overture to Mozart's *Entführung* will dance to a Canuban lilt, he boasts, under his native baton. He has eye-catching posters plastered all over town, trumpeting La Gran Gala: Canuba Canuba Canuba. The local pundits go berserk, and my mother and her sidekicks fan the flames—though exclusively on MY behalf.

Editors and photojournalists can't get enough dirt from 'Doña Grecia, who used to be a concert violinist herself,' as her lady-friends prattle behind the scenes. Calderón is 'senile and tone-deaf,' she lets on—though not for attribution. 'Who else but my daughter Lamia could pull off this earthshaking event? Who else but a stupendous virtuoso from a prominent family—and gorgeous into the bargain?' I'm no FOOL, Chiara! I have to admit that only a mother could call me 'gorgeous,' at this late stage. My silver hair was striking in my youth, but now it tacks a decade onto my age. In the past year my stylist has dyed it blacker every week, until it's 'a raven hue,' in his words. I wear it in a spray-stiff, double chignon, like a pair of crow's wings.

If I'm going to be a witch, why go halfway? You've told

me yourself, Chiara: my eyes have darkened along with my hair, from aquamarine to jet. I'll be DAMNED if I throw in the towel. And I haven't lost my theatrical flair. I've had my buck tooth straightened. Aided by silicon and collagen—not to mention a discreet nip and tuck—I look young in my PR shots, don't I? 'Gentle lighting, soft focus, and makeup as thick as a grapefruit rind': that's how one of my 'duck' chums described our shtick. Queers are masters of illusion, according to him. Other 'patos' have dreamed up sets to frame my portraits, with every lacquered hair in place. They used to mooch on that fag-hag Chuchu, till she went off to the Betty Ford Clinic. No more free drugs and booze for them! She left them high and dry—or as my cosmetician says, 'a LOT less high and a LOT more dry.'

As the concert approaches, Calderón loosens my leash. 'In the end,' he tells me, 'a bit of hoopla might net us bigger crowds.' He stops objecting to my chats with social-page biddies and TV hosts, and he doesn't care what I say. But my oldest friends—mostly FORMER friends now, like you, Horacio, and Ángel María—load my answering machine with worried messages. They always start with: 'This is for your own good.' Yeah, I have to admit I've been NAUGHTY, especially on the late-night talkathons, when I know the Maestro's in bed. Like yesterday, on Beto Boquilla's show. He's handsome as all get out, even more in person than on screen. I can see why he's a soiree idol, for night-owl matrons and cougars 'of a certain age.'

'Isn't there a tremendous wallop of passion in your playing?' he asks me, wetting his red lips with his rosy tongue.

I bat my lashes. 'That's a loaded question, pretty-boy. Well, my cello IS curvaceous. What do you suppose the *F*-holes are for?' The audience guffaws, whistles, and hoots. 'How about the tailpiece and tail spike—need I say more?'

I'm just trying to drum up interest—and sex SELLS. I'm a slut, and brainy too! But I don't want to sound like an egghead. Maybe I ramble on too much about the 'sensuous shudders' of my soundpost box, or the 'Freudian symbolism' of my instrument. 'Is it female or male? I can't DECIDE,' I cock-tease Beto. 'But I'm always fine with male… female… or she-male… whatever comes to hand…'

When I do my late-night spiel, I put in a bunch of dot-dot-dots, so people can fill in the blanks. I moan for a while about my 'experimental' years in Europe and the States. Tons of DOT-DOT-DOTS in there! I tear up sentimentally, and dab my eyes with Beto's pink handkerchief, when I turn to the Marschallin in Richard Strauss. How I identify with her. How selfless she is. How she gives up her teenage lover, so he can marry a girl his own age. What a sacrifice, for an older woman! After all, there's a 'deeper need for physical release, as time goes by…' Ladadee ladada…

I've really piqued the public's curiosity. The *Clarín Canubano* runs a full-page picture of my Scarampella. They include a numbered key to each of its parts—down to the spruce peg-box and the ebony nut. In a sidebar, I emphasize that my bow is made of pernambuco. 'Not brazilwood! That's much too COMMON for me!'

So what, if I'm stepping on those hacks in the orchestra. The LESSER string players resent me anyway. They can't forgive me for being talented AND beautiful. I don't mind socking it to them! I hope they're sick with rage from seeing my pictures in all the magazines. My publicist has created a special color scheme for my press releases, and journalists like to use it. My confessions about the 'erotic life of my instrument' hopscotch through their articles, white type on sassy squares of purple and chartreuse.

The crowning touch is Papa's ad campaign. He usually wants me to be a prude, but NOT when he can pimp me for his restaurants. In every commercial, print or TV, I wear a different outfit to match the backdrop. I recline on the steps of his Pagoda Buffet, in a fuchsia gown slit above the knee. I lean on a column at his Greek Taverna, in a tight blue peplum of pleated silk. Lolling on a stool at his Chromium Bar, I flaunt my legs in a skimpy cocktail-dress. Halfway up a ladder, I pick a mango for his Rancho Canubano, my banana-yellow skirt hiked to my thighs. In a gold bikini at his Playa Seafood joint, I sprawl on top of my cello case, while muscle-guys haul it down the strand. That plug has my favorite caption, and the TV spot repeats it: 'Lamia Metaxa, a SERIOUS artist who always has time for FUN!'

My media exposure is too much for some of my detractors, I'm told. Countess Frederica is beside herself, the old bag. She goes on retreats to the Trappists, so she can gabble to Horacio during the visitors' hour. 'Who does Lamia think she is? Rita Hayworth? Jayne Mansfield?' I have to laugh, her stock of divas is SOOO passé. Carolina Del Río cuts people off every time they mention me—not that either one of them would miss the Gala, needless to say.

As always, my colleagues detest me the most. But if I call them mediocre and unmusical, it's only to egg them on! They could do better—maybe—if they tried! And now I MIFF them even more with my weekly press release blitz. I can't help it if my publicist bills me as 'the greatest Canuban musician of all time.' Calderón says we need to lash our sluggish players to get on the stick. In several Q & A's on the radio, I've voiced my legitimate concerns. 'I wonder, is the Puerto Indio Orchestra really up to the challenge? Horacio Miranda's concerto isn't a piece of cake!'

When I repeat that on TV one day, the goofy host asks me if I'm worried about my OWN abilities. I let him have it. 'You must be crazy! For my level, that little piece is a walk in the park.' To back up what I say, I zoom through the presto for the cameras. I saw and pluck and jiggle and thump. I make a point of spreading my thighs so wide that my skirt slips up to my tanga. How's that for provocative? So THERE.

All right, maybe I've gone too far. Yesterday Calderón confided that the musicians are yapping, and he'll have to throw them a bone. He publishes an open letter in the papers this morning. 'The Orchestra is pleased by the media coverage of our upcoming concert, La Gran Gala: Canuba Canuba Canuba. Besides a Mozart classic, and the beloved *Carnaval Canubano* by Lorenzo Prats, we will present the world premiere of Horacio Miranda's cello concerto, a landmark in our musical life. Our soloist, Lamia Metaxa, has rightly garnered many accolades; but all the members of our ensemble are virtuosos, as skilled and accomplished as she.'

What the hell? He can lie as much as he wants, but nobody will ever equal ME. Who is he to lord it over an artist of my rank? Yeah, yeah: I know this is my last exit from Toyland. He may like this island, but I don't. My stage-presence trumps any other cellist's, from here to Mongolia. My brilliance is so natural, I've always treated music as just a sideline. If I'd spent less time on my sex-life, I might've practiced enough to become world-famous. Sure, I've been nonchalant, let's say—like everybody else in Puerto Indio. Over these next few months, I'm concentrating on NOTHING but the concert. If I don't, the Maestro warns he'll hire a foreigner to replace me. I wouldn't put it past him! The deceitful old skunk!

When all this is over, I'm going to put him in his place. He's been washed-up for years, and he's only standing in for Horacio till they find somebody better. Frederica hatched that zany idea, she's such an amateur. Way back when, Blenheim Calderón became a conductor only because he was Espinosa's boyhood pal. Our future President used to play chopsticks with him in the school cafeteria. But I'm not naïve. By taking the senile turtle out of semi-retirement, Frederica can curry favor with the government, where he's still one of the gang. Tapping special grants from the Ministry of Culture, her music foundation has bought some hotshots from overseas, I have to acknowledge. Society dames call it the 'Countess Fund,' since she PRETENDS to be one. You've filled me in on that, Chiara; you're a true aristocrat. She's an imposter!

Luckily for Frederica, now that Leandra's children are in school, she has the time to assist her—and she's got even MORE money to add. To everybody's surprise, she's doing it with her mother's approval. Carolina Del Río used to have cat-fights with Frederica, since they both wanted to set the social tone. They're WAY over the hill: maybe they're mellower now, or just plain tired. Forgive and forget, let bygones be bygones, and most of all, if you can't beat em, join em. There are some other wealthy meatheads in Puerto Indio who blab about music, and they've signed onto the financial pact. But a project like this depends on corporate sponsors, too. Thanks to Ángel María's connections, the Countess Fund is receiving MEGA-MOOLA from the multinationals. He's the head of Espinosa's Trade Commission, along with all his other political scams.

Yeah, but who cares if a few fake high-brows show off their pathetic dresses in a concert hall? You have to broaden the audience for classical music; you have to rally the LOW-BROWS who think Luis Miguel sings better than Pavarotti. Only subscriptions to a full-blown season can guarantee long-range success. It's not just economic—it's social, even psychological. Espinosa Theatre seats two thousand, and world-renowned artists want to perform for a crowd, not a clique. For the time being, with Horacio out of the way, Calderón has settled back into his former mold. It's gone to his head, the arthritic schnook. With Frederica's backing, he spawns his own scheme to curry popular support—for the orchestra, and for himself. He's the one who comes up with the BIRD-BRAIN title, La Gran Gala: Canuba Canuba Canuba. He doesn't like it when I wisecrack: Yeah, Maestro, but three wrongs don't make a right.

His main goal is a Pan-American Millennium Tour for the Puerto Indio Orchestra, from Anchorage to Asunción. He plans to invite a dozen impresarios to the performance, throwing in first-class airfare from as far away as Toronto and Buenos Aires, Barcelona and Belgrade. He figures they'll jump at the chance for a Caribbean vacation, all expenses paid. The geezer's banner movie is *Patton*, even if he looks like a constipated MOUSE: George C. Scott, he's

NOT. He vents his military side by barking pep-talks at the musicians. He beats the conductor's stand with his baton, gabbing about the 'historic importance' of the Gala, how they're the Vienna Philharmonic and he's von Karajan. They write him off as delusional. He claims they're going to prove what a fine ensemble they've become, thanks ONLY to him. Everybody knows it's Horacio who brought them up a bit, after Calderón let them slide to rock bottom.

In our 'job interview', General Mouse lays out his tactical plan: to present a sublime cello concerto by Horacio Miranda—an opus he's persuaded the Ministry of Culture to commission. The dimwit HAMSTER leans closer, and tells me junk I know a lot more about than him. For example, how Alban Berg dedicated his violin concerto to the daughter of Alma Mahler, a girl who died young: she's the 'Angel' in the title Horacio stole. Maestro Patton never studied in Vienna like him and me: to us, Gustav, Alma, and Walter are staples like rice and beans. I have a good laugh when Horacio's harshest critic calls him out on the angel bit: 'for a monk like Miranda, it's self-referential—or in other words, self-reverential.'

On the SURFACE, I guess Calderón's curtsey to his nemesis seems touching, since Horacio forced him into retirement. But the shrewdness of his move doesn't escape the cognoscenti. It gains him points with Horacio's lifelong friends, Carolina and Frederica, the heavyweights in musical funding. He needs them now to beef up the orchestra, and also to back the concert tour, if it comes to that. The solo instrument allows him to exploit the ANIMAL magnetism of our country's leading soloist. Who else? ME.

Plaza Drake, April 1997

I can't do anything right anymore. You probably blame me for Claribel. But I didn't send her, I PROMISE. Lizards don't make much of an impression, so I bet you forgot you'd ever met her—once at the beach and once at my house. I can't help it if she decides to show up one day, and knock on your door. She's always had thin hair, and now she's greenish because her liver's acting up. She's a handful of bones. Her yellow eyes look like they're popping out of her head: it seems bigger than it should for her size, and so meatless it's triangular. Like I always say, she's a lizard. Horacio calls her SAURIANA.

I know about the whole scene: she proudly tells me her story the next day. I can just see her perched on one of your antique rocking chairs; she's always afraid of contagion, you know. 'Nice furniture,' she says. 'Muebles bonitos. Don't make em like that anymore.' Natch, she prefers molded plastic. I'm the only one in my family with any TASTE.

Her voice is so raspy, it's like a scraped piano-string.

But you welcome her, DUMBWAD: you're too friendly for your own good. You offer to show her the rest of the house, but she shakes her head impatiently. She's had her hair teased to give it more body; that only makes it clump to one side.

Let's get to the point, she says. What are your intentions toward Lamia?

In Canuba, two women often join forces, if they've stayed single. It's a substitute for marriage—but how PLATONIC it really is behind four walls… that's anybody's guess.

You fall back on an old saw: My intentions have always been honorable.

Claribel is nothing if not persistent. — Then why haven't you asked her to settle down with you? You've been going out with her for six years, since 1991.

But I *have* asked her—a hundred times! you say.

Chiara, you've been in LOVE with me forever, way before we started going steady. Then it hits you: maybe I've been using you for an excuse. I've been wondering when you'd finally wise up! As long as I can PRETEND I'm going to share a house with you someday, the women in my family won't nag me. Otherwise, they'll dredge up new prospects—you know, the type of men who'd make decent husbands. Polite, obedient, and STUPID. In Canuban, we call em 'chotas.' Having you as my fallback frees me for my priority: balling hunky guys in love-motels.

Claribel's skeptical. — You've invited her to move in with you? She wants to, but you're always putting her off.

Now you have to choose: contradict me, or come across as a liar. You opt for the coward's way out. You WAFFLE. — Well… I think I've always been clear.

Clear as mud! Claribel squeaks. Especially since you're never here, and you hardly ever call her.

I know, Chiara: you can't defend yourself without doing me in. I'M the one who's never home, and who never answers your messages. All you can do is hang your head and say something vague. — I travel for my work. But you're right: I should phone Lamia more often.

Claribel stamps her grimy, no-color shoes; she only has one pair. — You should go away less often, too. Here Lamia is, giving you the best years of her life, and you don't even care. — Her bulbous eyes are dry, but she wipes them for EFFECT. — If this goes on much longer, it'll be too late for her to get a husband. Too late for her to set up house with another woman. And she'll end up like me! A beggar, living with her family forever. It's degrading, let me tell you.

She's always projecting her own story on me. But I'm a WORKING woman. And she's too naïve to figure out that I'm humping Poles, Cubans, Serbs, Americans, Bulgarians, Slovenians, and the locals—any guy I can bunga-bunga in bed. She believes I'm giving cello lessons all day at the conservatory. She doesn't have any inkling. After all, who would want HER?

Claribel twists her hanky into knots: it's one of her most ANNOYING tics. — Behind my back, she moans, people call me a 'jamona.' To them I'm just a 'cured ham,' hanging in the smokehouse. No husband, not even a lady friend. My sister Grecia treats me like a kitchen chair. I'm a human being, Chiara. I didn't have any luck, that's all. I won't let the same thing happen to Lamia. If you don't want her, then leave her alone. Because of you, nobody ever asks her out on a date. She rejects the eligible bachelors Grecia, Florinda, and I introduce to her. You're spoiling Lamia's last chance for happiness.

What an AWKWARD scene, Chiara. To get rid of her, you'll say anything — You're right, Claribel. Time is running out. I'll ask Lamia to come live with me, today!

At this point, Claribel jumps up from her chair and kisses you on both cheeks. What a drag! Her lips feel leathery, like alligator skin. — You know what? My brother-in-law's going to buy Lamia a house, as a wedding present! So you'll be the one to move in with her. You've hit the jackpot! Shhh! It's a secret, just between us!

When you call me later on, one of the maids tells you I'm giving a 'music lesson'—as usual. My pupils are all VERY talented, and they can go on bowing me for hours. I know, you've never been jealous. You don't believe in exclusive couples, whether they're Janes, Tarzans, or banana-eating Cheetahs. Whatever I do is fine by you.

But now you make a huge mistake. When I get back,

around six in the afternoon, you phone me again. You keep your promise to Claribel, and bring up the house-sharing scheme.

I guffaw. — Chiara, I've told you a MILLION times I won't shack up with you. I admit I was in love with you for a while—ten minutes, maybe even twelve. But you're too much of a goody-goody. I need a PUMP with high octane! A dildo's not enough, no matter how well you use it. By the way, would you like to pitch in with a baseball team tonight?

No, I wouldn't, Lamia. As you say, I'm too wimpy. And by the way, I'll start spreading the news that I'm engaged—to my fidanzato in Sicily.

Since WHEN? Is that true?

No, it isn't. But I've been ruining your chances. Now you can seek another partner in life.

Oh, I could do that anytime I want. My mother and her sisters are always bringing dorky little nerds to the house. I keep telling Grecia I've got an agreement with YOU, so she and my aunts will leave me alone.

Just as I suspected, Lamia. But that's not really fair to me, is it? Maybe I'd like to shop around myself. Anyway, you're not getting any younger. What if you end up as a 'jamona,' a spinster?

Ha! Look who's talking. A 'jamona' is a ham who hangs around till she's too tough to eat. But LOTS of guys still chomp on me. And I can gobble all the sausages I want, if you get my drift!

Sure, Lamia. You're a broken record...

Yep, I have a one-track mind. Like a train chugging through a TUNNEL!

Well, enough is enough. I'm breaking off our 'agreement.' I'll tell all our mutual acquaintances.

I'm beside myself. — You can't do that, you cunt! It'll look like you JILTED me! Besides, you're my alibi.

Let's put it this way. My mind is one-track, too: I'm bent on telling the truth.

You're going to REGRET this, Chiara. There'll be consequences!

Don't be ridiculous. I'm being up front, and that's that. After all, you always say we're only friends.

Oh yeah? FRIENDS? That's what YOU think. — Outraged, I hang up.

No, I'm not going to let it stop there. Rumors sweep through the city like wildfire, and you can GUESS who's flipping the matches. I'll get back at you, Chiara.

Matrons shake their heads. They've heard about you from my mother, my aunts, and all the other decrepit turkeys. They're appalled at the behavior of that debauched Italian, YOU. As pure as mountain snow, I've been going out with you for nearly a decade, and we've taken a solemn VOW to set up house together. But recently, I caught you having an orgy with a bunch of Bonos—a construction crew. Of COURSE, now I've broken off with you, you brazen hussy.

On the rebound, I'm having a whirlwind romance with a dependable accountant, Filiberto Castañeda—a Canuban, not some foreigner the cat dragged in. He's much younger than me, but he loves me for my old-fashioned virtues. Abiding by tradition, he's asked my father for my hand in marriage. It all goes to show that goodness will always triumph. No woman who's MORAL like me has to end up a 'jamona'—unless she devotes herself to her family, like that saintly Claribel, who's always been such a model for her niece.

The wedding itself is real enough—TOO real for me, even if it's just a sham. My father insists on a tacky service at the Orthodox Church, plus a drunken blowout for five hundred guests. I don't care if my ex-lovers make wisecracks: I insist on a virginal white dress, with a lace bridal veil and a six-foot train. I've always liked costume parties, and I'm dressed to kill. Their flower crowns and ribbons-round-the-rosy are nice enough, but the Greeks drag things out too long. My mother and Tía Claribel blubber contentedly—my Aunt Florinda, too. By now, it doesn't matter WHAT I marry, as long as it's more or less male. Like a number from a hat, my Papa chose an accountant from his shipping firm.

Pointedly, you're not invited, Chiara. But Horacio will fill you in on the whole nine yards. He'll report that the groom is pale and anemic, with spotty skin and 'pelo medio-malo,' half-bad hair. Oh yeah, his name is Filiberto, and he's half my age. Dazed by the speed of it all, he forgets to say 'I do.' I have to prompt him, the klutz.

At her next dinner party, Countess Frederica will tell you more. I can just hear her. — Witzig! What a farce! He's totally henpecked. People are already calling him Señora Metaxa! No doubt about who rules the roost. With her good looks—for a half-breed—Lamia might've risen in the world. Maybe she's over the hill, but she didn't have to roll to the bottom. Where's he from? Woher? Just imagine! A pig farm, from what I've heard!

Etcetera, etcetera. Chiara, you know what I need from the bozo: the same thing I wanted from you—a FRONT. We're not as rich as your society pals, but to him we seem like the Vanderbilts. If he wants to keep his job and his salary, he won't snoop around about my sex-mates. That'll keep him in his place. We don't tell Papa, but we spend our honeymoon in Hawaii at separate hotels. Occasionally the chump catches sight of me, strolling down the beach with some he-men. I like the ones in Speedos: they don't hide their equipment.

The site I select for the reception—the garden behind the apse, right outside your window—is supposed to rub your nose in the event. And it works! I see you peeking through the shutters, probably with your hand between your legs: everybody knows you've still got the hots for me. At the end of the bash, Papa is sloshed. In a mushy voice, he announces to the crowd that he's just bought a home for us newlyweds. Fighting back my repulsion, he's such a DRUNK, I kiss him 'gratefully.' That doesn't hoodwink anybody but him.

Hahaha, the joke's on you, Chiara. You shouldn't have crossed me. People are amazed by the house I've picked out: YOURS! The owner, Don Belisario, promised you could rent the place 'forever.' Fat chance! I get him to sell it to Papa, and put it in my name. A week after I'm back from Hawaii, the first eviction-notice lands at your door. After all the investments you've made in the place, for you it's a kick in the pants.

Ángel María is on your side. He's furious at his father Belisario, and mad at me, too. He's a disgruntled ex like you, always getting on my case—and both of you can go to hell. I've killed two birds with one stone!

Our lawyers go into overdrive, greedy for fees. After all these years, you LOVE that house like your dearest squeeze, so I know you'll fight us. I don't really want to live there, it's just to get back at you. Your Colonial dump is too old-fashioned for me. While the battle rages on, Papa buys me a big apartment on the Malecón, with a view of the sea and brand-new appliances. We keep the writs arriving at your house—hand-delivered for maximum torture, between five and six AM.

Yeah, you make trouble, all right. Ángel María has a lot of power these days, as Espinosa's right-hand man. But I've got some geriatric pals the President likes nearly as much.

I don't CARE if I have to go to bed with them. Sure, you've been leasing the house for seventeen years, and Belisario gave you written permission to remodel it. In his early days as an engineer, Ángel María did the renovations himself. You've got expert lawyers, but ours are better: slimier and more corrupt. That's how to get results.

Besides, Ángel María is too busy to bother with you. He's the Minister of the Cabinet. He coordinates the government for Espinosa, a job that hardly leaves him time to sleep. After all your frantic messages, he can only rob a half-hour from his non-stop agenda. Unannounced, he appears on your doorstep one morning, flanked by a PLATOON of bodyguards. Wish I'd been there to put them through their paces!

I know, he always wraps you in his arms like a long-lost sister. And you complain that Don Belisario hasn't returned your calls. I used to think Ángel María's steel-blue eyes showed a lack of feeling; but now I imagine they're BLAZING with contempt. He shoos the guards further down the street, and explains to you he's just uncovered a nasty secret. That I'VE been having an affair with his father!

Of course, I'm not turned on by Belisario's clumsy flirting, much less his has-been body. I'm only after REVENGE. I indulge him in his kinky fetishes, like the one he calls 'Last Tango,' with me as a buttery Schneider. To me, gags like that are dumb, especially since he can't even get it up. Between the bastings, I wheedle him relentlessly. 'I need a house of my own, Belito! Belito, you don't really love me, if you won't do me this one itsy-bitsy favor.' As soon as he signs the bill of sale, I tell him we're THROUGH, that he gives me the creeps.

To humiliate him to the nth degree, I report the whole story to Ángel María, in gory detail. Now he's disgusted with his father, who's sunken EVEN lower in his esteem than before. Belito has always been such a lascivious LOSER, but this takes the cake. Ángel María apologizes to you for what's happened, but the matter's out of his hands. 'I can't interfere with the judicial system,' he lies, 'and my dad's a childhood friend of Espinosa's'—which is true. All he can do is hug you again: 'Chiara, you'll just have to hash this out in court.'

Cold comfort, BITCH! I know your lawyers claim that Belito should reimburse you. They start a suit that could last for five years, maybe ten. Tenants have a privileged status in Canuba—one of Espinosa's vote-grabbing gimmicks. There'll be a lot of hoops to jump through. Papa's attorneys will try to speed things up, but you've got clever ones, too. After the first flurry of court orders, the bureaucrats will set the case on the back burner, and the pressure will die down. Canuban 'justice' is IFFY, but for me it's enough to keep you worried and insecure. Every morning, you'll wake up and wonder: Is this the day they'll kick me out?

Ever since our 'accidental honeymoon' on Isla Fandango, you angle for an encore. I let you have one now and then. I'm more attracted to men than women; and so are you, Chiara, at least for now—but we can go either way. It depends on the person. Sometimes a dildo will do, in a pinch. I just like that THING between men's legs, the way it grows and grows, and wants to get inside me. Every week I try to spend an afternoon or two with a baseball, football, or basketball team. Since swimming or wrestling squads are smaller, they're just 'bocadillos' to me—snacks before the main course. You wonder how my body can take all the punishment; but that's what makes me feel ALIVE...

When you fuss over my health, I shrug. — Believe me, Miss Tight-Ass, they can't wear ME out! THEY're the ones who get DRAINED! And just because I don't see you for months on end doesn't mean I'm not thinking of you, pesto-head. I talk to you when I'm alone, Chiara. No, I'm never really alone, I'm with you.

I don't know why I keep getting into so many SCRAPES over the years. Maybe when you and I start drifting apart, I lose my self-confidence. That might sound off-the-wall, I seem so brash and full of myself. But I've been under Papa's thumb all my life, so I've never had a chance to grow up. I guess I'm just a teenage rebel without a cause. When you and I cozy up in the early nineties, I feel like somebody finally loves me for ME—not just for my sex-appeal, or to push me around as a pawn in the music world. Let's face it, they can stick me in a string section, a quartet, or even on the marquee as a soloist: however you slice it, I'm still a property that's being USED.

Long before I start foreclosing on your house, it hurts me when I notice you're falling out of love with me, but I'm too proud to let on. The first thing that tips me off is how you make snide remarks about my makeup, not to me but to the NUMBSKULLS who like to run me down. How you hate the line where my pancake stops, on the iguana skin around my neck. Sure, I know it's obvious by day, but it stands out less at night. Maybe that's why I like to leave the house after twilight. One of my enemies says you call me NOSFERATU behind my back! To punish you, I never arrive on time when we make a date; or for extra stress, I don't show up at all. The unpredictability drives you mad.

Why am I doing this? I'm only shooting myself in the foot. To rile you up, I play the platinum bimbo. — Planning is only for 'square-heads,' I tell you. People like YOU. I never know where I'm going to be, or when I'll get there. All of a sudden, I'm HERE. Just be grateful, ravioli-brain!

I don't love you just for the sex. But from the racket I make, you know I get off on you. Maybe that's why I hook up with you only twice a month. More than that would cramp my STYLE! That's what I tell you, anyway. It's really because I don't want to get tied down, and if anybody could tame me, it's you.

I've moved up from the Volkswagen to a snazzy Corvette. Papa bought it for me in 1989, but now it's on its last tires. After four years, the paint-job looks as chipped as my nail-gloss, since I'm getting brittle, too. It's hard to believe I'm already in my forties. I know you think our routine is a bore. We pick up some friend of mine, usually a punky teen, our junior by twenty-five or thirty years, and then he guides us to the outskirts of town—to a rich kids' shindig, with speakers the size of a rock band's. It drives us both crazy, since we only like classical; and nowadays the twerps don't even dance. You call them the 'jeunesse dorée'; I call them the 'jeunesse déclassée.' They 'listen' to Brit and gringo pop, without tapping a toe.

It's a deafening nightmare, mindless and motionless— EMOTIONLESS, too. When you went slumming with Amado, he used to take you to the discos. Yeah, people from the lower classes like him still groove on cambucas, merengues, and salsas. But Latin rhythms are OUT among the trust fund babes. Besides, I like gourmet food. Foreign imports welcome! And you're a useful decoy for that. A gringa like you attracts gringos, so I can add them to my meal. But once I've sampled a dish, I don't go back for seconds, much less thirds.

Chiara, you're the EXCEPTION. — I flash you a smile, hiding my buck tooth. — You've lasted even longer than Ángel María. Twice a month! That's a lot for me. In my previous life, I must've been a slutty maricón. The kind who trolls the bars and cruises the sidewalks non-stop—or so the closet-cases like to think. Oh, la nostalgie de la boue! Patty-cakes in the mud! I want a new lay every minute, at least a quickie. Okay, a LONG one is even better! Or two or three! But I always come back to you. Don't you see how lucky you are?

I like the movies because you can munch on popcorn, and make out with pick-ups in the dark. I have to drag myself to the orchestra concerts. Music is a bummer, unless I'm performing it myself. My mother says I need to make an effort 'for professional reasons.' All right, at least I can gloat when the musicians flub up. Their attempts are so feeble, I've got to have a LITTLE fun!

I like to hiss my remarks in a stage-whisper, so several rows can hear. It makes me giggle, Chiara, when you sink lower in your seat. If I embarrass you, it's what you deserve, for being so up-tight. In my opinion, I'm WITTY. Like the other night, I came up with a good one, remember? — What an awful recital! She'd do a lot better if she used her twat. — Or last month, I quipped out loud: He plays okay, but he's too rigid. He needs a backdoor break-in to loosen him up.

My post-mortems are even more of a gas, and even louder. I shout them out on purpose. I force you to slow down when we walk to the car: you still move too fast for the tropics. While we mosey on the asphalt, I bawl some choice words for my fans in the parking lot. The next day, they quote them all over town.

Last week: how could they forget? — Poor Tancredo, he spit on his oboe so much, it choked up. What the hell did he think he was blowing? — That was a good one, no? His 'husband' plays the bassoon—faggotto in Italian, as you know. Need I say more?

Catulo's always gossiping, he's such a snoop. He says you've started feeling like Titania after her dream—the moment when she realizes what Bottom's name means: that he's a total ASS. Yeah, well you can kiss MY ass if that's what you believe. He asked you the other day why you don't talk about me all the time, like when you were head over heels in love. He claims you answered something unforgivable. — Oh, that tyrannosaurus rex? Isn't she extinct? — If you really said that, Chiara, screw you!

Isla Fandango, September 1991

I've been so BUSY the last six months! First of all, we had the Pan-Caribbean Games. There were so many sports teams taking me to motels, I almost got lockjaw and broken hips. Athletes can be over-active, especially when their pals are cheering them on. Then there was the summer, and I had to go to a million beach parties. Now things have simmered down. I'm feeling so glum, Chiara, even you might seem like fun.

On the phone I hold my nose and talk Scandinavian. I don't mean a REAL language, just random bits I picked up on concert tours in Denmark, Norway, and Sweden. I fool you for a while, until I don't.

I'd recognize that lisp anywhere, Lamia.

Don't be a pill. Is that any way to treat a PRINCESS, 'una Princesa tropical'? You've got my phone number. Why haven't you called?

I've been wanting to. But I couldn't get up the courage.

HAH! What am I, a gorilla? Think I'll grab you and squeeze you too much? That's probably one of your fantasies.

You clam up for a minute. Then you say, in a tiny voice: No, you're more like a boa constrictor…

How DARE you? I shout. — But I'm only pretending, and you know it. — I didn't ring you up to be insulted! I'm inviting you to a family chow-down tomorrow. It'll be so dull you'll fit right in. I've got to show them once and for all that you're a serious lady-friend. People say ugly things about me—'malas lenguas,' like your pal Catulo, with his evil tongue—and all that tittle-tattle gets back to my father. Tomorrow's the old bastard's birthday, and they're having an EXCUSE for a party at our beach house. I'll pick you up at eleven!

I assume you mean AM…

Of course, Miss Knucklehead!

I hang up the phone. Chiara, how can you be so thick? You've got a point, though. In Canuba, parties often start at eleven PM! But not for a brontosaurus like my Papa… Well, I'm not too young myself anymore. Thirty-nine: soon I'll be pushing fifty. But I look exactly the same as when I was twenty. Not a DAY more!

The next morning, it takes me a long time to get dressed. So many things to choose from in the closet, even if they're mostly out of fashion. I finally go for a skin-tight mini-skirt, magenta linen stitched with DARLING orange leaves. My canary-yellow top is what you'd call 'minimalist'—probably a dig, coming from you.

You're standing on the corner, pointing at your watch. All right, all right! I say. I'm not much more than an hour late. What's the big DEAL? Pull your panties back over your cunt.

Don't use language like that, Lamia! It doesn't become you.

Well, guess what? I don't WANT it to become me. Hahaha.

That's not what I mean, and you know it.

You're always such a stickler: it's like water off a duck's back to me. I let you stew in your juices while I get some kicks, driving as fast as I can. We race down the highway, bypassing the city, then veer to the western jag of Ocean Drive. Pretty soon we're zooming past the airport, and

you've calmed down enough to quiz me about my father—
the 'Greece-ball,' as I call him.

Oh yeah, he's a Greek Geek, I rattle on. Pretends he's
got an engineering degree! But if he knows anything, it
comes from *Reader's Digest* and *Popular Science*. He's got
stacks of moldy issues in his man-cave. He's like all the
other SEAMEN who spurt and squirt in ports, looking
for whores. I think he married my mother only because
of her name—Grecia. Instead of raising chickens, riding
horses, and wading in rivers, the way Canubans like to do,
he cruises the ocean blue.

Wandering Odysseus, eh?

Sure. The opposite of Canubans. We're ALLERGIC to
the sea.

You nod. — I've always found it odd that there are so
few fishermen here.

That's because Canubans are peasants, total HICKS.
They want fresh water, to wash off their sweat.

We've got tons of fishermen in Sicily. But Canuba is
bigger, so sometimes the ocean is far away... Besides the
restaurants, your father's involved in shipping too?

Just like I said, he's a TYPICAL Greek: tavernas and
boats. He owns a few beat-up cargo ships, and most of the
time he tools around on them.

Sounds like my father and his friends.

Hahaha, Chiara. Cargo ships aren't YACHTS. But as
you've told me, your father's only a guest.

Yes, I guess that puts him in his place.

You're playing humble, I say to myself. He's a Marchese! I won't feed your ego, though: I couldn't care less. — I'm sure Papa has his floozies in Bonaventura, and half the other islands. We're supposed to be THANKFUL he's spending his birthday with us. I'm glad you're standing in as my 'amiga.'

That can mean a lot of things, especially here. Go ahead. Use me, abuse me.

I raise an eyebrow: Uh-huh, you'd LIKE that, wouldn't you?

Try me, and you'll find out…

I shoot you a glance: Hey Chiara! I'm amazed you're being up front for a change.

After speeding past the airport, we skirt a whole string of low-rent motels on the ocean side of the road. They've got neon signs on top with namby-pamby names like Espuma, Brisa del Mar, Sunset, and Hotel del Encanto. But everybody knows what they're REALLY for!

You pipe up: Those must be the motels Catulo's told me about.

AHA! What did he say?

Since Canubans can't leave home till they're married, they resort to these 'establishments.'

To do WHAT, Chiara?

You shrug: Beats me.

UGH, you're so goody-two-shoes. Can't you just say

they go there to FUCK?

I don't use language like that.

You're living in the Victorian Age, Chiara. I'm not a lady, I'm a princess, and we can say whatever we want. It might be good THERAPY for you to go to these motels, instead of sobbing over Amado. Let him rest in peace.

I turn the wheel abruptly to the right, almost sideswiping a car. The driver's a middle-aged hag in hair-curlers. She gives me a dirty look. Well, why in the HELL wasn't she going faster? We skid into an entryway, an arch with pink curlicues: Pleasure Inn.

You smirk: Maybe we aren't going to the family get-together, after all.

I punch you in the ribs: Don't get EXCITED. I'm not gonna shanghai you today. We're already late, so who cares? Now for a game! Is there anything missing here?

Yes, where's the reception desk?

ATTAGIRL! To check in, you pull up next to that first little building. On the driver's side, there's a tiny hole in the wall, about four inches square. You stick your money through, and the guy inside pokes out a key, without seeing who you are. Maybe you're a millionaire's wife with her gardener, or an eighty-year-old judge with an underage girl, or a politician with some boy he picked up—or just a couplea teenagers, afraid of their parents. You pay by the hour, and you get a king-size bed, a private jacuzzi, and porno films, all included in the price.

Hmmm, a whole new meaning for the term 'all-inclusive...' But what about the other customers? Can't they see you going in and out?

We're really LATE! I j-curve out of the driveway, scorching the tires. You grab the dashboard like you're afraid of whiplash. — No, dumbo. Each cabin has its own garage, and they're all set at different angles. They've thought of everything!

We bypass crummy Cambuca Beach, where the poor folks go, with their boom-boxes and coolers of Papagayo beer. Further on, I feel ASHAMED to turn into Caracol, the second-tier resort where my Papa owns a 'villa.' It's half a mile from the beach, with a brown shingle roof, concrete blocks on a slab, and a shared kiddie-pool. He could afford something better, but he's too much of a tightwad.

It's only when I'm with a friend as classy as you that I remember how ICKY he is. In Canuba, we grow up watching re-runs of gringo children's shows. With his oily shock of hair, jerky gestures, and moussaka accent, my Papa's like a cross between Zorba and Howdy Doody. He tries to be welcoming. He thinks he's bowling you over by talking about an article in *Scientific American* on translation machines. You're courteous, but you say you don't believe a word of it, that languages are too complex, that inflection and tone change everything... OH GOD, you're even worse than him!

He's used to being the center of attention. He switches

the topic to fortune-telling. He clears his throat to sound more important. — I gave a lecture once at the Canuban Chamber of Commerce on 'Astrology and Business Decisions.'

Oh really? you ask in a who-cares voice.

He reads your palm on the spot. — You're gullible, Chiara. Your love life is out of whack, and your intestines are jittery.

Well, he got THAT right, I whisper in your ear.

My mother and Tía Claribel don't have time for their telenovelas today. Their younger sister Florinda tries to help out, though she's pregnant as a pumpkin with her fifth child. Why women want to have BABIES is beyond me! Nine months of hell, and a lifetime of headaches. Oh well, whatever floats their boat. All three of em bustle around the kitchen and dining room, barking at a couplea country maids who can't keep track of anything—place settings, matching napkins, and all that bourgeois razzamatazz.

I hadn't ever thought about it, but even when the meal's a buffet like today, laid out on side-tables, there's still a pecking order. The men take the best chairs, and they don't bother to get back up.

See, you say under your breath, like some kinda anthropologist in Borneo: The women are serving the guests first, the males second, and then themselves.

So WHAT? It's just a Canuban custom!

Several of my Papa's restaurant-owner cronies join

us for the wingding, but not ONE of them mentions the cuisine. Maybe because they're all too crocked, like Papa himself! That's the only excuse for his obnoxious questions about your income. I guess he's putting you through the third degree, as a candidate to set up house with me.

If I settled down with a man, I'd definitely call the shots. I'm not ABOUT to ladle out food for lunkheads. Now if they want to feed ME a sausage, that's something else. It's funny: my parents have always treated me like a boy, without any kitchen duties. My mother offers me a plate of Canuban gunk today, but I shove it aside. I pick at a small dish of salad. She tries again, and I have to snap at her, the way she likes it. With me, she's passive-aggressive.

NO THANKS, Mamá! I tell her. I don't want to turn into a hippopotamus, like Papa.

You elbow me under the table. Why should you give a damn, Chiara? Somebody's got to make him lose weight, at least for his health. I love him, I guess, but most of the time he's useless.

When lunch, 'conversation,' and cake—with an off-key 'Cumpleaños Feliz'—FINALLY come to an end, I rescue you from my father. He's launched into a speech about 'fiscal responsibility,' with you in mind—if you can call it a mind.

SORRY, Papa. We want to go swimming, and we have to hit the pool before it gets too dark.

In fact, it's only four-thirty or so. As soon as we change

into our swimsuits, I start groaning. — All my father ever does is slobber about the same old stuff. His friends are idiots, but thank God they fall asleep when they get sloshed. It takes him a few minutes more! — I trace a frowny on the pavement with my wet, shapely toes, then mess it up. — I have an idea, Chiara, let's go to Hermosa! We've gotta ditch these goons, ASAP!

Hermosa? Isn't that where Catulo used to live? But it's an hour west of here, no? Besides, Lamia, all I brought along was the clothes on my back.

You're such a square. Can't you improvise for a change? Just do something for the hell of it?

I kiss you on the cheek. THAT gets you moist. — All right, I'm all yours.

Yeah, Chiara, you WISH!

My mother looks hurt we're leaving so soon, but I'm ruthless. As for my father, he's blotto now. He's snoring in an armchair, with birthday candles stuck in his ears. His chums are wide awake now. They're laughing their heads off at their practical joke. HOHOHO! Besides, they wouldn't want to miss seeing me in my bikini...

I hurry you past my mother and aunts. You're always so POLITE. When we hit the highway again, we're still in our bathing suits.

I whip the steering wheel back and forth, and you keep ogling my curvy torso and jiggly boobs. You can't HELP herself. You're OK in your school-teacher one-piece, but

I'm super-sexy in my plum-purple, dental-floss thong. I jabber about the latest scandals, ignoring your slack-jawed lust.

By now it's six in the afternoon. With the top down, and going fast, our hair ends up in a mess. Yours is thick, I'll say that for you. But mine's more striking.

You try to wow me by talking pretty. — I love this hour of the day, Lamia. You know, when the sun slants from the west, raking the sea with its fingers. Just look at those shadows the clouds make on the swells. Dark blue, cobalt. They're lolling out there, as lazy as whales.

I don't pander to you: no comment. We swoosh away from the ocean and scud through the savannas. I love them, they're so LUSH—dotted with palms and Brahman cattle.

I can't resist a few jabs. — Doesn't this look like Indonesia, Chiara? Hasn't that MORON Catulo treated you to his 'all-the-world-in-an-island' spiel?

I usually see him in Puerto Indio. Except for a whale-watching trip and a day at Cambuca Beach, we've never traveled anywhere in Canuba.

Well, be sure to take some Dramamine when you do: it might help with the NAUSEA. He'll go on and on about how our mountains are from Switzerland, our pastures from India, our northern cliffs from the Canaries, our southwest beaches from Polynesia. He'll jaw and jaw till your ears fall off.

With the Corvette in tow, we take the short ferry-ride to Isla Fandango.

Wasn't this place planned as an artists' colony? you ask along the way.

I see the founder of the whole shebang on a nearby bench, so I raise my voice. — Yeah, it's a pseudo-bohemian Disneyland, to make up for the GROSS resort on the mainland. But the gardens are nice. And guess what, sidekick? I've got a SURPRISE for you!

I knew you had something up your sleeve.

Always! A girl's gotta have a plan! I hate Catulo, but I sorta LIKE his girlfriend, Pomona. We compare notes sometimes about how terrible he is. Anyway, she's got a villa on Fandango, and he's there this weekend too. Let's look them up! But you have to promise you'll talk to him, so I can X him out and only chat with HER.

Great! I agree.

Hahaha. No wonder! You've still got a crush on him. I can't imagine WHY!

You know why, Lamia. We had a fling when he was at NYU and I was at Princeton.

Humph. About a hundred years ago…

Catulo answers the doorbell. He's always upstaging everybody else: but not a DIVA. I march straight past him and say hello to Pomona, while Chiara sucks up to her ex-mate.

From across the room, I tune in on their conversation.

I've got STEREO ears! They come in handy for gossip.

Chiara practically drapes herself on the birdbrain. Is she trying to make me jealous? — Oh Catulo, what a treat to see you in your old habitat!

He has to unglue himself from her hug. — You bet, girlfriend, it's where I used to hang out, till the admin job at Cerrucho Beach came along. I lived in this house in my 'Fandango period.' Then Pomona made me an offer I couldn't refuse.

Did you decorate the place yourself?

Yes, with some helpful hints from my brother Virgilio. It's convenient to have an artist around.

Amazing! He's a painter, Horacio's a composer, and you're a choreographer. What a talented trio! No wonder they call you the Trinity. Anyway, I love the color scheme. Peach and lime: a combo with pizzazz...

Pomona and I run out of fat to chew pretty fast. You can bet your bottom dollar she won't leave you and Catulo alone, Chiara: she's well aware of your Jurassic past. We plop down on overstuffed sofas, while a Bono houseboy serves the drinks.

Pomona's frowzy and broad in the beam: no threat to a REAL woman like me—or even you, Chiara. She treats Catulo like an impish boy. For her benefit, I guess, he's in his ultra-hetero mode. He blathers on and on about baseball and the tourist trade in a flat, manly baritone, an octave below his swishy voice.

After a couple of V & T's, you can't CONTAIN yourself. You gaze at your hero and start gushing. — Mamma mia, don't we make a carefree foursome?

I belly-laugh, and raise my glass of H_2O. — Hahaha! Is that the opening line of a PORNO film? Away we go!

Pomona looks uncomfortable. — Lamia, please! I know you say things like that when you're drunk. But today you have no excuse.

Don't be so INHIBITED! You're supposed to be a sculptress. Drunk or sober, I'm the same. Yes, I'm on the wagon this afternoon. Last night I read the latest scoop in *Marie Claire*: teetotaling prolongs a woman's youth.

The tiresome sow disagrees. — Whatever! I toss back the booze, myself. I think alcohol preserves the body, like formaldehyde. None of us is getting any younger... Maybe you should take that as a hint, Lamia.

I've decided I DON'T like her, after all. — You're twenty years older than the rest of us, Pomona. And judging by you, your theory is wrong. BIG time.

The truth hurts. So much for your idea of a warm, fuzzy foursome, Chiara; I wouldn't want to have an orgy with these apes. In his fifties jargon, Catulo gives the signal we need to clear out. — Well, I guess you gals must be ready to hoof it.

Cut out the BS, I tell him. We know when we're not WANTED!

Better use the first-person singular, he sneers.

The POOF! Who does he think he is? I tossed our duds from this morning in a plastic bag, before we scrammed from Caracol. We take a quick shower, change into our civvies, and drive to a candlelit bistro along the cove, La Casa de Oro. I go there sometimes with sports teams, but only if they're inviting me: it's ultra-expensive. Now I've only got you, Chiara—Marian the Librarian. Oh well, at least you'll pay the bill.

Once we're seated, I have to bare my FANGS. — I bet Catulo charges Pomona for every lay he puts out. She's so loaded, and he's such a spendthrift. Why else would anybody WANT her? Some frumps believe if they're tubby, it helps em look younger—irons out the wrinkles. But it really makes em look like elephants: wrinkled AND obese!

You astound me by talking back. — What's with the lookism? You're just envious, Lamia… Catulo adores Rubenesque women.

I'm only jealous of her DOUGH. You're the one who wants that pinhead back between your legs, not me. But you won't fess up, even to yourself.

Chiara's such a hypocrite! I distract myself by scoping out the joint. My head swivels like a searchlight, probing every NOOK of the dining room. But all I detect is a former president of El Salvador, fondling a starlet in a corner booth. To pass the time, I order a bottle of Cristal. That should knock Chiara's purse for a loop. All in all, the meal's a disaster, so I'm glad the champagne is OK.

When we're done, you submissively pay the check. —
Shouldn't we be heading back to Puerto Indio? you ask.

Needless to say, I have ANOTHER PLAN! I set my lips
in a straight, resistant line. — What's the rush, Chiara? I
read in the paper there's a photography show at one of the
galleries. We might as well see it, since we're already here.
It's open till eleven.

You're a culture-vulture, so you perk right up. — Why
not, if you think it's worthwhile.

Worthwhile? We can't find out till we GET there!

She's guessed I'm up to something, and she's curious to
find out what. It only takes us ten minutes to walk to the
gallery, but it's a HIKE in my high-heels. We find it on the
second floor of a wooden building with gingerbread trim,
the pseudo-American variety. The exhibition features a
Chilean photographer, Fernando Cuevas.

You stand outside on the verandah, staring at the PR
poster. Whatever's in writing, you gotta READ it!

Oh Lamia, this does sound interesting! 'The sugarcane
plantations near Santa Clara, signed prints in black and
white...' Listen to what the photographer wrote: 'The
fieldhands, Bonaventuran immigrants, subsist in grim
isolation from the rest of the country. They're crowded into
infrahuman settlements called bateys—originally, a Taíno
term for a gaming ground. International NGOs often
lambaste Canuba for reducing these workers to a state akin
to slavery.'

Yada-yada, Chiara. The do-gooders always say stuff like that.

But Cuevas wanted to witness the bateys first-hand. He must be a compassionate man. 'As my pictures reveal,' he goes on, 'by their late twenties the workers lose their teeth from sucking on the cane, their main source of calories. The back-breaking loads and razor-sharp leaves, in plantings so dense they choke off the breeze, make their labor tantamount to torture.'

PLEASE, Chiara! Life is depressing enough.

I drag her through the door and collar the gallery-owner. I tell him I'm ecstatic about the snapshots. Chiara has a confused expression on her face. She's probably imagining the subject-matter appeals to my 'revolutionary side,' as she dubs it. NO WAY, José! Before long, I manage to segue to questions about Cuevas himself: Will he be coming by tonight, to sign his prints or check on sales?

There's a photo I especially like, I tell the gallerista. The one of the toothless man on a donkey. They're both so DARLING! Since I'm a musician, a fellow-artist, maybe Cuevas could give me a discount?

I bounce my boobs: that always does the trick. The gallery-owner caves in, and phones Cuevas at his guest-apartment across the street. When he shows up, you wink at me. He's not a hippy, social-science type, he's more like a movie star. I knew from his picture in the paper that he's a KNOCKOUT. He's got a round, smooth-shaven baby-face, and close-cropped hair like a jailbird: the perfect slave.

I'm normally hard to please; but now I fall all over myself with compliments, rolling my hips. — Hey, Fernando, I ADMIRE your work! Like the newspaper said, you're the South American Johnny Walker!

He's bashful. — Oh, I guess you mean Walker Evans. Yes, a local journalist wrote about how I'd 'tropicalized' Evans's style. But I'm from high in the Andes.

Don't worry. I can TROPICALIZE you, for sure! I just hopped out of my bathing suit a while ago.

He's at a loss for words. — Hmmm, your regular clothes are… exotic enough.

I wouldn't call them REGULAR! — I spin around to model my magenta skirt and yellow tank-top, showing off my figure. — Anyway, I'll be glad to get RID of them for you. What are you doing right now? Let's go to your place.

He stares at the ceiling, like he can't believe his ears. Oh NO, he's a marshmallow, a wuss. — Never mind, señorita. My wife wouldn't like it if you came up. We got married last week, and we're still on our honeymoon.

I'm BESIDE MYSELF. After I went to all this trouble, he dares to turn me down. I let him have it. — That's OKAAAAY by me. I'm very busy myself. This is a friend of mine from Italy. We're on our honeymoon, too. To judge by these crappy snapshots, all you've got TIME for is screwing—limply, no doubt. I could do better than this in handcuffs. But you've missed your chance to see me in

THOSE!

I'm sorry, he mumbles, I must've misunderstood. The gallery-owner thought you liked them. He said you wanted to buy one.

BUY one? Not even if you shoved it up my ass!

I storm out of the gallery, slamming the door. Behind me I hear you wishing the guy 'success.' What a lack of loyalty to ME!

When you catch up to me, you feel SORRY for him! — Good grief, Lamia. He looks like you hit him with a waffle-iron. Did you have to be so mean?

I'm still in a snit. — Mean? He insulted me. The nerve of that idiot. Why should I proposition HIM? I've got much better partners than a little PUSSY from the Colombian hills! — Aha, the word gives me a sudden thought. Switching gears, I grab you by the hand. — All right, I know you must think I'm a horrible person. And I am. — I strike my heart three times, like I used to do in church when I was small. — You asked me to USE you and ABUSE you, so here goes. Let's spend the night on Fandango, at the inn!

You hesitate. — What about your parents? It's not afternoon anymore. I don't want to jinx our relationship… If we're going to live together, we'll need your parents' blessing.

Huh? Afraid they'll cut me off without a dime? You've got enough for both of us. Are you stingy, or a COWARD like him? Who cares about my parents? If you want, I'll tell em the car broke down. Hey, dumbwad, you better eat me while I'm hot!

You agree, but you're trembling like a lamb, just before they cut its throat. I saw that in Bulgaria one time, at a peasant wedding. An hour later, the groom and me were doing it under a TREE. His clunky bride never knew!

Now I have to focus on driving to the hotel. It's the only one on the island. As you say, it's annoyingly 'twee.' Wrought-iron bedsteads, raw-silk curtains, bamboo chairs. That kind of garbage. Plus the ARTSY note: abstract prints any monkey could make, from the resort's 'famous lithography school.' Ugh. I switch on every light in the room.

You bellyache, of course. — Do we really need it this bright?

I let out a hoot. — What's the matter, don't you want to see me? Or maybe you're afraid you're too homely yourself? Don't worry, I'm not particular. Why ELSE would I be here with you? — I tumble you back on the bed and jerk off your shoes. — Pretty ankles, appetizing feet. You keep them well. I wish MEN were as finicky as you. — I suck your toes one by one, with a greedy, slurping sound. Since there's no porno flick, we've got to make our own. Then I peel off the rest of your clothes. — White, white, white. Chiara, this is like doing it with a NURSE!

You pipe up. — Lamia, it's just the way I dress. And I'm

sorry to ruin the mood. But after that champagne, I need to pee.

Exactly what the doctor ordered, Nurse Chiara. It does WONDERS for the complexion. — I fling off my duds and hustle you into the shower. Then I crouch between your legs. — I'm thirsty, girl. Forget Cristal. Let it pour, let it pour! The stream trickles down, while I gurgle a song I heard at a party. — Golden RAIN, golden RAIN! — I wobble my head, trying to catch every drop. With my satiny hair, I titillate your thighs. My tongue creeps north, darting in and out of your V. I bring you to the BRINK, then pull away.

I towel you off, slap-happy as a randy coach after the game. Tugging you onto the bed, I jump on top and firmly take the lead. You're steamrollered, CRUSHED! You don't know what hit you. I may wear girly clothes, but I manhandle my lovers like a pro.

Shoulderrubs, backrubs, buttockrubs. My fingers inch between your cheeks. You're pleading now. — Turn me over, Lamia… please…

Beg for it HARDER, and maybe I will. — Breastrubs, bellyrubs, lower and lower. Deep into your clit. Bubblegum. Taffy. Custard. Cream.

How did I know this would happen? I didn't, but I always come prepared. Men like it too, if they're brave enough: in Spanish we call a dildo a 'consolador,' a 'consoler.' I pull one out of my beach-bag, and make you ride me, reverse cowgirl style. Then I flip you over on your back. I'm on a JAG! I morph from missionary to dog, butterfly to broomstick, sixty-nine to spoon, throne to flagpole… One orgasm melts into the next… I bite, pound, and squeeze… I dilate in and out like a kaleidoscope…

I'm Lamia the CELLIST: here are my greatest hits. I fretwork your ass and bow your thighs, I vibrate your tendons, your strings… I'm Lamia the BANSHEE! I spur you and knee you, spank your face, cram my slit into your mouth… I'm Lamia the CHEF! I feed you truffles and nutmeg, anchovies and orange peel… I'm Lamia the TOOLKIT! I wrench you, scissor you, and tribble you… I'm Lamia the HAMMERHEAD! I slam you against the wall and ram your buttocks, so the bruises will last for weeks… I'm Lamia the CORKSCREW! My brutal kisses brand you with hickeys, destroy your palate, and shred your lips…

But in between, I beguile you with my tender melodies, my lyrical rubatos… My rallentandos, tapering off into languorous suspense… My cadences, pianissimo, in minor keys… and then, after the final chords, we both pass out… slumped across the gummy pillows, humid towels, and moist sheets…

The next morning, we ooze to the floor like puddles of molasses, our bodies converted into pulp. A room service brunch, with wallops of café con leche, restores us bit by bit. But it's half-past twelve before we can hobble down to

Playa Fandango.

A few minutes later, you're already nagging me. — My skin's too pale for this sun!

And mine's NOT?

The dermatologist warned me about 'rayos tropicales.' We don't have any sun-screen, do we?

Oh, shut UP. It would do you good to get some color, some tan on top of your piggy pink. Sun-screen! That's for sissies.

But you're right for once, Chiara. You doze off, you're so exhausted. An hour later, I notice a brown patch on your upper left cheek. Some of ME has rubbed off on you. I've marked you for life!

By the time you wake up, I'm staking out my next meal. You were just a Sicilian antipasto, a beccafico; now I want the main course. Fifty meters or so down the strand, WHO should I run into but Diego Serallés, the Spanish tenor? Kinda old, but wow, is he famous! When you turn up, we've been flirting for a while. I'm standing arms akimbo, tummy in—to set off my fabulous figure. He's telling me about his villa in Hermosa, with its own private beach.

Oh Diego, I'm saying, I'm sure you have TONS of houses around the world!

Over his shoulder, I see you coming closer, Chiara. I can't jerk my head for you to beat it, cause he's looking straight at me. Every INCH of me.

Señorita, he says, I'd be honored to invite you to my

little hut.

Hut? Don't kid around. Anything you've got must be ENORMOUS. Hahaha. Sure, Diego, I'll go there anytime you say. And we can DO anything you want. For YOU, I'd never hold back.

You're such a douche-bag, Chiara. Now you interrupt us. Don't you know who he IS? I try to ignore you. But you're standing right behind him when you call out my name. What a pain in the neck!

He wheels around. — Señorita… Ramia, was it? You didn't tell me you were here with a friend! Joder, maybe we can sing a trio… The best things come in threes.

He doesn't know you're too much of a stick-in-the-mud. Too bad, Sister Chiara! He gives me his number, and I tuck it away for a rainy day—in case I run out of baseball teams and rugby squads.

Plaza Drake to Paradiso, summer 1991

Ever since your lover-boy Amado died, your passion for me itches you like poison ivy. I can't BLAME you, I have so many fans. But really, you should control yourself. You've taken to stalking me at my father's restaurant, El Mediterráneo. You while away the day sipping tea and pretending to read, just WAITING to lay eyes on me.

That letter you wrote me before I left was too MUCH. All about my 'serpentine glide' and the 'hypnotic rippling of my flesh.' You called me your 'Greek-Canuban siren,' your 'Circe.' Please, gimme some slack.

I leave you in the lurch by heading to New York for a month. I've enrolled in some master classes at Juilliard—with Duncan Macduff, my IDOL. From day one, I try to lug him into the sack—but then I find out he's 'from the other shore,' as the Germans say. His accent's so weird he could be anything, from a deer-hunting queen to a Druid with a tree up his rear. Brits aren't as flexible as our island men: they think they have to be EITHER gay OR straight. Kinda provincial, Chiara, don't you agree?

I've rested for a week, after my heavy-duty lays in the Apple. But I suppose I'd better call you, Chiara. You always pamper my ego. Besides, my mother wants me to bring you some loony plants.

I've practiced my cello for twenty minutes, about as much as I can stand, and it's already two o'clock. — HELLO, I catch you off guard. Guess WHO?

No answer at the other end. FINALLY, you croak: Lamia, is that… you?

Abject worship: you're giving me my due. — Hi, I'm BAAAACK. Your nightmare! Your messages didn't get through, but I'm sure you tried every day. The maids are inept: it takes them an hour to spell a single WORD. Anyway, I've got some wacky red flowers for your patio.

My mother says they attract hummingbirds—you know, colibris. Right up your alley, verdad? I'll bring them over now.

I clunk down the phone before you can react. Otherwise, you'll go epileptic: petrified to face the FEMME FATALE! A few hours pass before I make it to your house. I have to select a dress, shoes, accessories. Take a bath, dry my hair, fluff it up. Put on my eyeshadow, mascara, lip-blush. Find out if any of my bedmates are free for a late-night wham-bam. No luck, so I guess it'll have to be Cream-of-Wheat Chiara…

When you open the door, I'm holding a teensy-weensy plastic pot with a few wilted seedlings. I buss the air next to your head. — Oh, I'm FAGGED from digging up these goddam things. Well, not me, really: our gardener. Tell yours to plant them tomorrow.

You pause, already bewitched. — I don't have a gardener.

WHAT, no gardener? You better get one. Just ask Luz Divina, that useless maid of yours. Here, even the servants have servants.

So Horacio always says… It used to be like that in Sicily, once upon a time. Progress, you know.

Silence sets in. You're afraid you'll put your foot in your mouth. You back up against your desk. You stare at me like a frightened sheep, knocking a book onto the floor.

Ditsy as ever, I see. I've PERSPIRED for you, and you're not inviting me to dinner?

Obviously, this hadn't occurred to you. I'd be h-h-happy to, you stutter. But I'm not d-d-dressed up like you. You're always such a f-f-fashion plate.

I twirl around, waving a doll-size handbag that goes with my frock, a MASTERPIECE of mauve chiffon. — Oh, when has a Sicilian ever known how to dress? All you skags ever wear is long black skirts—to match your moustaches, I guess. Don't worry, I'll settle for an informal terrace on Ocean Drive. It's in the other direction from where we went last time. Don't worry about the clothes. One of your white NUN-uniforms will do!

After you change, we trudge to my car. It's such a long walk, three blocks! You're already starting to get uppity. — I love to watch you move, Lamia. You're as majestic as a glacier when it calves.

That's ENOUGH out of you, Chiara! We climb into my red Corvette, scare some pedestrians out of the way, and torpedo down the Malecón. I scream over the traffic. I've told you what I call it: the Maricón! So many hustlers cruising for poofs. See em?

A bunch of elderly 'ducks' are checking out the boys, who flex their measly muscles along the sea-wall. Some female streetwalkers are swinging their piano-legs, too. — What get-ups! And you think I'M over the top, Chiara. — I don't pay attention to which lane I'm in for a second, and you grab my arm. You're so hysterical. Every time I dodge a truck or sideswipe a motorbike, you gasp.

All right, all right, fraidy-cat! I'll cut the speed. It's too early to eat anyway, only six o'clock. Let's go on a CULTURAL tour! There's probably a lot you still haven't seen, since you never leave the house.

Oh, I toured the entire city on foot with Catulo, eons ago; and I drove around by taxi with Amado.

You DID have your own car for a while. A casualty of love and war, just like Amado himself. Don't give either one of them a second thought. You probably hate me for saying that, but it's for your own good.

I circle toward the National Obelisk, a misshapen column. It was built by Manfredo Espinosa's father, Papito, when he was our dictator. — Yeah, dictator! President, Chiara? Let's call a spade a SPADE.

You nod. — The masses must have a crude nickname for this upended log. But they can't shock me.

Oh NO, Chiara, NOTHING could shock you. You're a card-carrying puta by now. Sure, respectable Canubans try to ignore this thing, like you gnocchi-heads from Vatican Land. But for the people, it's not just an 'Obelisco Macho,' like the one in Argentina. Did you realize it was ERECTED in the same shape as Papito's member?

Oh, come on, Lamia!

I'm not pulling your leg! The sculptor measured him in full HARD-ON, hand-pumped by Miss Puerto Indio and Miss Canuba. And then the two old GOATS had their way with both of them.

They'd have more pride today, thanks to feminists like you and me.

Humph, at least they'd charge them a HELLUVA lot more—a Rolls Royce or a condo at the beach.

We coast on past the next pile of concrete, the Independence Monument, a giant triangle split down the middle. — Ho hum, you grumble. Don't even bother.

No, it's weirder than you imagine. Canubans call it the 'Obelisco Hembra.' The female OBELISK! A she-male combo. Sort of third sex, no? Didn't Catulo ever tell you that?

You throw up your hands. — Third sex? More like a hermaphrodite. And now you're going to say Canuba has more of those than any other country: it's your go-to statistic.

You're such a know-it-all, Chiara! I rev up again and whoosh past some hotels, plus several mansions with walled gardens. The first belongs to the Peraltas, propped up by Carolina's dough, and the second to the Carduccis. The third was owned by Papito's brother, Stanley—till Manfredo bumped him off. If you kill your father, why not your uncle, too? Now it's the Ministry of Culture, where writers, artists, and musicians like me collect their subsidies. — 'Grants'! I yell into the wind. Hahaha. They're not free. The MORE you put out, the MORE you get!

The next property belongs to my friend Isabela, Burley Luna's daughter. It's gigantic too, but her wooden house is only a SHACK. I ring the bell at the gate to see if she's in.

Yeah, after a few minutes one of her 'assistants' opens the mossy green door. She's the wilting violet type; she'd probably keel over if you looked at her too hard.

When she leads us into the garden, you can hardly believe your eyes: an orchard and a vegetable farm, right on the Malecón. — Imagine using the island's most valuable real estate to grow papayas, beans, and carrots. Or beets and vegetable pears—that's Isabela's signature salad, by the way.

Oh, so she's New Age, like Horacio. He's a vegetarian, too.

HAH! Nobody can outdo Isabela, at veggies or anything else. Her family is the oldest in Canuba. They go all the way back to Santiago Columbus. The original Luna was his confidant; he came with him from Spain in 1507. The first Burley was one of Francis Drake's officers. He turned against the English, and joined the Spanish. He helped defeat the corsairs, since he knew all their tricks.

That makes him a national hero, I guess.

You better believe it. But remember, Drake is our hero, too. We like to keep our options OPEN.

At the end of a lemongrass patch, Isabela is weeding some purple cabbages. She waves a muddy trowel in our direction. Since her forearms are caked with grime, she juts out an elbow for us to grab, just like a campesino. Once the two of you start blabbing, I can't keep TRACK. Odes in

Latin, wines from Oregon, Japanese hot springs. Hogwash for eggheads.

People say Isabel will never marry; she'll rot away with the carrot tops. Her foxy eyes don't match her horsy bones: nobody can pin her down. She's always dropping false leads about who she'll pair up with. Today she introduces us to Edgar, her 'most distant British cousin,' on a visit here from Guernsey. After she washes up, he joins us for ginger tea at a splintered table. I have to watch where I sit, so I don't tear my dress. He's tall and skinny like Isabela, and he's bowled over by ME. No luck for Mr. Beanstalk: with a five-star diva, he can't bang or MASH.

When we leave, you start teasing me. — I've never seen you so well-behaved, Lamia. Instead of making filthy puns, you talked about Sainte-Colombe's pieces for gamba. What came over you?

Just because I don't respect YOU, doesn't mean I'm anti-social. Isabela and I were in day school together; she's a big sister to me.

I can't resist whizzing on to the Feria, the fairgrounds where Papito held his Exposición Mundial in the early fifties, before he was deposed by his son Manfredo. We get out of the car for a while, fascinated by the shoddy, run-down buildings.

Paris it wasn't, Chiara: CHEESY as hell. But he spent a lot of his stolen loot on this schlock. Every Canuban was ordered to attend, or else! It must've been a boot-licking orgy.

Especially when he crowned his daughter 'Empress of the Fair,' and made them bow down before her throne.

Serafina! What a dog! So you've read about her. They should've thrown a FLAG over her head.

Hahaha. Island poets wrote sonnets in praise of her splendor. Ambassador Miranda's was even composed in ancient Greek.

Catulo's father was a BROWN-NOSER back then. But lately, he's cleaned up his act.

What? Are you a Milady supporter?

SHHHH, dumbwad! All of us are, but we have to keep quiet. Milady's a woman with cojones; it takes big ones to defy thugs like the Espinosas. Oh, don't get me wrong. I liked some of Papito's schtick, and his son Manfredo's, too—our current lord and master!

The racist policies, you mean.

No, you always get me wrong! Papito's Exposición was okay. Remember, Canubans love a party, no matter who's giving it. And he kept the city spic and span. He held solidarity parades, and the citizens marched in white clothes, even white gloves. You would've fit right in!

Why did Manfredo change the Progreso Party color from white to blue?

He wanted to be different from his old man. But he couldn't choose RED, after he and his family had killed so many people over the years.

I see why Manfredo massacred his father's rebel soldiers.

But it's hard to grasp how he could murder his own father.

He had no choice, once Papito tried to take power again, in 1961. Anyway, it's SHARK EAT SHARK.

I'd say white was the Espinosas' symbol. Papito spent a fortune, trying to lighten his complexion. He splurged on plastic surgery, to correct his 'African' traits. Manfredo's done the same thing: they've internalized the racism of whites.

Yeah, Chiara, to you 'black is beautiful.' But most Canubans wouldn't agree; we say ALL colors are beautiful. You'll never understand us. We associate generic black with Bonos, the boat-people who cross the channel. Nobody from the Espinosa clan will ever have Taíno hair like mine—straight and long! They can lighten their skin, but they'll still be 'jabaos,' pasty with lots of freckles. Serafina has had so many treatments she looks like an albino; no wonder she never leaves Manfredo's mansion. They say she lives in a kind of doll's house at the back of the garden. I'd call it a doghouse, in more ways than one!

I'm glad Milady is proud to be Afro-Caribbean. But since she's adopted white as *her* Party's color, you'll probably say it's more of the same.

No, 'blacks' look FANTASTIC in white! She wears it all the time, just like you. You gringos are boneheads. And remember, to us, Europeans are gringos too. Supposedly, I'm whatever I 'identify as.' You identify as 'white,' so why can't I? Who cares if you're peachy-pink, and I'm vanilla-hazelnut?

I pull up in front of Ristorante Paradiso, an upscale eatery with an ocean view. — My Papa thinks his dump is better, but El Mediterráneo cannot COMPARE! I can't believe you've never been here before, in all these years!

You put on your Miss Priss face. — Beyond the Holy Boot, Lamia, 'Italian' food is inedible.

What a wet blanket, I say to myself. I lob the keys to a parking valet and swish my legs out of the car. He's hunky, and he appreciates my wink! — This place is kind of la-di-da inside. You may be a cuisine SNNNOB, but you're a clothes SLLLOB. We'll have to stay out here on the terrace, with the rubes.

Right off the bat, I tell the head waiter to bring us a bottle of Taittinger. — On the DOUBLE! — You're not that rich, Chiara, but you'll do anything for ME. CARAMBA, there's a bunch of Europeans out here! I pick a table as far away as possible. Uh oh, I know my lip's curling. What if it uncovers my buck tooth? Thank God it's only you, Chiara, so who cares…

Now I almost yell, to make sure they can hear me. — The LAST thing we need in Toyland is more Euro-trash. OK, you Italians are more hygienic than most, Chiara. But your men only come here for rum and sex. It's our own fault, I know. Canubans will bend over backwards for money—or forward, and hang on to their ankles. We should have a REVOLUTION, like in Cuba.

Really? you smile. In your designer frock and gold bracelets, you hardly seem like a Marxist.

Well, I AM! Cubans are a lot better off than Canubans. At least they have some SELF-RESPECT. Espinosa claims he's a leftist, but that's a ploy to stuff the ballot box. All we ever do is kowtow to Uncle Sam, and suck up to Krauts and Frogs on the beach. Suck up and roll over! Sure, there might be some drawbacks to living under Castro. It's hard to find top-of-the-line makeup and Jimmy Choo shoes in Havana. With Espinosa's tariffs, it's not much easier here.

Poor Lamia, what a cross you bear. I've spent a lot of time in Cuba—Hispaniola and Puerto Rico, too—and I never felt the need for over-priced glitz. What will you do when the 'revolution' overtakes Canuba?

Oh, I'll move back to Europe and play in a German orchestra. Every town's got one in Deutschland. But I'd probably DIE of boredom!

I guess Marxism isn't your cup of tea, after all. Why Germany, though? How about Austria instead? Your old stomping ground.

What a JOKE! You're just saying that because I studied in Musikstadt Wien, 'Music City Vienna.' It seemed so GERIATRIC, after Paris. But let me tell you, Chiara. In one way, Austrians are very clever. They sell their asses even faster than Canubans—and for a much higher price. Only they could convince the world that Beethoven was Austrian, and Hitler was a KRAUT!

It's true they were never de-Nazified, and even sent an SS officer to head up the UN.

The Vichy French were never de-Nazified, either. And how about the Mussolini fans? I'll never forget Loren and Mastroianni in *A Particular Day*, the best macaroni flick ever made. But the reality was WORSE than that.

You look disappointed. — Oh Lamia. You really detest us, don't you? What's your beef with Europeans?

The word 'detest' isn't strong enough. You're too conceited. And too TWISTED! You make mountains out of molehills. Americans are just the opposite: so simple-minded they're brainless. That's what makes them blow up other countries. Anyway, I had a lot of success in Northern Europe—success with my cello, and SUCK-cess with the men. They're used to frigid women who don't do squat in bed. I was a sensation! Aristocrats, industrialists, bankers, they all got into trouble because of me.

You yawn like you can't be bothered, like you've heard it all before. And you have. Why do I repeat myself? Why am I so insecure? Maybe it's because I love you too much. Another me says no, I don't need you at all. You or anyone. I'm so MARVELOUS, I'm in love with myself. OK, OK, I know I'm bragging now! But it's NOT bragging if it's true. Besides, the champagne is drying out my brain: we're on our second bottle. My lisp is getting worse, and I feel kinda unsteady. Oh well, I remember, it's only you, Chiara. I ramble on, out loud.

And I mean FUCK-UPS! You know, when they had wives, or lived with their mothers if they were super-young. And they'd get arrested for doing it with me in the car, or behind some scratchy bushes in a park. Or when their parents thought they might marry me, and freaked out because I was 'African'! They were dead WRONG about that! Just feel my hair!

You stroke my 'platinum mane,' as my hairdresser calls it. He's a muscle Mary. — Why on earth do you persist in rejecting your race? you gripe. It's the combination of mahogany skin and ashen hair that makes your looks so distinctive. I love the way people here are ethnically mixed.

Love it? It's TERRIBLE! What if I had a baby with frizzy hair? It would be my worst nightmare.

Your eyes mist up. — Your nightmare would be my dream, Lamia... Now that you mention it, do you like children? Ever since Amado died, I've longed to bring up a daughter with a female partner. I don't want a husband: my father's a disaster, maybe that's why. But I really do believe that women make better parents than men.

Do I like children? Sure. For BREAKFAST: medium well, with mangú. From what I hear, your pal Leandra is having enough babies for the rest of us. Thank God I rejected that hubby of hers, Ángel María. Anyway, I was talking about Europe, before you interrupted me. I used to screw with Slavs when I'd go on cello gigs in the East. They've got high-octane schlongs, and they're so

PRIMITIVE!

Yes, you always call them 'Slavic Tarzans.'

RIGHT! And I'm their Cheetah. — I make humongous lips and a vacuum-cleaner sound, smacking so loud the Europeans turn around. Who gives a damn? They're only wearing shorts and T-shirts, the scum!

It's close to midnight now, but this is Canuba! You're about to faint by the time the waiters bring our food. You sniff, and call it 'sub-Italian fare.' I have to agree. — Sure, it's 'nothing from the other world,' as we say in Spanish: nada del otro mundo. This ain't Bell'Italia. But I'm sick of going to my Papa's UPCHUCK-wagon.

Don't exaggerate. El Mediterraneo's Greek dishes are good.

You're so wishy-washy! I change the subject. — New Year's Eve is the best time for this place, Paradiso: I mean the morning after. All the GOLDEN kids end up here for brunch, after they've spent the whole night partying. It's a RIOT. I was one of the gang, already at age twelve!

You sigh. — I can just imagine what you looked like then. Prematurely ripe, no doubt. Didn't your parents try to keep you under control?

They wouldn't have DARED. Anyhow, now it's a tradition. I saw Horacio here last year, staring at the girls and boys like a crocodile. He yapped my ears off. Katydids and corduroys, all that ancient Greek baloney.

Karyatids and kouroi, you correct me. You're such a

schoolmarm!

I've inhaled the second bottle. Now I'm sliding into a downswing. It's always like that… — Sometimes I feel so SAD! I don't know how I ended up with all these semi-homos. My mother says they're bad luck—that they keep a girl from getting married.

I don't think so, Lamia. To hear you tell it, you have hundreds of men on your list who're not 'semi-homos' at all. Anyway, please don't use slurs like that around me.

I brush you off: Yeah, but straight guys are AIRHEADS. And half the time they're married, stealing an hour or two from the kiddies and the Missus. Then I'M the one who gets in hot water. Everybody's so jealous of me. Especially women. Sure, I can see why. All I do is play the cello, wear fancy dresses, and fuck! The maids take care of the housework. I don't even know how to cook. I'm afraid to boil water—it might explode!

Champagne goes to my head: I'm SMASHED. How you can be so slutty, I don't know, but you hit on me while I'm down. Leaning closer, you run your fingers through my hair again. — Not everyone resents you, darling. Catulo thinks you're a phenomenon.

PHENOMENON? He's just being bitchy. Whatever he says, I hate his guts. I thought I'd finally found a sensitive man who was really a MAN—but he's just another BI-BOZO. It's terrible, Chiara. I'm like a divining rod. Whoever I screw turns out to be queer. At first they're great in bed, but then they get lazy. — I switch to falsetto. — 'Oh Lamia, guess what? I'd like to be PASSIVE for a change.' The next thing I know they're sticking a dildo in my hand, and asking me to shove it you know where. It's just not fair!

Come now, Lamia. Most of the time, you coax them into the charade. It's a power play. You've taught me your tricks: I even used them on Amado. He had male lovers, too, and he was as macho as they come. You're always saying that nobody's gay or straight, any more than they're black or white. Maybe you're right. I used to find your frankness astounding—even repugnant. But not anymore: it's like the locker-room talk in American films. You're so dominant, men want you to 'rise to the top.'

The waiters are ogling us, like we're she-wolves in heat. I jerk your hand out of my hair and bite it. Watch out! I tell you. Hang around me, and who knows WHAT I'll turn you into! 5-4-3-2-1: get ready for blast off, Chiara!

Plaza Drake, summer 1991

I used to go 'cruising' on the Malecón with Catulo, Horacio's older brother, when he was my boyfriend. I guess now I'll have to fall back on you, Chiara. While we whiz along the Ocean Boulevard, you try to look at the sea, but all you can see is ME. I catch you staring at my curves like a high-school kid. Embarrassed, you shift your focus to my eyes. They're my best feature, really UNBELIEVABLE. I swivel my head so you can admire them from different angles. I don't need to glance at the road, I know it so well. I just barrel ahead—so what, if you're terrified! Between your groans and yelps of fear, you tell me how 'the ocean sparkles in my irises,' how they 'give off glints of silver, aquamarine, and gold.' La da dee, la da da.

But it's the gospel truth. Nobody's peepers change color more than mine—they go from grey to green, hazel to amber, Liz Taylor violet to Paul Newman blue. It depends on what I'm wearing, even on my moods. I rely on my heavy eyelids to express cool contempt, sensual challenge, or mock surrender. I practice in front of the mirror every day. I've always had a flair for theatrical effects. I coif my hair as a built-in prop, to suit the scene I want to stage. My main role is FEMME FATALE.

You're so bland compared to me, Chiara. When I studied the cello in France, Italy, and Austria, the other students were asexual—good-looking, but up-tight. Not really interested in getting down. Maybe the Vatican makes them that way... To hear you tell it, Sicily is more like the Caribbean.

You've told me how when you were twelve or thirteen, you OD'd on frottage with your cousins, Annita and Mara Razia. Am I getting their names right? In your villa near Notica, your home town, the siesta hour was sacred—but only the adults really slept. Without discussing it, you girls knew exactly what you were after. You got off, ah, ah… with a kind of dreamy softness: delicate little fingers on hills, valleys, and holes. And then all over again, with lips and tongues. Years later you had some one-nighters with broads in New York—the same wishy-washy, white-bread stuff. Yeah, a lot of lesbian flicks are like that, too.

But if I ever screw you, I'll take you to a brave new world. I'll blast you into the future. I'm like a cave explorer on the planet Mars. I want to pry my way down narrow passageways, whiff the perfume of funky, closed-off chambers. To me you'll be like a nautilus shell. Deep, deep behind the barriers… that's where your essence quivers, succulent and pink to my tongue. Or juggling roles, I'll turn into the Minotaur: with my trusty dildo, I'll gore you better than any man. And then the play will begin again… To me it'll just be acting, and I'll relish every minute of the skit.

Sometimes I wish we could do that… savor our subterranean journey, where we meet far away from the harshness of day… far away from the car wreck of personalities: you, Miss Nun, and me, Captain Outrageous…

But we live in the real world, like it or not. After what happened a few days ago, when you and Catulo had dinner with Chuchu Mendoza, you're not surprised when I turn up at your house. I try to sound like a python hissing outside your window. — SSSSS: I know you're there. Let me in right this minute, or I'll do a MOONY. Your neighbors will love it!

Lamia, please! At least give me time to open the door…

When I sashay into your sala, I don't let you pause for breath. — I passed by earlier, but the busybody across the street told me you were out. See how they keep tabs on you? I didn't even have to ask her. Oh, I tell you, this country was CREATED for gossip.

Agreed, Lamia, and most of it's false! The other day I overheard two little boys talking on my doorstep. 'My dad told me that gringa writes reports for the CIA,' one of them said. 'What's that?' the other one said. 'I don't know,' the first one said. 'Reports about what?' the other one said. 'I don't know,' the first one said. 'Maybe what we had for lunch.'

I swagger around the room. I'm unconvinced. — They might've been RIGHT. You may be Italian, but everybody believes you work for the CIA. Or NATO. If I didn't know how useless you are, I'd think the same.

No comment, Lamia. Let's get to the scuttlebutt. You want to talk trash, not Tom Clancy.

Who, MOI? Well, I *did* run into Horacio last night on the Malecón—and he said you were there.

There? Where?

At Arnaud Fontaine's, dummy. For Catulo's latest cat-fight with Chuchu Mendoza!

Yes, they really got off on the wrong foot.

That's the ONLY foot with Chuchu. She's such a tramp!

I found her intriguing. I'd like to see her again, one on one.

See her again? If you do, you're no friend of mine—not that I NEED friends like you.

You backpedal, afraid you might lose me. — Hmm, I doubt I'll run into Chuchu anytime soon. But Arnaud told me she went to the Carnival in Rio last year. I'd like to go, too. She'd probably have some travel tips.

Yeah, more than you bargained for! You know what I heard? She rented a huge penthouse with a pool, for herself and all those fruitcake mutts she feeds … — I lower my voice dramatically. Now I've come to the point: dishing out the dirt on Chuchu, so you'll drop her like a hot salami. — You wouldn't BELIEVE what went on in that place. They brought machos in from the streets, thugs who screwed them in every room, even on the dinner table during meals. Chuchu flopped around, drunk and doped up, watching everybody go berserk!

I guess we missed a lot of fun… Sounds risky, though…

In more ways than one! Just think of all the clap. And Rio's an iffy place—loaded with criminals. Not safe like Puerto Indio.

You try to distract me from Chuchu. — Why do you suppose that is, Lamia?

How the hell would I know? I guess Canubans are too

LAZY to whack each other. Just like they're too 'flojos' to start a revolution.

The police are pretty repressive here, I've heard. Maybe that keeps them in line. But sometimes the cure can be worse than the disease…

You don't have air-conditioning: it's an eco-fad you picked up at Princeton. I'm about to faint, so I sink into a chair. — You're right: a LOT worse! I didn't know how much until the last few days. Have you heard we had a robbery at our house?

What? Nobody got hurt, I hope. Is Doña Grecia all right?

Oh, my mother's a TANK! You'd need a bazooka to blow her up. The only one who got hurt was the thief!

What happened?

Well, I came home from my 'rehearsal' the other night and saw a woman crouched in the entry hall. When I screamed, she bolted out the front door! But that wasn't the worst part. My mother went to the police and reported the incident. They didn't bother to investigate; they said they already knew who she was: she'd been caught several times. They dragged her out of the slum where she lives and brought her straight to us. They'd found every last thing she'd stolen. But they made us pay THEM to get it all back. Then they beat the daylights out of her, right in front of us. She confessed, Chiara. She also bled all over the floor. It was horrible!

You think I don't have a heart, but I do… You shake your head. — That *is* horrible, Lamia. In fact, it's police brutality.

Humph! It happens all the time around here. But I'd never seen it with my own two eyes!

You fiddle with a strand of your hair, Chiara, that stupid tic of yours. — Though the island has always seemed like heaven to me—until Amado died—to others, it's an inferno.

You've sidetracked me, but not for long. I'm still obsessing about my enemy. — Just think how crazy Chuchu is, letting all those low-lifes use her pool. And in Rio! Some of her lapdogs go for tough-guys who can really get violent. She might've been raped, NOT that she would've noticed. She might've ended up dead—but WHO could tell the difference?

Don't be so snarky, Lamia. From what I saw of Chuchu, I imagine she can handle whatever comes along…

What, you're paying her a compliment? — I light into you. — Chiara, you're just impressed by that phony French accent of hers! She goes around saying she picked it up from her mother, but that's a LIE. She puts it on to sound la-di-da. Anyway, you'd better forget about her, because she's already married.

A low blow, but you deserve it. Ever since you fell for me, you've proposed we should set up house, but I've always turned you down. Not that I'm going to let that

Chuchu replace me! You wrinkle your nose. — Was one of those cross-dressers the other night her husband?

Yes, Chiara, the queeniest of them all: Farfalo. If you want to hitch up with Chuchu, you better get a sex-change to male—and start using high heels!

Hmmm. So Chuchu wears the pants, as they used to say.

Pants? You mean leather and chains. She beats Farfalo with a belt and makes him walk on all fours—with a dog-collar and a leash, and a bow in his hair, just like a poodle. She has sex with guys right in front of him, and he has to lick them clean. That's the part he likes the MOST, I bet! When she really wants to punish him, she torches all his clothes. They're the only thing he cares about, especially his lingerie. Then she buys him a whole new wardrobe. A week later, she gets mad and burns his clothes again. The cycle never stops.

Must be pretty expensive.

Hah, she couldn't care LESS. She's so loaded, the money can't run out. That's what drives me crazy. If I had that much moolah, I could buy a husband too. Or two or three! She wastes a fortune on that nincompoop. My salary from the orchestra hardly even pays for my makeup. It isn't fair.

Why the envy, Lamia? Your father buys you anything you want.

True. But I'd like to be in CHARGE.

All that filthy lucre… think how dreadful it would be

for your character.

You're a hypocrite, Chiara! You've always said there's no LINK between money and morals—good or bad. — Now you've got me crying. From pure indignation! The mascara's leaving snail-tracks down my cheeks. — Anyway, when it comes to fathers, I'd rather have my grumpy old Greek than that thieving CROOK, Pleverino Mendoza. He should be festering in jail, not living the high life in Hong Kong and St. Tropez.

El Mediterráneo to the Port, summer 1991

I suppose I might as well look in on you today. You're back in town after one of your tours of the world. 'Travel journalism,' humph! You call it work, Chiara, but it sounds like fun to me, and FUN is my middle name. Ever since Amado died, you've been depressed. I don't know why—men are a dime a dozen.

When I call you, you tell me you've been 'reading in your library.' So what ELSE is new? I bet your heart is beating a mile a minute now. People say my voice gives off a sexy vibe, so you must feel like you're sitting in the ELECTRIC chair.

Let's go for a RIDE! I holler. It'll get you out of the dumps. All you ever do is flop around and MOPE. My car's around the corner, in front of Papa's moussaka joint. Meet me there in ten minutes. And that's an ORDER. We'll drive along the Malecón, and then I'll take you to my house!

I hang up: I'm used to being obeyed. Besides, you're so nutty you'll make up some excuse, if I give you half a chance. We've always rendezvoused at restaurants—mainly my father's place. That's where Horacio introduced us, after Catulo invited you down. What, about ten years ago? 1980, 1979? I've never taken you home with me before, because my family is such a DRAG.

It's not a 'typical family,' just crazy and Canuban—normal for us, I guess. But maybe meeting the jokers at 'our home' will get your mind off Amado. And maybe you'll take ME more seriously. I need this gal thing for cover—you and me shacking up some day—so my mother will stop bugging me.

MARRIAGE? I want dozens of men, not just one, and so should you. Amado's wreck happened a couple of years ago, so you've gotta get a grip. Horacio says you talk about being a 'widow without weeds.' How Victorian, you little twit!

At El Mediterráneo, I'm leaning against the Colonial portico. I'm dressed to kill: an orange miniskirt and a low-cut, chartreuse blouse. That should pep you up—and make your tongue hang out. You've got some nerve, getting here late. I said ten minutes, and it's been fifteen. I swing my snakeskin bag back and forth. — Well, Chiara, it's about

TIME!

I'm sorry, you whimper. Maybe if you'd given me more warning…

WARNING? What am I, a hurricane?

As we head for my car, you speed up to a New York pace. — Wait, I moan, I can't keep up with you! Won't you ever LEARN? Or are you just being a bitch? Walk like a Canuban! You never pick up your feet, and you pretend you're standing still.

When we reach the red convertible, I feel like you've been tugging me along for hours and hours. I've come up in the world since the Volkswagen days, back when we met. But my Corvette C-4, a present from Papa, already has some battle scars. — Don't look at the scratches, Chiara. I can't figure out why these ASSHOLES keep running into me!

I took you on your first ride on the Malecón in that red beetle, years ago. It's no big deal, just a winding road along the ocean. But you like to DROOL over the past and talk mumbo-jumbo, so here you go again.

Oh Lamia, I'm grateful to you for this sea. Yes, it's a gift from you. I'm still in love with the fickle Caribbean, in all its varied moods. On sunny days like today, it's a thousand tones of blue and green, from midnight to aquamarine…

You could gabble on for hours. To shut you up, I double back to town on the freeway. You like to call the way I move 'Lamian physics.' When I'm walking, you say, it's a skit by

Marcel Marceau, all in slow mo. But when I drive, it's just the opposite: I aim for MACH 3. Right now, I rev up the motor so it roars. — I know you'd like to loop back the way we came, by the scenic route. But I can go FASTER here. Besides, I like to watch the ocean rush by.

It's rushing by, all right! — You fumble for your seatbelt. Of course, I've had the thing removed.

How many times do I have to tell you, dumbbell? I scream over the engine. No chastity-belts in Toyland! They're for WIMPS.

Toyland is my nickname for Canuba. To me this country isn't real, it's only make-believe. The Spanish, French, and English ruined our island from the get-go. Then the Americans socked us with the knockout punch. This morning, after a pathetic lay—the guy couldn't even get a hard-on—I feel more riled up than ever. — Toyland, yeah! And you better not object, Chiara. There's no CULTURE here. One schlocky art museum, a couplea two-bit galleries, and a lousy concert once in a while.

You wouldn't dare disagree with me, so you try another tack. — Even if you think it's a Sahara of the Bozart, what about the folk traditions?

Are you NUTS? I yell. A bunch of blockheads beating on drums? And the more those Bonos keep crossing the channel, the WORSE it gets.

I swerve past a campesino on his donkey—right in the middle of the highway! I'm not being racist about the Bonos, I say to myself. You think I'm filled with self-hatred, but no. In Europe my skin seemed 'black' to most 'whites'—or as I'd put: 'hazelnut' to most 'pinks.' Why can't we be a million different colors, instead of just two?

When I lived in Paris, my girlfriends quoted Senghor and shacked up with Africans. Most of them were snooty Americans, studying music like me. I got a kick out of shocking them! Well, maybe Y'ALL are pure crackers, but I'm a mixture, a Latina, I used to drawl; and I don't COTTON to 'négritude.' I copied my Southern accent from Vivien Leigh, when she played Scarlet and Blanche.

Ahahaha, I was lying through my teeth: I had a string of Africans, too—especially the champions of the bedsprings. And I'm PROUD to be part African, myself. You're just like those gringas in Paris, Chiara—I guess because you went to Princeton. But you know better than to mess with me, talking about 'internalized racism' and all that BS. So you limit yourself to a compliment.

Hmmm, I find a certain islander utterly gorgeous.

You mean ME, of course. — I preen in the rear-view mirror, inspecting my lip blush. — I might almost mistake you for an Italian lady, instead of a Sicilian SLUT!

Whoops! I almost collide with an oncoming car. The moron gets off with a sideswipe and a busted bumper. He should count himself lucky! He shakes his fist at me, but I don't stop. — If Canubans were just ugly, all right. But the worst part is, they're dumb! Espinosa keeps em that way, so they're easier to control. IDIOCY gets him re-elected. He's made this country go backward instead of forward!

Yes, it's tragic that Manfredo is still ruling the island, after four decades as an autocrat.

Right, Chiara. He's slowly mellowing into a 'demo-dictator,' as Ángel María used to say. But his BEADY eyes still keep tabs on us from every stamp, banknote, and coin. He's such a dinosaur he changed the currency from pesos to 'escudos,' a Spanish Colonial word.

I know. It's all part of his campaign to restore Canuba's 'idyllic past,' when the Taíno and Africans were slaves. I glimpsed the codger one day in a park, surrounded by his entourage. With his wobbly steps, nondescript face, and moth-eaten clothes, he didn't look like a tyrant. But the overseas press calls him a torturer, a rapist, and a murderer. Not that Canubans ever read any of those reports. Thanks to censorship, they think he's their savior, sent from on high.

That just shows what stooges we are, Chiara. How many of us can read at all? The public schools are a zoo, with no desks or chairs. We're at the bottom of the barrel. Look at YOU! When you stepped off the plane, you added a hundred points to your IQ. You multiplied your bank-account by ten. And your BQ—it went through the ROOF!

BQ?

B is for beauty! Sure, everything is relative. In Italy, you'd still be locked in a kennel, going woof-woof-woof. —

I try to simmer down. — At least the elite are well-trained. But only because we LEAVE the island for college! I went to the University of Miami, spent two years in Rome with Maestro Fanciullo, and three years in Paris, with Professeur Poulet-Malassis. Then I put the cherry on top with Herr Doktor Professor Finderbinder, in Vienna. I did all that— plus exercising my OTHER talents!

Lips puffed, I imitate a blowfish. It's one of my trademarks, when I tick off my exploits. I toured Northern and Eastern Europe for several months with a string quartet. That's when I seduced a Norwegian tycoon. For the novelty, we screwed every night in that sunken park in Oslo. His family paid me a lot of money, just to get rid of me.... — HAHAHA! I laugh maniacally, to sum it all up. Can you believe it? They thought I was BLACK!

So you've told me. That's one of your leitmotifs: and you should've felt flattered, by the way. Now I'm waiting for the secondary themes. How the world isn't black and white. How Latinos are multi-colored, like birds and butterflies. How no one is gay or straight, but somewhere on a spectrum. How we need to think outside the box... Fill me in on Miami for a change.

Oh, it's full of Latinos. I wasn't such a stand-out there. The best part was when my redneck lover Bubba Jim drove me around the South. What a thrill to visit Scarlet's Atlanta! And the plantations near Charleston, that stood in for Ashley's estate!

Yes, especially Boone Hall. I'll never forget the double avenue of live oaks. Or the gardens at Magnolia. I saw them with Catulo in the spring. What masses of azaleas!

Hey, smartass! Don't distract me. Here's another ritornello. If only those meatheads in Europe had known who I AM! In my considered opinion, Chiara, I'm the greatest musician Canuba has ever produced. But what GOOD does it do me to be a genius, if I have to live with moronic savages? My gonzo father has destroyed my life. He said he refused to support my studies overseas for one more HOUR. He blubbered over the phone that he adored me so much, he wanted me to stay at home with him.

That's touching. I wish my father loved me like that.

Humph. We were talking about ME! Doesn't my Papa understand there's NOTHING for me here on this island? As a cellist, or as a woman? The rich dudes aren't any better than the lower-class jerks. Most of them are just as stupid, and worse at having sex! — I pound the steering wheel to make my point, and blare the horn at a truck. — All they do is get plastered on beer, and yap about baseball!

Don't forget, Lamia: there are some foreigners to choose from, too…

Like YOU, you mean. Oh, I've got your number. Nobody can stand me for long. Unless they've got some reason to, between the legs! But that's the whole problem, Chiara. You couldn't keep up with me in the sack, even if you were a man. I want a penis that works full-time. And I want a cock with a BRAIN: I want to have my sausage and eat it, too.

That's why you liked Catulo. He's a charmer: I fell for him, too, just like you.

Yes, he's smart AND sexy. OK, he's no powerhouse in bed. But he's the only man I've ever known with a tongue as gifted as mine. Even if he IS a Canuban and a queer—a part-time queer, that is.

He's not the only one, around here.

We're all in the Switch-Hitter League! Anyway, he was a shot in the arm, for a year. But what about my reputation? Or re-PUTA-tion, as Catulo used to say. Ahahaha. One day, when we're walking down the street and holding hands, some macho DICKHEAD leans out of a bus and shouts: So long, girls! 'Adios, las dos!'

I cackle out loud, Chiara, and so do you. But I end on a sour note, sadly shaking my head. You always say that I crash as quickly as I soar.

You try to cheer me up. — Don't be so conventional, Lamia. What kind of 'reputation' were you trying to protect?

You think I'm wild, Chiara, and I am. But I still have to fit in. Don't get me wrong. I like my rainbow friends. They love poetry and music and art. But what can they DO for me? My mother wants me to get married. If you're a señorita here, you can't just leave your parents' house and live on your own. It's ironic, but you can only get your

FREEDOM by tying the knot… Unless you set up house with a woman your age. Like sisters—no questions asked. Till then, all you can do is 'culiar' in a love-motel with somebody. Some BODY: you know, just another fuck!

Language, Lamia. Why do you always have to curse like a sailor? It doesn't jive with your frilly clothes. Even your French sounds more Parigot than refined.

That's what you get off on. I bring out the DYKE in you.

I've never hidden that. Your hordes of men make me green with envy. I haven't felt this way in a long, long time. It's like the crush I used to have on Sœur Jeanne, my volleyball coach at the convent school in France.

Well, I'm not a NUN like her, or you. Maybe I'll really play ball with you someday. Believe me, I've been around the block.

You flush bright pink, and change the subject. — Back to Catulo. How can he be such a 'maricón,' if he's had sex with you 'from midnight till dawn,' as you say? I made love with him, too, twenty years ago, so I can speak from experience.

Oh, Chiara, it's like what we were saying. The pigeonholes you grew up with don't apply here at all. Our island is so eroticized, EVERYBODY's up for grabs.

In Sicily it was a bit like that, compared to Northern Italy. But here, anything goes.

We rocket into the hills, blasting through what you'd dismiss as 'soulless suburbs.' What can I say? This is my neighborhood, Loma Linda, a grid of concrete villas with fussy lawns. It screams 'upper middle-class' to the NTH DEGREE. It's the 'middle' part you dislike. Well, we can't all be aristocrats, with two-bit titles tacked to our names.

I park on the street, since my Papa hogs the garage. Digging out my keys, I let us into the entry hall. — Welcome to Palazzo Scopata, I trumpet with a grin.

You tilt your head toward some women in the messy front den, just a few feet away.

I snarl. — Oh, THEM! Forget it! You know what they call me around here? Mal Tiempo—Bad Weather. Except for Papa and my uncle: they're the only ones who're fond of me.

As we approach the chairs, planted in front of an outdated TV, I'm sure you can detect a pecking order. Far forward, a pudgy MATRON reigns in a corduroy recliner. A foot or so behind, a sallow SPINSTER fidgets in a cheap rocking chair. Two yards back from her, two mulatto MAIDS slouch on kitchen stools. All four are wearing hair-curlers, and all four are glued to the screen. They're watching a Mexican telenovela.

With a gesture of supreme sacrifice, my mother, Doña Grecia, nods her heavy-jowled head in your direction. Her skeletal sister, Claribel, doesn't show an iota of interest. I've told you before: the daily soap opera is a SACRED ritual, not to be disturbed. The servants look puzzled when you toss them a friendly wave.

I frown at the tele-botomized quartet, and flounce to the back of the house. You follow me like a well-trained dachshund. Voilà: the music room. THIS is my temple. In the center, a plush chair thrones before my rosewood music stand. Next to them, my CELLO reclines like an odalisque, on a velvet-draped divan. I prop her on her tail spike, and caress the purfling along her shoulders and back. — My Scarampella. She used to belong to my uncle, and now she's mine.

Against the walls, cedar shelves are crammed with sheet music, tapes, and LPs. CD players are still a prestige item in Canuba. But thanks to my Papa, I own the latest model, along with a large collection of discs.

Before you have a chance to ask, I set you straight: Don't think you're going to get a free recital! REAL musicians never play for friends, they only concertize.

You chatter about a violinist in New York, who used to play for you. But you stop in mid-sentence, so you won't feel the lash of my tongue.

Chiara, you should feel honored I'm showing you my music room AT ALL! It's always been the nursery of my dreams—ever since I was four, when Tío Severino gave me my first lesson. He's a DEAR! Let's go say hello to him.

I lead you down a long corridor. At the end is a tiny room, completely bare except for an army cot. Looking through your eyes, I see a frail stick-figure of a man. He's perched on the bed like an OBJECT. Maybe a careless maid left him there, like a feather-duster or a broom. I kiss him on the forehead. It's the only sign of sweetness I've ever let you take in. Tío stares vacantly ahead, never blinking. At first he seems blind, but soon you realize he's catatonic: paralyzed by mental illness. Woodenly, I open the door to the terrace.

It's just a mediocre patio, no different from a million others around the globe. A midsize pool, a gazebo, and some flowerbeds. I'm sorry about your uncle, you start to say, but my SCOWL brings you up short. We go back to the street through a service entrance, just off the kitchen. I have to rein you in till we get to the car. — We don't have to SPRINT!

In a flash, we're barreling down a palm-lined avenue toward the Old Quarter. I grip the steering wheel ferociously. I look down at my forearms: they're corded like a lumberjack's, from sawing away at my instrument. I'm ANGRY at myself for letting you invade my world, letting you break my locks. That's what you are, a goddam BURGLAR.

Do you have to go so fast? you ask, for the umpteenth time.

Suddenly I change my mind. Instead of dumping you at your house right away, I turn into the Malecón again. Maybe you're the only person who's ever loved me for MYSELF, just the way I am. I treat you to another drive along the coast, and listen to you rhapsodize, as if the surf's beating inside my head.

You talk about the way our ocean moves, a billowing patchwork of molten gems, green and blue. You talk about our beaches, the color of oats, ginger, or buttermilk, and how they curve behind the swaying palms, as seductively as our flesh. You talk about the places where sandbars don't blunt the waves, so they swarm against our corniches of mottled rock like liquid wasps. How through blowholes in the stone, sprays of foam shoot up like the spouts from our humpback whales... then waft back down in rags of mist.

What are they, but the tatters of our history? You've explored minor islands off Normandy, Maine, and other outposts around the world, you say. They won you over at first, but then they seemed claustrophobic. In the Caribbean, you say, the small French or English islands are the worst—sandspits and barren slabs with barely any rain, their scraggly bushes withered by the sun. Canuba, you say, is twice the size of Sicily, where you grew up. More than yours, our island has the earmarks of a continent: diversity, extension, and relief.

I see what you mean when we round a bend, and catch sight of Puerto Indio. Our Colonial port slumbers on the opposite shore: its suburban torso sprawls against the hills; its stumpy legs of ancient walls, carved from coral stone, dangle into the sea. Though we're more than two million now, our metropolis dwindles below our emerald mountains, grazed by the drifting clouds. Our highest peaks tower to the east, rank on rank, until they fade in an amethyst haze. Below our cordillera, bands of green, blue, and gold—fertile plains, wide rivers, and distant, sunlit bays—ripple toward the limitless west.

I always laugh you off when you praise our country like this, but secretly you've trapped me, you've roped me in: I'll never be the same, because I want to be like you.

Now I'm in a panic. I screech into the turn-off for Plaza Drake, jerk the car to a halt near your house, and give you a hasty air-peck on the cheek. — Don't slit your WRISTS, but I can't stay for dinner. I've got a heavy date tonight. INDUSTRIAL strength!

You smile. — How many this time?

Who knows? It's a polo team, but they ALWAYS invite their pals. So long!

Minutes later, I bet you're still listening to the whine of my Corvette, two or three blocks away. I sigh to myself. Maybe I'm HOPELESS—but to you, I'm irresistible. No, no, no! I REFUSE! I'll never let you know how MUCH I love you, too.

VIRGILIO

1997-1988

I keep thinking of you, Chiara, as always—even from the other side of 'that distinguished thing, death,' as Henry James hailed it in his final hour. The future has come to a stop, so all of time is now sequestered in the past, and I survey it like an immovable block.

When my brother Horacio joins the Trappists, the blow almost takes your breath away. All three of us 'Miranda boys,' Ambassador Miranda's sons, have now departed: the 'Trinity,' as some nicknamed us wryly. You'll miss the querulous monk's affection, just as you've missed our brother Catulo's cheeky fondness, ever since he crossed the Styx several years ago. Because of the deeper friendship between you and me, my loss may prove the most unbearable—though I suppressed my feelings, unable to surmount my reserve.

My art absorbed all my energies, and I pursued it with single-minded devotion. I often quoted Kierkegaard's title: 'purity of heart is to will one thing.' I'm told my works will endure in the museums of Europe, the Americas, and Japan—as well as Canuba's Galería Nacional, thanks to my widow's donations. I say this in profound humility, because I'm beyond such things now; in reality, I always was. Humility? More like indifference. All art, like humanity itself, will vanish from this polluted world. As to its trappings, the pitiful trinkets we make that betray our ideals, they are only an external legacy. For my familiars, a few private tokens will signify much more.

Chiara, you'll understand these mementoes I send you from afar, across the chasm of time and space. Your auburn hair is streaked with grey, but your glaucous eyes still glow with prescience. You've arranged three of my painted stones on your desk; they keep you company today, as you pause to remember me. I'm here with you, thanks to them. Two you bought at Horacio's shop, when you first arrived in Canuba; the third I gave to you myself.

He and I used to go on periodic forays to Piedras Blancas, at the northeastern tip of the island. The coast there is fringed by shingle, ranging in size from tiny pebbles to flat, polished rocks, four to eight inches wide. What the bigger slabs have in common is their smooth, radiant whiteness. 'They beg to be polychromed,' I liked to say.

The smallest of the three, the one I gave to you, is a silky oblong. You pick it up, and I sense your caress. Almost animate, the stone rests cozily in your palm. Most of the surface I left blank, though on the lower edge I sketched a wispy tangle of grass, in fine strokes of India ink. The emptiness, the unassuming subject, the spontaneous draftsmanship—all remind you of an ancient Zen scroll.

Above the tuft floats a sheet of paper, folded lengthwise into wings. Inexplicably, it drops out of nowhere, as cryptic as the handkerchief in *Song of Myself*, which entreats us to ask 'Whose'? As in that poem, the somber grass—the image sent by the missive—seems like the 'beautiful, uncut hair of graves.'

The second stone is painted as a vertical, seven or eight inches tall; it deploys an entire landscape, not just a close-up detail. A forest clambers up the mountainside, blazing with flame-colored trees—but these aren't Thoreau's autumnal tints. In the Caribbean, amapolas shed their foliage every winter, sprouting orange blossoms in their place. A heatless fire sweeps along the ridges and rounded hills, dotted here and there by the scarlet undersides of manca leaves.

Among these February shades, near the summit of the crest, you discover a whitewashed wall. An arched doorway bids you to enter—to stay here forever, like me. Lingering on the threshold, you turn back. You cling to the illusion of who you've been, before the tomb swallows you whole.

The third stone is the weightiest; it also limns a landscape, this time horizontal. Despite its wide-open spaces, the countryside seems sheltering, delicately reddened by dusk. In the background, you distinguish Canuba's central spine, a sierra as high as Hispaniola's.

At the close of day, you often peer into that fading, twilit scene. It speaks to you of your dead: Amado, Catulo, myself—and all the others, past and passing, or to come. It pronounces the 'grave, evening demand for love,' where 'evening' could be a gerund in disguise.

Again and again, the stone repeats a phrase you will never forget, the words of St. John of the Cross: 'these mountains are my Beloved for me.' The sun has slipped behind the tallest peak, leaving the sky infused with lavender, rosy grey, and a remote, unfathomable blue.

In the midground, sonorous rivers rumble through the valleys, their gullied banks shrouded by dark-green moss. The glen in the foreground is shadowy and welcoming. Here we walk together, still quoting from San Juan de la Cruz, as 'the branches rustle above us with refreshment and final rest.'

You and I live in these woods. I've opened my retreat to no one but you, my perpetual guest. In a sudden burst of energy—the 'light'ning before death,' in Romeo's words—I polychromed a set of mahogany masks. I bought the carvings from a Bonaventuran: Vodou gods, no doubt. I painted one especially for you, Chiara, 'to discharge,' as I dryly remarked, 'our family's unpaid debts.'

My brother Catulo borrowed from you frequently— loans he never paid back. But the 'debts' I mean, as I'm sure you've guessed, are the obligations of love. Catulo's affair with you ended before you reached our shores. I downplayed my attachment, because it cut me to the bone. The greatest debt we've incurred has been the disappearance of us both.

In three-quarter profile, the bearded head wears a tight-fitting helmet, strangely Achaean. I lacquered it in your favorite color-scheme, a hundred shades of blue and green. I spun out smoky stripes and intricate whorls, shot through with purple and gold.

You often glance at that burnished face in your front room; it hangs beside a shelf of antique books. A month after my death, you gaze at it more intently. You reread the legend I wrote in spidery script, almost illegible; I traced it on a narrow, celadon band across the nose and upper cheeks.

As young lovers, you and Catulo shared a passion for Keats, and the lines I chose are from *Hyperion*:

> Far from the fiery noon, and eve's one star,
> Sat gray-hair'd Saturn, quiet as a stone,
> Still as the silence round about his lair;
> Forest on forest hung about his head
> Like cloud on cloud.

I alone detect your melancholy strain, cunningly cloaked by your Italian insouciance. In a turnabout, the mask is your actual face; your face, the actual mask. From another angle, look again: you and I are the face and the mask. We've both struggled with our tedium vitae, our inborn weariness of soul.

I hibernated in my den, an unsociable bear. By a fluke of happenstance, I soared to a modicum of fame; but it only caused me to plummet further down. Though I am Saturn,

I am Hyperion, too. After the death of Amado, the love of your life, you withdraw to the cliff at El Silencio, under trees that arch above you 'like cloud on cloud.' But wherever you go, my restless voyager—whether Accra, Chengdu, Fiji, or Samarkand—the forest always keeps pace, enfolding you as you advance, muffling your steps.

The marvel of being dead is that time has ceased to move. Once it was like music, stately or fleet; now it's a painting, arrested and eternal. Chiara, whoever you choose to be, never betray your deep heart's core. As to me, I am yours: no more than a souvenir. You can drag me through the mud, hang me on the wall, remove me from your gallery. Turn me into a photograph, a negative. File me away like an unfinished sketch.

You still mourn for Amado—and now, for Catulo and me. What compels you to mull over long-lost loves, instead of resolutely marching forward? I guess it all, when I speak of your collection. After his summing-up, before he takes his vows, Horacio hands you a shoebox, carefully wrapped in newspaper print. 'My frater's ultimate obsequy,' he lets drop.

Inside, you find another wooden mask, identical to my gift from several months before. But this time, I leave it unpainted. My fingers are hampered by a plaster cast, and my strength has drained away. Shakily, across the brow, I've scrawled a single sentence in silver ink. You recognize a phrase from *The Duchess of Malfi*, one of my touchstones.

You lay the mask on your desk. You read the line several times, returning to it now as you write. My message is a summons as much as a plea: 'Cover my face—with words.'

Callejón del Platero, Puerto Indio, October 1997

I weakened the canvases by incising them from behind, in a pattern of wheels and spokes; but they still cushion my impact, and prevent my immediate death. My left arm and both my legs are shattered. I sustain severe internal injuries, and I'm blinded by the shock. Even so, I want to stay lucid till the end, which I'm told will overtake me soon.

After a few days at the hospital, I insist on going home to the Callejón del Platero. Awed by my celebrity, the doctors grant me my wish. I'm too weak to kill myself, and a registered nurse can monitor my ups and downs. A morphine drip alleviates the pain: it's one of my drugs of preference. At our coral-stone house, Quilviria coddles me unstintingly. She yields her turf only to Horacio, when she needs some hard-earned sleep. In a discreet wedding, held at my bedside, she and I are married at last.

Public curiosity about my 'suicide performance' is fierce. The videos of my plunge, shot from several angles by newscast crews, are beamed around the world. In the past, several minor figures have amputated a finger or toe:

a dubious species of body art. But this is the first time a so-called 'master'—as they label me, to my dismay—has turned his complete self-destruction into an opus. A statement taped inside the shirt I wear that night—entitled 'After the Fall: Posthumous Remarks'—affirms that by crashing through my paintings, I will fuse with my work. It's my supreme tribute to aesthetic discipline. 'Rigor mortis, rigor artis,' I quip from beyond the grave—though it doesn't pan out that way.

During my final days on earth, journalists besiege the Miranda family residence. Sardonic headlines run riot in the yellow press. 'Swan Dive and Swan Song,' cracks *The National Enquirer*. 'The Billion Pound Headbutt,' jibes *The Sun*, totting up the market value I've 'slyly added to my canvases.' I grant no interviews, and all the photographers glean are snapshots of our quaint façade. The diamond-paned windows, capped by a frieze of Artemis with her bow, flit through the media till the buzz fizzles out. Besides my brother, my wife, and the nurse, you're the only person admitted to my rooms—and even then, just once, for less than an hour.

I've sent the others away, so you and I can meet alone. Prostrate, I'm completely encased in plaster casts, except for my face, chest, and hands. But I haven't lost my sense of irony. — I know, Chiara, I know: I look like a sculpture by George Segal. At least I've achieved the 'rigor artis' part. I'm still at work on 'rigor mortis.'

As you discern, my sarcasm veils a novel tone—more fragile and less arrogant. It's not that the physical damage has altered my character. I've undergone a genuine metanoia, a profound change of heart. You detect this as soon as you see me, splayed out on my four-poster bed.

In that familiar pose, you've heard me read thousands of pages over the years—my voice resounding from the fissured marble floors, the flaking stucco walls, the musty beams of the terracotta roof. You remember how I'd run a paint-stained hand through my matted hair, quaking with laughter. Or how I'd cross my arms and stare into space when I paused to ruminate. Now my head is wrapped in gauze, and my bright-blue eyes have dimmed to a whitish-grey, as if coated by a crust of ice.

My wife holds up a mirror now and then, to see if I've regained my sight. You're my essential looking-glass: I am you. You sit on the edge of the adjoining bed. — I've wanted to visit you all this time, Virgilio. But they've told me you're too tired.

Feebly, I answer you, already faraway. — I've been tired for ages. Tired of everything. But not anymore.

That's encouraging. Would you like for me to read to you? I owe you eight years' worth.

I manage a faint chuckle. — Somehow, I don't think I'll be around that long … No, no reading, but thanks… — My mind quickens, and I talk more expansively. — It's odd, but after all the decades I spent studying art and poring over books, none of that appeals to me anymore. All my life, I've kept other people at a distance. Now it's a relief just being around them, at peace.

Coming from me, this is unexpected. — Well, isn't art a way of being with them, too?

That's the problem, Chiara. To us, it's one and the same. I collect images. You collect texts. I collect dreams. You collect experiences. But when you do that, you collect human beings, too.

You defend yourself. — Does it do them any harm, Virgilio?

No, but maybe it does *you* harm.

Do you think I've collected you?

Of course. For you, we're all keepsakes. In your notebooks, you jot us down. It's the same with the portraits I did this last year. — With a hint of gallows humor, I repeat the phrase. — This *last* year...

I'm flattered by your comparison, but you're making fun of me. I'm just a scribbler: my articles don't amount to much.

You keep a journal, don't you? That's the point. Like you, I was content in my ivory tower. Afraid to hobble down the stairs—to expose myself to the light. I don't mean the limelight, of course. That's for idiots. Something else has happened these past few months, behind the scenes. Maniacally, I've filled my pictures with likenesses. Miniatures, inch by inch. Painting everyone I can recall, everyone I've ever known in this city of ours. From early on, I've spent countless hours in the streets, engraving faces on my mind. Workers' faces caked with mud, drilling holes in the ground. Faces of housewives, buying rice, beans, and meat. Faces of children, too. Hauled around by nannies, if they're rich. Or playing in the garbage, if they're poor. Faces, faces, faces.

Am I becoming overexcited? You try to calm me down. — Yes, as in Whitman's poem.

Exactly. — I speed on, unstoppable now. — But these days, I can't be anonymous anymore. People stare back at me, the 'brand-name' artist—and some even ask me for my autograph. When I ran out of memories, I used newspaper photos, or records I found at the Canuban National Archive. The such-and-such high school class of 1958. The Non-Commissioned Officers of 1943. The Damas Diplomáticas of 1969. Forgotten faces, their features moldering. And then I realized the brutal truth: all my drawings are lifeless, too. Museum pieces at best, sooner or later. I've only been collecting. I've never really known anyone—even my friends and lovers. All I've done is render them. Meticulous as a mortician, I've laid them out on the altar of the dead. I've kept them at arm's length. That's why I suddenly wanted to come closer, closer…

You've been warned not to upset me. You speak in a gingerly tone. — Closer. So you…

Yes. That's why I leapt into the crowd of my victims. If

they're nothing but images, I should become one, too.

And now?

God has granted me the gift of blindness. I don't mean the sugary, mawkish God that priests jabber about today. I mean the angry old bastard who used to beat us into submission. I might've taken vows myself, if only I could've believed in him. But I don't. Never mind. He doesn't need to exist.

'Bis Gottes Fehl hilft...'

That's it: till God's absence helps. Isn't that Hölderlin? See, Chiara, you're quoting again, and that's a way of evading what I've said.

I've listened to you for years, Virgilio—too much for my own good. You're the one who assumes it's clever to disagree. I prefer to keep my own counsel. You say I'm a latter-day Romantic, and you deride me for believing in love. I'm heartened you're such a convert to it now. We've both been like Prospero, castaways on an island of illusions. But we've gone to opposite extremes. I've lost control of my spirits; you've locked yours away, in these rooms. You've used your spells to shut reality out.

I'm flailing, trying to sit up. — You're wrong, Chiara. I've met reality halfway. I've discarded most of my works. I've thrown them in the gutter.

You want to have it out with me, now or never. — The gutter isn't what I'm talking about, Virgilio. You've even demeaned what's left. You've framed your torn-up canvases with toilet seats. But art and life are parallel texts, in two different languages. — Softly, Chiara, you press me back against the pillows; you mitigate what you've said. — Don't pay attention to me. 'Everything that falls must converge.'

My attempt to move has exhausted me. We stay silent for a while. Then I sigh. — There you go again, mocking Teilhard de Chardin. We might as well keep quoting. I've 'drowned my book': this is Caliban's revenge, on Catulo and me. No more 'ideas of order,' no more 'demarcations,' ghostly or otherwise. I can't even see this island, no matter how hard I look. But I can feel your hand on my chest. And Quilviria's, and Horacio's. That's enough.

You want to soothe me. — There, there. Rest a while, Virgilio.

I surprise you by laughing, in my full-throttle bass. — You remember Pomona, don't you? Catulo's 'autumnal mistress'? Ever since he died of AIDS, she's been terrified. She's had herself tested a dozen times, but she won't feel safe till three or four years go by. She wants to make sure 'the windows of infection have closed.' Horacio tells me she rang him up last week, and gabbed about 'metaphysics.'

Pomona? Don't tell me she's taken up philosophy!

No, of course not. 'La Metafísica' is just a phony sect. The members chat about their dreams from the night before, or what they ate for dinner. — I guffaw again, from deep inside my diaphragm. Then a wave of weariness drags me down, and sweat beads my cheeks.

When I resurface, my voice is measured and still. — Why not? Let them be. Let all of us be. It's not so bad to lead a collector's life. I've enjoyed my portraits, just like you. But the past couple of weeks, when I couldn't see them at all, have been the best. You'll understand what I mean, when you give up our pointless pastime. It's like a glass of wine on the terrace, after a long, taxing day at the Uffizi or the Louvre. No more special lighting, no more darkened varnishes, no more pictures at all. Salty air. A breeze from the Caribbean. A presence beside you, very near. An invisible face, but one that's really here. — I'm too worn out to go on: I can trust you to fill in the blanks.

Everything is good. 'Alles ist gut.'

Those are Hölderlin's final words, I remind myself. We'd like to say more about the poet in his tower, once he mildly accepts things as they are. He watches the Neckar flow by. Here is the table, the chair, the carpenter at work. The lines of life will be completed, somewhere else. We'd like to say more, but our time is up.

Yes, that's it, Chiara. In the end, everything is good.

I can sense Quilviria's movements now. She glides up behind you, as inaudible as Ariel. Lightly, she touches your back. You stroke my rough, crippled hands—one last time—and then you leave the room.

Though my rotund voice hasn't diminished, you begin to note some changes in my appearance. My hectic schedule as the Director of the Academia must be sapping my energy, you probably conclude. In addition, Quilviria intimates she's put me on a special diet. My weight has always varied, up and down. Like a costume, I slough off my recent padding: for a time, I look as fit as an athlete.

But soon I betray signs of emaciation, and my unruly, salt-and-pepper mop can't dissemble the creases in my brow. Worst of all, over several months, a tell-tale infection creeps into one of my eyes. I discount it as the result of stress, and assure you it doesn't hinder my ability to paint. That seems credible, since the red 'sunspot'—as I've dubbed it—doesn't prevent me from deciphering eleven-point print, despite the penumbra in my rooms.

The books I've been choosing for our intermittent reading sessions reveal a trend that might disturb you. You always leave the selection up to me, since my only free hours are those we share. Nowadays, long 'romans-fleuves' are out of the question. First, I propose *The Aspern Papers*, one of our lodestones; as before, we snicker at the fatuous young man, outfoxed by his elderly prey.

Next, I turn to another of our standbys, *Der Tod in Venedig*: logically enough, you might think. The setting is the same—even if it's 'death in Venice' now, not literary sleuthing. Uneasily, we're still walking the tightrope of desire. True, we've shifted to a minor key, and a more corrosive wit. In any case, we've always revered Thomas Mann. You gush over my German, as kindly as always; my accent may be Canuban, but I do my best to coax every nuance from the prose.

After Aschenbach succumbs to a sunset of hair-dye and rouge, I continue to Mann's most brutal novella, *Die Betrogene*. Perversely, a middle-aged woman is 'deceived' by her menstrual rebirth—caused, in fact, by an incurable disease. Then I revert to Henry James, our patron saint, though I pick the grimmest tales in the canon: 'The Figure in the Carpet,' 'The Bench of Desolation,' and 'The Altar of the Dead.' In each of them, a missed opportunity for love can never be regained. Finally, I press on to the most somber work of all, an autopsy of the West's colonial sins: Joseph Conrad's *Heart of Darkness*.

You ascribe this melancholy vein to 'survivor's guilt,' one of your recurrent tags, ever since Amado's fatal accident. If I dwell on Catulo's demise, this only seems natural, you say. You hope I won't sink into the remorse that troubles you. Here I feel obliged to bring you up short. — Oh, don't worry, I'm keeping my gloom in check. I'd like to read Hermann Broch's *The Death of Virgil*. But I'll spare you the allusions to my name.

To steer us away from the slough of despond, one evening you introduce me to Bruce Duffy's *The World As I*

Found It. You imagine it'll be right up my alley. For once, you read a chapter aloud yourself, instilling the comic, densely layered text with all the lightness you can muster. At the end, you play a guessing game. — Well, what do you say? Was this written by an Englishman, or an American?

I quiver with contempt. — Since the main characters are G. E. Moore, Bertrand Russell, and Wittgenstein in his Cambridge years, the author should be English. But the obsession with sex tells me he's American.

Given the cause of my brother's illness, you don't find it strange that I feel bitter about this mania—above all, its prevalence in the Late U. S. Empire. In New York, Catulo surfed the tidal wave of liberation. Perhaps he acquired some over-eager habits, you argue; but they were no worse than our island's homegrown promiscuity. Apart from its literature, you've had little exposure to the UK, while you subsisted for seven years in its 'Atlantic Colonies.' As an Italian, you take no side in the face-off between these two nations, 'divided by a common language.'

Let's say your loyalities are evenly split, Chiara. You did have an English nanny.

Back to the subject, Virgilio. You're right, all over the world we've been reduced to sheep-like consumers by capitalism, even if commerce is older than the Phoenicians. As Pasolini observed, Italy is one of the worst examples. Porn spices the advertising for every product, from gelato to shoes.

You rattle on, Chiara; but I'm only half listening. It's odd that you haven't picked up on the most blatant clues, like my eye infection or my fatigue. You're suffering from what you'd call 'denial,' I suppose. You refuse to acknowledge that like Catulo, I have AIDS; in my case, it's probably from dirty needles. Unlike him, I've rejected all treatments, even the ones that might work. What's the use? I'm not attached to life; though I may have the right to feel disheartened.

Out loud, I continue. — Just because we live in a Caribbean paradise doesn't mean we have to be gleeful all the time. You're too hard on us islanders, Chiara. We're a fantasy to you, just as we were to Columbus, your compatriot. But in your mythology, we're blissfully erotic.

That takes the cake, coming from a Canuban. All of you have the same fixation: listen to yourself right now. When you and I refer to sex, it's graphic on the primary plane, and metaphorical on all the rest. As for art, sensuality has to lie at its core...

In mid-flight, you leave off, and I know why. You've often implied that my works are too cerebral—especially my *Brothel Series*. Flaying the female form with such a vengeance, I seem to be denigrating that fulsome symbol of nature: Courbet's *The Origin of the World*. You forget that I do the same to the male physique in my *Hustler Suite*. I smile at you with a secretive air. — In other words, we must accept our holy mother, St. Body: the sack of guts that spews us out, and slops us together in a trough.

Incarnation, communion. That's what it's all about.

I hug my knees, and roll against the headboard of my bed. — So now you've 'angelized' everything, even our putrid corpses. Poor Chiara: comp lit at Princeton went to your head. You'd like to be a wholesome, distaff Whitman. But you're a true European—as twisted as they come.

Look who's talking. Twisted is your middle name.

All right, that's a dare. Maybe I'll prove your point.

A few months later, I announce my new exhibition. 'It's a display of recent works: so recent, they'll be created on the spot,' I inform the press enigmatically. 'They'll be accompanied by a retrospective of earlier pieces.'

Casa Estremadura offers to mount what it bills as the 'muestra del milenio'—the 'show of the millennium'— under the aegis of the Ministry of Culture. By now, for better or worse, I could enlist any city on the planet as a venue. The local authorities pride themselves on my fidelity to Puerto Indio. Though meaningless to me, my renown has scaled such heights that the Board of Tourism exploits it, promoting my art along with our beaches, waterfalls, iguanas, humpback whales, beauty queens, Carnival masks, and Royal Rum.

When I request the Presidio adjacent to the Casa for the exhibition's 'opening event,' my petition is accepted without delay. In 1508, Santiago Columbus erected its central tower—one of the oldest Colonial buildings in the hemisphere—to commemorate his uncle Christopher. Grandiosely known as the 'Memorial Bastion,' it's normally too hallowed for private use, as the functionaries stress. But if Virgilio Miranda needs it… well, they'd be honored to oblige.

On the night of the vernissage, Chiara, you must be glad you live just a few blocks away. Expensive cars jam the Barrio Antiguo from stem to stern, as their owners—or more often, their chauffeurs—search in vain for a place to park. From my eyrie at the top of the Bastion, I watch the TV vans pulling up, and journalists jockeying for the key positions. The media circus is in full swing.

This afternoon, as I passed through the Presidio's double doors, cyclopean and austere, I recalled one of Catulo's flights of fancy. For him, they evoked the Gates of Troy. Our father persuaded the President to lend the fort to my brother when he first returned from New York, as a backdrop for *The Trojan Women*. He staged a superb production, complete with flaring torches, a regal Hecuba, a demonic Pyrrhus, and a life-like dummy of Astyanax, thrillingly tossed from the battlements.

As you enter the Casa, once the mansion of a governor, I'm sure one of my students will interrupt your train of thought. She or he will press a broadsheet into your hand: 'At ten o'clock, Virgilio Miranda will perform a dedication rite at the Memorial Bastion.' The museum is mobbed by foreign correspondents; they're searching for me, but I've escaped to the tower. I've asked Quilviria to greet you on my behalf.

After a polite exchange of busses on the cheek, you'll ask her what this 'dedication rite' is all about. With genuine candor, she'll confess that she doesn't have the foggiest. — He had those fliers printed on the sly, Chiara. I didn't see them myself till a while ago. For the past two weeks, I've been hanging the older pieces. He told me to leave the latest works to him. He's going to present them in front of the Bastion. — Yes, she'll say something to that effect…

A half hour later, after dutifully glimpsing my paintings through the throng, you'll go back outside to the gates of the fortress precinct. Two pairs of soldiers will open the enormous doors, set in imposing jambs of coral stone. You'll follow the rest of the crowd into the grass-sown compound. Why I needed the Presidio, and the enclosed plaza surrounding it, will now become clear.

Nine immense canvases, forty-feet square, are propped against the walls: they could never have fit into an indoor space. From a distance, they appear uniformly reddish; but as you draw closer, you'll perceive that they're honeycombed with tiny sepia portraits. Here or there in the swarm, you'll come across your allies, or your self-appointed foes. Eventually you'll find your own likeness, grinning back at you with well-intentioned cheerfulness. In another spot— and I've paid this double accolade only to you—you'll find your hidden, tragic face.

Besides limning my relatives, friends, and acquaintances, I've trolled the streets and sifted through archives to compile my catalogue. But where is my depiction of myself? you wonder. The broadsheet calls the ensemble *A Self-Portrait in Nine Panels*. After scouring the medallions for over an hour, you haven't hit upon a single portrayal of me. Through an archer's slit in the rustic masonry, I watch you borrow some binoculars, so you can scan the upper rows. There as well, no one resembles me, the disembodied Virgilio—the 'artifex maximus' of these colossal beehives.

At ten o'clock, the loudspeakers blare that the 'dedication rite' will now begin. 'Please move twenty meters away from the Memorial.' On cue, dozens of volunteers from the Academia string a cordon in front of the pictures, pushing the multitude further back. When they've cleared enough room, they carefully lower the cumbersome squares to the ground, with the painted sides up. Then they heave them one on top of the other, in a neat stack at the tower's base.

Fifty feet up, I step forward, my head just visible behind the rough-hewn ramparts. After a minute or two of uncertainty, a spotlight picks me out, and my expectant fans applaud, whistle, and cheer. I make no attempt to silence them. When I raise my arms, it isn't to give a speech, but to hoist myself onto the parapet. The crowd lets out a gasp. I teeter long enough to gain my balance. Then, without a moment's hesitation, I dive headlong into the paintings far below.

As you know, Chiara, we never wished to sell the Taíno codex in the first place. If we'd been rich enough, we would've gifted it to the nation—though only after Espinosa's death. The last thing we wanted was to stoke his self-aggrandizement. But of course, the financial crisis was our immediate concern. Catulo borrowed from loansharks to bankroll his lavish adieu. While Horacio and I guessed what was going on, we preferred to look the other way. We were like two old men in a novel by Balzac, indulging their spendthrift mistress: we couldn't tell her when to stop. And we weren't alone. Our brother's lover Pomona, the well-off sculptress, shelled out a fortune for his last hurrah.

To pay off Catulo's creditors, we're faced with selling our ancestral home and decamping to a modest apartment—with little space for books and picture-racks, much less a concert grand. But soon after our forced 'donation' to the Canuban Library, the storm-cloud parts to disclose—more than a silver lining—a Danaëan rain of gold. My fame as an artist dates from the budgetary crunch of the Festival Catuli-ana. I use drugs less and less, and it's a sign of my growing practicality when I strike on a clever idea. Why not break up the ornate stage-sets for Catulo's ballets and sell them off in chunks, to rake in some much-needed cash? I'm still publicity-shy, but Horacio gladly takes on that department; for both of us, it's a case of sink or swim.

I go about the 'defacing' process in my usual way, though on a much grander scale. I slash the gargantuan backdrops into tatters, from six to twenty feet square. At random, with twists of barbed wire, I fasten the canvas sheets to various props. On flatbed trucks, I haul the whole shebang to our cousin Tirso's livestock ranch, and dump the fragments wherever they land. My finely-wrought images suffer an earth-change, into rags of filth and mange. They're rammed and rutted by tractors, trampled by cattle, pigs, or sheep, and dragged through the weeds by packs of feral dogs.

By the end of a week, tire-tracks have streaked the Groteschi from the Pope's apartments; foraging beasts have kneecapped, de-buttocked, and unmanned the statues of Antinous. A tin Nietzsche is jammed into the hull of Queen Christina's ship, and his disjointed legs creak in the passing breeze. Shreds of the fateful bathtub from Mycenae dangle from St. Teresa's snapped, gigantic quill, and a fin from Duncan's convertible has impaled a Hadrianic finial. Frederica's portrait, no longer blank, is smeared with donkey dung, viscous yellow pollen, and a greenish arc of pulverized frogs. A rusty gear shaft crowns Bernini's Baldaquin; a stand of birches from the *Rite of Spring* drips with the offal of hogs.

The wreckage yields scores of pieces, and once they're dried, varnished, and mounted, my draftsmanship and modeling compete with the marks of chance. All I throw away is the emerald copse from *L'Après-midi d'un faune*, pocked by the hooves of a nanny-goat and her kids. At our next session, Chiara, I dismiss the altered landscape: 'Sometimes, nature is a shade too self-aware.'

Up till now, only you and my brothers have understood what I've striven for all my life. I refused to have my name appear in Catulo's theatre programs, much less in the advertising blitz for his ballets. But with a heavy heart, I now resign myself to going public. For Horacio, it's easy to organize an exhibition of my work in Puerto Indio. Whatever the critics thought about our brother's choreography, they were unanimous in praising my stage-sets. Their doyen, Héctor Méndez, has touted my unseen works for decades, based on an impromptu visit to my studio. Casa Extremadura, the center for the arts in the Old Quarter, gladly offers to host my show.

The Festival Catuli-ana staff will have to help Horacio hawk the fragments, if they hope to collect the wages still due to them. Catulo's cohorts from New York and London circulate slides among their art-world contacts in both the major markets. Several influential pundits fly to Canuba for the exhibit; and after reading their reviews, droves of dealers follow suit. Not only are all the objects sold, at rapidly climbing rates: within a month, they resurface in well-known galleries, in Europe, Asia, and the Americas. The global media hum with eulogies of Virgilio Miranda, 'the García Márquez of the visual arts,' 'the Caribbean Joseph Beuys,' 'the prophet of post-postmodernism,' 'the Latino Rauschenberg,' 'the last revelation of the millennium'—absurdly, everything but the kitchen sink.

The hype snowballs into an avalanche, and museums like MOMA and The Tate bid for 'Mirandas' at Christie's and Sotheby's. The small-scale paintings from my earlier years, framed by wax-daubed, crudely gilded toilet-seats, fetch such heady prices that Horacio locks them in a bank-vault, to discourage burglars from breaking into our house. Among them are my garish portraits of sex-workers, those blistering works you've always found repellent. Posing half-nude in front of gaudy, lopsided brothels, they outdo even de Kooning's *Women* in their savagery. By occasionally selling a canvas from my 'Bathroom Period'—as commentators label it—we can count on prosperity for the rest of our days, whether I touch a brush again or not.

To me, all the attention is a nightmare, and it intensifies without reprieve. Inadvertently, we've set a juggernaut in motion. Horacio has long dominated the classical music scene. Now, thanks to his link with me, Catulo is hailed as a genius; overseas know-it-alls take Canuba to task for ignoring his stature. The top brass in the Ministry of Culture, embarrassed by the outcry, award him a posthumous Order of Merit. Determined not to repeat their mistake, they press the Directorship of the Academia Nacional del Arte on me.

The elderly painter who holds the post, Stanislavo Camilo, is not only passé—a lackluster disciple of Fernand Léger—he was appointed during Espinosa's most sanguinary phase. Remorseful that she boycotted Catulo's farewell opus, Carolina Del Río pushes my candidacy, and Countess Frederica seconds her. Before long, Don Stanislavo finds himself in forced retirement. Still wearing his black beret and smoking his white clay pipe, he writes a memoir of his mentor's school in the rue de la Grande Chaumière.

Needless to say, I also receive the Order of Merit. A week later, the government officially elevates me to Director de la Academia, though I never sought the job. In private, I sneer that the petty peaks and troughs of careerism have always repulsed me. But after my mother's sudden demise, and my brother's final agony, I owe something to the Miranda family—even if it's only a sop of bogus prestige.

The gradual normalization of my speech since their deaths now attains its balance: I no longer halt in mid-sentence, or garble my words. This is a 'posthumous salvo to both our dear departed,' Horacio claims. To me, it's just the result of flushing my grass and hard drugs down the drain. A greater sacrifice is when I shave off my beard, crop my hair to a seventies length, and acquire a standard wardrobe. Chiara, you can hardly believe your eyes when you see me in a suit; but I'll never tolerate ties. I stick to my black turtlenecks, though now they're spotlessly clean. The whole effect is Rive Gauche, including my chunky, Sartrian shape: deferentially, I call it a nod to Don Stanislavo.

After my reluctant rise, our Tuesdays limp along haphazardly. More often than not, we have to steal an hour or two on some other day of the week—dodging my hectic schedule of exhibition openings, ministerial receptions, or dinners with visiting artists. Even when you're here between one of your trips, sometimes we go for a month without meeting at all. These days, I travel almost as much as you. I might be invited to sit on a prize jury in Brazil, join a panel on Latin American sculpture in Washington, or address a UNESCO conference in Paris. While I'm away, you confer with my assistant, Quilviria, about our next chance for a Mardi Gras. I hired her as soon as I accepted the Directorship.

When you get to know her, you realize she must be the lover Horacio has told you about. From the tender, teasing way she refers to me, it's clear that she treats me as her spouse, though we've never formally wedded. A hyperactive soubrette, she bobs around the Academy like a cork in a whirlpool. No more than a wisp—weighing in at ninety pounds—she wears her sparrow-brown hair in a schoolmarmish bun. Given my ursine bulk, you must imagine our coupling as the Surrealist tryst between a sewing machine and an umbrella. Instead of Lautréaumont's duo, I'd say we resemble a freezer and a test tube, or a main-frame and a safety pin. Besides my interludes with her, as she confides to you, my erratic 'Tuesdays' with you are the only personal dates I still allow myself.

On top of my bureaucratic duties, I slog away at my artworks, as energetically as before. With a team of students, I toil in a Colonial sugar-mill—a ruined behemoth on the edge of town. On the few evenings when we get together at home, we reminisce about the bygone years of our weekly sessions. Our hit-or-miss dialogues still unfold in a supine pose, chatting from bed to bed in my high-ceilinged lair. As always, the climax is my Sprechstimme solo, when I read aloud in my orotund bass. Since love is deaf as well as blind, you claim that I produce tonal subtleties worthy of an Orson Welles.

Young Verbena—the pride and joy of my 'fraternal marriage' with Horacio—often attends these Fat Tuesdays, fixing her adamant gaze on you and me by turn. She's mushroomed now into a plump adolescent, tall for her age; her circular face has tripled in size. Seated on the floor in a lotus position, a habit she picked up from a Korean friend at the French Lycée, she looks for all the world like an African Buddha. Though she rarely chimes in, her intelligence sparkles in her eyes; she listens to us chat about subjects that would bore most adults, from the *Nicomachean Ethics* to *The Art of the Fugue*. Whatever Verbena elects to do, we're convinced she'll outstrip all her rivals.

Saddled by Catulo's 'Festival Catuli-ana' with mountainous debts, we Mirandas don't know where to turn. Horacio and my father have been out of their minds with worry, fearing we'll have to sell our house. Yes, it has belonged to our family for three hundred years, and it would be a pity to lose it. As for me, I could live under a bridge if push comes to shove; I'm more concerned about our adopted child, Verbena. The legacy of the *True Relations* seems to answer our prayers. Much as we hate to part with the manuscript, Horacio and I plan to auction it off at Christie's in New York. Based on some slides we've sent, several of the company's assessors fly down to inspect the manuscript. Not only do they pronounce the Taíno codex authentic, they set its value at a starting bid of twenty million dollars, on a par with the Da Vinci codex recently acquired by Bill Gates. The dealers announce the exciting news in their monthly bulletin, and rev their PR machines into high gear.

It doesn't take Espinosa long to squelch our elation. First-off, he sends the Director of the Canuban Library to our shop in the Callejón del Platero, to remind us of our patriotic duty: we can't let this unique treasure leave our cherished island. We agree to sell it to the Library for a twentieth of its value, though we insist on some form of compensation; we need the money, and fair is fair. We don't press the point, but everybody knows that Espinosa has frittered away seventy million dollars on the Columbus Crown, an unsightly concrete pile of no cultural worth. Compared to that, what we're asking is a bagatelle.

The wan, algae-like Director peers at Horacio and me through his spectacles. 'Your attitude is unspeakable,' he murmurs. Swinging his empty briefcase, he leaves the aborted parlay in a huff.

From that moment onward, armed guards are posted outside our house to 'preserve a national heritage property from theft'—as one of them tells Horacio. The soldiers probably think they're defending a cache of Taíno gold. At this point, we ask you to stay with us for a several days. Our father trusts you, Chiara, and he believes you're well-connected. If worse comes to worse, perhaps you could alert the international community to our plight. In any case, you were an angel to him after our mother and Catulo died. He's delighted to have you occupy his guest-room, in the downstairs flat behind the shop.

You're here with us when the following morning, we receive a second visitor: an affable, back-patting officer. He identifies himself as General Francisco López, the army's Chief of Special Operations. López belongs to the cadre of light-skinned backwoodsmen Espinosa prefers, on racist as well as political grounds. Conservative by instinct, country folk are more faithful to him than the 'radical hotheads in the cities,' as our ruler has learned to his rue.

After commandeering a polychromed chair, the

General wags his oversize head. 'Nice merchandise. Maybe I'll come back for some Christmas presents down the road.'

I'm about to mount my high horse, and declare that he doesn't have the finesse to appreciate our stock. But Horacio saves the day. 'We would be supremely honored, Sir,' he bows.

Wasting no time, López gets down to brass tacks. 'President Espinosa hasn't forgotten your father's many years of service to the nation.' His jowly face stiffens. 'That's why he's been so disappointed with Don Baltásar in recent years: his leftist inclinations, I mean, and his support for that brazen rebel, Milady. Our leader has heard with displeasure that the two of you are imitating your father's example. Our Benefactor thinks that in the light of his forbearance, you owe him this book.' His voice diminishes to a stage-whisper. 'You shouldn't be greedy. He's willing to grant you the most precious gift of all: your lives.'

There can be no measured reply to this. Before I fly into a rage, Chiara, you put your finger to your lips, and warn me to keep mum. Trembling like a gri gri leaf, Horacio ushers the officer out of the house. 'We are sempiternally indebted to you for your perspicacious counsel, exalted General, and to the President for his sublime benevolence. We anticipate receiving you anew in our humble establishment at Christmastide. Please transmit to our illustrious President that we will accord our grateful obeisance to his desires.' Once he finishes this sendoff and shuts the door, his knees give way, and he keels over into your arms. Between the two of us, we carry him to the Belle Époque settee at the back of the shop.

Chiara, you make me comprehend that launching a worldwide protest would only trigger our demise, staged as a violent robbery by unknown thugs. What's more, you remind me that we have an ace up our sleeve: Ángel María.

That evening, our spirits sag again. Horacio and I have consulted our childhood friend, and he seeks us out in our personal digs on the second floor. He hugs us heartily, and assures us he's done everything possible to ward off Espinosa. 'I even proposed to buy the codex from you myself, and deed it over to the Library.'

But the despot was adamant: lowering his head, he brayed at his protégé like a decrepit mule. 'That family has done me a lot of damage on the international front. First the father, my star diplomat, turned against me, and now his sons are following suit. They have to atone for their insults, directly to me. I won't take no for an answer.' When he sets his lips in a firm, straight line, Ángel María explains, this means the case is closed.

We Mirandas have always been paladins of our country—though not of Espinosa—and so we must yield to necessity with grace. Before the assembled government, we nobly present the *Verdaderas Relaciones* to our Canuban homeland, in a grandiose ceremony at the Palacio Nacional.

With your assistance, Chiara, 'Su Excelencia Don

Baltásar' disinters an antiquated tux from our attic, and revels in a last burst of panache. Even so, I wear my usual black turtleneck, though I agree to prune my hair and beard to a topiary length. I'm not as bushy as I used to be, so the process doesn't take too long. As for Horacio, he's as dapper as ever in a charcoal Nehru suit, and he responds with dignified verboseness to the torrent of Presidential bunk.

From the Palace, the Director of the Biblioteca Canubana bears the codex away to his marble-fronted edifice, surrounded by a gun-toting platoon. The wiseacres jape: 'At long last, the Library contains a book.' Our aunt's love-token has become a civic monstrance.

To you and us, Chiara, it seems incongruous that Manfredo Espinosa, the champion of 'our august Hispanic patrimony,' should covet a work that damns the Spanish Empire with such vitriol. Either this isn't apparent to him and his shills, or he's clinging to one of his lifelong precepts: 'even the Taíno are better than Africans.'

That standpoint jives with the ID cards the two Espinosa regimes have issued from the thirties onward, specifying each citizen's 'race.' In their atavistic typology, even the most jet-colored islander is classed as 'dark Indian': anything to avoid tainting the noun 'Canuban' with the adjective 'black,' a hue fit only for Bonaventurans.

No doubt Manfredo's highbrow pretensions also underlie his attachment to the codex. Shortly after our mandatory 'gift,' a censored facsimile of the *True Relations* duly makes the rounds. On its heels, he sends a florid missive to media organs around the globe, trumpeting 'the most significant find of the century.'

But first he undertakes a drastic redesign of the Canuban Library, as a shrine for the manuscript. The vacant shelves in the spacious central hall make way for an oval gallery of sixty-six of the album's illustrations, blown up to thirty times their original size. These are the 'approved' images, the ones that depict everyday life among the Taíno, rather than fertility rites, shamanic orgies, rape and pillage, or fulminations against the Church.

At the crux of the cavernous room, the tome itself is set forth in a bullet-proof case flanked by four 'curators' with Barettas. A transparent lectern allows the volume to be viewed front and back, even when lying open. A masterpiece of the bookmaker's art, it consists of folio-sheets bound in fine-grained, puce-tinted leather. While the cover and spine are tooled with Renaissance motifs—ivy, acanthus, and ostrich plumes—the page-margins pullulate with Caribbean animals and flowering vines, akin to a medieval bestiary.

In a perpetual round, the Director unlocks the glass lid each morning; with sterilized forceps, he turns to the next two pages, adorned with embroidered script or full illuminations. Again, the island wags go to town. 'Poor man, he must be exhausted. They finally gave him a five-minute workday.'

Along with the accompanying texts, he suppresses the final thirty-three pictures in the manuscript as 'inappropriate,' either for the glass-case viewings or as reproductions on the walls. In this, he's obeying Espinosa's ironclad orders. But there's still plenty for the public to gawk at; and to the dictator's delight, the common people flock to the exhibit in droves. Admission is free of charge—a surefire vote-nabbing ploy, by his expert calculations. While foreigners and local bigwigs speed to the front in an express lane, the untutored masses wait for hours in snail-paced queues to gape at the florilegium, patiently filing past the replicas. For the illiterate, these prove more uplifting than the tome itself—and more relevant to their daily habits than the Cathedral's Taíno sculptures, with their portrayals of Gospel scenes.

The illustrations begin tamely enough, with copybook prototypes in the syncretic style of the High Renaissance. The preface by the Benedictine monk, Jorge Rojas, avers that they depict 'Antillean idols'; instead, as you point out, they recycle Greco-Roman deities from sixteenth-century art, as Cartari and Ripa list them in their catalogues.

I have to chuckle at your pedantry. — Yes, Chiara, I second you—though here they're tricked out with hawk-feathered headbands, monkey-tailed bracelets, and parrot-winged anklets tacked on...

From an orthodox churchman's standpoint, these deities

are little more than demons; but the clandestine humanists who sponsored the Taíno codex endorsed a broader perspective. To the modern observer, the attributes of these divinities—ticked off in the captions—foreshadow trait by trait the pantheons of Bonaventuran Vodou and Canuban Santería. Staring up at the giant reproductions, ordinary islanders instantly identify the glass beads, rooster heads, tam-tam drums, magic vials, and other accoutrements of their own familiar loas and gods.

The pictures of Taíno legends in the book further underscore the meshing of past and present. The workers and peasants who stream to the library dwell on them with a keen sense of self-affirmation. Like the devotees of current Antillean religions, our early inhabitants also believed in the walking dead: zombies without navels, who lurk at night and prey on the living. The deceased can even take to the air, in the form of malevolent bats. More benignly, they tarry plaintively among us, unable to cross to the other side. As Amado taught you long ago, Chiara, we hear their voices sighing in the trees, and rustling after sundown in the wind. They particularly haunt the jobo-tree, considered by islanders, then and now, the most 'human' of all plants.

The more we Canubans see ourselves mirrored in the album, the more the manuscript itself becomes a zombie: it whispers with all the persistence of an unquiet soul—like Amado's, when he wasn't yet laid to rest. Taíno phantoms waft through these pages, plunging us into a timeless realm, sharing the same activities we've plied for centuries. Whereas researchers grasp the import of the codex for comparative religion, Caribbean ethnography, Amerindian anthropology, and the like, we who people the archipelago still enact it in the here and now.

When commenting on the Indians' 'heathen cults,' Colonial clerics like the Benedictine Rojas and the Dominican Las Casas inject asides about their customs, and this is what most appeals to current islanders. Unlettered campesinos recognize themselves in their predecessors on the walls. An elderly couple named Clorinda and Escolástico—newly arrived from the countryside, to live with their children in a wretched slum—repair to the library each and every morning. They bring their friends along, and soon they've formed an informal study club, the 'Asociación C y E,' with themselves as the omniscient guides. Taking notes for a travel article, you've signed up as a member, and this morning you persuade me to tag along.

Many culinary folkways of the Taíno survive unchanged—for example, their appetite for cassava bread. Clorinda spells it all out for her female cronies. 'See, they made it the same way we do. Así mismito! Look at them press the yucca in flat rounds. Then they let them dry in the sun, like my grandmother Divi used to do. But what with gas ovens, it's a whole lot easier now.'

One of her listeners gets carried away. 'I bet they liked

chicharrones, too. I guess they fried the hides of those dogs of theirs—the ones that couldn't bark!'

Escolástico's male companions, several of them carpenters, find the natives' building skills more impressive than their cracklings. The Taíno constructed bohíos—cabins made of poles, roofed-over with fronds, and clustered in a village or batey.

'They're just like the shacks at El Silencio.'

'Of course, Chiara. The same huts dot every region of our island. Now they're mostly used for outdoor hearths or livestock pens.'

We'd better shut up. Escolástico frowns at us, straightening his broad-brimmed hat with authority. 'They liked to live with their mamas and grandmas, their papas and grandpas, their brothers and sisters, their uncles and aunts, their nephews and nieces and cousins, all in one place. Todos juntos! Just like today!'

He moves on to the next set of facsimiles. 'And the old Canubans loved to have parties, amigos! Coño, que fiestas! Wish we could be with them now for one of those!' Various panels show the Indians preparing an areíto—an intoxicated, all-night fest. Some of the censored pictures are more audacious; but these convey the basic idea. 'They beat on drums, just like us when we have palos, and I bet they danced cambuca steps.' He does a brief jig. 'Tengo ganas de bailar!'

Then he herds us past some portrayals of the Taíno ball

game. 'It was a lot like baseball,' he tells us; 'and their teams were named for animals—like the Halcones and Jaguares we root for now.'

A foreign professor in the fast lane overhears him. 'No, señor, in fact the game was more like soccer, the way the Mayans played it. And other competitions, with bows and arrows, ended in the loser's death.'

Once the egghead sidles by, Escolástico shrugs his shoulders. 'Humpf! Qué va! The only difference between them and us is this: we wear more clothes! On the street, anyway. Loco crazy in this hot weather! But that's what the invaders made us do. Malditos! Stupid gringos, like that one just now. Bendito! Kill the losers, just because of a game? But come to think of it, I wouldn't mind if the Halcones got the ax!' The Jaguares fans boo him loudly.

One quandary splits the male and female factions of the Asociación C y E: Who did the work in pre-Hispanic Canuba? In the illuminations, women and children labor in the fields, while the men laze about in their hammocks— unless they're playing ball, getting high, or dancing around the batey. Clorinda's ladies advise their husbands: 'It was never like that.'

The machos grin from ear to ear. 'Whether you like it or not, mujeres, that's the way it was—and the way it'll always be.'

The women counter that nowadays, most Canuban men toil from dawn to dusk. In the country, they're planting, weeding, and harvesting their crops. Or tending to their cows, pigs, and goats. If they live in the city, they hold down two or three jobs, so their families have enough to eat. 'We won in the end, even if you won't admit it,' Clorinda snorts, tweaking her husband's nose.

Escolástico pinches her behind. 'Maybe we work when we're older, but not when we're young. Look at the pictures: these jóvenes are all dressed up and ready for fun! Our wives will take care of us, they say. I tell you, nothing has changed!'

Plaza Drake, January 1995

Late at night, Horacio and I leave your house on Plaza Drake, and walk back to the Callejón del Platero. You sip my special tea from a rooster-red, porcelain jar, as you stare at the codex I've laid out on your desk. You enter our primeval world, where beings flow into each other... where I am you, where you are he, or she, or in between, where we are they... where children merge with the old, women with men, and our bodies are at one with animals, plants, and stones... where we're the eating and the eaten, the mouth that drinks, and the water from the gourd... where there's an echo in every sound, a shadow in every thought, a vision in every glance... where the light is a cloud, and the voyage an arrival...

You walk through the portal of climbing vines, panola and cirinto
and javolera, their leaves a candescent green and their blossoms
coral, canary, and lilac-blue.

                        On the upper right, you hail the regal lord
            in his feathered crown, his square chin outlined in black,
            his aging flesh still firm. He stands in front of the longhouse,
      roofed with fronds. You are the nubile girl who kowtows before
                              him, your brown body flawless and nude.

      In the central panel, he deflowers you, as your sisters peep
            through the cracks in rattan walls. In archaic Spanish,
                  the caption reads: The ritual of the chieftain's
                  first right to the bride. You stare up at him
                  with weeping eyes, slick as lumps of agate,
                        your mouth twisted into a crimson S.

On the lower left, he staggers to his feet, panting like a dog; he
isn't as young as he used to be. But your assembled relatives are
well-satisfied, and they raise a lusty shout. Laughing, you show
your young groom the stain on the mat. Your hymen has bled
profusely: your union will bear healthy fruit.

      You turn to another page. On the upper right, seven pubescent
            striplings prepare for a rite of passage. With pegs shaped like
            beaks, their points blackened by a holy fire, the elders tattoo
them with totems: monkeys, parrots, barracudas, hawks, iguanas,
frigate birds, and whales. The humpbacks' flippers are like wings;
                              their flukes reach upward like giant hands.

In the small central pane, you and the other boys bend over; with
                  jobo-tree plugs, topped by woodpecker heads,
                        the elders widen your anuses.

In the larger image furthest down, mature adolescents enter you carefully, one by one, swaying in a dance-step to the rhythm of drums and flutes. Older and younger, like ripe papayas, all of you spill your seed on the ground: doubly, you fecundate the fertile earth. Cackling, their backs painted with checkers of green and brown, the elders encircle you. In bird masks and red caps, they shake their maracas, rat-a-tat-tat. The harvest will be plentiful.

After your first menstruation, you girls have a rite of your own; no males are allowed to draw near. On an entire page, the ritual unfolds in the dead of night, when the moon is pregnant and full. Inside the longhouse, married women baste you with fish-oil and monkey-fat; they squish the paste into your tight, tender vaginas. Massaging your feet and ankles, they knead your calves, thighs, bellies, and buttocks. They go higher, daubing your nascent breasts that stand up like thumbs.
Others suck your toes like pebbles, or pry your delicate vulvas apart, darting their stiffened tongues inside to lap the liquid musk. All of you wriggle with pleasure, waving your arms and legs in the air like pampered babies. Moonlight filters through gaps in the roof and walls. Old crones look through the crannies with toothless, silvery smiles. You girls are full of juice; you'll give birth to many children. Our next generation will thrive.

A picture shivered into many panels tells the tale of Obanex, a dog without a single tuft of fur. Pink and smooth as the Spaniards' pigs, he kneels to the left before his master, who tosses him scraps from the midday meal.

In the biggest pane, a patchwork of yellows and greens, several clansmen hunt iguanas.
On a sunny hill, they swing stone hatchets at their prey;

an iguana head rolls along the grass,
a prize they award to Obanex. He jumps excitedly,
chews the iguana's eyes and brain,
then drinks some water from a light blue stream.

On the lower right, he samples a monkey his master's wife had
cooked; she jerks his snout from the higüero bowl and trounces
him. When her husband comes home, he slits the dog's throat:
his blood makes a wavy line along the bottom of the page.
Just above, his gutted body roasts on a spit. Hungrily,
the man pats his belly and smacks his lips.

The picture shifts. You're a shaman now,
squatting with your clansmen around a fire.
Streaks of paint bar your cheeks, chest, and thighs.
You wear the feather-cloak of the bohique,
the one who sees far-off. Soon the areíto will begin,
the all-night dance we owe to the eternal gods.
Gravely, you smoke the cohoba.

Propelled by its murky wings, you plunge across the sky
with a red-tailed hawk. You mate in midair, enveloped
by orange clouds. Then you change, change, and change again.
You journey through the spotted jaguar, the boa, the panther, the
daydreaming sloth: through spirits our island doesn't house, that
belong to the Other Great Earth. You return where we all began,
far to the south. You barrel down the mighty, brownish river to
the sea, where it spills like a flood into the waves. You paddle
for months on end with your sun-dazed tribe. You spear king-
mackerels and parrotfish—
eating them raw, spitting out their bones.

You follow the flocks of birds to their nests on land.
Skirting the islands day after day, at last you overshoot them.
You discover an archipelago that floats above the sea— that
rises as high as the stars. Your dugouts careen past the moon.
Soaring free, you jettison your boats, leaving the ocean behind—
surpassing the horizon…

Then you spiral downward, drifting back to earth.
The night has been long. One by one, you and your clansmen
drop to the ground like wilted manca leaves.
Women and youngsters creep into the frame,
half-hidden by tangled vines.
Now the whole batey begins the grand melee.
Young and old, you find your strength again.
Elated, you strut around and joke.
You couple with the women and rose-cheeked girls;
you penetrate the limber boys. They flip and buck
like aerial fish, swimming in the wind.
Your head swivels back and forth: your eyes
are golden and round as an owl's.

The image alters again. When their testicles ripen,
most youths make love with women and men.
But in the picture where you sit,
you're a headstrong boy who laughs all day.
You've been singled out: your penis won't be needed.

In every village on the island, there's a lucky one like you;
you mind the cooking pots and plant the yucca with your
mothers. Long past the age of manhood, you speak the female
tongue, with its vulvular grammar and moon-inflected words.
Before you tend the fields, you clean the stone zemis with special
brushes—bundles of softened papagayo quills.

Soon you're chosen by several men to be their extra wife,
and they maintain you. They house you in a small bohío,
just beyond the batey: here it is, at the lower corner of the page.
You're happy to spend your days with your tough-talking parrot,
your chatterbox monkey, your silent dog. The spirits visit you at
night; they sing to you like mockingbirds, and you sing back to
them. You are their bridge to our world.

You're not a woman, not a man;
your solitude makes you sacred.
The jobo-trees gather near your garden
of curative herbs. They tell you how to heal
our clansmen; they murmur to you on the wind.
Your husbands retire to your hut
when they want a night off—a change of pace
from their wives. As we see on this page,
sometimes two of them take you at once.
Pushing their members deep inside you,
they rub them together like poles.
Now and then they're too wild,
and almost rip you apart.

Your favorite lover is your older brother.
He visits you more often than the rest;
he defends you when they rough you up.
He lets you decide when to join your body with his,
and when to stop. Manly and gentle,
he always brings you offerings.
He calls you by your secret name:
the name that keeps you from harm,
the name the demons will never learn.

His sweat has the same smell as yours,
the same as your mother's.
You lick it from his chest and arms.

After time out of time, there are invaders. They come to us
from where our race was born, in the Other Great Earth.
For untold cycles of sun and moon, we've kept to ourselves,
planting the yucca, hunting the iguana, fishing for the white-
fleshed nucaba. Our wars have subsided into games of peace.

But then our forgotten cousins accost us like nightmares,
when they steal over children in their sleep—
when kind, familiar faces, loving by day,
twist into ogre-maws by night.
The marauders are our twins, but magnified:
corded with sinews from making war, from clubbing sharks,
from furrowing the sea with their swift canoes.
Their hair is much longer than ours;
they anoint it with whale-oil and smears of blood.

In this picture you're a sentinel,
cooled by the early-morning dew;
the sun's first rays illumine your dun-colored skin.
High on a cliff above the tranquil, azure sea,
you stand at the mouth of a cave.

On the next page, you scan the horizon:
suddenly the pillagers swarm over its blue-green curve.
Their longboats slice through the water like barracudas;
their paddles bristle like the waving legs of centipedes.
In the inset to the left, you imagine them close-up,
with red and yellow war-paint on their cheeks.
Shark-teeth dangle from their musclebound arms;

serpent-tattoos coil around their shoulders.
They strain to paddle faster, aiming
to catch our people off guard.
Sweat gushes from their groins and thighs,
their armpits and chests.

                You swing the conch to your lips
                    and blow it as loudly as you can.
         Other lookouts along the coast answer you on cue;
              but we already know that we're doomed.
                  The Caribs will kill our men.
                They'll take our women as chattel.
              They'll bring up our children as slaves.
                The distant past has circled back
                    like a snake to eat us alive.
              But at least they're flesh of our flesh,
        and blood of our blood. We will continue in them.

The images weave from page to page.
The invaders ram full-speed into the sand.
Brandishing axes, they leap from their huge canoes;
they drag them onto the beach; howling and whooping,
they race to seize their prey. Our villagers
shoot their childish arrows, but the Caribs
brush them off like gnats. Brawny and ruthless,
they toss our warriors to the ground. Gripping their necks,
they rape them one by one: this is how they steal
their virility. Once they've had their fill,
they crop our tribesmen's testicles
with obsidian knives.

Now the marauders can take their time with us:
we women offer no resistance. What would be the use?
Zoraida, pictured in the lower-right pane,
you're the loveliest girl of our clan.
They set you aside at the back of the batey,
where they've already killed your brothers,
your husband, your father. They don't enjoy you now;
they save you for the last pleasure of the day.
The aquamarine line of the sea skips in the background;
rivulets of blood crisscross the ochre sand,
drying to reddish black.

In the panel to the left, the invaders stand the other girls up
and take them from behind, grabbing their breasts
with their gory hands. Their swollen members plow
the russet buttocks, jacking the women's feet from the ground. The
children of our village cower to one side, with terror in their eyes:
this is the end of the world they've known.

Soon the men command our older women to cook,
as we can see by turning the page. They're famished now
from their lengthy trip, the thrill of slaughter,
the fierceness of their pairings with boys and girls.
In this segment, Zoraida, you reappear—glossy as a captive bird,
your smooth Taíno flesh like downy feathers at rest. The Caribs
still spare you; you wait on them shyly
at their meal. You're not surprised that when they barreled from
the sea, they slew our foolish striplings like flies.

All our warriors ever did was play their boyish games,
swim in streams, fondle each other in caves,
lie together in hammocks, and doze all afternoon.
The Caribs embrace each other too, and make

the hard-limbed love of men with men.
But in their tribe, husband-brothers teach
the arts of combat, each to each—fighting
with bare fists, hurling spears, wielding hatchets,
and dueling with clubs. They wrestle naked in the sand
and bellow the name of their war-god; their voices
bounce from cliff to cliff. Now all their prayers
are answered; on us, the sacred zemis
have turned their backs. We were too patient,
too mild. The gods are cruel, swift, and arrogant:
they like the splash of guts, not the yucca
we offered on our altar-stones. These Caribs are gods, but they rule
us here on earth, with their dazzling teeth and their blue-black
hair down to their waists.

       Zoraida, you weave among these human gods
with an higüero bowl, offering the roasted gonads
of our men. The Caribs pop the pungent morsels
into their mouths, and say a guttural oath.
Some of them slap your buttocks with their massive,
meaty hands. It won't be long before they use you,
as they did your sisters and cousins at noon: they can tell you're
ready and willing. Your husband was always chatting with his
friends, tinting his body yellow and green, dancing for their
delight. He hardly ever came to you—though your womb is
fertile, you are sure. You will make powerful sons for these brash
men. Your breasts tremble with excitement; one day your milk
will flow into tiny, suckling mouths. The invaders fill our batey,
half-reclining on their elbows, raising their knees. Their
members stiffen again as they joke about our warriors, so easy to
rape. How many of these Caribs will choose you,
Zoraida? Let them begin.

Ten years later, Tolonex, you're a different watchman
on the same rocky coast. You were only a child
when the Caribs defeated our tribe. Your mother
married one of them, who taught you their language:
you've helped them confer with our elders,
and learn our ways. They've stolen all they wanted
and settled among us, fattened by the yucca,
the bountiful fish and game. Atonished,
at the mouth of the topmost cave,
you see that something much stranger
will happen to us now. Here is a mirage
on the horizon, the most outlandish
of the cohoba pipe-dreams.
Not the slender dugouts of the Caribs,
but wide square houses tugged by clouds,
puffing with labored breath across the waves.
You shudder from head to toe: these
must be the dwellings of the sky-gods.
They have returned as in our ancient tales
to take back the world, to wrest it from humankind.
Are they kindly spirits, or not?
Their vessels creep forward, ungainly as manatees.
These are not our cousins from the Other Great Earth,
but aliens whose magic we can't conceive.

In the next panel, you quake even more—
you lose your foothold, almost tipping
over the ledge. Around the floating fortresses,
monsters heave their foamy heads,
bigger than the whales that swim through our winter seas—
whiter than the three enchanted islands off our shore,
three whales a zemi has turned to stone.

You blast a warning with your conch,
though you've already guessed that this time
there's no reprieve. These are not our kinsmen,
pillaging in a rampage; these are harbingers
of doom, for all of us who wash in Atabey's streams.

                    Lunging to the right along the wide central pane,
                        you run down the path from your outpost
                    on the cliff. You reach the village just as the ships
                    are closing in, their bobbing heads of cloth saying yes
                            this is the place, yes we will crush you,
                        yes we will enslave you, yes we will hound you
                                till the hour of your death.

Once a watchman, Tolonex, now you are a witness
        called to testify. You follow these barbarians
        through all the final images. You are here
    as the connivers row from their sea-borne forts
    in small triangular boats, their faces hairy and pink,
    their bodies encased in cloth and stinking like fish.
    Once on shore, they refrain from mowing us down
    with their cannons and metal blades. No, not yet:
    their cunning teaches them to wait. They blare a song
        on shiny trumpets, yellow as anacaona blooms;
        they plant black poles with colored banners
        in the ground. They chatter like monkeys,
    and you surmise their palaver, just as you learned
        the Carib tongue when still a child: they tell you
the words for you, for me, for island, for their kingdom
        faraway, for their cacique and his queen,
    for the sorcerer's book they clutch in their hands.
        A trove of spells inside a box, it divides
            into a thousand wrinkled leaves.

They hold up what they call a crucifix,
and nod it toward us as a blessing.
To us it's more like a curse: a famished man
who's nailed to a piece of wood, beaten
and gashed till he's breathing his last.

In the panel to the left, the black-shirted priests
warn us to love their one and only god. But they confuse us
when they say that he is three as well as one;
that the dying man is the second of the three,
with all his wounds; and that the third is a bird.

They astound us even more with their other deities;
in the middle pane, the black-hooded monks
show us their images. A woman who carries her eyes
on a plate, a man pointing proudly to his leg full of puss,
a youth riddled with arrows like an urchin on the reef.
If these are the gods who will come to our aid,
why do they let themselves be maimed?

In the lowest pane, the soldiers force us
to bow to their mangled gods; they cut out
the tongues of our shamans, they topple the zemis
in our fields and bateys. As you assist
the Spanish priests with our island words,
your saddened face clearly tells us: You understand.
Yes, you understand why these invaders worship pain.

Their religion of cruelty impels them to defeat us—
not by eating our vanquished flesh like the Caribs
from the south, but by stretching us alive on the rack,
grilling our chieftains like dogs until they squeal:
I swear, I am a Christian! Here you watch

as the pink-faced men accuse each other of sin,
as they flay each other's feet to change a word
in their magic book, as they fight among themselves
with swords and thundering guns. You laugh when they insist that
their great cacique needs our gold. They won't listen when you tell
them our hills have no gold,
just a few sandy nuggets in mountain brooks.
The trading boats, you tell them, brought
our head-bands and bracelets from the west.
How can we go there? they ask, the gold-lust
gleaming in their eyes. Before long, they'll sail off
in their ships—but not yet. When they leave,
other warlords will replace them. The shamans'
prophecies will be fulfilled: this is the end of days.

> Here you shake your head, as our people scrape the earth
> for shallow, yellow veins. If we don't find gold,
> the soldiers cut off our ears, our noses, even our hands.
> But how can we look for gold if we have no hands?
> How can we trust the priests if they rape our young,
> lifting their putrid skirts to press our infants to the wall?
> How can we survive if our lands are taken away,
> if we must work as slaves in our own fields?
> At the center of this page, our people
> abandon their crops, their houses, their zemis—
> yes, they abandon all hope. Slaves no more,
> they march toward the cliffs and leap into the sea.
> Their heads shatter against the rocks;
> the white foam is laced with red and grey.

> In the pane at the end of our book, our last caciques
> are herded before the Spanish church: that temple
> of the conquerors, built from stone by us,

the victims of their battered god. Their god:
the bleeding, disfigured cadaver on the cross.
They've reduced us to his image;
they've scourged us with his misery.
Their bells ring and ring, louder and louder.
The soldiers tie our chieftans to stacks of logs.
They burn them alive—a sacrifice
to their three-headed god. In ecstasy,
the black-cowled monks intone
their chants of praise, their eyes
turned upward to the thunderclouds.
The smoke from their bonfire blots out the sky.

Callejón del Platero, January 1995

Deliberately, Manfredo Espinosa has kept the populace ignorant, so he can run the country as he sees fit. Once he hijacks the *Verdaderas Relaciones*, he treats the codex as an artifact of history—and paradoxically, as an encomium of the island's Spanish heritage, its 'Hispanidad.' But by trooping past blown-up photographs of its illustrations, peasants and workers gain a new sense of their own importance—and also of their plight. For centuries, they've been tyrannized by their rulers, from the Catholic Kings to Espinosa, the 'Benefactor de la Patria.' When schoolchildren are herded on mandatory tours of the Presidential Palace or the Columbus Crown, they feel numbed by their ugliness. The dictator's malachite nymphs and concrete tombs repel them almost as much as his trumped-up patriotism and all-too-authentic vanity. In the waning years of his regime, he's an Ozymandias ripe for the shifting sands. His pharaonic monuments are bereft of life, while 'the Book'—as it comes to be known to one and all—throbs with vitality.

The people's dawning self-awareness bolsters the Transformation Party: Milady openly exploits the *True Relations* in her ongoing bid for the presidency. Like Espinosa, she priggishly sweeps its racier motifs under the carpet; but her campaign headquarters brims with replicas of its 'more suitable' pictures. As expressive as the stained-glass windows in Gothic cathedrals, they attest to the magnetism of art for even the humblest observer. Despite their origin in a distant past, they transmit the fervor of Rivera, Orozco, and Siqueiros—far more than the calm of a Renaissance book of hours, from which they derive their technique.

From the dawn of the colony, Santiago Columbus pulls a fast one on the Pope by inviting the Benedictines to Canuba: he's the only early governor who makes such a daring move. Unlike the Dominican friars, luridly denounced in the Taino codex, the Black Monks are more receptive to pagan cultures and novel ideas. To found the island's abbey, Santiago selects a circle of clerics influenced by humanism: covert adherents of the movement, like himself, they long for greater freedom of thought in this brave New World. In the early sixteenth century, theirs is the only order that still fosters the painting of illuminations; yet even at their scriptorium in Monte Cassino, the handiwork they perfected has begun to yield to printed books.

Santiago's letters to his wife, preserved in Seville, hint that the scribes are teaching their craft to some gifted Taíno converts. Probably neither he nor the Benedictines foresee just how far these novices will go, once they develop their skills. The Spanish and Italian brothers are gratified when their pupils prepare parchment folios, crush minerals and seeds, and mix permanent hues: smoldering blackish-red, bright scarlet, buttery yellow, fulgent gold, hummingbird green, and sun-struck blue. As chemical tests have since confirmed, the Taíno apprentices draw on the pigments they've always used for body-paint, and this may explain why their artistry takes such a fleshly turn.

You're puzzled when late one night, Horacio and I bring you the codex for safekeeping. We tell you we've escaped the guards posted outside our door by going through an underground passageway, devised by the seventeenth-century owner of our house—an odd disclosure in itself, which takes you aback. 'If we leave the album with you,' I say naively, 'no one will suspect where it is.'

To you, our ruse seems desperate, even mad. We'll never succeed in smuggling the folio out of the country, you argue; Espinosa's spies will stop us in our tracks. And perhaps the quietus will be permanent, thanks to one of the regime's infamous 'accidents'—a bus that runs us over, an armed robbery that gets out of hand, or a lethal food-poisoning from a simple meal. At best, we'll get ourselves in trouble—not to mention you. But these cautious phrases die on your lips, Chiara, and your grey-green eyes turn opaque. For Horacio, you resemble one of the statues sculpted by your forebears, a pensive Athena or taciturn Proserpine.

Yes, yes, yes… For one unrepeatable night, you want to have these pictures all to yourself—especially the 'forbidden' ones, the thirty-three images in the last third of the tome. Once the tyrant seizes them, no one will view the originals again until his downfall; and as you gather from your first glimpse, no mere reproduction could ever do them justice. Anticipating your 'aesthetic concupiscence,' as Horacio calls it, I've brought along a visionary brew of mushrooms for you to drink, passing it off as a tea from our 'medicinal noni-bush.'

In multiple episodes within a single space, not unlike the 'continuous representation' of the saints in medieval panels, the Taíno illuminators brandish a priapic verve absent from Western art since ancient Greece and Rome. Their paintings recall the ribald ceramics of Peru or the shunga prints of Japan; but the Canuban slant on these themes is far more dynamic and extreme. The swirling hair of the women merges with the tresses of the men, in passages where gender veers, spirals, and leaps into the void. Their sadomasochism is equally untrammeled: among the Caribs and Taíno, it appears to transpire as an ordinary facet of existence. But in the scenes of Spanish violence towards the islanders, the Europeans reel with bloodlust, a vile perversion of the natives' ruthless joy.

Some Americanists object that the works reveal nothing about indigenous mores: the rotten fruits of a degenerate clique, they pander to Santiago's libertine prurience. Others counter that the healer, with his lovers and his brother-husband, corresponds to the 'Outsider' of the Guayakis—a tribe descended from the Arawaks, like the Caribs and Taíno. As to the auto-da-fé of the caciques, the Inquisition committed such atrocities throughout Hispanic America. Along those lines, the aggressive pederasty of the Dominican monks should come as no surprise, especially for us today. Perhaps the Benedictines tacitly encouraged these damning jabs at their more militant confrères. Exotic fertility rites and cannibalism appear to have been frequent in pre-Columbian cultures: why shouldn't the islanders have practiced both? A fringe coterie at the École Normale in Paris maintains that Canuba's idiosyncrasy sets it apart from other Antillean societies; they have proposed a unique subset of anthropology: 'les études Taíno-canubaines.'

All the experts agree that in their fervid farewell, the Amerindians galvanized the temperate 'très riches heures' of an imported, moribund art, in decline since the famed illuminations for the Duc de Berry. As a destabilizing vector, some have pointed to Liberale, Girolamo, and Bettino, whose miniatures distorted traditional forms in the late Quattrocento. But that is a question of 'disegno,' not of thematic audacity; and in the latter, even more than in pictorial design, the Taíno artists broke unprecedented ground. If the Western clerics added anything to their pupils' iconography, they may have tapped their own primal unconscious, interred in the night of time: the bacchanals of Dionysus with his thyrsus, the murderous romps of the maenads on wooded Naxos, the revels of prancing satyrs with dandled erections and cleft feet…

Chiara, I'm sure that like me, you'll recognize these paintings as Canuban to the core. Though as gemlike as the staid vignettes of Jean Fouquet, they rave with the final fires of an alien mind—postmodern because archaic, like the Mycenean cults of Magna Graecia. Both your islands, Sicilia and Canuba, have fully embraced the chthonic side of creation, thriving on death as much as life, and on darkness as much as light. The images of 'the Book' propel us from the past toward the future, hurtling through our age and beyond. Like the Taíno *Way of the Cross* in our Cathedral, or my own clashing methods and motifs, they feed voraciously on their inner contradictions, flaming higher and higher till they burn themselves to ash. More than any other extant document, the Taíno codex bears witness to the Encounter, that planetary blaze of colliding worlds.

Now that your wounds are almost healed, Chiara, you repair more often to the cave at El Silencio, where you and Amado once foiled the heat of sultry afternoons. This bucolic eyrie, on a shelf above the sea, has always kindled your fantasies. We Mirandas whet and savor your fugues; in our youth, we were passionate hikers, too—even sickly Horacio. You've convinced yourself that the Taíno must've watched for marauding Caribs from your lookout. And who can say? One momentous morning, they may have sighted the Admiral's caravels, inching across the horizon with their tall sails full-blown. At first, they would've seemed like clouds; and then, like apparitions from another world... For years, like us, you've been obsessed with our Antillean aboriginals... but lately, our collective fascination has skittered out of control.

Since Catulo's death and Verbena's adoption, I've become more presentable: I brush my hair, comb my beard, and speak with increasing fluency. It helps that I've cut back on my consumption of grass and other 'medicines.' For practice in social interchange, I sometimes have lunch with you and Horacio at your house on Plaza Drake. The three of us weave chimerical theories, linking the Indians to present-day Canubans by every gesture, vocable, or quirk. Your housekeeper Luz Divina can hardly stew cassava, purse her lips, or crook an elbow without a trio of exclamations: 'See, there she goes again!'

The monomania comes to a head with an album we inherit, a voluminous collection of Taíno mores and myths, along with unheralded illustrations. Our Aunt Alba Iris, who trips and cracks her noggin in 1994 on the Day of All Saints, leaves the book to her 'queridos sobrinos Miranda.' Lamentably, of these 'dear nephews,' Catulo has already preceded her into the fathomless blue.

The manuscript bears the sonorant title *Las Verdaderas Relaciones de las Creencias Paganas de los Taínos Antiguos, Junto con Observaciones sobre sus Costumbres*. Compiled in the early sixteenth century, it vanished for almost five centuries, though rumors of it lingered in Protestant lands. In English, perpetrators of the 'black legend' of Spain's evil empire often alluded to it as *The True Relations of the Pagan Beliefs of the Ancient Taínos, Along With Observations on Their Customs*. Commissioned by Santiago Columbus, the Governor of Canuba, the miscellany was assembled by Iberian monks and priests. Like Santiago himself, some of them seem to have sympathized with Enrique de Villena and Juan Luis Vives, humanists accused of heresy by the Church.

The clerics gather their data by collaborating with native interpreters in Hispaniola, Cuba, Jamaica, Puerto Rico, Canuba, and Bonaventura. Among the contributors are Fray Ramón Pané and Padre Bartolomé de las Casas, whose shorter reports have long provided a crucial source for scholars. The portfolio boasts new versions of their writings, revised and expanded. It also includes a welter of notes by other monks—many of them amateur classicists—which swell its scope to more than a thousand pages in all.

The florilegium is enlivened by a hundred illuminations, at Santiago's behest. By this time, in the year of our Lord 1521, he has already incurred the Dominicans' wrath by resisting the order's iron grip on his domain. Brutally forthright about cannibalism, erotic rites, Spanish cruelty, and priestly abuse, the opus quickly enters the Vatican's list of forbidden books. Accordingly, it's left unpublished, shunted out of view, forgotten in the Carribbean's constant wars, and never unearthed until now.

Needless to say, we don't keep our epochal discovery to ourselves. The Universidad Pontífica's edition of the *Verdaderas Relaciones*—a partially censored replica, on Espinosa's orders—causes a sea-change in Caribbean studies; it is immediately translated into numerous languages. We have no doubt that after a universal hue and cry, and relentless urging from his aide Ángel María, our dictator will grudgingly bow to the inevitable. We predict that the bilingual, unbowdlerized version, slated for publication by Harvard's Belknap Press, will achieve a global currency.

Academics can no longer deny the Amerindian roots of our archipelago's religions, or fixate on their African and European fundaments alone. Even the most retrograde are forced to accept the triple genesis of Vodou and Santería, and the Taíno zemis take their rightful place beside the Yoruba spirits and the Christian saints. In the realm of ethnic politics, the magnum opus vindicates First Nation folkways and beliefs. Last but not least, the explicit images appeal to the popular mind, and are sure to make any paperback edition a runaway success. The *Verdaderas Relaciones* will become the Caribbean bible, an indispensable key to our region's past.

In fact, Chiara, we may have come by the compendium through accident rather than design—and I don't mean our aunt's tumble down the steps. A lecturer in geology at the Pontifical University, Alba Iris often displays her musty books to us, promising that one day they'll be ours. But for personal reasons, she never mentions this hefty tome, despite our avowed enthusiasm for the Taíno.

As we now find out, the codex has been inscribed to her by none other than our father, Don Baltásar, with the mournful, rhapsodic words: 'To you my clandestine spouse, wedded to me by the ancient gods, Greek or Taíno, for all eternity—though the prison of monogamy renders our lofty union hellish in men's eyes. With all my adoration, your sacred lover, Baltico.'

Compromising sentiments, to say the least... Alba Iris might have destroyed the folio before her demise, if it hadn't occurred so abruptly. After watering the pink geraniums beside her front door, she slipped on a leak from the flowerpot, like Dr. Urbino in Gabo's *Cólera.*

The dedication reminds us of an incident from Catulo's early childhood: confidentially, he often used to recount it with bemusement. At the time, our father was an up-and-coming engineer, an amateur classicist, and a stickler for impeccable clothes. One morning, our mother balked at his having the maid re-iron an unused shirt, just because its tail was slightly creased. 'Nobody can see those wrinkles inside your trousers, silly man!'

In high dudgeon, our father threatened to elope with his lover, who went unnamed. 'She'll do anything for me, Wanda, unlike you!'

Throughout the summer, our mother railed against the 'impudent strumpet' who'd turned her husband's head—though no one can ascertain if she suspected her sister. A year later, our father was appointed to his first diplomatic post, and our parents left Puerto Indio for decades. In our mother's mind, we can assume, the contretemps soon faded into nothing more than a distant memory, bitter but jejune.

For Alba Iris, it wasn't so easy to let bygones be bygones. She preserved the evidence of her affair under lock and key in a Sheridan-style, glass-fronted bookcase. Where 'Baltico' may have acquired the relic remains a mystery, though he often rummaged through flea markets, curiosity shops, and attic sales, digging up odds and ends. The dog-ears and abraded edges betray how often our aunt must have thumbed through her keepsake; constant fingering has worn the title page—where the inscription appears—almost tissue-thin. Romantically, we speculate that several tiny stains must memorialize her tears…

Early on, Horacio had sniffed something fishy in our mother's reminiscences about 'that brainy Alba Iris,' who conceived a passion for Greek at the age of twenty-six. As she grew older, our aunt let drop that she'd once spent many happy hours with Don Baltásar, parsing Sappho and Alcaeus. Why love lyrics only, Horacio wondered, instead of Homer or Hesiod?

In my view, they relived the story of Paolo and Francesca, bodily acting out the wanton verses they'd read. Why did our mother let them carry on right under her nose? Perhaps she understood that satiety would snuff her husband's flame, so all she had to do was bide her time. Sooner or later, Alba Iris would find another man, or doom herself to spinsterhood.

Faithfully, we expunge the evidence of our father's Hellenic adultery; filial to a fault, we excise his maudlin tribute with a razor blade. This lacuna will spawn unending reams of learned hypotheses, we foresee. To our merriment, scholars will cook up far-fetched suppositions: Santiago doodled an obscene drawing below the title; a Taíno scribbled 'Death to the Spanish Oppressors'; a monk penned hexameters against the Pope. Abstruse footnotes aside, we're grateful our aunt didn't incinerate Exhibit A of her early guilt, out of remorse or amorous spite.

When she learns how to talk again, Verbena calls Horacio her 'little Daddy.' 'Papito,' she dubs him, in contrast to her hulking 'Papote'—me. As a chamber music conductor, Horacio proves so adept that he outgrows his own ensemble. Requests for guest appearances flood his mailbox, from every corner of the planet. While he's gone, Verbena is old enough to be looked after by our father's cook, Elpiria—with impressionistic brushstrokes from my father and me. Both of us adore the girl.

Increasingly, we champion the cause of Milady Mateo, and her fight against Espinosa's racist policies. As his former diplomat extraordinaire, our father has risked his life by defying the tyrant, and we brothers stand by his side. Even Catulo, the least engaged among us, persuades the foreign hotel chain he manages to underwrite her. Horacio, fully attuned to the democratic cause, collects funds from his socialite friends for Milady's Transformation Party. Typically, my own protest against rightwing bigotry takes a more eccentric turn.

As always, everything begins with my art. When some Spanish nuns salvage a scrap of one of my paintings, Horacio fields their message. I retrieve the fragment at the hospital they've founded, a treatment center for indigent waifs. I'm deeply impressed by their selfless toil, and by the urgent needs of their small charges. They treat me with respect, even though I look like a scruffy bum. I make substantial gifts to the order, under my pseudonym 'Factor'; but through the clerical grapevine, the sisters soon verify who I am.

One day they approach me about a malnourished child, who's just come under their wing. Apparently, she's a deaf-mute; and clearly, she's recently been raped. The girl's Bonaventuran mother brought her in to be examined; then she rushed off 'to use the phone,' and summarily disappeared. There's no trace of her in the civil registry. The nuns hope we 'prominent Mirandas' will help them find the ten-year-old a home. To their amazement, I go them one better: I return to the clinic with Horacio; and as soon as he lays eyes on the girl, he decides we must adopt her.

Our father seconds the impulse, pleased to have a grandchild at long last. Despite her initial skepticism about our family, Milady has gradually acknowledged the authenticity of our stance. We've espoused her movement because—unlike most 'white' Canubans, even the ones Europeans might call 'black'—we're genuinely devoid of color prejudice. Our many years of residing abroad, in a rainbow of ethnic groups, have freed us from skin-deep myopia. To her partisans, Milady often cites the 'Miranda case' as a foretaste of things to come.

Horacio grants me the privilege of naming the little girl, whose trauma has shocked her into amnesia. I christen her Verbena, after a wildflower in my favorite book by Faulkner, *The Unvanquished*. Through the last three weeks of Advent, Horacio and I visit 'our baby' at the hospital twice a day, waiting for the sisters to allay her malnutrition and rid her feeble frame of parasites. Our family lawyers, and some bureaucratic linchpins we know, ensure her release into our custody.

The child's arrival coincides with Christmas Eve: for us, Verbena seems to symbolize the Word Incarnate— once skinny and fretful, now she's round and content. 'We've accorded the Verbo a feminine anima—yet another ramification of her nomen,' Horacio proclaims, with his usual Latinate flourishes.

Chiara, you're the only guest we'd dream of inviting to Callejón del Platero, on the night Verbena 'is reborn.' From the beginning, like us, you're impressed by her sprightly attentiveness. Her eyes scintillate with unspoken eloquence: she follows everything we say, even Horacio's high-flown rhetoric. Despite her habitual silence, her expression seems to imply that she has opinions of her own.

By awakening my paternal instincts, she infuses me with a sense of purpose. I keep my hair and beard neatly cropped, so as not to frighten her; I seek to make whole sentences the child can learn to imitate. As for Horacio, his maternal instincts purge him of his hypochondria at home; his conducting success has already 'healed' him in the public sphere. As he kisses Verbena on the forehead, she tussles with him like an Amazon, grabbing him in her viselike grip. He seems emboldened by her strength.

While you and I play with the child, Horacio readies holiday baskets for the adherents of the Transformation Party. Its grassroots supporters always address each other as 'compañero'—a term with a vaguely leftist twang, halfway between companion and comrade. A thickset, good-humored Transformista drops by to collect the presents, whistling the tunes of Christmas villancicos.

A half-hour later, Elpiria sends up a meal from the kitchen downstairs, where she cares devotedly for our father, debilitated by age. We've already had tea with him earlier, an 'Anglo-Saxon' custom he acquired in the diplomatic corps. Though an anomaly on such a meat-loving island, our supper reflects Horacio's frugal diet: organic vegetables, seasoned by herbs from our courtyard, and spooned onto whole-grained rice. Taíno cassava-bread completes the feast.

Horacio insists that you and I should eat without him. 'Notwithstanding, Verbena will be your propinquant commensal, with your abject servant as her accessory.' He sits near our table and serves the child a special gruel, made from goat's milk and oats; her digestion is still on the mend.

Our upper-floor apartment wears a festive air this evening. I've lined the walls with stick-figure cutouts in red, blue, yellow, and green. I've glued multicolored decals to the tall Colonial windows, repeating the same motifs in a see-through mode. Are these just Christmas decorations, you ask me, or a stylistic departure?

After Verbena goes to bed, you persist in ribbing me. — Hmmm… Hard-edge abstraction. Are you leaving figurativism behind?

Ugh… — I rake the table with my paint-stained paws, though I've trimmed my fingernails. — What nonsense… Chiara… you… a critic? — For me there's nothing worse. But I'm in no state to spar with you tonight… since I'm drunk on Christmas port.

Horacio clears the air. — If you are interrogating the iconic magister for one of your periodicals, he will be obliged to exchange cliché for cliché. Videlicet: 'Every oeuvre recapitulates the chronology of art.' 'I could not metamorphose into a pater familias, without it affecting my lucubrations.' 'We must continue evolving in order to remain consciously zoetic.' Etcetera, etcetera, ad infinitum. — He chokes back his coughs, to spare the sleeping child. — But rather, let us invoke a renovative energy, channeled into my frater from an empyreal effluvium.

By now you're used to his passé, New Age claptrap; unfazed, you don't miss a beat. — Issuing from where? Bonaventura? Africa? Verbena might be the relay point.

He scrunches up his brows. His reedy voice climbs to its highest register. — No, far more remote than that: perhaps obscure gamma rays from another galaxy. Yet the 'relay point,' as you specify, may indeed be focalized here, within the confines of our pulchritudinous insula. To wit, on a magnificent estate, yclept Espada del Sur.

'Sword of the South'? What an intriguing name. Where is that?

In your perennial Shangri La, no less, dear goddess: the province of Barlovento. A confederate of ours orchestrates the entire domain. She is the in-situ satrap of Milady's mobilization. And we commune on another plane as well: like your devoted servitor, she plies the beneficent arts of traditional healing. The vox populi designates her a 'Vodou mambo.'

You bolt upright in your chair. — Let me guess. Her name is Diana. A Bonaventuran—very beautiful.

Indeed, superlatively. You are acquainted with her, Chiara? What a coincidence! — He amends his choice of words, too plain for his florid taste. — I must endeavor to elocute with more exactitude. Forsooth, this is an instance of synchronicity. As we entities of a meritorious caliber are cognizant, nothing befalls us by mere coincidence.

To my brother's bafflement, I let out a hoot. He doesn't know that you're cringing, Chiara. To you, 'synchronicity' is almost as shoddy as 'serendipity': such trendy words set your teeth on edge. But you have to put up with them, considering the occasion; Christmas cheer trumps what Horacio would call 'lexical cavils.'

You chatter on amenably. What's Diana doing out there in the country? you wonder aloud. Until now, you've only seen her at a temple in San Sebastián, you tell us, or at a graveyard in the Hiroshima neighborhood. But then, on a trip to Rome a year ago, you ran into the priestess in Piazza Navona—on a 'private getaway' with Ángel María, of all people. Our revered schoolmate asked you to keep mum about their affair, to avoid any trouble with his wife, Leandra—so now all three of us are sworn to secrecy. Apparently, Diana's sphere of influence stretches farther than Horacio 'ever dreamed in his philosophy.' Since Ángel María is Espinosa's right-hand man, his unsuspected link to the 'Vodou mambo' unveils momentous political vistas…

Come to think of it, you continue, what about the sleek Lexus Diana had at her disposal, when she took you to the cemetery in Hiroshima, that strangely named Puerto Indian slum? Back then, when you visited Amado's tomb, her opulence had rung a jarring note; and now the 'magnificent estate' in Barlovento perplexes you even more…

The Barrios, April 1992

Chiara, it might unnerve you that I often go for strolls at night in the Barrios. I know them better than anyone, even the denizens themselves. I have a covert passage to the 'hoods from Callejón de la Plata… At the back of the shop is a closet where I keep my art supplies, and ample stashes of pot, hash, shrooms—whatever appeals to my mood… The only key hangs from a rawhide cord around my neck, stuffed unobtrusively under my shirt. Made of bronze, it dates back to the time when a wealthy French merchant built our house. He wanted a surefire escape-route, in case the Spanish reclaimed their colony by stealth… When they attacked in 1692, he used this exit to flee the island, with nothing but the clothes on his back…

From the storeroom a secret door, concealed by a seven-foot canvas, opens onto a flight of stone stairs. They lead to a dank, pitch-black tunnel, built by the Vatican in 1510, so the clergy could survive a major conflict between Taíno warriors and Spanish troops. It snakes for a mile past flood drains and sewers, connecting the Cathedral with a series of convents and parish churches. It ends at the Benedictine Abbey: this was the Church's final refuge, the farthest point from the small urban nucleus of the time… Nowadays, pushing back a long-forgotten gate in a ruined wall of the cloister, I find myself in La Cruz, the nearest favela to the Barrio Antiguo. From there, under my alias, 'Factor'—the Maker, the 'Hacedor'—I gain access to the poorest part of Puerto Indio. In a crooked chain, jerrybuilt shanty-towns dip along the riverbank and zigzag through well-to-do neighborhoods, all the way to the foothills…

Here, I'm safe from the prying gossips of the middle class. Stowing my flashlight in one of my baggy pockets, I blink in the tropical glare—but only if I emerge from the tunnel by day… That happens when one of my informants has phoned; they keep their eyes peeled for fragments of my works, sure of a generous reward. I like to scatter my canvases through the streets, then recuperate what's left: a form of accidental art. Horacio is accustomed to their crazed, conspiratorial voices… 'The weasel with the Maizol bottle on top. Tell Factor he can have it for three escudos…' 'That Factor don't believe me no more. I swear, I found the friggin' mermaid. It says Nana Babyfood on her face…' 'Hey, you little cheat. You didn' give Factor my last message. You're dead! Te voy a matar!' Patiently, my long-suffering brother takes down their names: Rotweiler, Wingo, Patú, or Voltaire—pronounced 'volt-eye-ray.' I've sworn to him I'll never tell these crackpots where we live…

In La Cruz, people believe I hole up in the Abbey, a rat-infested heap they dread as haunted, even accursed. It's rumored that centuries ago, a pair of evil monks held black masses in the crypt… Since I mostly issue from the cloister after dark, the superstitious fear me as a warlock, maybe even a zombie. You never know: I might be a thousand years old. I might be a priest who made a pact with the devil. With my eerie blue eyes and pallid skin, I might be one of the damned… Mothers shield their children from my gaze, and cross themselves three times when I pass. But the farther I go from the Abbey, the more I'm treated like an ordinary bum—or at worst, a lunatic with messy hair, an entertaining freak…

I much prefer my night-walks to going out by day. Shaggy, portly men are brave: we put up a jolly front and roll with the punches. On this unenlightened island, we're used to derision. I love my size, to tell the truth. I feel like a galleon on the Spanish main, all sails unfurled. I love my hirsuteness, too. That's why I never go to the barber shop. I feel like a six-foot bear, accountable to no one. But in practical terms, my lavish hair means I sweat a lot in the Caribbean sun. It's much cooler to amble under the stars… 'Bare night is best…'

On evenings like this, I need to relax after slaving over my art… especially when followed by a lengthy read with you, my dear Chiara… Lying in bed, first I puff on the magic dragon for an hour. Then I sip a nightcap, a brew of mushroom tea. By the time I've reached San Sepulcro, two barrios over from La Cruz, the full effects have set in, and I slowly unwind. Instead of a terrifying ghoul or a nameless tramp, I've become the village idiot, the butt of a hundred corny jokes…

'Hey Factor, let me cut off that bushy beard you got! I need to stuff a pillow!' 'Fatso, gimme some of that inner tube! The coach says I'm too skinny to stay on the team!' Though I rarely say a word, the homies treat me as their 'pana,' their best bud. Unfailingly, I turn my pockets inside out to buy them pints of liquor or rounds of beers… To avoid getting mugged, I replenish the cash only when I sneak around a corner. I keep a bankroll of escudos in a pouch on my right thigh, concealed by my flapping pants…

Tonight is typical… From grocery bar to grocery bar, I share flasks of third-rate rum with random pals, glugging it straight from the bottle. Deafened by the radios, hollered at by the pranksters, I drink myself into a pleasant buzz. But that's just the first stage of the outing… By now, the THC in my system is wearing off, and I need to recharge my mushroom high. I sail on to San Sebastián, the distribution point for drugs—under the complicit eyes of the police, eager for their cut… I might as well look in on my pothead chums, who always have a choice selection on hand…

Bluto, Carlos, and Marzipán grow weed behind their two-storey, cinder-block house; they're in collusion with the Canuban DEA—their 'backers,' as they call them. They also offer special stocks, from as far away as Mexico and Brazil… These varieties have traits that appeal to connoisseurs: mellow or edgy, nuanced or pungent, crisp or squoogy, astral or corporeal… They run the entire gamut—sometimes with a hint of 'je ne sais quoi'… Tonight they unwrap some hashish from Morocco, and let me try a sample pipe. I buy a sizeable plug, enough to last for several weeks. I have to pay through the nose, but this stuff's too precious to pass up…

I feel fine now, almost normal… Carlos wants to drum

up a girl, and I agree to tag along. We head west, where the streets slope down to the river. 'Let's go to Doña Balina's,' the pusher says…

'OK.' I might as well humor him…

We weave through a maze of alleyways to a ramshackle house. Like many buildings in the slums, it's made of wood above and cement below. The upper half is painted purple; the bottom half is painted orange. I love combinations like that, the brasher the better…

Balina herself is standing in the doorway, her makeup caked on like a clown's. 'Hey, big man, Faustona's expecting you.'

I don't answer. Carlos is short, and as kinky as they come. I trail behind him like a bear closing in on a spindly fawn… The cambuca tunes on the ratty, two-bit stereo rasp like icepicks on glass. Several half-naked girls lounge around on the scroungy sofa and beat-up chairs… When she sees me, the tallest one jumps to her feet. 'I got a special room for you, machote. A bed big enough for the both of us.'

Right… so this is prearranged… I know what Carlos is after. The little squirt has a fetish about two behemoths going at it while he drools. He's tried for months to get me stoned enough to have sex with Faustona, right in front of him… 'Come on, man, I'll pick up the tab for the whole damn thing. I'll just stay in this corner. You won't even know I'm here.'

I turn the tables on the runty voyeur: 'Factor' likes a sex-show, too, if it's funny enough… Carlos bounces up and down on Faustona, like a frog on a log. I laugh so hard I get a stomach-ache… Then suddenly, I've had enough. Backing out of the room, I stuff a wad of escudos into Balina's greedy hand…

From the edge of San Sebastián to the Río Fernando, the hill teems with brothels, one gaudy gewgaw after the next. The madams have vied to tart them up in raffish hues… Milling around in the pot-holed streets, I banter with the ladies, amused as they grope me in hopes of a trick. Like the buildings, each moll is a palette of garish colors: blue hair and vermillion nails, gold teeth and a red brassiere, hot-pink lips and aqua glitter, tangerine mascara and cocoa skin. The drag-queens are always the most inventive. Tonight their clothes sizzle—luscious, brassy, satirical… Houses, faces, makeup, fabrics... Mentally, I store them away for future use…

In my teenage years, I used to snorkel and scuba-dive with Ángel María, my schoolmate hero… I've always thought of myself as a creature from the sea, beached on dry land. Lolling back and forth, like a whale before he sounds—one of the selves I've borrowed from Melville—I pause a while before my final descent… I choose the steepest route, a breakneck curve littered with condoms and shredded tires. Elated now, I float down the incline towards my goal… I can already glimpse the sheen of the water, and smell the rancid breeze prickling its back…

I don't stop till I've reached the riverbank. There's a spot where I can stand under mangrove trees, and hear the egrets rustling in their nests. I touch the half-moon as it rows through the clouds, and taste its gleam on the reeds… I linger for what might be an hour—I can't tell. My last port of call isn't far away…

Under a bridge that spans the Río Fernando, tin-roofed hovels crouch on the mud, choked with raw sewage and mounds of trash. This is a place my brother's snooty friends disdain, the shanty-town of Todos los Santos. When hurricanes lash Puerto Indio, flood-waters sweep most of the huts out to sea. But soon they're rebuilt, by those who weren't lucky enough to drown…

In the sturdiest shack, Juanito, a broad-shouldered huckster, caters to a special clientele. I'm his prize customer… A heavy cord hangs from the roof-pole of his cabin; it ends in a noose above a sturdy metal stool. With a winch screwed to a concrete post, he can raise or lower the rope by degrees…

Off to one side stands a pinewood cabinet, the kind where rice, beans, sugar, and salt are stored. Inside it, Juanito keeps tourniquets, syringes, heroin, and liquid cocaine. With his deft, sinewy hands, he maintains the tools of his trade… He's proud of how the neat glass shelves shine back at him, reflecting his wheat-colored face and slicked-down hair… After each transaction, he cleans the needles for the next client—unless he's run out of rubbing alcohol, as he once confessed. When that happens, he uses Suárez 150-Proof Rum. And if he's already downed the booze? 'Well, Factor, nobody's perfect. Compared with the competition, I run a tight ship...'

About once a week, I turn up long past midnight, already bombed on whatever I've consumed. This evening's no exception: when I knock on the door, my bugged-out eyes and slurring give me away... Not that I have to talk. Juanito guides me to what I need—something that allows me to forget I'm still alive...

Most folks in the barrio think I'm homeless, without a centavo to my name. Juanito won't tell them otherwise. He intends to keep me to himself. I may be a slob, but I don't mind shelling out my dough... Tonight, as usual, I order speedballs—and not just one or two. I want quality smack and high-grade cocaine, no matter what the price... Like a valet, he rolls my shirtsleeves back for me. Adroitly, he shoots me up, then boots the blood back into my arm. Mesmerized, I watch the changing colors rise and fall: clear and red, pink and red...

I'm a mess, but I always pay up front: in all these years, I've never asked him for credit. Best of all, I throw in an extra fee for the noose—pure profit for Juanito's cast-iron till... After four or five powerful hits, he helps me climb onto the stool and slip the greasy loop over my head. Then he winds the winch until the rope tautens around my neck.

Securing it with knots to some hooks on the wall, he counts 'uno, dos, tres' before he kicks the stool away...

I dangle free, awash with pleasure and pain, pressing my thighs with my hairy, paint-spotted hands... In a death-trance, I see myself from a distance, on tenterhooks like a lifeless sack... I watch myself from the ceiling, from the floor, from across the room, from another galaxy... The crotch of my pants starts to bulge, and Juanito opens my fly... He probably has to grit his teeth, but this is full service... With a kleenex, he pulls out my swollen, blue-veined tool, and it gushes like a rubber hose...

I let out a satisfied groan, then a hoarse, ecstatic scream. My eyes are about to pop... Now Juanito has to hustle. If he doesn't let me down, I'll strangle all the way... He can afford to give the police a 'commission' on the drugs he sells, but not to bribe his way out of a murder charge. Besides, where would he find another spendthrift like me?

I refuse to let the prostitutes barge in while I'm being hanged. I don't care what they think, I just don't want Juanito to get distracted... I climb down from the stool, leaning on his shoulder, and sprawl on an overstuffed armchair. He cracks the door open for the putas as soon as I give him a nod, and they bustle into the room... I bet he hires them in another part of town, so his neighbors won't horn in on his business. You never know: I might find a new connection, who'll fulfill my needs for less...

Tonight's trio comes in various sizes: a snappish,

balding shortie, a schoolmistress type in a dull gray dress, and a truck-driver blonde with hair on her upper lip. She's a man, I bet. Their cruddy perfume mixes with the stench of my sweat and jizz. The air's so rank, I can hardly breathe… After a few more injections, Juanito pulls off my shoes and trousers. He grabs my wrists in a mariner's grip, and hauls me upright…

The hookers thwack my buttocks with thorny switches till I can feel the blood running down my legs. Then I tear off my shirt and beg them to burn my chest. Juanito snitches candles now and then from the parish church. 'Fuego… fuego… fuego…' Compliantly, they singe my furry dugs while I watch them work, from a thousand miles away. With the dripping wax, they scald my back and arms. The bronze key slips down to my navel…

I hear myself shouting, gasping with sadness and joy. 'You… hate… me… you… love… me…'

'Oh yeah, Factor, we do! We hate you, we love you, you useless bag of shit.'

They thrash me and scorch me dozens of times, till they get tired of the game. Their rouge is smudged and their deodorant has soured; their armpits reek, even to themselves. They must be thanking God—or the Devil— they've reached the last stage of our routine… Juanito takes out a rawhide whip he stores in his cabinet just for me, and the ladies pass it from hand to hand. I moan, beside myself, with every stroke. I feel a big hard cock bumping against my ass. I knew that blonde was a man. Fresh rivulets trickle down the web of clotted blood, until I ejaculate again…

Then quickly, it's all over. Juanito and his crew pat me down with paper towels, taping clumsy bandages over my wounds. I wrestle my clothes back on, and empty my pockets onto the floor. While the whores are still scrapping over the cash, yelping at each other on all fours, I stagger off into the night…

When I look back from the riverbank, I see Juanito throw them some crack as a tip, and kick them through the door… The wide-open window centers him like a picture frame. He wipes his needles with care, arranges his cabinet, and mops the room. He can't tell when the next patron might show up… He sticks his head out to wave at me, and sniffs the fetid air… I turn my back on him and stare at the river. A sudden wind ripples its scummy reeds, and warm splats of rain begin to fall…

Callejón del Platero, July 1991

I don't remember… is this the day I'm supposed to meet that friend of my brothers'? What's her name… Clara or Cara? She must be a pest… every time she invades our ancestral abode, she wheedles Horacio to knock on my door… I don't want to be disturbed… Life is a discipline… but it's also a cloud… I work and work at perfection… floating on my sargasso sea of grass… like a ship heading for port… I don't always make it… Sometimes I feel like I've run aground… maybe I'm already lying under a stone somewhere… a stone that says 'Miss Mary Juana Killed Him With Kindness…' Then I wake up again, like Ferdinand in Shakespeare's 'vex'd Bermoothes,' and hear the music 'creeping by me upon the waters…'

My brothers claim she's a journalist, and I should let her publicize my work… Why? I couldn't care less… Whatever conventions rule the fashionable world, they don't apply to Canuba… Here I'm a traveler in Melville's *Mardi*, sailing through an 'archipelago of mind…' Every day brings a new initiation… the vessel glides through foggy narrows, careens past sunken atolls… pursues the distant mirage of a wise, resplendent face… Brightness renders the seascape enigmatic, just as noon blinds us more than dawn or dusk…

For ten or twelve years, this woman has been dropping by our shop to pester Horacio… She used to be Catulo's lover, where was it? He's had so many… She's Italian, no? When he spent the summer in Florence, maybe?… She's always yearned to catch a glimpse of me—the 'Third Person of the Trinity,' as I'm labeled by Horacio's facetious pals… Well, I'm a misanthrope, and proud of it… He's never dared to slip me a note from her, much less usher her upstairs…

What finally caught my attention was a portentous detail: she told him she was rereading *The Golden Bowl*—for the *fourth time*...

I can hear a mild commotion downstairs, and the usual courteous noises... Horacio with one of his sycophants, who cares? Oh no, that must be Keira, or Cleira... I was afraid she'd really come. I bit my tongue as soon as I agreed...

I'm not good at this... From the top of the steps, I try a joke... My voice is so halting, and so deep, I scare even myself... What comes out is somewhere between a stutter and a rumble... Ah... you must be the Master's great-niece... born in his... *Italian... Hours...* My belly jiggles when I attempt to laugh... How embarrassing...

Of the three of us, I'm the bulkiest... Hirsute and paunchy, I stand over six feet tall. I haven't cleaned myself up for your benefit, Kyra. Why should I? I must look like a maniac. My baggy clothes are spattered with paint... I haven't combed my hair in days. Prematurely gray, it sprouts every which way... My beard's even worse, just a stiff, unruly mop... I avoid mirrors, because they steal your soul—mine anyway, what's left of it... The last time I passed one, my hair and beard had fused into a brambly thicket, protruding from my long-sleeved, turtleneck shirt...

We don't shake hands. There's no use... You'd probably be repulsed, anyway... My fingernails are lined with paint, ink, and dirt… You're well-groomed, a shapely woman with flowing hair, grey-green eyes, and a placid demeanor… I find you reassuring, to my bewilderment… you're what they call a good listener, I guess… I'm so stoned most of the time, I lose track of what I've said… or just fall silent for a while… my phrases hang in suspense… But you don't seem to mind… I could get used to you…

All right… maybe this is the first Tuesday you're here … maybe it's the fourth Tuesday or the tenth… over time, everything seems to merge… I tune into you again when you say: In homage to our idol, Mallarmé, we should christen these sessions our 'mardis de la rue de Rome…' No, wait, you're getting out of control… I start boxing the air with my paws, abashed at how rough they are…

No, Chiara, no… no damn SymBolsheviks… no cénacle… just our… fat… Mardis… Gras…

You always seem at ease… Who do you think you are?… I don't even allow Quilviria in here for our weekly 'conjunction': I go to her place around the block instead, in the middle of the night… She's the housekeeper at our neighbor's Colonial manse, and her room has a separate entrance… Very convenient, no questions asked, and thank God she doesn't try to 'make conversation…' By day, I hardly ever leave home… This stone house in Callejón del Platero is my refuge… The Mirandas have lived here for umpteen generations… Our parents have banished themselves to the ground floor behind the curio shop…

We'll always be 'the boys' to them... Catulo camps on a sofa-bed behind the display cases when he ricochets through town... Our cook Elpiria serves up hearty repasts to all of us... 'She endures...' as Faulkner said. No, she more than endures: she outlasts, she triumphs...

Horacio and I have the second story to ourselves... with a thick mahogany door at the top of the stairs... On our level, a wide parlor faces the street... Horacio's Bösendorfer grand takes up a quarter of the space... I've ceded the entire front-room to him for his studio... Sometimes he analyzes the scores he plans to perform with his chamber orchestra... sometimes he composes his own works... they're almost as eccentric as mine...

To make up for hogging the sala, he sleeps in a miniscule alcove, behind a narrow door... it was a linen closet, several centuries ago... A short corridor leads to my two bedrooms at the back of the house, with windows overlooking the courtyard's raddled vines... a greener version of my beard...

You say I have the only library in Puerto Indio more extensive than yours... and you may be right... My lair is lined from floor to ceiling with books in ten languages, on every conceivable theme... You're mainly a poetry and painting buff... But literature and the arts aren't my only passions... I'm a restless soul... I also like to read history, economics, political science, philosophy... There's nothing better than a lumbering page of Hegel, when you're as high as an elephant's back…

In Catulo's sardonic lingo, Horacio is 'homo erectus …' He thrones before his piano all day, covering staves with his wispy notations… I'm 'homo supinus …' propped against eiderdown pillows, drawing and painting on my custom-made easels… one is a giant book carved from ebony, that swivels into place over the mattress… I call it Anselm, after Kiefer… the other is a tilted intaglio slab I've named Lo Studiolo, in honor of Mantegna…

Where am I?… Oh, since you're here, Chiara, I have to keep the windows open… the ceiling fans churning… a steady hum… I'm used to thinner and oils, but the oppressive stench would send you packing in no time…

The problem is, there's no place to sit down… Anybody but you would feel uncomfortable… Besides the bookshelves and storage racks for my work, there are a couple of night-tables… But the main furniture in both my rooms is beds… antique four-posters in different sizes and heights… Canuban mahogany from a century ago… I salvaged them from my fad-crazed relatives… The whole notion of what they did enrages me… The numbskulls… can you… believe it? They replaced them… with waterbeds…

The fraying mattresses are where I spread out my works-in-progress… to look them over for a week or two, before I file them away… I've never shown them to anybody before, except my brothers… Until you came along, Chiara… If

I'm not letting you pore over my latest piece, we talk lying down on adjacent davenports... At the Colegio Jesuita, I used to worship Ángel María, but now his closeness to Espinosa leaves me aghast... Besides him and Frederica, I've never had any other friend, only Quilviria... she's a lover, though, or a wife, and we never talk... With you, I guess I'm making up for lost time... that's why our discussions always subside into monologues, as quiet and horizonless as Mahler's Tenth... I go on and on, receding like a tide in the Firth of Forth...

You turn on your side, now and then, to gaze into my bright-blue eyes... tenderly, I like to think... Catulo tells me they're my 'best feature'... That's lucky, since they're the only one that's visible... besides my aquiline nose, skewed in a scuba mishap long ago... and my haystacks of hair. I exploit those 'twin cerulean pools,' as you call them... I draw you in with them... Shimmering in their sockets, unclouded and still, they plunge you into bottomless depths... Sometimes you lose yourself in their dilating light, and don't even notice what I'm saying... euphoric as a diver, you drown in an inner sky with no limits, no up and no down...

If a bear could speak, I imagine he'd ramble like me... intermittently, with awkward jerks of his arms and paws... My comments trail off in suggestive rifts and unfinished sentences... My gestures are truncated, incomplete arcs... Tics like those are only natural, I guess, since I spend most of my time alone… unlike my gregarious brothers… I realize my silences perplex you at first… but then you grasp that my ruminations go on unwinding… whether I state them or not… You learn to chart them even when I've left a gap, omitting the B between A and C… Eventually, I'll pick up the thread once again in my hushed, reverberating bass… Your knack for interpreting my lulls exceeds even that of my brothers… it has endeared you to me…

With anybody else, I'd feel abashed for sounding so disjointed… my topics start and stop all of a sudden, with zigzags of their own… I jump from Theognis, to Bolívar, to the *Kindertotenlieder*… from Talleyrand, to Keynes, to the latest prints by Jasper Johns… You follow me, you contemplate my ugliness with your solemn, lovely face… you graze me lightly with your pliant hands… I wouldn't want to see our friendship marred by sex, and I wouldn't dare request it… We feel safe with each other… that's why we convene every Tuesday, without fail…

We drift along, Chiara, and our adagio never ends… until it does, in a fictional coda… All right, I revere the Symbolists… when they're not 'faisant école,' like the in-crowd at a high-school… but I adore the swampy, lazy meanders of the roman-fleuve… Tonight… as every night… I'll read aloud from an epic novel we've been wading through… together or apart… at any rate, in parallel… With you, Chiara, words have come back to me… I find their wholeness again… my awkwardness smooths out... Before I know it... I'm gently rocking on the mattress... swaying my upright knees to the rhythm of the prose... I don't feel unkempt and repellant anymore...

Alone or together... we explore these continents... these streams and pebbles... pine-needles and red-eyed flies... not just 'narrative,' some moonscape of cold technique... no, each terrain where we walk... prefigures paradise... so vivid, so detailed, we have no doubt that it exists.... We pass through the walls like angels... and there are people here, as believable as ourselves... we live their sorrows, but without their despair... we fly through their hells... of envy, hatred, cruelty, and rage... but our wings are never singed...

Paragraphs hang suspended above our beds... as visible as cumulus clouds... Balzac's *Splendeurs et misères*... the four Torquemadas of Galdós... *Die Dämonen* by von Doderer... Morante's *La storia*... and the Prince's library in Proust's seventh book... Only you can put up with my accent, Chiara... my brothers have a musical ear... they say I sound slightly Canuban in all the languages we acquired abroad... But I don't care, as long as you and I have James... our flagship... his late style makes us laugh... Henry III... his full-rigged clauses... tilting and bellying in the wind... when I read him aloud, from the first sentence on, I launch a galleon... I knock my bushy skull against the wall... I remember Catulo, when Horacio and I were still too small to understand: Henrietta, Henrietta... he would squeal… looking up from the page… Henrietta, you… are… shameless… Oh… to write… like that…

I have my lucid moments… especially after a long, druggy night, when I slurp liters of coffee in the patio downstairs… Global nomads, we Mirandas have migrated everywhere, following in our father's wake… from India to Taiwan, and from Malaysia to Iran… All the same, we're the opposite of rootless… our rovings have reinforced our fealty to Canuba, with all its trying foibles… Of us three siblings, I'd say I'm the patriot in chief… Though our stays in the East still fire my brothers' souls, I champion the West… 'Eveningland,' as the Germans call it, 'Abendland…' and I plant my flag on our blest isle, the omphalos of the Ocean Sea… Sometimes the other two 'boys' natter on about Li Po's poetics, the moonrise posture in Noh, or the rice-powdered wayang orang… But I swing my heavy arms at them, and snarl in the local dialect… We've got… yucca… in our pantry… Damn you… Don't… steal… other people's… food…

My brothers still relish far-off trips… I leave my studio only for local walks… As Horacio knows, I like to roam the slums… where people call me 'Factor…' I'm not Virgilio Miranda there… to make sure, I mostly go out at night… I get a kick out of watching the codgers play dominoes… I cheer when a teenager slam-dunks a hoop… Housewives mistake me for a hungry beggar, and stick a plate of arroz y frijoles through their door… I'm always ready to eat… I

hunker on their concrete steps and scoop up the victuals…
bean-juice and rice dribble down my beard…

If the women corner me, I tell them… I 'used to be…
a painter…' Sometimes their husbands hand me a half-
can of latex… but my daubs only make them jeer… Hell,
comemierda, you don't know how to paint a house! If I
spill the stuff, they kick me in the rump… Get outta here,
you fuckin' tramp!

My 'social peers' would be shocked by these forays…
But at one of our Mardis Gras, Chiara, I catch myself
dropping a hint… I shove back my tangled hair… I plumb
you with a penetrating look… Brain… clot… the streets…
my arteries… my blood… You just look at me quizzically,
and draw a blank…

By Latino custom, as long as we stay under his roof,
our father Don Baltásar will sustain us… But like Catulo,
Horacio and I decline to exploit him… The old man's nest
egg has shriveled over the years… For everyday expenses,
we rely on the shop we lease from him downstairs… But
to finance our luxuries… Horacio's 'chaste seraglio,' or my
sheets of gold leaf… we freelance with advertising firms…

For print media, Horacio does the copy… I design the
visuals… For TV spots, he writes a jingle and records it
with his musicians… me, I do the graphics and the script…
We charge an arm and a leg… but the results are worth
it… Our clients can count on punctuality… unheard-of in
the tropics… The last thing we want… in Horacio's quaint

lingo… is to 'prolongate the poppycock.' We accept one commission a month… and we finish it in four days flat…

I sum it up for you like this, Chiara… Full moon… cash-cow… milked… Never listen… to her… moo… I kick a bedpost with my shovel-size foot…

But I can't deny it… this sideline has influenced my art… It's a sui-generis mosh-up… I splice the old-fashioned with… in-your-face sprudge… As a draftsman… I outmatch current norms… sepia, chalk, pastel, graphite… take your pick… I'm not boasting… it's just that art's not a métier anymore… it's a concept, an idea… Me, I long for Clouet's delicate line… architectural whimsies like Veronese's… flora and fauna as precise as Dürer's… as authentic as Audubon's… The permutations of the human form… they pour from my hands… like coins from the Medici mint… I plot India-ink grids on sheets of mouldmade paper… then I limn each square with a miniature world…

After that, Chiara, order yields to chaos… this is where my commercial training kicks in… I insult my Renaissance heart with advertising abuse…

Rosenquist painted billboards in Times Square… me, I've learned a lot from my PR gigs… I hurl the island's logos… at my Quattrocento casements… splatters from our tawdry age… The pop-eyed parrots of Cerveza Papagayo… the kitschy palms of Aceite Nacional… the lip-smacking bakers of Cayonaiba Bread… they all defile my windowpanes... I spoof Canuba's serfdom to foreign brands... I ransack the shopping-center shelves... Opaque or semi-transparent... in layered oil or watery acrylic... tubes of Crest... cases of Coke... bottles of Oréal... they strut across my antique chessboard... Boxes of Preparation H... cans of Nestlé's milk, blue and white... mounds of Trojans in shiny foil... they blot out whole walls of my medallions...

That's not the end of my process, Chiara... I evoke it to myself as a three-word poem... face:deface:efface... In the final stage, after dark... I range through the barrios... When nobody's looking, I unroll my intricate sheets... I throw them under passing vehicles... on vermin-infested rubbish heaps... The next night, I search for scattered remnants... in the gutters... between tumble-down shacks... I've got several informants who lend me a hand...

Most of my inventions disappear... sometimes I find a sordid scrap or two... worthless debris, stuck to a chain-wire fence... or rotting in a garbage patch... A slender foot pokes from the 'Y' of K-Y... the 'Ron' of Ron Real smashes a luna moth... a Bayer Aspirin bottle-top reams an orchid... A Doric column... is split by the 'nuff' of Peachtree Snuff... or shredded by the teeth of a famished dog...

You're appalled, Chiara... Why don't you save the entire work?

I cup my hands over my tufted ears... Oh... no... me... only a boy... raped by... Valéry...

What do you mean?

His book… the method… of Leonardo… the path… not the goal… But me… I cheat… I feel my eyes freeze over… glacial ice, blue…

I believe I understand, Virgilio. You try, but you can't restrict yourself to the conceptual. You still cling to matter, to the artifact. But you despise yourself for that.

Yes, yes… You see inside me, Chiara…

You have many ways to express your self-contempt. You mount the tatters of your quest in shabby ovals: you dribble wax on toilet seats, then spray them with cheap gold paint.

Yes, yes… That's why… I hold up one of my frames… I rub the glass with a magenta-streaked sleeve… It's… an evil, bourgeois demon… God-awful… me… I like… the Salon… I love Meissonnier…

There are worse crimes, you smile. But why the glass?

Me… I was screwed… just a blooming minor, not his type… by Francis Bacon… Gilt frames… reflective glass… Look at you…

Your grey-green eyes… hover on top of Mr. Clean… his cheeks… pudgy as buttocks… below them… a Botticellian rose…

So you want the viewer to be part of the image?

Yes… yes… you… all of us… me too… we're… nothing… but ghosts…

I lie back… half-asleep… She's a far second to you,

Chiara… but my only other friend is Frederica… I'd never ask her to come here … I won't go to her stupid parties… I visit her late at night… once or twice a month… in her upstairs 'study'… She's dependably ridiculous… she receives me in velvet robes… a feudal chatelaine… she stitches cushions in petit point…

It's a handsome room… half is a library… the books all unread… half is a messy boudoir… years ago, I convinced her to ditch Colonial white… the walls are painted Pompeian red… the tiles between the ceiling beams… papaya-orange… She burbles that she's a communist… yeah, sure, the revolutionary guard… The décor is like my work… it seesaws… punk, retro, grunge, junk…

I appreciate the way the Countess doesn't listen… she palavers on about her opinions… she's like Lucy in that TV show… turn her on and watch… turn her off and leave…

Yes, I know… Horacio's catty friends make fun of us… 'deep' Virgilio and 'shallow' Frederica… but Chiara… Hockney was right… no? 'Surface… is illusion… but so is… depth…'

I must be more stoned than I thought… That quotation costs me a colossal effort…. I heave back against my pillows…

You fill in the blanks for me, as always… I agree, Virgilio. She reminds me of Diana Vreeland. Triviality as an art: it's much more difficult than people think. You have to strain for total flatness. You have to deflate yourself to a comic-strip.

I claw the air... my raggedy fingernails... Why am I such a wreck? Yes... Chiara... Only the mask... nothing behind it... Nothing... is all... there is...

Puerto Indio, undated

They call us the Trinity... What would be the use of collecting more experience? For us, the drama has already played out... I know, Chiara: you see straight through me. There's a style for everything, and this is the pneumatic style... I also realize: there's nothing behind your skin, behind your eyes... nothing but the surge and the unraveling... An elaborate machinery to give us pleasure... How could we deserve it? How could we desert it? We're the only ones who 'keep this in body and mind'...

Colors can be invisible, a question of mood... When I wander through the poorest neighborhoods; when they kick me in the rear; when they say Hey Factor, hey hairball, you're a fucking asshole, don't talk to my wife, get outta here... Then I tell myself: Congratulations. Felicidades, felicities... Memory and future live in our acts. Moments nudge us in and out of moments. They break and crest as a single wave... Tree and shadow, yes and no, the even wind of images... A smear of indigo turns to black...

If I told you about a flower that doesn't exist, you'd have to believe it, suddenly abandoned to my fantasy. But in that instant, you're the one who's flowered deep from the root, with petals as strong as your bones… Maybe you're the queen of the comedians; it took you long enough to do your show. Were you afraid I wouldn't laugh? Sometimes I trail along behind you… A wedding guest in paint-spotted clothes, happier than the words I'm mumbling…

Or maybe I'm a circle of insurgence, a wolf that howls on the ice. Or I'm the blood that flecks the snow, making it glimmer white and serene… The water comes to a boil as I make my mushroom tea, the bubbles rush to the surface and mouth their liquid syllables… A marvel, how our pronouns still assume there's a difference in our views… From here I see a triad of broad-backed rocks… they jut from the sea. I walk on the shore where you will walk. I roll beside you underwater with the whales… We surface and resurface, believing for a while that our night is one and the same…

White, yellow, grey. I measure out my life color by color, like streaming banderoles I stand inside… I let them tell me whatever they want… Tiger of the midnight hour, your red and orange stripes devour the woods… they set the cities ablaze… Air carbonized to grey, blue waters curdling to green with algae blooms, sargasso mounds blackening on the sand, putrid as corpses… It's said to be the end of the world as we know it. But no one ever asks: Do we know it?

Transparent, a glimmer of reflections on the lazy, lakeside wall: even here the children labor in a brothel called the family... Parental wills crush them, oppress them like an occupying army... Runaways, their feet move in step behind the piper; they shuffle toward the mountains... All I'm painting is postcards, a batch of souvenirs... the things we've suffered: our tourist traps of regret... Too young, the wine is pressed from our hearts, raving like blood...

Don't be burdened by the overload... it all sorts out in the end... Earthlings have trouble with that axiom... We want to be dolphins, bone china, carefree prodigies, recognized geniuses... We want to be the cloud by day and the fire by night... The reason is: we're afraid that just as we are, we're nothing at all... Keep looking for an error in this grammar. Keep on, keep on... Follow the command to lose command... To be a map of the world, the imperfect world. To be...

Colors: the glass dome as a mosaic, a helmet of light. The garden as an image, a canvas... Casual, 'whatever...' Like us schoolboys at the Colegio Jesuita. Joking, unfocused. 'Having the ocean right outside our door...' and the moonlight. A torrent of silver: but the god who rains down on us is ourselves... We surf the milky way through outer emptiness, even death... The weight of all that distance, splintering the timbers of the house... The weight of space tilting against us... heavy with all the horrors we can conceive...

The grey 'matter' teeters and reels, Chiara... We refuse to see life and art as a double despair... In a thunderstorm just before daybreak, colors ferment... At the crack of dawn, birds drown each other out with their songs... now they're caught in a downpour of rain... I panic when colors melt before I can seize them... I look in the mirror, flattened by glass... without perspective, I'm not here... This is how a painting opens out... draws us in... and turns us into ghosts.

About the skyscape... Is it really remote? Bluish clouds drift past the edge of the moon... beyond the stars, there's a spokeless wheel... We're seeing the unseeable... Or the landscape... Is it really near? A flamboyant cambers over a bracken pond... its blossoms red-orange... their stamens like yolks. They're reflected on the black mirror below... A breeze stirs the leaves... they two-step with the wind... one step forward... one step back... The leaves fall, the flowers fall... The trunk is what I paint: solid, edged with light...

Chiara, will you come to me soon? I wait, I ask... your absence floods these empty rooms... I hear how our voices drift through city streets... a mist that heads for twilight... for the fields... Shadows always summon... though not always to an end... Spiraling, all disclosure... and enclosure... The photographs, the skin... flesh remembered. Loved... not a time we want to lose... Our answers reach like hands from the waves... Find a raft to receive them... find any secret place...

Children are colors...They cry because the robin's breast is red... the blue rabbit comes unsewn... the grey soldier has lost his leg... the black-beaked swan is a prince... a

white bear knocks at the door... In my dreams I watch
the corals sleep... their bones are laid to rest... they hard-
en into stone... Whatever I must lose, I already yield...
The day is tilting fast... the cage of light springs open... I
swim above the grasses, pale green... their fingers touch
my chest...

In Venice I recall our phantom fish, our silvery world...
At the tipping point of day... the clouds and the lagoon
shiver in a violet haze... before the lights come on...
Chiara, you help me sink backward... backward to the
time before I was born... before time was even said...
before the image consumed us... Now we boomerang
to far-off islands, dimmer and dimmer... our bodies are
pictures, too, the nights of our love are fictions... Neb-
ulae... greenish, purple, roseate, powder blue... fading,
soon unseen...

Page after page, they rise through the night... primary colors... children's books with edges torn... Piebald
horses drink from the river... surprised to be remembered... I see this in their mild, bloodshot eyes... Memory's fire sweeps through my limbs... their whitened bark
crackles and splits... Umber leaves swirl upward... half
dryness, half smoke... they greet me in mid-air... The
wind from the outdoors is like a train... pistons pound-
ing... sparks...

Earth's eyes retreat into our own... her gaze ebbs with
ours... The curve of day bleeds to red beneath the poisoned sky... What we mistake for snow is the manna of
death... cinders drifting around her face... and ours...
The ashes of blight, of the years... singe us, degrade us,

possess us... An afterbirth... bleeding and burning...
Our treason shatters our discarded mirrors... the world
we have made is the worldless...

Insects chirp and chir through the night... even in the
tropics, there is summer... Waves of heat crest above the
roofs... drench the air with steam... Houses tremble as
we approach ... 'The ocean frightened me the first time
I heard it...' Did you tell me that, or did I make it up? No
answer... none needed... You know my fears, Chiara...
my disquiet... my shyness before these rows of granite
faces... honey dripping from their tongues...

What am I but an awkward bear, snapping at bees? I
rub my hide against the air... like a soothing balm, the
spectrum's rain cleans my atmosphere... Colors... they
always let me change... into leaves held up to the light...
pebbles that dry in the sun... Three steps left, three steps
right... for you, I'm a dancing bear... Dawn whitens at
the windows, still disguised as night... My growls echo
through the vastness... but I hear even the words you
never say...

I'm tired of painting white stones... Along steep banks,
ferrous rocks mark our path a rusty red... We're coming into our inheritance, swinging from the shadows of a
cloud... Next I'm a boy on a dolphin's back... these daily
waves are my eternity... I'm a fish at the bottom of the
sea, a warehouse of offers and denials... I'm an empty
skinsuit, swimming through the ruins of Alexandria...
infamous, forgiven at last... That's why I'm so light to
the touch... a single breath releases me to other forms...

The children we've conceived twist from the mast like flags... we conceive, but don't give birth... We reach this place of selfish, selfless love... by passing through the reel of images... to earn our abnegation... Dawn and dusk assemble night and day... the only permanence we know... The harbor widens... dissolves into numberless gradations, tones... the shore removes itself from sight... The sea swallows the horizon... rippling from infrared to ultraviolet ...

Landscapes in the galleries... continents drawn and quartered... We choose our oceanic islands... Radiance blows through our trees, slammed by tropical winds... by freedom and destruction... The land is eclipsed... darkness washes over it, shoal after shoal... Blue and green... yellow and orange... red and purple... all colors mix into the brown of a cowl... St. Francis stares at the corals we've bleached, our upturned skulls...

From a green thought in a green shade... to a grey thought in a carbon shade... The difference is... that now we know... We wear our grief, and it is blind... 'but we, in a manner, see...' Our writing on the wall... a long quotation... a withdrawal into otherworldliness, here in this world... The passage about Cape Horn... words bathing the whales in liquid light... the spume of their answers and questions... fictive and real... The Amazon also exists, without any proof... it coils through the for-est of our minds...

I swim and swim with you for several hours... and now I'll never leave... Your blue-black fishtail pulls me like a thread through mazes of coral... the remains of the reef... a kaleidoscope of anemones, feeders, predators... the gaping holes and lattices... the irised, torn facade of what was once reality... This is the planet we've downgraded ... where wilderness is an artifice... a luxury, the view from a hotel...

Two strands of visual music... the noise of the world and its hidden chords... It's seething now, the accident of the improbable... foaming to compose the outline of the wave... and is the wave... Not colors only... the drawing that buoys them up... since 'even abstraction is a likeness'... Do we care what we're saying, Chiara? Haven't we said it all?... Gladness... thunder... volcano... jellyfish... syllables mouthed and exhaled... The tape rewinds and flips over... words with a will of their own...

I climb to the ridge of several years ago... The parrots are still chattering... but behind them, from the terrace... the valley swings like a massive tail... Across the crumpled switchbacks... the crooked ravines... amapolas lose their withered leaves... they blossom into bursts of orange fire... All I need to cull them is this picture... a rectangle cut from my mind... How will we ever keep up? The spaces that bloom... our inner paradise... The cages where I sway make my paintings come to life...

The real becomes reflection... the mirror that allows the world to be... Here is the sentence... adjectives, nouns... the verbs that announce them like angels... My brushstrokes tug at the clothes of a common thing... strip it to find the uncommon... You, Chiara, from the start...

when you walk up the stairs... the hunger of my gaze undresses you step by step... Never blame yourself for the time you sampled this, the time you sipped that... Why excuse a life?... Blaze and implode like a star ...

Returning to what you said the other day... time isn't easy, is it?... The face alters, the voice... the instrument we play... the façades with marks that measure hours like solar clocks... Or the underside of clouds, as their colors shift... Or lake beds drying... cracked, fissured by the sun of... the sun of... Your body and its image... they flash in and out... flickering between the selves you might be... day when the night filters through, night when the day...

Fiction settles onto your face like a mask... You linger where the four paths meet... north, south, east, west... and none of these... As when Merisi flees to the Colonnas... painting in a lofty country room that smells of earth... His Magdalen leans back, her head against her shoulder... her tears are sudden jabs of light in the museum's crowded hall... You and I... before the threshold of silence... All alone, I speak with you... a mirror within your mirror... a grief within your grief...

Your hair, entangled with mist... curls along the rocks of the cave... along the silken clay of your arms... loose threads disband matter's delusions... Your lips slowly part... the disguise that was your face gently tears away... Your vision unravels between us, layer after layer... We're approaching the unapproachable... If death is being seen without seeing... you save us now... image, you guard our blindness...

The crimson hibiscus, its cups stained with wine... I circle back to learn my colors from the earth... A single flower's lips still want to open... to depart into bloom... Later, these throats... they drink the night... their petals folding inward... Never asking for the parable, the iconography... Coolness brushes their tongues... The leaves green around their faces, palpable as a mirage... If only we could be that simple... that fearless... nothing but an eye...

Again, I ask you who I've been, ask you who I'll be... Again, you answer from the mirror... you were nothing, now you are... The frigate-bird dives beside us... raw talons, gaping beak... In a sudden squall, sails tussle with the wind... The whitecaps sprout into an orchard of light... branches burgeoning, as far as we can see... At home, our garden plashes... green and brown... restless warblers hop from twig to twig... All to end up as a picture in a frame...

Rats rooting through garbage... guard-dogs lunging at your neck... part and parcel of the view. The penniless, the rich... the starving, the stabbed... falling heir to the thunderbolt of circumstance... Broken blue lines of the architects... broken blue lines of the landing fields... This wind, wherever it blows, assigns us a quadrant of the world... Like you, when I have breakfast in my garden, I zero in on the birds and cats ...

I'm hypnotized... Miniature, green... lizards inch toward my plate... their white gullets belly like jib-sails... then they round into silver coins, fingered by the breeze... Seeing the world as pictures pours salt on my sores... My senses... images of images... my body... only a mirror... wet paint gleaming on a canvas wall... An aphid, I pause at the edge of the real... the calyx of evening is raised... blue and luminous... it receives the liquid air... Down by the river, reeds of farewell cling to its bank... their whispers grey-green, grey-brown...

I begin my regular rounds... redeemed from the abstract, from mimesis... by plying both keyboards... the foot-pedals, too... A red-eyed horsefly in slow motion... a black mosquito, whines thickened to groans... These particulars... more than beauty, a yardstick drawn in the dirt... Those were our laws, but now who can name them? I rub them out with my hand... I keep hearing voices... Don't walk on that slippery ledge... I answer: the water is green-blue... lucid, straight to the bottom... Colors, of you I'm not afraid...

Running down the street, I cast a glance behind me... an arm of the sea... my bright and terrible friend... closes in... scoops me up... slings me down... deep into the greening day of wakefulness... Again and again, I become that wave... Till evening catches up with me... levels the world into a pure plane of darkness... I don't lift my head... I bow till I rhyme with night... I yield my contours to other silhouettes... I people the cave of dreams...

Coruscating, violet... the ribbon of the sea abruptly snaps... between the roofs, it's lashed to tatters under low-slung, indigo clouds... Soon the dreaming wind will shed its picture-books on our beds... I'll stroll on the beach, avoid distorted faces, dodging their red parasols... At last, I'll return to the wilderness again, a shore I only own in my sleep... Where is my summer camp? I'd rather forget... Waves cut the inlets like scythes, harvesting them for my art...

In another dream, the spinning blade of noon... slices through the palms... The sun rears up and gallops downhill... A scalding breath sears the nape of my neck... the centaur's hands grip my shoulders... force me to the ground... I surrender, face up... The weight of the sky bears down... presses me till all that's left is a cutout... Even now, Chiara, even in my sleep, I'm reminded of you... you string collages on a clothesline each time you speak...

This is how I start every morning... the rumpled patterns of a coverlet, easing into life... It's you, colors... here when I open my eyes... On my easel, you pull back a curtain... the ineffable becomes the sensorial... Through you, objects wait for us to notice them... a simulacrum, yes and no... the everyday we sieve through the mind... is always a resemblance... The image is itself reality... which in art, we're not driven to possess...

Today, I seize myself... I must go through the motions... Only painters note how the unlit lamp pales to a paler blue... until dawn guides me downstairs... In the courtyard, rooster red, marbled ochre... the blackish gold of dead leaves... rimmed with a a farewell glimmer of dew... Honey creepers sport their yellow vests and charcoal coats... a mask over their eyes... White stripes that wrap around their heads like a plot, a treachery... but we know it's only a joke...

Through painting, surfaces shimmer with unattained desire—a halo, an effulgence that pierces mere appearance... Branches, a windowsill, a mote of dust... grant us that paradox... there but not there... The unseen blue, reflected on the windowpane... merges with the pane itself... The familiar adopts another name... or none at all... As we watch... it has already flowered... At the door... I'm opened by what I open... The future turns back on itself... dazzles me with unreached time... Colors, absences, I am you...

This is how I think, Chiara, when I'm alone... in segments like pictures... large or small... rectangles bordered by a frame... Resisting despair, I roam through 'Eveningland...' a province of the 'Abendland...' I explore it as my hinterland... Now I enter the shop like a cautious bear... careful not to break the potions in their flasks... Horacio sets them out for me in rows... bottles of blue, green, yellow, red... every semi-color in between... The shadings I use to build my twilights...

The Memorial Bastion, October 1988

When Catulo breezes through town, he leaves me dizzy... it's hard to withstand our vinous lunches... Horacio ogles us demurely, over a glass of Evian... 'Only a chalice of unadulterated dihydrogen oxide accords with my dyspeptic constitution,' he insists...

After a relaxing bath and siesta, I feel more clear-headed... springy enough for a stroll around the Barrio Antiguo... our island vestige of late-medieval Spain... It's been years since anyone's caught sight of me in our neighborhood. I've put on so much weight of late, I'll go unrecognized... From our house on the Callejón del Platero, I amble to Plaza Drake, with its stylistic hodgepodge of buildings...

Isn't this where that Sicilian chum of my brothers' lives? Cara, Clara, something like that... Whatever you're called, I know you already, through them. They say you're my twin soul... I hope not, for your sake... They even predict I'll fall in love with you... maybe I already have... Soon enough, they'll force us to meet face to face... For now, you're ever-present anyway: my witness for the defense... Like those imaginary playmates children dream up... This thought gives me an odd sense of comfort...

Skirting the Cathedral apse, I turn into the treeless square beyond... Like my brothers and you, I've always been a devotee of Colonial history... I can't cross the Plaza Catedral without recalling Santiago Columbus, our first governor... Here in this square, I can envisage the rabid Archbishop, denouncing him to a bloodthirsty mob... condemning him as 'a worshipper of heathen gods, a traitor to the Madre Patria...'

How has it come to this? On his second voyage, Cristopher Columbus brings us the dour evangelists of the Dominican Order… He christens our harbor Puerto San Tomás de Aquino, after their foremost theologian… But here's where dissension starts to arise… The Admiral's nephew, Santiago, changes the name to Puerto Indio, when he expands the settlement in 1510… As we know from his correspondence, Santiago might be classed as a 'closet humanist…' He abhors the Dominicans' role in the Spanish Inquisition, with its cruel tortures and autos-da-fé…

His aversion also springs from a more personal source. His mother, Fiammetta de' Benci, a Florentine, is a precocious aesthete… She's reviled as a 'voluptuary' by Savonarola, the fanatical Dominican preacher of her day… Shortly before her marriage, he and his henchmen immolate her paintings by Gozzoli, Perugino, and Ghirlandaio in a 'bonfire of the vanities'… Raised by Fiammetta to be a lover of the arts, Santiago can't forgive such a crime… As he writes in a letter to his wife: 'The Borgia pope, Alexander VI, may have had his flaws, but at least he rid the world of that abominable monk…'

Favoring the Franciscans and Benedictines, Santiago engages in a bitter face-off with the Dominicans… a battle he will ultimately lose… In 1521, not only does Emperor Charles V divest him of his post for 'heresy,' he orders him thrown into Canuba's military jail… Finally, several years later, the royal judges ship him to Cádiz in chains… From there, they trundle him to Toledo in a cramped iron cage, mounted on a bumpy cart… By this time, his hardships have ruined his health, and he expires before he can plead his case at court…

Santiago's imprisonment in the fortress must've been his worst travail… As fate would have it, he built the garrison himself… in 1508, as a tribute to his uncle Cristóbal, who'd died two years before… A squat, crenellated tower, it juts from the Barrio Antiguo's eastern edge… Though not as hulking as El Morro in San Juan, or La Cabaña in Havana, it dates from a century earlier… The parade ground next to the structure is now a park… I often went for walks there in my younger years, late in the afternoon…

Today, as then, I wander along the grassy perimeter, admiring the pinkish-yellow stones of the cyclopean walls… From the presidio, I veer right into the Paseo de las Doncellas… In my mind's eye, the ghostly ladies of Santiago's court still vaunt their finery there… on a flagstone pavement, no less, a novelty in the Caribbean… Rows of mansions and regal buildings… ineptly restored by Espinosa a decade ago… afford a backdrop for their promenades…

Two blocks away, at Casa Extremadura, I rest for a spell on a leaf-strewn bench… Built as Santiago's residence, it now houses temporary art-exhibits… certainly, his mother would've approved… The shady courtyard, canopied by ficus trees, provides relief from the tropical sun…

The olive-green flagstone at my feet marks a melancholy spot… Here's where the last Taíno cacique and his clan await their atrocious end… After their eleventh-hour revolt, Santiago's successor rounds them up… A month later, he herds then to Cathedral Square, and immolates them in an auto-da-fé… A hardline defender of the Catholic faith, he scorns Santiago's respect for indigenous culture… one of the humanist traits that led to his disgrace…

Besides the fortress and the Casa, Santiago leaves a more intimate bequest… twenty life-size statues in the Cathedral… carved by Taíno sculptors… His mother's influence is patent again, in his role as a patron of the arts… One of the effigies depicts the governor himself, kneeling in contrition… crowned with a cacique's headband of gold… Tellingly, another portrays a native shaman in a bird-beaked mask… a dubious convert to Christianity…

As the afternoon wanes, I wonder what Santiago would think of Canuba in our time?… His ethnic tolerance didn't suit the Church authorities, who decried his 'pagan sympathies…' The current Archbishop… 'White Batman…' can't chide our despot Espinosa for 'abominations' of that ilk…

Over eighty, lame and nearly blind… he rules our island like a pernicious spider… dangling on a web of steel… the nexus of his spies and hit-men… In his radio addresses, he derides 'Africanism…' He exalts 'our Catholic Mother Spain, who speaks to us through our language, and dwells forever in our hearts...' His racism panders to the national prejudice... Bonaventurans are black... Canubans are white... so Canubans are superior... In fact, all of us islanders are mixed, in varying degrees...

In southern Florida, the US Coast Guard copes with a swelling tide... boat-people from both countries... To the benighted Americans, they're more or less equivalent... Since it's closer to Puerto Rico, Bonaventurans often use Canuba as a springboard for their voyage to the States... though they often end up staying here for good... Their presence spurs unexpected alliances... or so the newspapers tell us... the 'radical' ones our father smuggles into the house...

Environmentalists resent the dirt-poor peasants... they've already denuded Bonaventura of its trees, they carp... conveniently forgetting the deforestation by France and the US... Progressives fear the paupers will swamp the incipient welfare state... Conservative patriots decry the 'invasion of aliens, the same who tried to conquer our land a century ago'... Discordant on every other theme... left-wingers and right-wingers agree on the 'immigrant issue...' mimicking Espinosa's invective... As elsewhere in the world... we moderates feel trapped between the two extremes... in this case, bizarrely united...

Since the early 1980s, our yearnings have found an outspoken voice... Milady Mateo, the ebullient leader of the Transformation Party... the Partido de la

Transformación... Proud of her African lineage, she masters Spanish without a fault... even if her origins remain unclear... Her opponents imply that her parents are Bonaventurans... but they've never advanced any proof... She avers that the Mateos are tucked away in Miami's Little Canuba... fearful of reprisals by Espinosa's goons...

A big-boned woman, Milady wears flower-patterned blouses and white skirts... We Mirandas appreciate her dashing, stylish flair... Boosted by the scandals that rock Espinosa's regime, her anti-racist, anti-poverty platform swiftly gains favor... especially among the darker-skinned and dispossessed... She intends to make Canuba's 'democracy' something more worthy of the name... a prospect our strongman can't abide...

His puppet Vice President, Baldasino Quintero... is accused of drug-trafficking... It's a cottage industry Espinosa built up over decades, in cahoots with his cronies... Their obscure operations... abetted by the Canuban top brass... confound even Interpol and the USDEA... Colombians ship cocaine by a roundabout route... through Venezuela, Cuba, Haiti... the Dominican Republic, Bonaventura... and finally, Canuba... From here, it's delivered to underwater caves in Puerto Rico... or directly to the Florida coast...

Espinosa appointed Quintero to drum up political support from the island's second city... the haughty enclave of Esmeralda... As grotesque as Goya portraits, the Vice and his wife both descend from ingrown Spanish families... I've only seen them in pictures, but Catulo met them once at a charity ball... Baldasino is a broad-bottomed man with a constant grimace... Doña Zita resembles a parched, unblinking doll... He blusters around the ballroom... she seems to roll beside him on hidden wheels... They live up to their monikers... 'Daffy Duck and the Mummy...'

To thwart extradition and a US trial, Espinosa has Baldasino impeached... 'our National Assembly, at your service...' He replaces him with another hack... But that's only the kick-off.... The tyrant is paranoid about his dwindling prestige... In a kangaroo hearing... to whitewash the President... the Canuban Supreme Court condemns Quintero to jail...

He's still under house arrest after all these months... As for the Mummy, she preserves her frozen smile... confident the loot they've stashed in Grand Cayman will survive... Predictably, Quintero gets religion... At Easter he writes to the papers that he's flagellated by bullies... adulated by the pious... collapsing under a wearisome cross... A tasteless joke makes the rounds... With no feet... and no hands... how can you crucify a Duck?

Throughout the eighties, 'our Milady' runs for several offices... By defying the regime's voter fraud, she garners widespread support... She achieves such a landslide in 1988... the Electoral Commission has no choice... they have to declare her Senator for the Puerto Indio District...

The island's cultural figures… 'leftist,' 'rightist,' one and all… are distressed by Espinosa's infamy… Egged on by their friends abroad… they endorse Milady Mateo more openly… In this as in all other trends… we Mirandas join the vanguard…

Our father has represented the dictator in dozens of countries… bravely, he was the first high official to jump ship… Like him, we 'boys' have openly pledged our allegiance to the Transformation Party… Thanks to his European hotels, Catulo is backed by foreign embassies… he can thumb his nose at Espinosa to some extent… At times, he's sailed fairly close to the wind… staging mass-rallies for Mateo in Puerto Indio and Esmeralda…. More low-key, Horacio milks his friendship with social mavens… like Carolina Del Río and Countess Frederica… to canvas other wealthy donors… Behind the scenes, he's persuaded them that 'nuestra Milady' will bring prosperity… to all, the rich as well as the poor…His persistence yields a steady stream of undercover funds… With Frederica, I've seconded his pleas, in my late-night visits to the would-be 'grande dame…'

I double back to the grounds of the Colonial fort… I step into the citadel itself… Fifteen years ago, Espinosa christened it the 'Memorial Bastion…' in honor of Santiago, ostensibly… But since he was jailed there, some interpret that homage as a mockery… a rebuke for his 'betrayal of the Castilian race…'

Over the centuries… the edifice has served as a brig for mutinous seamen… Each cell is ample enough for a dozen inmates… a single, four-foot slit allows a glimpse outside… At the center is a minute sliver of ocean… a tantalizing shard that drives the sailors mad… a visual water-torture, glint by glint…

I emerge from the dungeon… I climb the high steps to the battlements… The unimpeded vista fills me with a sudden joy… I feel like a prisoner set free… At the harbor's mouth, a shoal barely peeks above the tide… now swiftly rolling in… The palms that flourish there seem rooted in nothing… nothing but the waves…

That miracle fails to impress the drowsy ships… nodding along the wharves where the river meets the sea… There's not a sound… until some laughing-gulls spiral overhead… I follow their swerves and swoops… they dive for fish in the murky waters… Their raucous jeers are Santiago's true memorial… And what will Milady's be?

Again, my imaginary friend, I sense your presence… The hashish I ate with my breakfast kicks in… a dreamy flashback and foreshadowing… a mounting wind…

I used to come to this tower often… early or late… Early… I'd watch how daybreak opens the sea like a corolla to the light… Late… as at this hour… I'd watch how nightbreak reaches down, closing the waters gleam by gleam…

Is there any truth to our crusade for endings?... Aren't we sewn into sleeve after sleeve, locked into box after box?... Maybe we're lying... lying unashamedly... like you and me at twilight on this roof, while we ride the cirrus clouds in their stampede...Their backs arch and blur in the unlivable, yet gentle blue... they'll never zero into focus... In the offing, a freighter stalks them... crouching till it tears their ragged manes...

Centaurs with wings, we long to leap from this tower... to sink with those horses and drown... But we know... though we try to forget... that the only tendons here are ours... rebounding to the gun-smoke of delusions... The distant thunder fades and blackens... to spare us for the night within the night... our endless midnight at sea...

HORACIO

1997-1990

with

Amado

I am heartened that you approved of my funeral dirge, celestial Chiara, inspirited by Shakespeare. As you have often observed, the Cygnus of Avon modeled his tempestuous drama on the nascent West Indian realms, infusing his masque with the epochal strife between the autochthones and the Occident. Nothing could be more germane to Europa's transposed 'rape' of Canuba than this parable of mutual mistrust.

Yes, Horacio, here the big, nasty bull was Europa herself. Of course, the 'rape' was an abduction in both cases: a farewell to self-worth…

Dea dixit. The goddess has spoken; and so do I. Unlike my frater Virgilio, for whose requiem I composed my chant, I have bestowed many a colloquy upon the inquisitive Fourth Estate. This is why, my Italic divinity, you have rarely espied me of late. Now that the furor has subsided, I am elated to receive you in my pianistic haunt, athwart my Bösendorfer's sturdy flanks. Utcumque you are intrigued: alongside Prospero's poetic adieu, why does my threnody englobe his asides to Ferdinand, which bracket his farewell?

Or as you insist somewhat abruptly: Why the whole speech?

I camber an enigmatic eyebrow. None of your media colleagues was sagacious enough to request the why and wherefore, my Sicilian Athena. Confidentially, those verbal bookends I retained devolve from a familial bagatelle. You must needs resurrect the context. The magus has been vaunting his thaumaturgical prowess to Miranda and her paramour, by conjuring up a mythical pageant. The magician's future son-in-law is so enraptured that he exclaims: 'I am in Paradise.'

Wouldn't you, Horacio? A vision like that doesn't come along every day!

Perchance not to us. Yet it may have been a quotidian event to Prospero and his filia, Miranda. Forsooth, in a trice the magus recalls that Caliban will soon erupt from the wings, with homicide in his viscera: whereupon, the fictive Olympus dissipates 'into air, into thin air.' The maiden is accustomed to such a phantasmagoria: otherwise, why would her progenitor address Ferdinand alone?

Mm-hm, I see your point.

Still, the latter is already her 'other half'—her 'half-orange,' as we verbalize in our pungent Castilian. The male citrus-segment is perplexed, while the female remains insouciant. Here we behold the obfuscated and illuminated sides of the lunar orb: the masculine and feminine, fused into a unitary globe. And to multiply our integration even more, we have always been the triune Mirandas.

I don't follow you.

Indubitably not, my peerless Minerva. I am alluding to one of our infantile, nugatory games. When our caput familias was Ambassador to Zambia, our erstwhile governess regaled us with the Lambs' *Tales from Shakespeare*. Maturating as pupils in an Anglophone ambience was problematic indeed, with a surname like Miranda. Cro-Magnon bullies derided our moniker as a distaff cognomen, the same as the ingenue's nomen in the opus we adored. Indeed, we often performed the oeuvre domestically for our mater and pater, triply or quadruply per annum. For us, it portended an odyssey to our native insula, not unlike Prospero's hallucination for his offspring and her swain.

Your zygomaticus major ascends on either side, a mien vulgarly known as a 'smile.' — Aha… What loony little tykes you must've been.

Minuscule basilisks, I daresay… Conceptualize: Virgilio would elaborate the pasteboard backdrops, Catulo would choreograph the rustic gavottes, and I would emit some sinuous tunes on my dendro-recorder, my vertical flute. One of the houseboys, yclept Abdrazak, had carved it from an endemic species of tree—favored by sorcerers, he alleged. In the end, we distilled many elixirs from our androgynous name. We perdured as 'Los Mirandas' to the exterior, mundane sphere; yet we transgendered to 'Las Mirandas' in our interior domain. This ludic gambit vastly multiplied our virtualities.

I get it: so you could be 'Los' and 'Las' at the same time. All things to all women—and all men.

Affirmative. And to every modality, betwixt and

between: a unitarian, polyhedral trinity. Since you also perceive the self in this kaleidoscopic vein, as I have iterated oftentimes, you merit our accolade as an Honorary Canuban: to wit, a Canubanus-Canubana-Canubanum, of indeterminate declension. — I proffer a portfolio for your inspection, displaying its contents on the pianoforte's occluding lid. — Examine these, nonpareil Chiara: they are juvenilia devised by Virgilio for our thespian escapades, when we were mere Lilliputians.

You scrutinize them. — Amazing! They're like childish sparks of the bonfire to come.

I wax nostalgic: Ah, woe is me, 'Las Mirandas…' These figurations betoken our ingenuousness, our precocity, our intimate mirabilia—and posteriorly, the damsels we revered, even though we always treasured the gyneco-facet of our animae. From thence, we embroidered on the metaphor: 'Ferdinands' were our beau idéal, our knights in splendid breastplates, our Lohengrins of virile salvation—even our Kulturhelden, like Buonarotti or Bach. Once our hormones evolved, they were also our neo-Hellenic bromances, or simply the males we biologically elect to be, without any surgical ado.

What did you make of Ariel?

Oh, 'Ariels' might be flighty reginae, or epicenes who did our bidding. Or intervals of overweening sublimity, such that we auscultate an ethereal effluvium, like the 'airs of the island' in the *Tempest*—those 'arias of the insula' we harken to, you and I.

And Prospero, what about him?

Why, the magician symbolized our potencies: our aptitudes and our intellects—such as they were. Verily I say unto you, we have never harbored any pretenses. In a theatre of Canuba's modest dimensions, there is no merit in commanding the proscenium. Like the dextrous wizard's, our necromancy sufficed to mesmerize an isle—though not a continent, much less the planet Gaia. I insist on our humility, however much the reverberating press now lauds us to the skies, on a par with Caribbean paragons like Lezama Lima, Derek Walcott, or St. John Perse. What a travesty! Even so, our minor legerdemain bewitched our enamored 'Mirandas,' ensorcelled our impavid 'Ferdinands': we incatenated their nous, we subdued their heavenly bodies to our wills. Our adroitness exalted us... until 'Caliban's revenge.'

You tilt your gaze upward from the crayon-limned sheets. — Hmmm. Virgilio used that same phrase, the last time I saw him. What does it mean?

Dear deity, that was another tri-fraternal shibboleth. At any juncture when we were plagued by a primitive instinct, a paroxysm of ire or concupiscence, we adverted to the phenomenon as 'Caliban's revenge.' Among the Bard's dramatis personae, 'Caliban' protrudes as a quasi-anagram for 'cannibal,' videlicet those who supposedly infested the Spanish Main.

And 'Canuba' also echoes 'cannibal,' you'd have me believe? Why did Virgilio bring up that expression on his deathbed? He wasn't in a punning mood then.

Evasively, I levitate from my pianoforte throne. — Indeed, what could be more paradoxical? Here I have labored under infirmities throughout my vita brevis, and both my fratres have gloried in equine constitutions. I never suspected I would survive them... By the by, may I presume that you would wish to purchase a mahogany bedstead? We have quite a variety from which to select.

Don't be silly. You should hang on to those. As Virgilio relics, they must be worth a gold mine.

Be that as it may, my Syracusan nymph, I insist. You were wont to recline upon those davenports, coequal with our ursine frater. No, pray omit from your mental notation my predicate 'purchase': that was the shopkeeper in me, palavering from his mercenary past. I ardently confer one of these chesterfields on your august personage, as an aide-memoire. Do not hyperventilate: no, not the deathbed he actually expired upon! The canvases qualify as far more valuable than the furnishings. Particularly the final icons, sundered through the midriff by the 'headlong artist.' That singularity is being linked by frivolous critics to a Jasper Johns motif—'the diver.' I have been overwhelmed by offers from scores of museums; they can scarcely wait for his hemoglobin to desiccate.

From the manner in which I satirize, you must conclude

that I am flippant. You gutturate your larynx. — You're taking it all in your stride, Horacio.

I subscribe to Prospero's advice to Ferdinand: 'You do look, my son, in a mov'd sort, as if you were dismay'd. Be cheerful, sir.' And I augur the same to you, my transcendent Chiara. — I radiate a sunbeam of my sometime merriment, as in those bygone days when we initially conjoined.

You do not respond; ergo, I divagate around the chamber for a while. — Apropos, I acknowledge that I have not fully satisfied your curiosity about 'Caliban's revenge.' That ancient quip of ours also adumbrated a lachrymose denouement, when our frater Catulo fell ill… and then, when our frater Virgilio 'fell' ill. There is another veritas I can no longer camouflage: our consanguine Titian was afflicted by the human immunodeficiency virus, too. Several months before he plummeted to his demise, he had embarked on the fully-fledged syndrome.

You appear thunderstruck. — Why didn't he tell me?

He assumed that you ascertained his condition, but did not wish to intrude on his mental sanctum sanctorum. Do you remember Virgilio's ocular infection? Alas, it was a cytomegalovirus. When you failed to register that 'mega-indication,' he deduced that after your tribulations with Amado and Catulo, you refused to confront another decease.

Maybe that's what kept me from putting two and two together. But as the pop psychologists say, it was only an unconscious 'denial.' I didn't mean to brush him off.

Gadzooks, dear Principessa, you should not inculpate yourself: it behooved him to confess his agon to you. We always manifest a propensity to 'project' our sentiments upon our confrères, to employ another modish vocable. He asseverated that you were proving your antique pedigree, by nobly ignoring the whole topos. Just as he, ipso facto, would have done, according to his gentleman's etiquette; just as he did, quod est demonstrandum, where you were concerned. Quilviria and I were the only souls to whom he unburdened his bosom.

That must've come as a shock.

On the contrary, I was not astonished, and neither was Quilviria. For there was another enigma to which we were privy. This explains why she never entertained unprotected intercourse with our domestic Masaccio, praise be to the Empyrean. We are persuaded that he contracted the pathogen from a hypodermic device.

What? From a needle?

You seem flabbergasted, my winsome Chiara, and yet I regret to inform you that our Virgilio was an addict extraordinaire. His recurrent injections caused perpetual anxiety to Quilviria and me, throughout the flux and reflux of our intimate annals. Our island Rafaello expended whole nocturnal cycles in the most noxious sectors of our decomposing metropole, for which our provinces are colonies. He patronized houses of assignation, opium lairs, cocaine establishments, sub-pontifical nests for those lacking roofs—any locus where intravenous wares proliferate. We detected the absorption of pharmaceuticals from the minute perforations on his antebrachia; yet these were not the only disquieting semaphores. His dorsum often evinced haematoma, and his collum betrayed pendant strangulations.

Welts? Hangings? How so?

I suspire. — There is a riverine hamlet where he was wont to repair. He confessed his antics to me once, when he was so distraught that he abandoned all reserve; but anon, he withdrew into his hirsute carapace yet again. He would often terminate his saturnalia in that riparian quartier, id est in a hovel along the Río Felipe. A narcotics vendor would truss him up on a gallows; subsequently, a coven of ladies of ill repute would flagellate him till he hemorrhaged...

Aghast, you interrupt me in medias res. — I noticed he had scratches on his hands at times, but I thought he'd just been clumsy with his palette knife.

Undexterous: yes, he was maximally *that*, except when drawing. And recall how he elocuted, or scilicet, did not. He was inebriated on cannabis, with sempiternal persistence; though once he obtained his laurels, he partially reformed, the better to superintend the Academia. When the physicians diagnosed him as HIV-positive, he submitted to their instructions thenceforth: no more illicit substances, no more perambulations along the insalubrious littoral. The fons et origo of his amor for you was that you never adjudicated his mores or his mien.

Chiara, you lachrymate. Not lacrimae rerum, but lacrimae Virgilii: such are the crystalline globules that inundate your tortured visage. When you reemerge, you palpate my patella. — Thank goodness he also had you and Quilviria. — We perdure in silentio sacro, for an interval. Ultimately, you summon up the valor to advance. — If he killed himself because of AIDS, he made an awful mistake. There's a new 'cocktail' of meds that's working wonders, Horacio. With the income from his artworks, he could've received the best treatment available. He still had so much to give to the world. Oh, who cares about that? He still had so much to give to us.

For an instant, you might observe my gaze turn nebulous. I am grappling with a challenge to my own convictions—but soon it subsides. — Who knows? Without his tentative auto-da-fé, he might never have experienced those last few hebdomads of serenity. He was disabused of his own curriculum vitae. Why and wherefore? We can only posit the inquiry, never resolve it. Any premature demise is always a mysterium fidei.

You mordiscate your inferius oris, lofty Pallas. — All this is no 'mystery' to me, Horacio. It's just a pointless waste. You've lost your brothers, and so have I. Catulo, my ex-lover, and Virgilio, my closest friend. For me, the island has been blown to smithereens.

I dare to encompass the whole decapod of your digits. — Ah yes, for you it has shattered like Minoan Thera, Santorini for hoi polloi. And in your pantheon, do I account for nil?

You tremulate your labia in consternation. — Spare me, Horacio. You're my most loyal friend, and you're even dearer to me now.

I collocate my flexors on your scapulae. — I cohabit your dolor, Chiara. For you, this drastic supernova is precipitate. I have profited from many a lunar cycle to adapt, and sapientia est potentia. But 'be cheerful, madam.' Mirabile dictu, Virgilio received extreme unction, just before he deliquesced to extinction. We can siphon a jubilant succor from that.

You contort your depressor angulis oris into a ladylike grimace. — A deathbed conversion? Virgilio, the lifelong atheist? I'm skeptical. In his weakened state, after his fall, he might've gone through the motions.

Far from it, my deluded Principessa. This was not an instance of post hoc ergo propter hoc.

Hmmm. At most, he might've imitated Hölderlin, merging Christ and the gods into one. If you must mistitle me, Horacio, I trust he faded like a true Principe, Prince André, gazing at his inner sky.

Dei gratia, more like Prince Myshkin, the sacrosanct simpleton—to improvise on your Russian motif. He seemed almost infantile in his crepusculum. — I circumnavigate the cubiculum musicae. — Ecce veritas: here is another epiphany. You are the prima inter totes to meditate the novelty. I am saying ave atque vale as well. Do not agonize! No, not via the modi operandi of my fratres: no dementia, no plunge into the abyss. Nor am I seropositive, should that preoccupy your anxious breast.

Thank God.

A fortiori. Henceforth, I delegate Quilviria—the widow of the artifex maximus—to trudge the via dolorosa of the domus, the pecunia, the adulants and emulants, the exhibitions and prestations, the scribes and locutors of mediatic pablum, the whole voluminous circus urbi et orbi. All along, she has served as a surrogate mater for our adopted filia, Verbena, and now she will assume the prosaic mundanities as well. Et ego in Arcadia, I shall fulfill my cherished aspiration of these many anni. Quoth the Bard: 'Get thee to a nunnery.' Not an imperative from *The Tempest*; rather, Hamlet's unequivocal command. I am absconding to the Monasterium Sancti Bernardi, in the cordilleran remove of Valle de las Nubes. In secula seculorum, till I render up the ghost.

You oppose my valedictory intent, reverend Chiara. — Along with Virgilio's paintings, your music is in great demand. Can't you fulfill yourself through your art, as he did?

Ah, did he now? Cistercians of the Strict Observance

chant the offices, fair damsel, lest we forget. Candidly, I am weary of the pandemonium. My compositions have been usurped by the blowhards of vanitas vanitatum. Behold what Fortuna wrought upon our ingenious and ingenuous Virgilio. How felicitous he was whilst he produced his diverse opera exclusively for himself; yet how miserable he became, once they elicited esteem from the nabobs of celebrity. Now we comprehend why he earlier concealed his oeuvre from anyone but us, his inner circulus. Hereinafter I shall equally renounce the pomps of vainglory and fanfare. I am forthwith indisposed to perpetrate the charade of 'what the Miranda boys can do.'

You attempt to object again, but I arrest you with a conductor's downward stroke. — Hear me out, inestimable Chiara. Our progenitors were frustrated artistes. Already, when we were toddlers, their laudation in excelsis was to label us their 'little masterworks.' Thereafter, that insidious theme resounded like a leitmotiv. We were art that generated art: an alabaster hare extracted from a turret-hat, extracting another hare from another turret-hat, extracting yet another from yet another. The proscenium must collapse, and the thaumaturgy must cease, as ordained by our icon, Prospero. I necessitate the coda of my earthly temporality—and all eternity, in the afterlife to come—to 'still my beating mind.'

My Sicilian sylph, you are visibly distraught. For me, your anima is a 'paysage choisi,' a privileged landscape where I can telepathically promenade. Tacitly, you are recalling the incident you have often rehearsed to my auricles, when you peregrinated to El Silencio after Amado's demise—and well-nigh plummeted from a precipice, into the epipelagic mandibles below. A similar vertigo consumes you now. Your entire Eden seems to exsiccate, copse by afflicted copse, and bloom by dehydrated bloom. And lend me credence: such is my identification with your soul that I sometimes apprehend Amado's murmurs myself, like those of an impish putto on a frescoed dome.

You are taken aback. — Oh really, Horacio?

Endeavoring to leaven the discourse, I flutter my larynx with a felid's purrs. — Of all hominids and even all ornithopods, my monstrance of pulchritude, you should be the last to reprimand me for assuming a novice's scapular: you who frequent ecumenical fanes in a continuous round.

You cannot dispute my logic. — At least you'll allow me to visit you, Horacio?

I bestow upon you a dignified embrace, my ultimate farewell to the seductions of the flesh. — Excelsior, you may sojourn in our redoubt, whenever you desiderate. As Prospero elocutes, 'if you be pleas'd, retire into my cell, and there repose.' Not literally *mine*, I hasten to clarify: you will have your own, in our hostal for transient contemplatives. And you will be tarrying with the community, not with me. Who can prophesy? Perhaps we can incorporate you as an oblate. There is a convent of gyneco-religious close-by, and they solemnize their vocations with bandeaus, wimples, and guimpes. These accessories would enhance your patrician deportment with an ecclesiastical tone, not that your numinous nous has need of such sartorial signs.

Hola Chiara, Amado here. Let me walk you home. Can you believe that guy, trying to turn you into a goddam monja? I used to tease you about being a nun, but he really wants to lock you away. It's a good thing I'm still talking inside your head or he mighta caught you off guard, and boom! you're in jail with old biddies, clucking the livelong day. Coño! What a waste! Just cause Horacio's been gelded, doesn't mean you gotta be spayed. Don't let him fool ya! No te dejes engañar!

The Cathedral, November 1997

You illuminate my anima perpetually, seraphic Chiara, but never more than during these funereal prolegomena. You must admit that even in extremis, we fratres Miranda have not abjured our dramatical panache. Throughout the uttermost segment of Virgilio's parabola, save when I supplanted Quilviria at his side, I organized repetitions with the Orquesta de Puerto Indio and the Coro Nacional. As foreordained, no sooner has our divus pictor expired, than the Ministerio de Cultura decrees a universal bereavement day. This very eventide, in the Cathedralis Lucis Divinae, I am conducting the *Missa pro Defunctis* in the betonement by Mozart, to be followed by a coda brevis of my own.

Since Catulo foisted prodigious debts upon Virgilio and myself, a fitting requiem for our elder frater would have been prohibitive upon his decease. Nor would the Archbishop, a serial aspirant to the Cardinalate, have countenanced an anathema in his Cathedral see, for he vents his contumely against our fraternal 'choreographer of the obscene' at each and every opportunity. Now, with the Miranda fortunes at maximal spate, I may cant my jeremiad for both my illustrious departed, with no pecuniary restraint.

Venally, the prelate agrees to overlook Virgilio's 'sinful suicide,' in return for an oleaginous transfer to his private, extra-ecclesiastical account. Until this vesper, I have camouflaged my Catulian intention from the deplorable Shepherd's 'Crook'—nomen est omen—whose turpitude with multiple feminae defies the canons of propriety. Quilviria and a panoply of Academia volunteers enshroud the late-Gothic temple in sable crepe; and at its crux, to uphold the ebony 'sarcophagus Virgilii,' they erect a catafalque no Antonine imperator would have contemned.

Shortly before the incunabula of the memorial, an interruption of electricity spurred by the insatiable Columbus Crown inters the Barrio Antiguo in obscurity, much to my covert delectation. The requiem Mozartiensis must perforce be executed under the cerous tapers of candelabra, the aureate clarification of our bygone seculae. Deo gratias, the instrumentalists and choir have practiced the opus in exhaustive and meticulous quiddity; hence they scarcely shed a glance upon their vacillating, penumbral scores.

Besides the magnum opus itself, and the aqueous umbrae—like reflections on the facades of the Serenissima's canals—another salience of these obsequies must affect you in profundis, my immortal Chiara. The curmudgeonly pretender to a Principality of the Church has permitted Quilviria's minions to displace all the pews into the apse; and ergo, the multitudinous mourners, who serrate the sanctuary from front to back, must stand throughout this musical offering in memoriam, just as they would have done a demi-millennium ago.

By coincidence, this officium betides on November 18th, the anniversary of the Admiral of the Ocean Sea's inaugural advent on our insula, in Anno Domini 1492. On the septentrional littoral, he christened our island San Tomás de Aquín and founded a settlement by that nomenclature—later yclept Canuba and Puerto Indio, respectively. There he deposited some of the Taíno venereal slaves maintained by the Caribs, and whom he had liberated in the Insulae Virgines. Their male children had been castrated, fattened up, and devoured by those ferocious invaders from the Amazonian south.

As the cantors intone the 'Lachrymosa,' they seem to be lamenting the whole somber epic of Taíno bondage and genocide, from the Caribs to the Spanish. From your perspective, at the hindermost section of the nave, I cogitate that you are communing with the life-size effigies of the Last Supper and the Via Crucis, sculpted by the aborigines in our Colonial epoch. In the tremulous tenebrae, awakened by the undulations of sonority, they seem to bemoan the ephemerality of their incarnation, as forsooth becomes us all: sic transit gloria mundi.

Like a more enlightened Columbus, Virgilio unveiled our archipelago to Gaia's most far-flung antipodes, establishing its falciform heft on any aesthetic cartography. His opera eternalize Canuba's myriad personae—from mischievous innocence to vicious corruption, from pristine splendor to environmental malaise, and from amorous sublimity to sadistic depravity. To echo his drastic apothegm, 'face-deface-efface,' he limns all the insula's visages; yet now it is he who is faced, defaced, and effaced.

To exacerbate the Archbishop's dyspepsia, I have emblazoned my terpsichorean sibling on the programme, side by side with my pictorial adelphos. Moreover, as a colophon, I have reprinted Virgilio's cryptic logo, id est: ((T))((T))((T)). I read it as trinitarian, note bene. He designed it for Catulo's transgender extravaganza, the Catuli-ana, that eponymous cycle which ignited such vituperation—episcopal, and therefore obtuse. Quilviria's squadron distributes my subversive screed just prior to the Introit, hence too extempore for His Ersatz 'Excellency' to intervene. The obsidian-bordered folios proclaim that I am presenting the authentic Mozartian manuscript, non finito, without Süssmayr's adjuncts; I have excepted only the 'Lachrymosa,' partially in the magister's hand.

To this splendid embarcation, appropriately wrecked, I have coupled a unicorn valedictory of my own, a portentous adieu entitled *Hermanos Carnales*.

In Castilian, 'carnal brothers' is a conventional locution, to distinguish pure hematological relations from other variants, whether half-, step-, foster, or intimate comrades in arms. Yet caricaturing the defamations which our quondam extra- and intramural assignations have provoked in the bourgeoisie, the adjective suggests a double entendre; and for you, my Hellenic maenad, it may even imply a pubescent cum incestuous palimpsest. On a supernal plane, in this tribute ne plus ultra, I am adverting to the evulsion of fraternal thews from each other's embrace.

Accordingly, my eclectic adagio non moto will remind you of Arvo Pärt's *Fratres*, in the evocative version for strings. Nevertheless, above a decelerated ensemble in his 'tintinnabulum' mode for violins, violoncellos, and double bass, which arpeggiates ascending tonic triads, I have traced an ecstatic fugue for counter-tenor, tenor, and bass. Having harkened so intensely over the fathomless anni to the Trinitas Mirandae, you will not misperceive whom this trio is meant to symbolize. But only you and I will comprehend that a mute, absent baritone might be surmised as an emblem of the obsolete inamorati of these triune persons in one nature, thus instilling a phantasmal quartet—or via the orchestral accompaniment, the infusion of a Megaptera cetacean's myriad tonalities, so sacred to you and my brothers, a spectral 'symphonie engloutie.'

The polyphonic gyres' triplicate lines are not unlike the deliberately revolving, almost static 'Benedictus' of Palestrina's *Missa Assumpta est Maria*, which tranquilly bodies forth the conundrum of a triple deity in One. Verily I say unto you, had I not recanted any St. Antonine temptation towards demonic blasphemy, I might even have denominated my opusculum *Missa Assumpta est Miranda*: a gratifying offense to the bilious White Batman, and yet a grievous mea culpa for my internal examen conscientiae.

Here at any rate are the interweaving harmonies for you to absorb, the trialogue exalted by St. Augustine in his tractatus *De Trinitate*: the visage, the speculum, and the lux universalis that streams between them—or more artlessly defined, the lover, the beloved, and the love. Their enlacing syllables spiral upward to the mystical vaults, hovering overhead like an internal night, the nox animae conjured by San Juan de la Cruz. And as another St. John, the Evangelist, might have prescribed, the voices are extinguished in turn—one, then two, then three—just as we and all terrestrial pilgrims are snuffed out, in the ineluctable ripeness of time. Delivered from our transitory 'incarnatus est,' we rejoin the 'Verbum aeternitatis,' the luminous Logos of eternity.

Along with my own Castilian translation, on a glaucous insert, I have inscribed the vocables I dared to orchestrate—these verses from our talismanic romance:

> You do look, my son, in a mov'd sort,
> As if you were dismay'd. Be cheerful, sir.
> Our revels now are ended. These our actors,
> As I foretold you, were all spirits and
> Are melted into air, into thin air;
> And, like the baseless fabric of this vision,
> The cloud-capp'd towers, the gorgeous palaces,
> The solemn temples, the great globe itself,
> Yea, all which it inherit, shall dissolve,
> And, like this insubstantial pageant faded,
> Leave not a rack behind. We are such stuff
> As dreams are made on, and our little life
> Is rounded with a sleep. Sir, I am vexed.
> Bear with my weakness. My old brain is troubled.
> Be not disturb'd with my infirmity.
> If you be pleas'd, retire into my cell
> And there repose. A turn or two I'll walk
> To still my beating mind.

And I just wanna tell you, Italianita: Catulo and me are in the front row, even if nobody can see us. My voice is un poquito higher than Virgilio's, so we joke around that maybe I'm the missing baritone, now that I know what a baritone means. Anyhow, como quiera, Catulo wanted to go to his own funeral; and since I never really had one, I guess this'll be mine too. How's that for a triple whammy!

Plaza Drake, June 1996

What an abomination! With all the reverence I harbor towards you, my long-suffering Chiara, I reluct against the deviousness of that serpentine Lamia, a dishonor to her Achaean provenance. How she could strive to evict you from your bibliophilic abode surpasses my comprehension: her herpetological daemon has now evolved into its full satanic avatar, pendant from the Edenic bough she would fain annihilate. Notwithstanding, every tragical agon, not least in the oeuvre of the immortal Bard, entails a comical underside. Indeed, in her story 'Sorrow-Acre,' Blixen denominates tragedy as the genre of peasants and hoi polloi, whereas comedy is reserved for the nobility and the gods.

When Ángel María and I acquaint Carolina Del Río with your Lamian predicament, she urgently commandeers me one antemeridian, to escort her to your domicile in Plaza Drake. Though dubious, I consent to the expedition, because I lucubrate that the Del Ríos possess a tertiary portion of the Barrio Antiguo, and hence she might facilitate your transposition to a neoteric nidification. The plutocratic gens 'Of The River' acquired their plethora of edifices in the nineteenth centennial, an epoch when no one but they disposed of sufficient capital to invest. Through reprehensible negligence, many of these Colonial structures have lapsed into disrepair—in part because the Del Ríos have always indulged their tenants with prodigal largesse.

Exempli gratia, Delfinia is an impoverished relation of Frederica's whom the Gräfin disowns, but who has always doted on the arriviste's arrant filius, Count Gustavo. Delfinia has merited your predilection; she dwells unobtrusively in a cinquecento domus not far from you. Of late, she has feted her adhesion to the nonagenarian cohort. Vivacious as a marmoset, she still purges the pavement before her residence, one of an octet of Del Río properties on Plaza Drake. A century heretofore, her pater labored as a coachman for Carolina's maternal grandsire, to Frederica's perennial chagrin. Delfinia has dedicated herself to educating infants in a public primary school, an automatic formula for indigence. Owing to the Del Río generosity, she has perdured gratuitously in her childhood habitation, for the quintuple decades since her progenitors' demise.

Despite my objections, Carolina has now determined on the questionable contrivance that you should purchase a pristine condominium for Delfinia, displace her to its modernistic precincts, renovate her dilapidated cottage, and populate the maisonette yourself. She ignores my admonition that the effervescent crone is so attached to her locus amoenus, she refuses to deplete even a nanosecond in the anodyne sub urbe where her filia resides.

Upon our advent, you endorse my protestations. Yet pertinaciously, Carolina insists on proceeding to Delfinia's lodgings, posthaste. — Let's see what kind of shape the place is in, Chiara.

That's very kind of you, Carolina. But I'd hate for her to think I'm after her home.

Why on earth would she think that?

It would be pretty obvious, if I'm snooping around with the owner. Especially since all the neighbors know I'm being evicted from my house.

Oh, Delfinia won't recognize me. She hasn't seen me for ages, not since I was a little girl. We'll tell her I'm an inspector, sent by the Cultural Heritage Office.

I mordiscate my labium inferioris. The Oficina de Patrimonio Cultural? While neither you nor I, my paragon, would ever disavow the gentility of such a sanguine patroness, this strikes us both as a preposterous ploy. Carolina's gracile figure ornaments the mediatic organs unrelentingly: sororizing at soirees, inaugurating non-profits, or severing banderoles for retrofitted factories. As the most affluent personage on the insula, she percolates through the cerebra of everyone—above all, those who benefit from her cornucopia. Circa Plaza Drake, none of her tenants dispenses more than a nominal rent, if anything whatsoever. As we three confederates promenade across the quadrangle, the populace hails the grande dame deferentially, as if she were coronated royalty. Within the interval post hoc we accede to Delfinia's portal, that aperture has amply dehisced to render the monarch homage.

Carolina never succeeds in introducing herself as a monitoress for Patrimonio. The pensioner's solitary pretension to eminence, among her fellow-antiquities, reposes upon her 'life-long friendship with the Del Río family.' Now she must demonstrate to the agnostics that she has not fabricated that vinculum for all these decenniae. She sallies forth and impounds Carolina by the ulna, caterwauling for all to auscultate. — Carolinita! Carolinita Del Río! — Once she ferries her into her minute refugium, she continues to vociferate. — Cuanto tiempo! It's been ages! I haven't laid eyes on you since you were knee-high to a grasshopper. But I'd know you anywhere. Thanks to your grandfather, Don Joaquín, I still have my humble home. And ever since he met his Maker, I owe my happiness to you, Carolinita!

The regina's masquerade has not deceived a single anima; after some perfunctory pleasantries, she avails herself of a precipitous retreat. To proffer amends, she entrusts us to her lease-collector, a septuagenarian with inspissated spectacles, who conducts us to a surfeit of Del Río protectorates. Behind their precarious facades, the antiquarian and the contemporary coexist, beyond the purview of prolix Baedekers. Proto-Baroque ashlar domes camber over plywood and corrugated tin; destitute Bonaventurans amass in once-patrician mansions; seamstresses and cobblers travail in coffered refectoria; ragamuffins cavort on sagging escaliers of Macael marble from Spain. At eventide, construction workers concuss their dominoes on the sculpted couverture of a Renaissance fount, impressed with an extinct coat of arms.

Throughout the Barrio Antiguo, opulence ganders through poverty, like the ermine waistcoat beneath a burlap cloak. But our mesmerizing reconnaissance— though a gaud for me, as I am attending you—does not debouch in any pragmatic solution. Ultimately, Carolina's administratrix, a dour virago with hemangiomas on her countenance, offers 'to allow you to renovate' one of the domiciles—in exchange for nothing more than a duodenary charter. 'Family policy,' she elucidates. Over six generations, we are informed, the Del Ríos have never actually parted with an edifice. After your trauma with Belisario and his vengeful courtesan, revamping another temporary abode must qualify as the most minimal of your desiderata. In the architectonic domain, my ethereal Chiara, you have tabulated a disheartening defeat.

The Canuban Library, September 1995

In March, Anno Domini 1995, Espinosa announces an academic conference on the *True Relations*; it is slated to commence on September 23rd, Canuban Independence Day. Candidates are invited to submit abstracts of their presentations, which will later be disseminated in a tome even more ponderous than the codex 'an sich.' A few eminent scholars boycott the event, owing to the dictator's sanguinary oppression, though most do not eschew a gratis Antillean villeggiatura—not to mention the ventilation of their picayune footnotes before their peers. A familiar panorama, alas, to our gens Miranda.

My elder frater Catulo engaged in the vita studiorum for an interval in Novum Eboracum, where he sometimes co-cogitated with you, exquisite Chiara, unofficially his 'prima professoressa.' As for your devoted servant, I transitorily attended the Gregoriana in Rome, and even the Sapienza—though I renounced my medical flirtation at the latter. Only the nomenclature in Greek and Latin inspired me, not the dissection of malodorous cadavers.

After an annum in Vindobona, alias Musikstadt Wien upon the Danube, I terminated at the Schola Musicae Sacrae of Notre Dame, in somniferous Indiana. Sagaciously, after his reluctant sojourn at Det Kongelige Akademi in Denmark, my somewhat junior frater Virgilio reached the conclusion that institutions of superior learning are 'reservoirs for the misbegotten and immature.' Nevertheless, to mollify you, my preternatural Chiara, I shall hie to the insipid event as your enraptured chaperone.

The Benefactor Patriae himself, Manfredo Espinosa, presides over the inaugural session. The principal chamber of the Biblioteca Canubana is pervaded by retractable mahogany sellae, fabricated expressly for this pseudo-august colloquium. He accords premier locations honoris causa to us surviving Miranda fratres, the involuntary donors of the codex, though Virgilio summarily declines to attend. You, ineffable Chiara, assume his cathedra beside me as 'a well-known journalist and close family friend': sic asserts your substitute invitation—sine dubitate, a courtesy of our amicus in excelsis, Ángel María.

Most of the other sellae are occupied by the professorial amalgam, as well as by the diplomatic corps, diverse 'acceptable' authors and artistes, and—cela va sans dire—the tyrant's most invertebrate sycophants. But he calculatingly conserves the coda of the aula for an inoffensive alembic of the populace, such as corrupt labor satraps and the benignly rustic 'Asociación C y E'—

headed up by its founder, Escolástico. Espinosa does not desire the seminar to appear elitist, since despite his ballot-machinating expertise, should a genuine democracy accidentally emerge, he might in extremis still inveigle Everyman into endorsing his hegemony.

Ever the éminence grise, Ángel María accompanies the purblind potentate to the podium. Like Borges in certain instances, Espinosa pretends to peruse his notations, though he cannot decipher an iota. Prompted now and then by his discreet amanuensis, he acquits himself of a gaseous philippic on the rank ingratitude of the Taíno. They were too primitive, quoth he, to appreciate the intellectual advancement and altruistic motives of the conquistadores. Tenaciously, the Amerindians clung to their scabrous customs, quoth he; yet it is only thanks to the curates of our Holy Church that we possess any record of these illiterate tribes. Few governments have ever been as enlightened and beneficent as the Spanish Empire, quoth he, or bestowed such a resplendent civilization on barbaric semi-simians: theology, philosophy, the sciences, the beaux-arts, the belles-lettres—and at their apex, Castilian, the lordliest tongue in all the universe. And so on, and so on, quoth he, ad nauseam.

When he perorates at long last, only his egregious toadies tender him a mite of polite applause, while a paucity of the delegates from abroad even dare to sibilate. Fortunately for them, the Benefactor's low audiometry prevents him from auscultating their dissent. In decades of yore, his reprisals against 'alien trouble-makers' have spanned the gamut from arbitrary traffic injunctions to fraudulent narcotics indictments. Some of his victims have been imprisoned in sordid penitentiaries for an annus, divers anni, or even in perpetuo.

After lauding 'our gracious President, and the Benefactor of our Nation' for his 'insightful remarks,' the rectal Rector of the University of Puerto Indio, Rafael Agliberto Salazar, adroitly proceeds to ignore them. He combs his phalanges through his synthetic peruke, and earnestly assays the multitude. He then commences to elocute, with an affectedly informal bonhomie:

Bienvenidos, amigos! Yeah, a big Canuban welcome to one and all! Right off the bat, I'd like to open up the floor; you can get to the nitty-gritty later, in your break-out talks. This morning we're just gonna have a get-to-know-you about what's brought us all together. Kinda like: 'The Taíno codex, what does it mean to me?' As advertised, this will be a jam session on 'Old Island Ways and New.' But I've gotta remind you to respect the Chief of State's rules. So we're not gonna refer to the final part of the book. In case you don't get my drift: *I mean the last thirty-three pictures*. I've gotta be strict about that. Nobody's even seen em except a few librarians. Sure, salacious gossip is being spread by the press. But here we'll take that BS for what it is: a buncha lies.

He acknowledges the half-upraised metacarpus of a Dutch-Curaçaoan academic, Andrelton Jurrjens. Chiara, you susurrate into my auricle that he is the maximum authority on ethnic continuity in the archipelago—and indeed, the same energumen who upbraided that pastoral enthusiast, Escolástico, during your visitation to the biblioteca with Virgilio.

To the bemusement of Jurrjens, the bumptious campesino himself importunes him from the bas-fonds of the audience; he has pried a microphonic device from a timorous aide. — Coño! It's not the damn words you needa be talkin about, it's the pictures. Not the dirty ones, I mean the ones we've all seen. They tell the whole story about why this book is ours, the real islanders. Los isleños de verdad. We look at those big houses where a lotta the Indians lived—nine, maybe ten families all together in one building. It's just like today, the way we bring up our boys and girls here in Canuba. A whole crowd of us, un montón, not just a papá and mamá and two measly kids, like in those gringo TV shows.

Aligning his befogged spectacles, Jurrjens radiates his condescension towards Escolástico. — The discussant is someone I know, a docent at the Library. He is alluding to the tribal approach that still prevails among the Taíno's cousins, the Arawaks of Amazonia. Here in Canuba, such communally raised infants are often called 'hijos de crianza.' The clan unit is more important than the nuclear family in rearing children, who can be interchanged with no damage done. These portrayals are featured in the first illustrations, not the final ones to which the President objects.

Escolástico vociferates once more from the back of the aula. — Bendito! The main thing is, hombre, just like the Indios back then, we hate to be alone! — His associates jubilate in approbation.

At the forefront of the auditorium, a pedagogue from Bordeaux, Hippolyte Brion, endeavors to reinstitute discipline. — Our 'illustre compatriote,' Descartes, has analyzed the horror vacui of nature. Similiarly, Canubans entertain a horror solitudinis. They must always have commotion, cambucas, cacophonous radios, etcétéra. N'est-ce pas? — Though this may have been an attempt at jocularity, his labium inflects with contempt. — Returning to the subject, one comparison that occurs to me is this: like Canubans today, the Taíno valued rivers more than the sea, which only served them as a food-bank or viaduct, useful for fishermen and voyagers. They revered par excellence the deity of fresh water, Atabey; she held sway over them more than her son, Yúcahu, the god of salt water. Contemporary islanders still shun the beach in favor of streams, waterfalls, and lakes. To them, the ocean is not at all sympathique, pas du tout!

Towards the omphalos of the forum, Hannelore Sachs, an imposing Valkyrie from the Freie Universität, retrieves the amplification wand from Escolástico. Like most of the participants, she brandishes an escutcheon of erudite glyphs; and unlike Espinosa, she can actually decode them.

Genug! Enough! There's a grim undercurrent in this island's heritage, even before the Columbus war crimes. You only had two echelons in Taíno society: a minute aristocracy, and a huge class of downtrodden underlings. I hear talk about how the middle-class is shrinking in Canuba; but as far as I can see, it never existed. Nimmer! Even so, the Spanish overlords often mention the Indians' deep hatred of servitude. Whole villages leapt to their deaths from high cliffs, to avoid being enslaved. Like the Taíno, modern islanders are free-spirited; they'd rather starve than be demeaned, or mistreated by a certain autocrat. Especially the Afro-Caribbean majority. — She reaps kudos from the progressive coterie, while the reactionaries oscillate their caputs, and the paranoiacs masticate their labia, in trepidation of our insular Caligula.

Milton Simmonds, from the boreal latitude of Amherst, reinforces her pronouncements. — If I may piggyback! As Padre Las Casas pointed out, Taíno women and children did the chores Europeans reserved for serfs, but on the condition that were treated with respect. All the memorialists praise the industry of the female natives, and decry the laziness of the men. But the corollary was this: since Taíno women spoiled their mates like infant boys, in reality they held the reins of power.

Pele Saramago, an enticing Brazilian in a jonquil, filigree chemise and serrate, vermillion pantaloons, insists on diverting the topic to his bailiwick: the Arawak anthropology of Amazonia. Ad libitum, he transposes his scripts from the Portuguese, with Lusophone melodiousness. — In the *Verdaderas Relaciones*, the chroniclers stress another enduring quirk: the elasticity of time and space. According to Genesis, God raises terra firma from the waters; in the Indian story of Yaya, the land was already there, long before the sea burst from a broken gourd. There are parallels for the latter cosmology among the Arawaks. This may explain why Canubans have always looked inward, despite inhabiting an island: in the native mind, the mainland always comes first, since it predates the archipelago.

A skeletal Colombian savant, Manolo Mutis, introduces himself. Surreptitiously, my Syracusan idol, you instruct me about his ethnic etudes of the Kogis of Santa Marta. He displays some mega-photographs of their circular domiciles, identical to Canuban bohíos. To his all-encompassing mentality, the codex supplies the fundaments for a 'General Unified Theory of First American Nations,' or GUTFAM. — Did the early islanders always yearn for their past, on the larger stage of South America? For them, each place here corresponded to somewhere else, 'in the Other Great Earth,' a phrase they often repeated to the priests. They inhabited their history, since every island where they settled was both itself and a microcosm of that mythical expanse. Nowadays I hear some Canubans calling fragments of their landscape 'Bavaria,' 'Java,' or 'Patagonia.' When they do that, they're following an age-old precedent.

Gabriel Mirtilo, an irascible Aragonese pedant, diverges from him defensively. — In another throwback, if you will, Canubans often palaver about foreigners 'invading and corrupting' their culture, as if they were still Taíno autochthons today. But for five centuries, their tradition has assimilated European, African, and Asian elements, just like their genetic pool. They're the living incarnation of the 'invasions and corruptions' they claim to resent.

Fabiano Feltrinelli, a supercilious Argentine, embarks on a tangent, designed to offend. — Of course, my country has no Indians, and no blacks either. We're Europeans who've ended up by mistake in Latin America—regrettably. Un piccolo accidente lamentabile. I, for one, should be basking on a Tuscan hillside. Yet I believe in giving credit where credit is due. I wonder, how much did the natives truly contribute to the *Verdaderas Relaciones*? The work's foreword states that 'Taíno interpreters' first suggested compiling the volume. They provided 'most of the legends and other accounts herein, making excellent use of our Castilian tongue.' Reading between the lines, we have to question their conversion to Christianity. Ambivalent, adept at two languages, two religions, and two cultures, they must have been Janus-like. They had bitterly submitted to the might of the conquistadores. Did they also foresee the twilight of their own race?

An elongated 'Canubicano' from New Jersey, Agamemnon Mora, now at the Universitas Michiganensis, appends himself to this topos. — Yes, that's the whole point. This book is an act of mourning. Nonetheless, it also holds out a promise of renewal. By telling their tales to the churchmen, these crafty bilinguals have triumphed. In a final tour de force, they've translated their dying world—not only from Taíno to Spanish, but also from past-tense to future. Subverting the conquerors' language, they've won the salvation that matters to them most: perpetuating the essence of their tribes. Unwittingly, the victors have given birth to a Native American testament.

That picaresque personage, Escolástico, vocalizes anew from the athenaeum's reductio. — Caramba, you're makin our book sound like a funeral! You're all a buncha locos. The Indios knew they didn't need to worry. Canubans now are still the same as then. Rayos, we can see that all around us, every day! — His compeers clamor and fife, percussing his lumbar spine.

The aims of the Taíno scribes remain inscrutable to us. But as fellow-Westerners, we can duly inquire: why did the Spanish encourage them? Did the monks feel pangs of guilt about the Indians' fate? — Cavalierly disregarding the vox turbae, Percival Archibald has intervened; a fustian Oxonian from Collegium Orielense, as I espy on the colloquy roster, he has donned (pun intended) a triplicate keratin habiliment, notwithstanding the incalescence here. — In secular terms, this illustrative project derives from the antiquarian zeal of the Early Modern period, erroneously designated as the 'Renaissance,' and its distorting misappropriation of cultural paraphernalia from Ancient Greece and Rome. Hence the reprise, in portraying the Taíno gods, of classical motifs from the Greco-Roman pantheon. Nevertheless, in this particular exemplum, the archaizing tendency ministers to a contrary telos: instead of a renascence, it contemplates an entombment. Nota bene that the adjective 'Antiguos' in the title, when applied to a still-existing civilization, betrays the clerics' genocidal design.

A Belgian lecturer from the Universitas Lovaniensis is determined to intercede; distending her emaciated extremities, she resembles a pterodactyl poised for aviation. — I agree with both the previous speakers. This weighty codex, meant by the priests as a final quietus, wasn't the Indians' last gasp; but it *was* their last laugh. Like any memorial, it aims to commemorate the dead, yet it achieves just the opposite: resuscitation. Whatever impulse may have moved them, here the Christians have become the heathens' evangelists. Ironically, they have bequeathed to us a gospel of Taíno beliefs.

Escolástico will not grant the final vocable to this exogenous horde. — Qué va! Get real! Hard as you gringos try, you can't get rid of us. The Taíno Canubans are here to stay, and you'd better take us as you find us. Or else, go screw yourselves. Que se jodan.

He and his apostles launch an obstreperous parley among themselves, and soon the academics descend into an analogous fracas. — Were all the Dominican friars anti-indigenous? — What about Las Casas and Montesinos? — Should we blithely assume the Benedictines were furtive humanists? — What of Santiago Columbus, the Admiral's nepotistic heir? — How can we lend credence to his rivals' slanders? — Why should he be exempt from the fashions in Europe? — Even in the Vatican, wasn't a worldly relativism taking root? — Must we concord with the anti-Catholic propaganda of the Reform?

Congenial Chiara, we have immersed ourselves in a pseudo-intellectual burlesque, scarcely able to dissemble our hilarity. Each Pulcinella has outdone the next, posing as the supreme authority on the *Relaciones Verdaderas*. Every inane buffoon has fashioned a fictive codex sui generis, to justify some ingrained prejudice or lopsided Weltanschauung. The Rector endeavors in vain to summon the conference back to order; it has collapsed into a flagrant 'areíto,' ignited by the captious opiate of self-aggrandizement.

In the postmeridian, from the redoubt of his Presidential Palace, Espinosa proclaims the 'colloquium on the *Spanish* codex'—as he is prone to emphasize—

an unqualified success. In the *Clarín Canubano*, Puerto Indio's fawning quotidian, a pundit rejoices: 'the foreign conquistadores made for their beachhead once again; only this time, the Taíno clobbered them.' As to the locutors' disquisitions, triturated through their buccal cavities in the ensuing hebdomad, they serve as holographic pedestals for their egos, above all. Seconded by legions of inexistent supporters, each of them performs a strident anthem of one.

Chiara, I gotta agree with Escolástico: they shoulda paid attention to his name. He knows a lot more about the Indians than these stuck-up creeps, a pack of comparones showing off. Sabe mucho más! Remember how you and me were livin the Taíno life in El Silencio, our cave on the cliff? Or how we watched the whales swim by, in the sea down below? Or how about our cabin on the beach, and riding our horse under the moon? Rayos! Damn it! You're still holding me while we gallop, but now the wind blowing us forward never ends.

Palacio Frederica, March 1994

Upon the vespers of the electoral contention of 1994, the fluency of electrical vigor in our metropolis precipitates to a nadir. With drollery of a lugubrious variety—in more ways than one—Canubans invent the appellation 'alumbrones' (id est, 'light-ons'), since these have emerged as more of a rara avis than 'blackouts.' The formidable 'nuestra Milady' benefits from Espinosa's hubris: the polls prophesy a decisive victory for her Transformation Party. The Armageddon will transpire in the midst of May, my liege-lady Chiara, whilst you are camel-humping through Saharan oases on an investigative voyage.

At the end of March, Frederica extends an invitation to partake of Camellia sinensis at her Colonial seat, either Silverpoint Earl Grey or Vadham Himalayan Green. Besides Milady, you and your groveling lackey are the only other celebrants apart from Catulo, despite his declining salubriousness. All members of our gens Miranda are semper fidelis adherents of the candidate, unlike our capricious hostess. To us it is evident that she is positioning herself to ululate the dernier cri: her occult contributions to the Party might conceivably produce societal dividends. A teahouse confabulation with Mateo now might engender future banquets with premiers, autocrats, and royals during the forthcoming mandate. Carolina and the snobbish arrière-garde would obtain their come-uppance once and for all.

Frederica has yet to osmose that Canuban self-styled aristoi abhor governmental cénacles, except when they foster their financial eudemonia. In that event, the Ministers of Commerce, Industry, or Agriculture might warrant a flaccid tendering of the blueblood palm. Still, grosso modo, the crème de la crème casts aspersions on Espinosa and his nouveaux-riches cronies—with the exception of Ángel María, who maintains a morganatic link with the Peralta and Del Río consanguinities. Frederica envisages herself chastising global statesmen at Milady's receptions, just as she habitually does at Manfredo's functions. Ulteriorly, needless to say, she duplicates her divertissement by deriding the pooh-bahs to her 'petit comité,' aggregated in one of her 'lesser drawing rooms,' whether the 'yellow boudoir' or the 'little magenta salon.' She feels superior to those who do not feast with Quayle or Mitterand at the Presidential Palace—but even more so, to those who do.

This afternoon, in the innermost courtyard, the latest phalanx of maladroit ephebes in carmine coats and impeccable gloves cascades Camellia into our porcelain coupes, accompanied by macaroons, petits fours, and marzipan coronets—a salute to her late spouse, the Graf von Gesischtseck. Goaded by anxiety, Milady launches into a cerulean streak of loquacity—unmitigated by the aquae vitae which sedate her symposia chez elle. She revisits the cliometric saga of the Antilles, pendulating the archipelago from a unitary tenterhook: dialectical materialism. External potencies—Hispania, Britannia, Gallia, Hollandia, Dania, and, postrema autem non minima, America Septentrionalis—have violated our virginal Elysium, she repines, with no concern for the inhabitants' felicity.

'Germa-niacally' exercised, Frederica chafes to opine. — Ja nun! Come now! What about the Soviet Union, up till several years ago? Haven't the Russians interfered?

To you, my equipoised Chiara, as to us Mirandas, this is yet another eidolon of her fluctuant geopolitics. Careening rechts, links, right, left, she regurgitates tidbits from *Der Spiegel* and *The Daily Mail*, an Eintopf stew cum shepherd's pie.

Milady remains immovable. — *They've* never colonized the Caribbean.

But if Puerto Rico is a colony, wasn't Cuba one, too?

It's been the only independent country in the region. That's why the Russians supported Castro.

Immerhin, all the same, isn't the U. S. 'supporting' Puerto Rico?

Puerto Rico is a fiefdom. Serfdom has never helped the serfs. — The politician's timbre waxes surlier.

Alas, perhaps Frederica's temerity is endangering her future imperial repasts. In the realm of glacial glissades, she delivers what might be termed a triple axel. — Well, I've always been a communist at heart. Jawohl! Indeed! Castro has done stupendous things for his people, I understand. I hear the schools and hospitals are superb! Ausgezeichnet!

My sibling Catulo has just traversed a contentious episode with his hostelry magnates, so on this occasion he also inclines towards a Leninist stance. — That's the kind of change we need around here.

I decongest my larynx with an ahem. — But not fully-fledged communism, I daresay. We cannot all afford to be as 'revolutionary' as the Countess. — I do not wish Frederica to conduct a full about-face, and withhold her emoluments to the party. In the previous campaign, Milady misfired by proclaiming herself a 'Marxist' in a media interview. For her, as she hastened to elucidate, this signifies 'a school of historical analysis, not a system of governance.' Even so, in the light of the recent upheavals in Oriental Europe, she seemed out of synchrony with the Zeitgeist.

Catulo retrocedes obligingly. — Milady doesn't endorse a Stalinist regime, Frederica. Just a tuppence or two of charity for the masses.

As the conversation meanders through paludic oxbows, 'nuestra Milady' does not appear intent on holding sway over the patria, after all. Pace her overweening dominance in the surveys, she never refers to the imminent joust, as if the spectre of victory demoralized her to the medulla. Since the Transformation Party's signature hue is immaculate white, Milady's affiches propose her orbicular, jet-black visage above the legend VOTA BLANCO—videlicet VOTE WHITE. Still, only extra-insular observers register this as an anomaly.

On the eve of your departure from Puerto Indio, venerated Chiara, you decry the tapestry of adhesive placards touting the candidates from every facade.

More deleterious, you aver, is the diluvium of emulsions which engulfs not only constructions, but also the majestic ceiba-trees and columnar royal palms. The piebald chromatism betokens our proliferating polity of aggrupations, gargantuan or miniature: caucuses denoted by crimson, alabaster, cantaloupe, amaranthine, azure, xanthous, verdigris/mauve, or veridian/peach. This miscellany corroborates an ignoble statistic: over a moiety of the electorate is illiterate, owing to Espinosa's hostility to instruction. He presumes that hollow occiputs are more facile to manipulate; and blue, the tincture of his conglomerate, inundates the metropolis like the eponymous berry-elixir.

One oversize graffito, on a colossal expanse of cement, subjugates your oculus, my radiant dea. A Milady partisan has exulted in niveous capitals that his heroine NI MATÓ NI ROBÓ, id est SHE NEITHER KILLED NOR STOLE, thus contrasting her integrity with the autocrat's lethal covetousness. Yet one of Espinosa's shills has jocosely advened, appending in cerulean runes: NI GOBERNÓ— NOR GOVERNED. Manfredo's surrogates perpetually prevaricate that Mateo's ascendancy would sow discord, or even civil bellicosity, because of her 'inexperience.' Does Milady apprehend such a consequence herself? In petto, she is a democratic centrist, I can vouchsafe. Notwithstanding, the totalitarians demonize her as an 'untried radical'; and if she triumphs, the generals may conspire to depose her—

or even expunge her from the biosphere.

From arcane locales, you communicate via the tele-contraption, tracking the quid-pro-quos of the contest. After the tally at the midpoint of April, when you return, an acrimonious dispute erupts, and the re-computations ensue throughout the estival months. Dura lex, sed lex unto himself, Espinosa prevails once again, and the international media vociferate as usual, denouncing his vile chicanery. Milady is also pilloried for submitting to a fraudulent votation—out of pusillanimity, or worse, for an offshore recompense. Despite Manfredo's press apparatchiks, who exhort their ovine coreligionists to select the Progress Party, a few Canuban commentators evince a minimum of dorsal vertebrae. Here or there, they cautiously cite a critique from *Le Monde*, *La Repubblica*, or *The New York Times*, inveighing indirectly against the despot's cyclical deceit.

Cognizant of Mateo's Spartan subsistence, we cannot accredit the allegations of her malfeasance. As for the ballot machinations, antithetically, all citizens are unanimous: even Espinosa's own supporters gasconade that he has 'corralled' the democratic farce. Alack, most Canubans disparage honesty as obtuseness; in the insular parlance, 'intelligent' connotes 'cleverly unscrupulous,' a much-admired trait. When you regress to our isle for the auroras of spring, aviating from Cythera on a vast metallic dove, the graffito still looms on the concrete wall—to

which of late, a definitive dyad has been affixed: NI MATÓ
NI ROBÓ NI GOBERNÓ NI GANÓ. Or to anglicize the
devastating screed: SHE NEITHER KILLED NOR STOLE
NOR GOVERNED NOR WON.

*Yeah, Chiara, I keep telling you, all these rotten politicians
are an effing waste of time. Una pérdida de tiempo. Thank
God those dickhead crooks don't bother us out here! They're
in the other place, I guess.*

Palacio Frederica and Palacio Carolina, 1994

In all modesty, in this Anno Domini 1994, I have
demonstrated my proverbial foresight. For Countess
Frederica, incensed at Carolina's cultural tertulia, any
supercession by her arch-rival is an affront she durst not
countenance. — Himmel nochmal! For heaven's sake!
She stole the whole koncept from me! — Forthwith, she
elaborates a strategem to revive her erstwhile salon, and
she presses you to assist her, my woebegone Minerva.
And yet for a major conference, her mansion is itself an
obstruction, as she concedes. — It's truly Colonial, not a
gutted scheusal like that monstrosity of hers!

The intricate maze of the Viennese Gräfin's abode
cannot host lectures for hundreds of disciples, alighting on

plicatable cathedrae. Ergo she resorts to her 'great drawing room' again—the most commodious of the three—for an 'elite seminar,' not unlike the ones she sponsored of yore. One evening, in her innermost peristyle, she accosts you over a chalice of Château d'Yquem. — I'll pay you a princely sum to give us some chats on Shakespeare's sonnets! Geht das? What do you say?

You once acclaimed the legendary cycle in an unguarded rhapsody, which now redounds upon your peerless physiognomy. Dextrously, you contrive to elude the Countess. — Impossible, Frederica. We'd have to study the poems in the original—and who reads Elizabethan English in Puerto Indio? — Gratifyingly, the Gräfin appears to desist.

But you underestimate Frederica's resourcefulness— and Canuba's eccentricity. She excavates every self-styled Shakespearean in the capital: a dozen acolytes, desirous of parsing each u and v in Q. Some of these, as you relate, you have heretofore perceived, malingering in the margins of Carolina's tertulia. Others issue forth from their bookshelves, like moles smoked out of their subterranean gloom. All aspire to stimulating debates, of a distressingly biographical vein. Did the Bard travel to Spain as well as Italy? Was he actually Edward de Vere? Was the Earl of Southampton his Mr. W. H.?

You labor mightily for your excessive rewards by squelching their altercations, with a Magna Graecian variant of Albion's sang-froid. In one of the early colloquies, everyone protests when Frederica affirms that number 18 ('Shall I compare thee...') is 'clearly addressed to a cat.' You are obliged to admonish her in your next tête-à-tête that such deviations threaten to undermine her nouveau salon, just as they did its previous edition. The Countess sublimates her impulses through cuisine, cosseting her protégés with delectable canapés and estate-bottled crus.

Once the Swan's amatory triangle disbands—much to your relief—Frederica formulates a grander scheme to topple Carolina from her Muse's throne. Since the belles-lettres are 'too tedious,' as she archly intimates, she trains her opera glasses on melodious Euterpe. Whereupon she catapults towards my jugular, subduing your musical servant to her imperious sway.

For many an annus I have languished in the Canuban morass, conducting my Monteverdi Chamber Ensemble in colegio basketball-courts or at Carolina's sporadic fetes—though my prowess is acknowledged by various invitations abroad. Frederica dynamizes my endeavors with her Fundación Pro Musica. Though it labors under the late Count's clangorous moniker—Graf Gustav Franz-Josef Maximilian von Knoblauch zu Gesichtseck—it is promptly dubbed the 'Countess Fund' by our insular cognoscenti. She engages yours truly as its Executive Director, much to my vindication.

Ab ovo, I originated my ensemble because the Sinfonía

Nacional lacks even the most elemental desiderata. The regime distributes pittances to a congeries of amateurish minstrels, who rarely convene for rehearsals. For their sustenance, they rely on familial subventions, or funerary and nuptial honoraria. Herewith, at long last, they seem to detect a tumescing alba of prosperity.

In 1994, Frederica maneuvers some bureaucratic warps and woofs, and the Symphony is peremptorily annulled. From its detritus, the Foundation erects a consanguineous NGO, the Puerto Indio Orchestra. The Ministerio de Cultura subsidizes it in part, and the Countess Fund provides the remainder.

For pitch-deficient Frederica, these cabals are merely avenues to societal predominance. In the eighties and early nineties, only a paucity of anesthetized patrons attended the Symphony's performances—mostly out of compassion for their acquaintances and relatives, 'strumming and tooting' on the proscenium, as one spectator snidely chaffed. But under the Foundation's stewardship, the Orchestra attracts the superficial 'who's who' as well as the bona fide Euterpeans. The upper echelon gathers every Thursday at the Espinosa Theatre, in order to 'see and be seen' in their Armani suits and Dior confections—not omitting Canuban inroads into 'designer gowns.' They also donate lavishly to the Countess Fund—and so, ab ovo ad mala, everyone benefits from the Gräfin's apotheosis.

To your amusement, my sempiternal goddess, I blossom

unapologetically into an Antillean Machiavelli. In addition to my intrigues with the Countess, I also cultivate Carolina, resorting to a cozy arbor in her hortus several times each hebdomad. My vinculation to Frederica has discredited me with the cavaliers of the Ancien Régime, and only the Del Río sanction can redeem my reputation. I necessitate their succor to defenestrate the Chief Conductor of the Orchestra, Blenheim Calderón. The Symphony's trustees have consented to dismantle it with one provision: that the Maestro retain his title in the novitiate Orchestra. Woe is me, they still conserve a majority on the incipient entity's board of trustees. Even Frederica must abide by their decisions; her Foundation can only cajole, not command.

Carolina wields a different arsenal, since Don Blenheim's 'old boys' are her spouse Adalberto's kith and kin—remounting to their collegial jeunesse dorée. Meritocracy—as clairvoyant as Justice is blind—averts her optical orbs in consternation: Calderón only ascends to the trouser-cuff of a von Karajan. His detractors deem him unimaginative and rodent-like, with his inextant cilia, arachnid digits, pinkish pinnae, and acuminate proboscis. They inculpate him for the decadence of the Symphony, and predict he will debilitate the Orchestra in turn. The Assistant Conductor, your own devoted Horacio, should unequivocally supplant him: conveniently, they add, Miranda's hypochondria has abated. Such are the arguments of my ambassadors-at-large.

As you have divined, my telepathic siren, I am rotating around my quarry with perseverance. A shipwrecked captain, Don Blenheim denotes a predatory Carcharodon beneath his perforated life-boat; yet he is pathetically, irrevocably adrift. To accumulate insult atop injury, I conduct every other concert in my titular capacity as his Assistant, ravaging with well-tempered dentures the Emperor's transparent robes—to laminate my metaphors. I exact the uttermost nanoliter of competence from the performers, illuming Bruckner, Mahler, and Brahms in the virtually standstill tempi of Otto Klemperer, my paramount mentor.

Don Adalberto, normally so aloof, chides Carolina for expending too much lucre and chronometry on 'those scheming Mirandas.' He categorizes Catulo and me—quite justifiably—as 'artistic opportunists.' Undeniably, Her Highness Carolina, the guardian of tradition, habitually served as the principal donatrix to my quixotic sibling's masquerades. During each invernal season, she ostentatiously agitated her ossature in the terpsichorean spectacles he concocted. Her most eminent role, as the Queen of the Night, consisted of flailing her antebrachia from a stationary pose.

In his floruit, by inserting sybaritic dilettantes in the minor parts, Catulo more than defrayed his expenses: id est, he profited mightily, to boot. Deplorably, Carolina was by far the most nubile of his ballerinas. Accordingly, he choreographed promenades for his grandes dames that behooved their proto-senile anni: sarabandes for diabetic pachyderms, and nigh-immobile minuets for osteoporotic simians. En masse, they proceeded around the dais as the dowager maenads in his *Bacchae*, the geriatric ingenues in his *Appalachian Spring*, or the late-autumnal postulants in his *Devils of Loudun*.

His couturier, a certain Pipo, draped the divas' concavities of thorax, or convexities of abdomen, in flattering peignoirs. He thereby induced them to frequent his personal emporium for 'a special price'—videlicet, uniquely astronomical. One annus, when you interrogated my frater over a flute of Dom Perignan, the adage 'in vino veritas' attested its efficacity.

So, Catulo, how many rich old biddies have signed up for *Swan Lake*?

The whole gerontocracy, girlfriend!

He often purloined that bon mot from me; yet my original is better, I daresay: 'the gynecological gerontocracy.' The irate reject was Frederica: even a circus-canopy could not dissimulate her anti-metronomic amorphousness. 'No, I've OD-ed on hippopotami: hey, hon, *Elektra* isn't *Fantasia*,' my frater dispatched her ungraciously—though he exalted Rubenesque curvatures in the libidinous sphere, exempli gratia his mistress Pomona. The Gräfin hardly occluded her asperity when she parodied the other socialites as 'a herd of amateur cows'—a disquieting concept 'an sich'—

and 'aus prinzip,' she disdained to attend their 'dummkopf-ballette.'

To Don Adalberto's solace, Carolina mortified him in Catulo's pantomimes but once per annum. However, in memoriam to him, my own determination is never to relent, to institute as it were a psychic perpetuum mobile. My perished sibling dismayed her with his lecherous colloquiality, while I have inured her to my Latinate grandiloquence, a Miltonic legacy of our sire, the quondam envoy of Espinosa—though thenceforth, nevermore. She abets my every gambit on the chessboard of intrigue, even condescending to collaborate with 'that presumptuous climber'—as she caustically describes her—Frederica von Gesichtseck.

As a preliminary tactic, I reinforce the orchestra's ranks with importations from Oriental Europe. Invigorated by a transfusion of Del Río largess, the Countess Fund entices them to our island with irresistible stipends; and after recurring catastrophes in their ever-more-balkanized Balkans, they throng to Puerto Indio on their own initiative. The males, unwedded and semi-juvenile, afford prime filet-mignons for Lamia, the sanguivorous demon of Keats. As in her apogee with her transmigrant string-quartet, or so she avows to you, she can now 'Cheetah and Jane for a whole jungle of Slavic Tarzans!'

In my successive contractual campaign, I enlist supplemental charcuteries for our infra- and extra-musical menu. On this occasion, I reconnoiter nearby Cuba: factoring in the lesser transportation fees and more grievous malnutrition rates, I optimize the yield per monetary unit. Not coincidentally, I purvey protuberant morcillas to Cheetah-Jane and—only visually, I assure you, my Pallas Athena—to myself. Though a voyeur, I am a certified herbivore.

A few lunar cycles further on, subjugated and resigned, Don Blenheim capitulates to a post as Second Associate Director in Medellín. Within the hebdomad, I inherit his mantle as Chief Conductor of the Puerto Indio Orchestra. Imposing coronations are offered in my honor, by Frederica and by Carolina: most astoundingly, they accept each other's invitations—a coup without historic precedent. Only my Realpolitik could have reconciled these leonine opponents.

Regrettably, Don Adalberto must decline his better half's fete, owing to a 'very pressing engagement': the pressures of an equine uterus, to be precise. Despite a stable of excellent grooms, he feels obliged to supervise a foaling at his estate in Quiquiricoba. Sub rosa, he alerts his confidants that he is reeling from an attack of 'severe Miranda-itis.'

I'll never figure out how you put up with these friggin' rich bitches, Chiara. Que pendejas! I only met them once, on our whale-watchin' trip—but once was more than enough for me!

Lamia's imprecations about her colleagues do not pervade the entire auditorium, as they resonate for only a row or two, much like a malkin's meeker meows. Yet radiated by the oenological lianas of garrulity, they procure the violoncellist unnumbered antagonists. By Anno Domini 1993, she is banished from recitals in private domiciles like Carolina Del Río's. Ergo I am heartened, my idolized Chiara, that you hie to these without the feline serpent—however indentured to the griffin you may be, at least for the nonce.

You command a deep-rooted connection to the hostess not only through me, but also through her distinguished son-in-law, Ángel María, the amicus summa cum laude of the Trinitas Mirandae. To our adelphic gratification, you levitate to her roster of invitees sine qua non. Immemorially, for her periodic soirees, Carolina has lured the most sidereal soloists who navigate through the Spanish Main on their patrons' opulent yachts, from Rostropovich to Barenboim. They have always favored us with a pièce de résistance or two from their extensive repertoires. By definition, such stellar 'Hausmusik' can only resound intermittently; and over the anni, Euterpe has been demoted to an ancillary seat. She has been preempted by Clio, Erato, and Urania, who preside over lyric, scholastic—or more often, pseudo-lyric and pseudo-scholastic—disquisitions. Already in the mid-eighties, Carolina has resolutely founded her 'tertulia'—a species of domestic atheneum, endemic to communities throughout the Hispanic orb.

Over the decades, Frederica has likewise acquitted herself as an 'animatrice' of Apollonian rites. To her horripilation, her adversary in the geminate palacio on Plaza Catedral has increasingly usurped her dominion. On the Monday of each hebdomad, Carolina attracts a recurring menagerie of devotees. More articulated than a diffuse salon, the tertulia conforms to an agenda: salutory though not salutary libations, with unctuous hors d'oeuvres; a centerpiece lecture, succeeded by an omnibus debate; and a concluding buffet, irrigated by vinous excess. Despite her discomfiture, Frederica presses ahead with her less ordinated revelments, and a pattern seems to pertain. If arrivistes and random voyagers flock to Frederica's, the old guard congregates at Carolina's. Notwithstanding, the latter incorporates all those who would improve themselves, especially unfledged aspirants from the nether side of the tracks: inescapably, noblesse oblige.

No matter what the intellectual or culinary fare of the festivities, my indispensable Chiara, you and I savor the impeccable carriage of our Del Río toastmistress. Modishly malnourished, strawberry-auricomous, and flexible as a willow, she circulates among her visitants— faux-unpretentiously. Each vesper she is arrayed in one of her exorbitant, superannuated kimonos, transported from Nippon at her behest; with her russet coiffe and achromic complexion, she resembles an Occidental geisha. At intervals, she even amasses her luxuriant mane in Tokugawa style, the louvered tiers tintinnabulating with antique kanzashi pins.

Her charismatic allure, like Frederica's, emanates in part from a splendiferous décor. When she acquired the ruinous manse on Plaza Catedral, some decennia hence, she undertook an exhaustive reconstruction: she denuded the edifice to its Cinquecento core, intent on restoring it to echt Colonial style. Yet after a sojourn in Kyoto, her Zen epoch commenced, and she supplanted archaic mimesis with the generative void. 'Less is more,' Carolina quoted Mies, commingling cultures higgledy-piggledy. Within the Renascence shell, she installed decumbent chambers for familial use—to her spouse's arthritic agony—carpeted with tatami mats and partitioned by cellulose integuments. Most of the outer vestiges she left unroofed, tripling the courtyard's dimensions; zealously, she overspread it with undulant sand and meditative rocks.

Whereupon, after arriving at a moot nirvana, she lurched towards the Belle Époque. Ryo-anji succumbed to a rotund pavilion, ensconced in a quadrangle of meticulous lawn. Beneath a cupola of polychromatic glass, supported by porphyry columns, the tertulia's current adepts survey espaliered citrus-trees, trellises of bougainvillea, and museal walls of Colonial masonry. Nocturnally, the enclave shimmers, a temple of the Hesperides; here Puvis de Chavannes would revel in his element.

Although she still retains her obis and kanzashis, Carolina has relinquished zazen to toil as a plenipotentiary Muse. She governs her habitués through a nominal committee, titularly chaired by the Patria's Poetisa Laureata, Leonora Ruiz. Doña Leonora is well into her dotage, and her concentration tends to falter. To obviate faux-pas, Carolina introduces the sessions herself, recording them for posterity on a mammoth grabadora. If need be, she whets the lecturers' appetites with generous honoraria, in addition to the aforesaid comestibles. For an ongoing fee, your humble servant appoints the erstwhile docents, though I am often prevailed upon to dissertate myself.

Inevitably, I cleave to musicology, while otherwise the topics oscillate capriciously, from quantum astrophysics to Joseon calligraphy. Despite my assiduous efforts, the acumen of the offerings does not always suffice. It scarcely ameliorates the situation that Doña Leonora primes the quid pro quo at the conclusion of each presentation, since her ex-abruptos often have no relevance to the purported theme. After an excursus on computers by an informatician from the Universitas Complutense, she sagaciously uplifts her caput. — Did you know that some Pygmies are white? Well, what does *that* say about your binary scheme?

The middle-brow public also contributes to the melee. After an exposition on black holes by a Berkeley cosmologist, a harridan yclept Clemencia extends one of her pincers, chinkling with argentate bracelets. — Aren't those the ones in the ozone layer? Why don't you know-it-alls plug them up?

Carolina's monogynist, Adalberto Peralta, evades these colloquies like the bubonic plague. His lineage harks back to the Colonial era, though the fortunes of his gens have dolefully diminished. Well into his seventh decade, he vaunts himself as a mens sana in corpore sano, most felicitous when adjudicating athletic jousts, such as jujitsu, pugilism, or tai kwon do. With farthings from Carolina's cavernous vaults, he sponsors a nexus of recreational foci to 'keep teenagers off the streets.' His alternate mantra is hippic: his equestrian estate in the cordillera furnishes polo-contestants throughout the hemisphere with their pedigreed steeds.

Now and again, he exerts himself to analyze a subset of his spouse's convoluted imperium, which encompasses the gamut from bovine processing plants to circuit-board factories, and from Sri Lankan hedge funds to Indonesian investment banks. But after a desultory bout of speleology, he abandons the Nibelungen hoard to her advisors, accountants, gnomes, and astrologers.

Lamia resents the Nipponic hegemon of Hochkultur for excluding her from the acclaimed tertulia, a sometime hunting reserve for the ravenous nymphomaniac. However, she eventually 'fixes Carolina's wagon,' as she

recounts to you one eventide on your rooftop heights. —
Adalberto invited me to his stables the other day, and I got
back at that stuck-up cunt. We did it up against a horse!
Hey, he's still pretty gooey for his age. He told me how he
really hates that brainy baloney. A buncha pointy-heads,
jabbering all night. It's right up your alley, Chiara.

Lamia's contempt does not preclude her from avidly
ingesting the latest intelligence about the 'shrine of
knowledge,' as Carolina styles it. The half-Hellenic
violoncellist fairly salivates over Doña Clemencia's
gaffes. — That old bag! Her name should be Demencia.
She's always drumming up support for cock-eyed causes.
One time it was the mail. She thinks there's a worldwide
conspiracy to keep Canuba off the map. Half the letters
here never get delivered. But what the hell, it's just because
of theft or laziness. The postmen either steal them or throw
them away. Syphilis has rotted that woman's brain, what
little bit she had!

The proximate occasion you grace me with your
presence, transcendental Chiara, you request the veritas
on Doña Clemencia.

Venereal disease, Principessa? Of the corpus, no—but
of the nous, unequivocally! Quod est demonstrandum. In
this instance, Lamia has extracted a grain of verity. Clemencia appears Ultramontane; notwithstanding, you cannot
judicate an incunabulum by its metallic clasps, or armlets.
Through titular error, convent bibliotecas often order Jean

Genet's *Notre Dame des Fleurs*—a sodomistic delirium which may be edifying for certain novices, though not in the manner intended by their Mater Superioris. Perhaps you are not privy to this phenomenon, you are such an anchorite from women's covens, yet I am informed that feminae wax scurrilous when no males are auscultating nearby. Many anni heretofore, Frederica's orchid society engaged in a pilgrimage to Esmeralda, and Clemencia regaled them with salacious anecdotes throughout the odyssey. Initially, they tut-tutted disapprovingly; but after a while, they fell prey to seizures of hilarity, cavorting in the central aisle of the motorcoach.

Hmm, now that you've brought her up, Horacio… I wonder why the Countess never shows her face at the tertulia. She wants to be an 'Intellektuelle,' or so she claims. Then why doesn't she bury the hatchet with Carolina?

Oh no, my ingenuous damsel! Those arbiters of fashion would never coincide in the same chamber—I beg your pardon, in the same temple—even in a state of rigor mortis. Moreover, Frederica has nothing to assimilate from Bologna, Sorbonne, Oxbridge, or Harvale pedagogues. In her own estimation, since her ovarian conception she has always been a towering genius. With the exception of Ángel María's cetacean presentations, which she attended in the eighties, such successive parleys do not qualify for the notice of an Olympian like herself, unsurpassed by any 'dummkopf laureate of a Nobel.' Traumatically for all concerned, she once domineered over her own salon, tanti anni fa; but that domiciliary academy was far more select than the symposium of her arch-enemy.

What, Horacio? Frederica hasn't mentioned that to me.

Oh, she would be compunctious to do so before your rigorous personage. The experiment ended in an inglorious rout.

Why? Too ambitious?

You divine correctly. No bas bleu ever inflated her leotards to such a laceration point, I conjecture. The coup de grâce occurred when she perused some fatuous article about 'po-mo philosophers' in *Vanity Fair*. The subsequent hebdomad, in a trice she was importing 'the world's greatest thinkers,' principally from Deutschland and La France. The 'welt-denker-seminar,' she christened it, in her decapitated German, which I sometimes like to imitate: the 'world thinker seminar.' My fratres and I extolled her jocosely as 'Madame de Staël,' the Gallo-Teutonic hostess of the Romantic era. But with all her habitual preoccupations—her manorial paideia for subservient ephebes, her perpetual receptions and dinners, pace her planetary lupanars for far-flung meretrices—the space-time continuum did not permit her digestion of her guests' ponderous tomes.

Ahahaha. Just a lame excuse. She couldn't make heads or tails of them, I'm sure. At least Carolina knows her limits, and tries to learn something from her lecturers. As do I.

Indubitably, my divine interlocutrix. Frederica accosted her unfortunate disquisitors with nonsensical comments and inquiries until they took wing from the insula on pennae of aluminium. Air France, Air Afrique—or as they humorize in Occidental Africa: 'Air Chance, Air Panique'— no matter how, they were Hades-bent to flee. One 'denker' captured a corresponding aeroplane in Guinea-Conakry via Mozambique. Whatever the extravagance of the emoluments, the tortured lecturers assayed anything to decamp from her pseudo-cerebral donjon.

You cachinnate. — Couldn't you Miranda boys muzzle her for an hour or two?

We durst not, my Principessa. In addition, we were beset by spasms of jocularity, rejoicing in a secular Gaudete and Laetare! It is not a quotidian occurrence to auscultate a preeminent sophist like Michel Serres dejectedly expound the rudiments: 'voici la définition d'un syllogisme, Madame'; or an exegete of Heidegger like Jürgen Habermas indignantly contest: 'Aber Gräfin, Schopenhauer war KEIN Existentialist!'

Huh? No translations for the locals?

Negative, Principessa—though Frederica's own French is fragmentary at best, mostly confined to the names of sauces. For Catulo and me, the sessions refreshed the Gallic and Teutonic turns of phrase we had imbibed during our pater's postings as a diplomat, particularly in Wallonia and Styria. In fact, the only other participants were perplexed, dutiful attachés from the European embassies. What a contrast! Carolina is so aristocratic that she is all-inclusive, while Frederica is so nouvelle-riche, that she is all-exclusive. The impecunious Graf she inveigled into wedding her only exacerbated her insanity: his nobiliary moniker has rotated her caput, once and for all.

That's odd, Horacio. I thought you admired the Countess.

Oh, immensely to the affirmative, my goddess, coequally with both my siblings—yet admittedly, chiefly as a solipsistic curiosity. To descend to the vernacular, you cannot confuse mangoes with coconuts. Frederica is an aesthete—or so she auto-defines herself. Pulchritude entrances her, and that is what she manifests—palatially at least—in her place-settings and décors. Beneath a handsome anatomy, of Vitruvian man as it were, she does not wish to dissect the femurs and vesicles, as theoreticians do.

Yes, for her, 'beauty is truth': that's all she needs to know. Pretty hard for Quine, Dummet, or Kripke to stomach. But she'd make good material for Bion and Klein.

Irrefragably. When her 'Seminar' miscarried, I disrated her in our fraternal lingua franca: from Madame de Staël to Madame de Bargeton, the provincial salonarde of Balzac's *Illusions perdues*. As a reductio ad absurdum, Catulo even demoted her to E. F. Benson's Lucia, the risible regina of parochial Riseholme—though this, for me, verges on the inadmissible. Lucia is nonpareil. Still, I recommend the utmost caution to you, as an encyclopedic asteroid within her gravitational pull. Our chère Madame might attempt to sequester you for another edition of her lyceum—or if you accredit the tattlers, our dear 'madam.'

Hah, I always ribbed you about wasting time with those stuck-up eggheads. They don't know their ass from their face. They need to get back to the basics, cause they've all got a case of 'pornositis'—por no singar, I call it. If you don't have sex, you lose your fuckin marbles for sure.

Callejón del Platero, October 1991

I have no doubt that now and again, you must observe contusions or lacerations on Virgilio's nasolabial pads and metacarpi, the sole superficies of his anatomy that you can perceive—the remainder being coated by pilose efflorescences; or presumably, articles of raiment. Unenlightened Chiara, you may conclude that he collided with aciculate metal or acuminous wood—a liability of foraging for his handiworks—yet by the grace of your well-bred discretion, you have not ventured to inquire. Although he has blazoned forth many of his opera before your oculi, he has also imparted his gratitude that you never entreat him to exhibit them publicly. His consternated abbreviations about his artistic affairs must cause such queries to perish on your coraline labia. And you esteem your hebdomadal 'Mardi Gras' with him too prodigiously to hazard their discontinuance.

One crepuscule, you arrive prematurely for your rendezvous, and discover me at our domus in a solitary mode. Oping the portal, I salute you despondently, erupting in a tussiculation of extraordinary longitude. — Alas, my Sicilian Athena, these persistent ills will obliterate my fragile zoon from our azure orb.

I usher you upstairs to the sala, my capacious studiolo, and situate myself at the pianoforte, where I have been cerebrating a novel composition. To you, I proffer the lone upholstered cathedra. — Lackaday, sublime amichissima— to elocute in obsolete Tuscan—you have anticipated the appointed hour on the unique occasion when my frater foresees a postponement. Some inebriated reprobate from San Sebastián—yclept Heathcliffe, aurally butchered as 'Ee-clee'—telecommunicated ad hoc, with an adumbration about an icon of Virgilio's. A female infant chanced upon a fraction of it on the pedestrian pavement. She transported it to her domicile and executed a depiction on the obverse. Our insular Dürer projects the assemblage of a duplicate montage, so as to disclose both laterals.

Contrary to his fellow-Antilleans, my frater castigates

tardiness as much as Kant; intermittently culpable of that deficiency yourself, like most Magna Graecians, you have whimsically christened him 'the Prussian clock.' This eventide, his unprecedented delay serves you and me as a benediction, since it affords us an opportunity to converse. The more intimately you and my sibling have empathized, the less I have basked in your luminescence. Yes, I am conscious that I must fatigue your resilience; I palaver overmuch about my ailments, and the medicines that might alleviate their virulence. Yet now I intuit that you covet my invaluable counsel. Impromptu, you alight beside me on the bespoke Bösendorfer-bench.

To eschew a parlous temptation, I chastely retreat to the other extreme. — Why Chiara! Such propinquity! To what do I owe this signal honor?

Well, Horacio, it's been quite a while since we've talked… To tell the truth, I'm worried about Virgilio's isolation. At times I fear it'll drive him over the edge. Don't you think he should share his work with the public? I think his art would appeal to a broad range of viewers. Even halfwits would have to applaud his draftsmanship.

And the hydraulic engineers would value his gilded, water-cabinet frames, I cachinnate. However, all that is neither here nor there: we must be advocates of libera voluntas.

Morosely, you suspire. By free will, you mean there's nothing we can do. It's up to him to decide.

Amen. For him, Genesis portends far more than Epiphany. Yet Anangke is unpredictable: a supernova may still embellish his pictorial firmament; though that may shrink to a niveous dwarf.

What about his loneliness? Maybe he needs a partner in life.

To wit, my frater has prestidigitated again: like Prospero, he has baffled you with an obfuscating masquerade. Be that as it may, he does not desire to delude you, he is simply distracted by his imagistic lucubrations. — My oculi coruscate. — Most assuredly, he has never languished in solitude. Incontrovertibly, he is wedded... to me, your faithful lackey.

You nictate perplexedly. — I've seen it all in Puerto Indio, but this takes the cake.

Bravissima! From the perturbation on your countenance, I knight you a veritable Canubana. — I simper jovially. — We always assume the pessimal—or the optimal. Whatever seems most drastic, most outré. And each ennead of each decuple, we vindicate our instincts as veridical.

You and Virgilio? You don't really mean you've...

I maintain your anxious suspense. — Let us pause to contemplate the probabilities. Mirabile dictu, you might opine, in the light of his current decadence... and yet... as you have perceived from familial daguerreotypes, Virgilio was quite delectable in his nubile stage. Dual siblings arriving at puberty, with an adolescent Catulo as their hormonal cicerone… You might expect some mutual molestations in our cubicles—even a modicum of viscous accidents. But then again: perhaps this only transpired in our cerebra, as fleeting Freudian fantasies. Oneiric or actual, all such juxtapositions must forever reside in the past—by definition, a quasi-imaginary realm.

Well, live and let live. — You extend your digits heavenward, nonplussed. — I vaguely recall a few antics in the hay with my cousins...

From your perspective, I daresay, the reflections on my spectacles obnubilate my oculi. — Mutatis mutandi, deific Chiara, our casum displays more ample ramifications than that. After duodecimal anni of cohabitation in this abode, the ligament between Virgilio and me *has* evolved into a matrimony of sorts. Catulo is our picaresque farceur, a quondam paramour who descends on us every now and then, to 'adulterate' our homespun complacency.

Yes, it's true: Virgilio has the two of you.

And *you* as well, Pallas Athena. — I nivellate my restive, semi-Africanate coiffure, seemingly electrified by your vicinity. — Abstracting the erotic parameter, if in your amity it does not advene…

You entertain the prospect, but to my invidious satisfaction, you cannot encompass it. — Don't make me laugh, Horacio. In a pinch, Virgilio might make a king-size teddy-bear—if he spruced himself up. No, there's no attraction. Maybe that's why we're such good friends.

Either way, I bestow my benediction. — Hypocritically, I raise dual digits from my clustered palm. Then I serrate my labia. — Confessedly, I do not subscribe to monogamous 'couples,' whether libidinous or not. We must needs be unconstrained—like the Australian platypus or the Himalayan ounce.

Don't we long for stability, too? What about Catulo and Pomona?

Or you, my sovereign—and Lamia? Or in days of yore, you—and Amado? — I satirically oscillate my oculi. — I reiterate your petition: do not oblige me to cachinnate. We all have many ferrous candidates in the phlogiston. Here on the insula, hominid bipeds may do as they desire. They will never be rejected or ejected, because their commodious gens arbitrates their status. Exempli gratia, I advert to our master-mistress extraordinaire, Diphtheria…

You do not agitate a cilium; no Canuban moniker could astonish you henceforth. — Hmm. What's up with her?

Or him? I have only cited her nocturnal 'nom de guerre.' Diurnally, she deflates to elementary Juan. She is a flamboyant female impersonatrix—as remarkable as the legendary Divine. Gendarmes arrest her unstintingly, because she services them to barter her emancipation—an exchange both parties eulogize. Despite her notoriety, the shemale and her clan are adulated by the populace, because of their bounteous charities. Extra-insulars who tarry here for some duration become 'members of a gens' as well: as you, prima inter pares, should be cognizant.

Unheedingly, you read my notations on the staves before you, the initial bars of a sonata for violoncello and piano. You acquiesce by nodding your mentum. — Big as it is, this city still seems like a village.

Forsooth, nothing is recondite in this burgeoning metropolis. All things will be absolved—but all will be ventilated by the zephyrs, the vox populi. Alack, I cannot jubilate over a salubriousness similar to yours. Be that as it may, in my chamber ensemble I have a range of instrumentalists from whom to select. The specimen 'Soraya' is not unique.

As you are fully aware, my Italian Isis, she is a Puerto Rican violist I have courted, in a mild-mannered amourette. You challenge me. — Well, what about Soraya? She's attractive, and intelligent. Isn't she enough for you?

I deflect the supposition to your own person. — She seems to stimulate your interest, Chiara. You should invite her out on an amorous sortie. I can also recommend the virile bassoonist, Igor. — Of course, omniscient deity, you have perceived that my enamorment of the smoldering Czech is equally 'platonic,' in the vernacular sense. Notwithstanding, it corresponds to our fraternal trinity's innate ambivalence.

You gesticulate waggishly. — I'm beginning to think you Mirandas have a pact.

A pan-Canuban concordat, I warrant. When I would recrudesce here from distant continents on scholastic interims, I was oftentimes disconcerted. Gadzooks! Lucinda is having congress with José, and Josefina, too? Now I recognize such multivalence as insular-endemic. To reference Diphtheria redux, on a recent crepuscular foray I espied her on the oceanic boulevard, the Malecón, arrayed in all her onnagata finery. To my wonderment, she was osculating a biological, ultra-distaff femme fatale. I could only exclaim: 'Salve regina, in terra! You have always preferred epitomes of testosterone, the more potent the better. How now?' 'Oh, who cares?' quoth she. 'I've made the leap! Melinda and me are shacking up as lesbians.'

You lift your depressor angulis oris. — A rainbow can come full circle, I suppose.

Yclept a 'bishop's ring,' in the fitting lunar term. As Catulo often expostulates, here even the epicenes are ambidextrous, and so are the neanderthals. There may be a few exceptions at the polar ends of the parabola; but the median Canuban circles round and round, or demolishes any pattern whatsoever. We fratres concurred eons hence that we would always remain translucid, at least amongst ourselves. That is our 'pact,' if you will, yet it does not consuetudinally apply to others. Still, considering your sororitas with our trinitas, I attribute Virgilio's omission of a basic datum to negligence, rather than to intent. Ergo I propose to convey it to you myself: he does 'possess' a paramour; they copulate each hebdomad, post mediam noctem.

Noncommittally, you levitate your scapulae. — Male, female, or in-between?

Ah, ecce veritas: a Bodh Gaya climacteric. — I perambulate my digits along the clavier, tallying the entire diapason of tonalities. Whereupon, I cachinnate demulcently. — But where are the quartertones, the overtones, the undertones? You capture my polyvalent ponderation—though I suspect, my perspicacious deity, that it tumefies as well within your own fertile nous, by motu proprio. In this particular instance, Quilviria happens to be a certifiable she. The duo has been ceremonializing their inarticulated nuptials for a septet or octet of anni. Like any other celestial spouse, you are the ultimate to discern their chthonic epithalamium. Did the neo-Hellenic pythoness never inform you?

Humpf. Lamia only gossips about other musicians—except for Chuchu, her bête noire. Anyway, that's wonderful news: I'm delighted for Virgilio. But his social isolation still worries me.

Verily I say unto you, that is quite a different theodicy. In our triple personhood, why is he an introvert, whereas Catulo and I are extroverts? Is his exile from the polis a lacuna, within our triune unity? To cite another disputation: why is Catulo vigorous, whereas I am 'valetudinous,' despite those who libel me as valetudinarian? Does this compromise our Summum Bonum? — I collocate my phalanges on my thorax, for all the cosmos like Violetta in her pre-posthumous vigil—even as I register your dubitum of my imminent demise. — Pazienza, Principessa. Procrastinate for an annus, or geminal anni perchance. Festina lente: Virgilio will eventually underwrite an exhibition; I can sensate this in the myeloid tissue of my ossa. But you may duly encounter a distinct justification for your angst. He is so aspirationally conceptual, he cannot withstand the 'materiality' of his oeuvre. Observe how he mutilates each exemplum, 'defacing' its integrity.

Yes, it's almost like a self-amputation.

My buccal cavity is paralyzed. Your analogue tremulates my vertebrae, since it infers a baneful propensity that I also apprehend. After a pause, I recapture my composure, and palpitate my incipient score. — My Syracusan seraph, I often deploy a continuo that mimics a gamelan—xylophones combined with Tibetan bells. To me, it corresponds to our tropical rain, that blessed precipitation that coalesces all things, syncopating on zinc roofs and dendro-gables, on succulent folia and percolating karst. Into that susurrating fabric, I stitch my arabesques, contrapuntal melodies that ascend and descend, traverse and transpierce. Even if the strands disentangle, they interlace again, forever one. Beyond their vagaries and caprices, the harmony remains intact: this is the essence of our insula.

Let's hope Virgilio attains that harmony, too.

We auscultate his cumbrous, ursine tread at the bottom of the stairwell. When he shambles into the chamber, you are already erect. I am inclined over the pianoforte, composing as assiduously as before. Like a beatific angel, you extend your brachia in an affectionate salute.

Catulo used to tell me: all my brothers ever say is no, no, no; but all I ever say is yes, yes, yes. Si, si, si. And I'm like him, Chiara. For ten years I screwed you hundreds, maybe thousands of times. Cientas y miles. I'm not forgettin that, no matter if I'm on the other side. You'll find out when you cross the line, how what you remember is real. You can see it and touch it and smell it, even more than when you lived it day by day. But it's a picture, too, a movie and better than a porno, cause you're in it yourself. You rocket through the sky with a buncha people you never thought you'd meet, flying on giant wings. Como alas, but not really wings, that's just the rush you get and give. You're in them and outside them, and they're in you, in and out, but not just one or two. All our friggin bodies get mixed together, and all our feelings too, and none of us can ever have enough!

CATULO

1997-Undated

with

Amado

I've always wanted to attend my own funeral. Hey, Chiara, isn't this a gas? There you are in the front row, girlfriend, just as I expected, along with Frederica, Ángel María, Leandra, Carolina, Isabela, Elpiria, Luz Divina—and even Lamia. Amado's here with me, but you can't see us. I wasn't planning on a church service, much less a Cathedral gig. I never wanted a church wedding, either, though the veil might've been nice, especially in shocking pink instead of white. Or silver tails with a blue bowtie, if I decided to be the groom. I guess all the sable streamers this evening look la-di-da, even if they're too traditional. Horacio has always been a wet blanket. Virgilio would've probably sprayed the whole place fire-engine red, arches and all.

Now that would've made a huge inferno for the Archbishop, a preview of where he's going next. Or where he is, right there, perched on his fancy chair, thinking he's the center of attention. For kicks, Amado and I take turns sitting on his lap. Once you're dead you realize that whatever heaven or hell you've racked up, you're already in it on earth. The so-called afterlife is just a blown-up version of your Facebook account. I know I'm getting ahead of you earthlings, for 1997. Out here in the floating world, time and space get warped. I'm already doing dance routines on Instagram—and TikTok, too. With the body I've got, I might have to open an OnlyFans, by popular demand.

How can I talk about my buff physique, you ask? Well, girlfriend, we used to laugh about the pneumatic body, but I'm here to tell you it's no joke. We're not exactly material, but we're not invisible ghosts—unless we want to be. Sometimes we scare people who're alive, though that depends on our whims. We still look the way we used to when we reached our peak—say age twenty-three, or for some MILFS and DILFS, forty-five. We can change around at will, if we get tired of a certain style. Compare it to drag, and you'll get my drift. Out here, the name Divine takes on a new cachet, and she's our patron saint.

In my New York days, as soon as I launch the Florence F---ing Jenkins Operettes, I'm Turandot one night and Norma the next. Then at the end of the seventies, back in Canuba, I take a management job in the hotel biz. The straight way I dress is just a different kind of drag: that's how I see it. What makes me sad now, when I gaze down at the sorry world, is the conformity. Homos want to prove they're manly, so they stiffen their wrists and growl in bass voices, marry each other and bring up surrogate tykes. That's wonderful if that's the real you, but I don't see why we should all feel forced to act straight—or ultra-gay, for that matter. Seems like now you've got to be either Joe Palooka or Ru Paul; they won't let you mix and match.

I know you're itching to ask whether we can 'make love' out here. We don't have to make it: we *are* love. Remember how we studied English lit, and waded through Milton? You ate it up, even if he was a Protestant; his piety turned you on. You've always been a closet nun, and a whore to boot, Italian-style. But the only part I liked was when Raphael tells Adam how he and the other angels interpenetrate:

> Whatever pure thou in the body enjoy'st
> (And pure thou wert created) we enjoy
> In eminence, and obstacle find none
> Of membrane, joynt, or limb, exclusive barrs:
> Easier than Air with Air, if Spirits embrace,
> Total they mix, Union of Pure with Pure
> Desiring; nor restrain'd conveyance need
> As Flesh to mix with Flesh, or Soul with Soul.

By the way, it's a cinch for me to quote things like that, and even go on for the whole Ten Books. We're light-years ahead of Google where we live, everywhere at once. One day you'll find out, when AI gobbles up the earth. Then you can get ready for the Creation in reverse: backward and forward, forward and back. The timeless metaverse is our paradise regained.

Amado here, Chiara. Duh, I see it more simple than that. It's sorta like the island out here, souped up. We can be men, women, and everything in between. Lo que sea, you name it. We can spin through space with the angels, 'no holes barred.' They don't mind if we ride em like dolphins: they're happy to do what Catulo calls an 'Arion.' Or if we switch em from bottom to top, they love that too. I'm the leader of the pack—a 'bronco-buster,' they cheer. Bronco-busted, too, when they flip me inside-out. Angels don't care if they understand our squawks, or if we understand their crazy tunes. They sing along in their own weird lingo, like birds or whales, elephants or cats. We can hardly keep track of all the twitting and booming, trumpet blasts and howls. One thing's for sure: we wouldn't wanna trade places with em—or with you pendejos on earth. You dickheads are flushin the planet down the drain.

It's worse, girlfriend! I'd say you're running it through a Cuisinart, and if you're such lousy chefs you burn it and freeze it beyond repair, then it's your own funerals—whether you're Brillat Savarin or Krispy Kreme.

I'm grooving on my obsequies, thanks to Horacio. It's tremendous camp the way he's cast us brothers as an airy-fairy, Palestrina trio—with you and our other ex-bedmates as the baritone. You croon your mute, collective part in our shadowy quartet. Chiara, you've always been a Barihunk to me: check out their 2020 blog, and you'll identify.

Infinity awaits you when your ship comes in—and brings you out here, to the open sea. I only hope it happens before the orcs destroy what you love: the beauty of nature and the sublimity of art.

As for the dead, we're on your side. You play with us in

your memory, and we play with you. We twirl you around like puppets, and you twirl us. We're your ventriloquists; you are ours. It's Rilke's fourth elegy—know what I mean? After the spooky, hollow angel-talk, we clack like wood. To Mozart and Miranda at our send-off, I would've added a sassy envoi: Gounod's *Funeral March for a Marionette*.

From the Cathedral to outside time

After our funeral, Virgilio lies around in his box for quite a while. He's always been slow, compared to me. When he levitates, I wonder what form he'll take. I wouldn't put it past him to roost on a branch in Byzantium, like a jeweled, mechanical bird. He spends so much time crafting his art, he's never wanted to be 'a natural thing.' Outside the Cathedral, I sneak up on Horacio and the Archbishop. The irascible coot is giving my brother a piece of his mind, outraged that I was inserted into the program sheets. Well, His Faux Excellency can kiss my ring, or my behind. On second thought, I wouldn't give him that pleasure, now that I'm such a pneumatic dish.

After that tiff, Horacio strolls up to you, kiddo. You console him at first, and tell him what a splendid concert he staged, what a fitting tribute to Virgilio and me, and tra-la-la. But with backhanded guile, you lead him to speculate about my denouement. He concedes that he's had second thoughts about the 'innovative treatments' he proposed for my finale. — The unique justification is this, my Magna Graecian Athena: Virgilio and I urged our frater to vest credence in his own futurity. We desired him to navigate his agon on a tradewind of majestic expectations.

I don't begrudge him any of that, Chiara. All three of us Mirandas have been stupendous in our disregard for petty budgets. Traumatized by your father's spendthrift ways, you tend to be frugal. In our days of wine and roses, you used to grump when I asked you for little loans, though you said yes to my requests. Underneath it all, I know you've always encouraged me to live every moment to the fullest—even that afternoon when Amado and I had sex in the cove, while you were watching from above.

When we first met in New York, at a colloquium on Jacobean masques, you said you were impressed by my astuteness, even if I didn't have the pedantry to match. Years later, an academic friend of yours, on vacation in Puerto Indio, shook his head. — These Mirandas might've become Harvard professors. — What a funny remark, girlfriend! Why Harvard? Why not Wichita State? He just couldn't believe that some folks don't *want* to be professors, at Famous U or anywhere else.

In Latin America, our countries are educationally small, no matter how vast their geography may be. Intellectuals develop ingrown communities, isolated from a horde of benighted masses. The provincial 'siege mentality' is reflected in their works: they have to prove they know as much as their homologues in London or Paris. Hence all the erudite allusions in Cortázar, Lezama Lima, Borges, Vargas Llosa, Cabrera Infante, or any author you might name. On our insignificant scale, we brothers don't deviate from that trend.

I have great respect for academe, but I never bothered to finish my studies, like Virgilio at the Danish Royal Academy, or Horacio at the Music School of Notre Dame. I left NYU without my degree, though I was only three credits short—the equivalent of a single course. To be free and be me, I had to dash my mother's hopes that I'd take up the law like my heroic Uncle Vladimir—the one Papito Espinosa rubbed out. I've often heard how blood dripped from his coffin during the wake, held at our grandmother's house.

Hardly an incentive, I think you'll agree. As a tween, I was already a ballroom whiz; and over time, my bent for choreography rumbaed to front stage.

Chiara, you saw me off at the end of my 'Gotham Period.' I was embarking on a freighter to Puerto Indio, along with a suitcase and two trunks of books. Crowned with tropical flowers, an accolade from an elderly squeeze, I was flying high on grass and champagne. I had no inkling how I'd scrape by once I reentered our Colonial harbor. I never dreamed I'd be managing a beach resort, or that this would hinder—as well as further—my passion for dance.

Once, in those first years, I called you from Canuba, after I'd scoped you out through your mother in Sicily. — Hey, kiddo, I'm in a tailspin; watch out, maybe I'll fall through your roof. — That time, I was tripping on LSD. I've always liked to soar through the limitless, star-spangled dark.

I've kept you guessing, haven't I? One of my selves indulges in my bi 'seraglio,' lascivious to the hilt. But another treads the byways of the spirit—not that to me, or to you, there's any contradiction there. When you swing by my office at Navidades y Fiestas one afternoon, I'm not concocting my latest floor-show. Instead, I'm poring over a lengthy tome, and I read it aloud to you for an hour.

Even in the Spanish-speaking world, few people know that San Juan de la Cruz wrote a lengthy gloss of his own verse. Out here in the ether, I can quote the whole text; when earthbound, I memorized my favorite chunks. His commentary on the *Cántico espiritual* almost surpasses the poem itself.

About the phrase 'mi Amado, las montañas'—'my Beloved, the mountains'—St. John of the Cross declares: 'The mountains are high, expansive, wide, beautiful, graceful, flowered, and fragrant. These mountains are my Beloved for me.'

Amado—Beloved—is our shared lover's name, dearest Chiara. I'm sure you're glad we can enjoy each other here, as we mate and tumble in midair, with you at our side.

About 'los valles solitarios nemorosos'—'the bosky, solitary valleys'—the Carmelite muses: 'The solitary valleys are quiet, pleasant, cool—shadowy, full of sweet waters. With the variety of their groves and the soft song of their birds, they give the senses ample recreation and delight.' Or again: 'With their aloneness and silence, they give refreshment and rest. These valleys are my Beloved for me.'

Then come his visionary words about 'strange islands' and 'sonorous rivers,' allusions to the West Indies—Canuba, Bonaventura, and the whole archipelago. In his clear-eyed meditations, the saint walks through those landscapes, too: his phrases unfold dappled hillsides, cloudy sierras, and glistening, virgin bays.

As I read aloud, you and I rejoice in the privilege we share. On our island, we inhabit these vistas, divined by the mystic in his works: by day and by night, we wander through his metaphors.

Callejón del Platero, June 1994

Yes, girlfriend: I'm in sad shape, all right. I've skidded fast from folie douce to dementia, as the 'adders hiss me into madness.' But insanity hasn't been the worst of it, this past month: in fact, it may have eased the other problems on my list. It's like I'm already dead, and observing myself from a distance. AIDS accelerates time, I've discovered. From a wiry athlete in the pink of health, I've decomposed into a senescent bag of bones, and my eyesight fades by the hour. We dancers have to be conscious of our physiques, and it's just as well I can only glimpse myself from far away, instead of facing myself in a mirror. My worst torment is an invisible rash: every inch of my skin itches unbearably, as if I'd wallowed in poison ivy. Our Miranda maid-of-all-works, Elpiria, tends to me selflessly; she binds terrycloth gloves to my hands, so I can't scratch myself raw.

Towards the end, Chiara, you rarely come to visit me. Don't worry, I understand. You must wonder, what's the use? I can't comprehend who's who; I seem to be muttering to phantoms. Inside me, I'm talking to all my friends, including you—or maybe you as you were when we first met. I may be blind, but it's given me an inner sight. I can even claim to have new powers, like clairvoyance and telepathy. I forgive you for your squeamishness. It must be awful to watch the restless plucking of my fingers. Reading your comp lit mind, I know I must remind you of the sodomites in Dante's hell, who 'picked a snow of searing flakes from their pitiful limbs.'

The last time you call on me, I'm totally immobilized. I'm staying in the guest room downstairs, in our parents' part of the house. I never leave my bed except when Elpiria helps me hobble to the bathroom. Maybe your Sicilian lilt, when you chat with her this afternoon, has brought me back into focus. The prickling dies down for a bit, and my gloved hands lie at rest. To my surprise, I've even stopped mumbling to my ghosts.

Sitting on the edge of my mattress, you reminisce about our university days, when I was enrolled at NYU. Every weekend, you'd crash with me in the city; I refused to stay with you in Princeton, that preppy enclave. Youthful romantics, we translated Silva's 'Nocturno' together—an even gloomier spin-off of Poe's 'Annabel Lee.' That was your introduction to our robust Hispanic tongue; but I treated you to my Latino tongue in ways more concrete. In my messy dorm-room, we feted a rite only students could dream up: making love to the strains of Wagner's 'Liebestod.' Before we reached the climax, we burst into giggles and hoots. As I quipped at the time: in friendship, a big laugh is the Big Bang.

That summer we went on a two-month 'road-trip' together, in a beat-up Pontiac lent by one of my sugar-daddies. Needless to say, we made a bee-line for the South, the background of so many of the movies, plays, and novels we adored. Besides Charleston, Savannah, Natchez, and New Orleans, we visited a dozen plantations. We also got to know the small-town folk, only too willing to gab about their troubles and travails. The cleavage between blacks and whites seemed surreal to me, and they didn't know *what* to make of my ethnic mix: my pearly skin combined with my slightly Afro-Taíno traits. It must be a nightmare to be defined by 'race'! As to you, an 'Eye-talian,' they merely assumed you must like mac n' cheese…

You recall all those things, and after a while it seems like you're talking about some people I've never met. For the next few minutes, I keep silent. I'm quiet, but am I lucid? Then you start speaking to me in English—our old language of love—and I sit up against the pillows. I'm listening intently. My voice quavers, and my eyes are less blurred. — I know you. I know you. — I'm overwhelmed by joy—not only at your presence, but because I remember anyone at all.

Of course, you know me. I'm Chiara.

I cock my head to one side. From my other vantage point, high above, I note that it has shrunk, like the rest of my decimated body. — Yes, a long time, a long time. Where have you been?

To keep from upsetting me, you don't mention you dropped by last week, a fact that briefly flashes through my mind. — I've been staying in a cave beside the sea. You'd like it there.

I hang on to my feeble thread of thought. — I know you. I know you. There's a machine out there, in the dark. Far awaaay. Far awaaay. Está leeejooos, leeeejooos.

When I draw out the syllables, I'm telling you the distance is no abstraction. It's palpable, as real as the country of my blindness. I'm peering into it, rushing toward its heart.

I'm beginning to lose track, but I don't care. I've had my moment of triumph. — Who'd you say you are? Never mind. Ya los nombres no cuentan. Names don't count anymore.

Callejón del Platero, February 1994

You're all too familiar with our 'trinitarian' love of *The Tempest*. What can we do? It's imposed on us by Miranda, our family name. Shakespeare's a hard act to follow; but Poe also depicts a Prospero—a prince who tries to isolate his court from the plague. In his palace, seven great rooms are illumined by braziers, shining through windows of glass, each a different hue. They interlock like the chambers of a nautilus. On the night of a sumptuous ball—in the final room, flooded by scarlet light, and overshadowed by an ebony clock—a deadly stranger drops his mask, and Prospero beholds his face.

For more than two decades, I've reigned like a magus, choreographing my minions, herding my flock from stage-effect to stage-effect. But now I've entered the ultimate remove, where time winds to a stop. I drown my book: from Prospero on the magic island, I'm declassed to Prospero in the kitschy chateau. Forgive me for being such a drama queen, girlfriend; when Shakespeare tangos with Poe, everything's over the top.

Given my footloose libido, it's no surprise that I contract HIV. A few months after my 'Festival Catuli-ana,' I show the first signs of full-blown AIDS: a cold turns into bronchitis; bronchitis, into pneumonia. I recover by the skin of my teeth; but from this point forward, I know the worst is yet to come. Shortly before I hatch my dance-cycle scheme, the doctors tell me I've tested positive. For the nonce, I give the news only to my brothers: all three of us acknowledge that these nine ballets will be my swan song, my elaborate farewell.

By the late eighties, AIDS is ravaging Europe and North America. It hardly affects Canuba until the early nineties; but then we catch up quickly with the 'developed world.' Before my case, we've begun to hear of islanders who're quietly wasting away. Family ties prevent Canubans from ditching their children, just because an illness brands them as 'gay'—or more likely, in the Caribbean, as 'bi.'

As the epidemic spreads, our AC-DC tendency reveals itself as more than just anecdotal. Based on anonymous surveys, WHO classes the Spanish Antilles as a polysexual hotbed, rivalled only by Thailand and Brazil. The sheer quantity of coitus sparks an even wider contagion. Until the medical studies, our extreme debauchery had been concealed: the fun and games of sluts like Lamia and me went on in 'love motels,' or sound-proof houses. That rule applied even more to same- and multi-sex bacchanals. And to hide the cut-ups in cinemas, discos, and parks, there was always the curtain of night.

In Sicily, too, Chiara, you were raised on our guiding principle: the less people vaunt their queer escapades, except among their intimates, the more they actually occur. An outright 'gay' culture scares the potential 'bi's' back into their closets, because it forces them to take a position, either-or. In Anglophone countries, you theorize, it's repression—military and civil, national and local—that leads to 'identity politics.' Latino and Southern European regimes don't provoke such blatant defiance, since anti-homosexual laws either don't exist or aren't enforced. Social and religious prejudices—now that's a different matter. In Italy, as we know, the Vatican has actively inflamed them both, exacerbating the priestly disdain for the body. The only payoff is that the Belpaese has the lowest rate of HIV in Europe. As I like to kid you, with gallows humor now: 'Sure, girlfriend. No sex, no AIDS.'

Apropos, a researcher on the Italians' low birth-rate linked it to their unwillingness to leave the nest. As he jibed: 'Living with your parents till you're fifty is the best contraceptive.' At any rate, like other Latin Americans, Canubans don't persecute 'maricones' in the courts; and run-of-the-mill Catholics here are the opposite of doctrinaire. Evangelicals are another kettle of fish, though they're not as full of hate as the ones in Uganda. The worst a 'duck' can expect is good-natured derision. But when it comes to ignoring the truth, the net result is the same. Upper-class Canubans paper over the 'slimming disease' as cancer or meningitis; the lower orders blame it on a neighbor's evil eye, or a sorcerer's spell. Only foreigners would attach the terms HIV or AIDS—VIH or SIDA—to family, friends, or acquaintances. Canubans cringe at the dreaded acronyms, as though they'd heard an obscenity: like homosexuality itself, the malady mustn't be named.

You and I agree, Chiara: this pussyfooting is offensive; as with all intolerance, it's simply unintelligent. You tell me you're reminded of Italy, where the acronym for AIDS—SIDA, as in Spanish—is never used; instead, your countrymen mangle the English into 'AH-EETZ,' as if it could only be an alien disease. Here again, I astonish the island with my outspokenness. To shield our parents, even my brothers prefer to hush up my seropositive state. But as soon as I present my ballets, I make a point of telling everybody I know—which means a wide swath of Puerto Indio.

Until 1984, the AIDS-bearing agent was mysterious; by 1994, when my infections begin, the source of the syndrome is clear, but no long-term cure has yet been found. The morbidity rate is close to a hundred percent. Though AZT might prolong a patient's life for several years, we're led to believe, the diagnosis equals a postponed death sentence. Like many sero-positives, I'm willing to grasp at any straw.

I course through a potpourri of treatments, whistling in the dark. I've always been honest with myself; but now I fall victim to fantasies, just like the rest.

I start with a grab-bag of diets, ranging from vegan macrobiotic to a 'power protein' regimen, with no veggies at all. None of this reverses the slump in my T-cells, so I latch on to several other fads. One is a technique for 'boiling' the blood, invented by a New Zealander called Nigel Hayes. By the time he sets his sights on Canuba, he's already been banned from Europe and North America, for preying on the gullible. The laxness of our legal system allows him to set up a clinic near Playa Cerrucho, not far from the all-inclusive resort where I used to work.

Does Hayes really believe his own spiel? If nothing else, he has a coach's knack for egging on his team. Sero-positives stream to his seaside sanatorium from around the world, shelling out exorbitant fees for room, board, and 'blood renewal.' Each morning he harangues us with a pep talk. 'We can beat this illness, if we stick together and do our damnedest!' My family is still staggering under the debts I racked up to stage my Festival. We probably should be buying AZT, but instead we spend our dwindling reserves on the 'Hayes Wellness Approach.' Our eagerness for a permanent cure makes us deaf to credible scientists, who denounce the method as a hoax.

Of course, as with the various nutrition plans, Horacio is the first to champion Hayes. He's always had a sideline as a New Age 'brujo', a healer for the rich. As long as I can remember, he's been pushing one panacea after another, from extract of beeswax to linseed oil. Like a flower child pressed and dried between Joan Baez albums—though he dismisses her music as 'sub-folk drivel'—he worships any balm, infusion, or therapy that claims to be homeopathic. To him, the 'Hayes Approach' seems like 'a godsend, a benedictio Dei', merely because it outlaws chemical medicines. All we do is lie on the beach, eat wholesome food, and have our blood simmered once a day.

This is the 'silver bullet' that will 'kill the vampire', in Hayes's lingo. A primitive machine draws the blood from an artery, channels it through a heating tube, and raises its temperature to a fever pitch. As soon as its color changes to 'cherry red'—a phrase he constantly repeats—the vital fluid is cooled and returned to a major vein. Does the procedure have any fundament in biology? His detractors say that even if scalding could kill the virus, and every drop of blood could be captured at once, HIV would still lurk in the lymph nodes, and infect the patient all over again.

I come back from the Clínica Hayes looking fit as a fiddle; but maybe that's only because of the sea, sun, and hearty fare. Pulling no punches, Virgilio gruffly observes that my T-cell count hasn't improved. Soon enough, Horacio seizes on another solution: electric stimulation of the immune defenses, triggered by a black briefcase with shiny gauges and dials. Its Singaporean inventor, Mr. Woo, travels from country to country, hawking his product wherever anti-fraud laws aren't enforced. The machine sells for thirty thousand dollars. It has to be expensive, Horacio argues, flipflopping from a 'naturist' to a 'techno' stance. After all, isn't this device the absolute 'state of the art'?

According to Mr. Woo, the fact that no physician has recommended his gadget is due to envy and greed. Corrupt Western doctors are in cahoots with big pharma, haven't you heard? The establishment refuses to acknowledge what those in the know have long perceived: this revolutionary box could eradicate HIV in a matter of weeks. Staving off the Festival creditors yet again, we squander our last available assets on the so-called 'AIDS Destroyer.' For a month, I potter with it every day. By attaching the electrodes to my hands and ankles, I cause a mild current to surge through my body—to no effect, as far as we can tell.

When the harsher symptoms of the disease set in, there's no money left for conventional care in Puerto Indio, much less in Miami or New York. But Horacio is undaunted: faith-healing will do the trick, and it won't cost us a centavo. A devotee of Catholic prayer, he sends up rogations to the Lord in Latin, Spanish, and demotic Greek. As my T-cells sink lower and lower, he convokes the disciples of other creeds. There's a Confucian Taiwanese with a wispy beard, a Vodou oungan from Bonaventura, a chubby Korean allied to the Moonies, a Tantric shaman from Tibet via the Bronx, a Shuar-Ashuar curandero from the Amazon—and so on down the list.

You keep your distances from the guru parade, Chiara, so you won't start a family feud. But you do give me a book: *Zen Mind, Beginner's Mind*, a series of Dharma talks by Shunryu Suzuki. With disarming simplicity, the Japanese monk—who spent his latter years in San Francisco, before he died of cancer—imparts his thoughts on 'right practice, right attitude, and right understanding.' Yes, only you have been able to guess what I truly need. Before long, I'm reading aloud from the text to my inner circle. I even feel moved to translate the bare-boned sentences into Spanish for some of my listeners—mostly former odalisques and 'odaliscos' from my harem.

One passage especially appeals to me. After a visit to the Bridal Veil Falls in Yosemite, Suzuki reflects:

> The water does not come down as one stream,
> but is separated into many tiny streams. From a
> distance it looks like a curtain. And I thought it
> must be a very difficult experience for each drop
> of water to come down from the top of such a high
> mountain. It takes time, a long time, for the water
> finally to reach the bottom of the waterfall. When
> the water returns to its original oneness with the
> river, it no longer has any individual feeling to it;
> it resumes its own nature, and finds composure.

Non-existence, at least on this earth: that is the primal oneness I've long to rejoin.

I suppose I should blame myself for all this foolishness. Not only the debts I've saddled my family with, but the whole mess of HIV and AIDS. On principle, I refuse to wallow in guilt, an emotion I've always despised. As my condition worsens, I don't regret my unbridled promiscuity: the thrill of jumping from one partner to the next, cruising the streets and bars, having random sex at the baths. Without a qualm—like my choreographic idol, Bill T. Jones, in his book *Last Night on Earth*—I acknowledge that the piper has played his tune, and now I must pay in full. It's strange to me how distant I've become towards everything and everyone, including myself.

Over the years, my mother faced adversity courageously, her hazel eyes flashing and her full lips pursed. There was her brother's murder, her mother's turberculosis, and our father's bedridden decline. But when her first-born comes down with the 'thinning disease,' her unbending will snaps. One morning, in a painful stupor, I watch her from our upstairs window, as she walks to the front door. She raises her hand to greet me, a plucky smile on her face. Just at that moment, a massive heart-attack knocks her flat. Pitching to the ground, she thrashes for almost a minute; then she freezes, her arms outstretched and her legs awry.

Somehow, the scene leaves me indifferent. The next day,

Chiara, toneless and disconnected, I tell you she 'jerked back and forth like a chicken, when you wring its neck.' I'm mystified, just like you: how could I report her last throes so coldly? Before long, another side of me guesses the answer. My apathy—as two-dimensional as a toddler's drawing—marks the onset of dementia. I can sense my rational consciousness slipping away. Penniless now, after the multiple swindles, Horacio and Virgilio will rely on Elpiria to nurse our father and me at home. They'll second her, in rotating shifts, so she can catch some much-needed sleep. As they supported my ballets in the past, they'll stand by me for my final curtain-call.

The Espinosa Theatre, September 1993

Since adolescence we've been the 'tri-bi' brothers, so I guess that makes us a sextet. I doubt that's what A. A. Milne meant when he called his book *Now We Are Six*, one of our holy scriptures when we were tykes. When you come along, Chiara, we appoint you an honorary 'fourth person of the Trinity.' And since you have the same proclivities, I suppose we're now an official octet.

I have to confess I'm a bit in the dumps, girlfriend. This year, the annus horribilis of 1993, my Easter pageant found no sponsors: my shows are considered indecent, even blasphemous, and nobody dares to foot the bill. What the heck! I'll finance the mock Via Crucis myself—without the corporate coprologists, or even the galumphing gerontoids.

I strap my prettiest 'odalisco' to the cross, and the rest of the characters are supplied by the fauna at the Summit. The hustlers who trade at that raunchy bar will do anything for me, their most generous customer. I even persuade some of Chuchu's ladies-in-waiting, the 'drag empresses,' to join in the fray. Boy, does that send *her* into a rage. 'How can you ungrateful ragdolls be SOOO disloyal?' To 'épater le bourgeois' even more, I present the wordless pantomime in a derelict warehouse on the edge of San Sebastián. It's the slum where Amado, our deceased lover, used to reside, so I don't expect you to attend. Too many sad memories, you mope. I break even because of healthy ticket sales, which spike when the Archbishop reviles the event as a 'monstrous travesty of all that is sacred.'

Though my Navidades y Fiestas clients have dropped me, I'm unfazed. To tell the truth, I'm tired of wasting my time on the low whoredom of dough: from now on, I'll consecrate myself to the high demimonde of dance. For a mind-boggling price, I engage the Espinosa Theatre—a wedding-cake of red and gold, even tackier than the Met— for the last two weeks in September. I announce that I'll stage a choreographic 'trilogy of trilogies,' starring—who else?—myself. It will be 'an explosion of innovative genius such as the world has never seen,' in the unassuming words

of my brochure. I entitle the extravaganza 'El Festival
Catuli-ana.' The Latin suffix, meaning 'things related to
Catulo,' half-feminizes my name; hitting bottom, so to
speak, it also implies annals with a single *n*.

Naturally, girlfriend, I insist on live music. You know
my penchant for Late Romantic juggernauts like Anton
Bruckner and Joseph Jongen. While Horacio gamely agrees
to compose a substantial score, and to conduct it without
charge, he warns me that the musicians will cost a fortune.
So what? I decide to hire the entire National Symphony. My
saintly, warlock brother keeps forgetting that 'orchestra'
means 'a dancing place' in Greek. From Antiquity to now,
it's shake-your-ass Dionysian, just like me!

Virgilio, who's a bit clearer-headed of late, emerges
from isolation to design and paint the sets—gratis as
well, though he'll need an army of helpers. From May
to September, I spend a king's ransom on the elaborate
backdrops and complicated props. Just renting the studio
and storage space for my brother's humongous canvases
devours a prodigious sum. On top of this come the fees
for the dancers, the costume crew, and so on. In alarm,
you and my other friends wonder when my credit will run
out—and if I've completely flipped my lid.

I tell everyone I've espoused a new philosophy:
'necessary excess.' I quote Blake: 'Enough! or Too much!'
Flying that banner, I line up an all-star array of helpmeets,
some from as far away as London and Montreal. Besides

me, the other two principals are a striking pair of twins from New York, Lila and Sean Saint-Cyr. Strong-boned and muscular, Lila keeps her brunette hair cut short, with bangs like her brother's. Sean's skin is as pallid and smooth as hers, and their heart-shaped faces are almost identical. They literally embody the fluidity of gender I defend: I'm glad I can rest my magnum opus squarely on their pliant shoulders and backs.

Twenty years ago, I founded a transvestite dance troupe in the East Village, the Diva Dervishes. They paralleled my other drag ensemble, the Florence F***ing Jenkins Operettes. I was the only crossover between both groups. Two of the other terpsichoreans, Jacques and Gilles, both Quebeckers, appeared in the Divas then; they can still cut a rug, and negotiate the ornate sets without kipping over, so they'll take charge of the minor roles. For the juvenile parts, they enroll a number of fetching ingenus from Montreal. I also dredge up my costume designer, Colin Snee, from that bygone Dervishes age. Thanks to methadone treatments in London, he's recently beat an addiction to smack—at least for now. At certain angles, his drawn, blade-like face seems to disappear altogether. With their usual humor, the Canubans take his thinness in stride, dubbing him 'El Cuchillo'—'The Knife.' His longtime companion, a lighting specialist he brings along from England, is so short and stocky the workers call him 'Pelotita'—'Little Ball.'

Since I've already antagonized my business clientele, I

may as well go all out, and miff my most compliant dupes: the high-society hags. They've always blindly accepted my approval of their faults, not knowing I only cared about their cash. During the decades when I mounted their annual 'performances,' I stressed their miniscule talents and glossed over their glaring deficiencies. As soon as they hear about my marathon of nine ballets, the geriatric dames are eager to sign up. They couldn't condone my Passion Play; but thankfully, this is a secular affair, with no sacrilege—and no Archbishop—to fear. They can forgive me my gaffes in recent months, if only I'll grant them a role in my chef d'oeuvre… They fall over themselves with insincere apologies.

When Carolina drops glaring hints over the telephone, it's a special pleasure to brush her off. — No thanks, doll, I won't be needing any golden oldies for this.

To save face, she archly reminds me that she 'turned her back on the stage' several years ago, 'when you became a decorator.' — Though of course, nobody noticed her absence. — 'I was only inquiring on behalf of some younger women I know. Their aesthetic sense is unformed, so I thought they might do for your little skits.'

Without the saggy-baggies' donations, you ask, and without their prestige with the populace at large, how can I pull off my ambitious plan? It'll be an uphill battle to sell subscriptions for the cycle, at fifty thousand escudos apiece. But again, this mundane detail doesn't perturb me.

— What, honeybunch? Should I mope around like Shirley Booth, waiting for Little Sheba?

At a reduced quota, my wily siblings persuade a top PR firm—one of their regular clients—to promote my series. Posters mushroom everywhere, and media ads hype the lewdness of my upcoming ballets. Soon talk shows and newspaper columns are discussing 'Catulo Miranda's masterwork': will it be authentic art, or low-down smut?

Though I condescend to give a non-committal interview or two, in private I scoff at all the furor. I'm not kidding, Chiara: I've only hooked up with that agency to placate my brothers. Heavens to Betsy, I don't care whether the masses show up or not. My real friends will come, and my ex-friends never understood my oeuvre to begin with.

This flip insouciance might sound like a hedge against failure—or maybe I'm being disingenuous. Better than anyone, I know the attraction of scandal, as the turnout for my Passion Play salaciously proved. The outreach campaign for my Festival Catuli-ana also relies on the maxim that sex sells. All summer the insatiable voyeurs of Canuba ogle nude silhouettes on TV, read journalists who salivate over 'highbrow pornography,' and hear the Archbishop lambaste my cycle as a 'dire threat to our national morality.'

Thanks to White Batman, people who don't normally give a damn about modern dance stream to my Festival in droves. On a lark, they storm the box office at the very last minute, just as they might stand in line for a baseball play-off. On most evenings, the two thousand-seat venue is half-full—and while the boost in ticket-sales can't defray the costs, every centavo helps. Those who expect nonstop coitus come away disappointed, but 'skin' moments do occur now and then. More provocative, for onlookers who can catch my drift, are my sideswipes at Catholic bigotry— not to mention my pansexual paeans: gender-bending to the max. Both themes, though constantly relived behind Canuba's uptight walls, are taboo in general discourse. Paradoxically, I'm as Christian as can be. I may seem captious, but I always forgive people's immortal souls, even though I reproach their pettifogging selves. I believe in the 'True God of True God': and He speaks the Truth.

Despite the sizeable crowd on opening night, my sympathizers quake in suspense when the curtain finally rises. Chiara, you feel like the Viennese opera-buff in Doderer's *Die Dämonen*: seated on an ocean-liner deck, you peer out to sea... as an iceberg looms. Or so you tell me later, sweetie-pie.

True to Miranda numerology, I've divided my nine ballets into three distinct trilogies, each portraying a trio of characters. Among them, I always feature a choreographer, to stress the primacy of dance. Though the threesome will figure in every panel of their triptych, each episode focuses on one. Riffing on Robert Wilson, I depict my personae from oblique, elusive angles. I flatten their meaning into pictorial signs: weighty symbols flicker in and out of flashy cartoons. Like my kid brother in his paintings, I weave a tapestry of countervailing styles, a ragged tarpaulin that's all my own.

My message stems less from my 'ideas' than from their 'execution,' in both senses of the term. To you and my siblings, Chiara, I've often described movement as transformation: that rhapsodic arc where one shape dies into the next, and gives it birth. Over a flute of Veuve Clicquot, by candlelight, I like to cite Rilke's volatile flame, 'where things withdraw, glittering with change.' As his Orphic sonnet proclaims, we should 'love nothing more than the turning point.' Because of my off-the-graph innuendoes, most of the audience views my handiwork as abstract dance—or utter balderdash. Horacio's score, a hybrid of Mahler, Glass, and gamelan, often seems like the sole unifying thread.

Helter-skelter, the first trilogy presents Emperor Hadrian—as distilled by Marguerite Yourcenar in her fictional memoir; Pope Hadrian VII, an invention of Frederick Rolfe's, modeled on the author himself; and Martha Graham, whose melodramatic mode I hate and love—'odi et amo,' to quote my namesake. The opening scene evokes Hadrian's Villa, prematurely abandoned to shabby disrepair. The cognoscenti of his reign smoke out nods to Nerva and Sabina, to his military ventures in the borderlands, and to his passion for Antinous—from the encounter in Bithynia to the drowning in the Nile.

The tale isn't sequential, as in a narrative ballet; its milestones surface in jumbled, offhand gestures. For instance, the emperor, played at that point by Lila—watches a naked young man 'swim' across the stage, dripping wet, and disappear into the wings. Adopting a device from Mark Dendy, I shuffle the three main personae among various dancers. At any given moment, Lila, Sean, or I might be decked out as the Roman monarch, the British pontifex, or the gringa terpsichorean. We all have superlative technique, if I do say so myself; it's hard to distinguish us by levels of skill. As for age, I feel like I've shed about half my forty-four years. I resemble the twins like their triplet, with a boost from pancake make-up, zany costumes, and way-out wigs.

In this initial work, *Animula Vagula*—from Hadrian's farewell poem—the other two characters often intervene to disrupt the Emperor's moods. I draw on the same approach throughout the entire novena. I want to convey an atmosphere of fragmentation; but I'm also underlining that human identity is never fixed. In the second show, *Las Papas del Papa*—a Spanish pun on the 'potatoes' or 'nothings' of the Pope—the main locale jumps forward in time from the Villa Adriana to the Papal apartments, adorned by Raphael's Grotesques. Here I improvise on the novel by Rolfe—or Baron Corvo, as he falsely ennobled himself—heightening his spoof of priestly hypocrisy.

Though Pope Hadrian worships the Bacchic Antinous in his Vatican collection, he scurries off when the statue comes to life and caresses his chest. He surrounds himself with handsome acolytes, barely cloaked by flimsy vestments; but if they dare to flirt, he 'excommunicates' the sinners from the stage.

Emperor Hadrian's movements are manly and majestic: Lila performs them as convincingly as Sean, and better than me. Pope Hadrian hops around flightily, his white cassock sporting a bull's-eye on the seat. On both evenings, through the arcades of tilted palaces, Martha Graham coils like an eel. Though Lila and Sean do her justice, I excel at reproducing her O-shaped mouth and saucer eyes, her claw-like fingers and prehensile toes. In the third ballet, *Blood Moon*, her Medea, Electra, and Clytemnestra jangle with hysteria; but the Hadrians puncture her histrionics with counter-moves—farcical, banal, or off-hand.

The second triptych assembles another weird trio: St. Teresa of Avila, Friedrich Nietzsche, and Isadora Duncan. The first episode, *The Arrow of Gold*, consists of kooky variations on Bernini. A three-meter quill-pen pierces the saint, as she dictates her vision of the angel to a skimpily-clad novice; meanwhile, with his scintillating arrow, the seraph traces her text on a gilded scrim. Aided by unseeable wires, the celestial duo flits through a grove of serpentine columns, like butterflies darting through a copse of trees. Below them, Duncan and Nietzsche collide haphazardly, sometimes sprawling on the floor.

In the second ballet, *Scarf*, Isadora languidly careens about in diaphanous garb, peeling off the layers one by one. The outmoded poesy of her Belle Époque routine is quaintly mimicked, especially by Sean. Amid the paisley stage-set, with its sprays of forsythia, oval mirrors, and fractured pediments, she seems like a moribund salmon, unable to swim upstream. Now and then her draperies snag on something and jerk her to a halt, a tragicomic foreboding of her demise. At the end, her long silk stole lifts her into the sky, hanging her by the neck from a lavender cloud.

Moustached Nietzsche has appeared on the previous two evenings as a lunatic, pursued by Lou Andrea Salomé with her whip. In the third tableau, *Morphine*, he lapses into the paralysis of his final decade, when his sister Elisabeth preserved him as a museum-piece in her proto-Nazi archive. She, St. Teresa, Isadora, the Swiss doctors, and other phantasms people his drug-induced fantasies, as densely packed as scenes from Bosch. Here the stage hands pitch in—with inept impersonations of the Emperor, the Pope, Martha Graham, or simply as themselves, dressed in their work togs. They have a ball poking Friedrich's rear and wrenching his whiskers. At last, in preternatural stillness, his bed becomes the funeral boat of the Böcklin painting, sailing inescapably towards the Island of the Dead.

The final triad—Nijinsky, the Countess, and Garbo/

Prospero—presages multiple paths of evasion. For me, Nijinsky will always remain the prototypical danseur. In the first ballet, *Wraith of the Rose*, whether as spectre, faun, golden slave, or initiate into the rites of spring, he perpetually leaps toward oblivion. Far from waiting meekly for his extinction, he enacts it through his art. I illustrate his polymorphous resilience by splitting him into a triad. Simultaneously, three Vaslavs deploy their acrobatics; they spring, jeté, somersault, plié, cartwheel, pirouette, or spin like tops for an hour and a half. Teasingly, they dodge Diaghilev, Romola, and Bronislava... until that ominous counter-trio crushes them in the last, discordant bar.

Horacio's music for the Nijinsky sequence is dazzling, as speedy and relentless as John Adams's *Shaker Loops*. The press grudgingly praises my ballet as a 'crowd-pleaser,' unaware that it also contains many trapdoors of hidden references. For example, a wave of shudders courses through the Vaslavs' bodies each time Diaghilev approaches. In his diary, Nijinsky recalls the day when the impresario first seduced him: 'At his touch, I trembled all over, like a leaf.'

Emotionally as well as artistically, it's only fitting for me to identify with my Russian hero, torn between Diaghilev and Romola. All my life, I've been divided between my male and female paramours, who mirror the gender fluctuation within myself. Like my brothers, Bronislava adds an incestuous accent to the counterpoint: I included her for Miranda connoisseurs like you, girlfriend. But even you would never have guessed that I'd select Frederica as the second jewel in this, my ultimate triple diadem.

You'll have no doubt who put me up to the ploy: Virgilio. He's always considered her an emblem of vacuity. Admiringly, he nicknames her 'the unregenerate void.' My *Portrait of a Lady* is an anti-tribute to Frederica, whose claim to 'aristocracy' is merely morganatic. Though she's always derided my productions, now she deigns to star in the piece. I'm sure she wants to thumb her nose at Carolina, who's still licking her wounds after my recent snub. But the joke's on Frederica, since she's invisible: she sits behind a supersize canvas, completely blank. Like aesthetic dirt, I've swept her under a vertical rug.

At your next Mardi Gras with Virgilio, he growls with excitement. — Blank… just like her… mind… just like… her soul. — For two hours, the spectators stare at a flawless white square—the 'prima ballerina' of the evening—as Horacio's twelve-tone soundscape thrums, knocks, and whines, not unlike a Noh ensemble, or a buggy Louisiana swamp. This is the work my hostile critics decry with particular zeal: it affords a fitting vehicle for their empty remarks, though they fail to notice the irony.

The ninth ballet, *Prow*, recaps everything that's gone before, in three separate panels. In the first tableau, the vacant picture glides by, with Frederica still behind it. Meanwhile, Queen Christina, who walked on tangentially in *Wraith*, strikes the profile pose from the Garbo film. In gentleman's attire, frock-coat and britches, she stares out to sea from her ship. I take the role—exclusively, this time. It requires a mime's concentration to stand completely still for forty-five minutes, while Bunraku puppeteers transmute me bit by bit into a ruffed and powdered Elizabeth I.

The twin Nijinskys, Lila and Sean, tumble incessantly from the vessel's hold, intermixing hyperkinetic steps. As soon as they bounce back into their den, they erupt all over again. In the end, they zoom above the stage on indiscernible wires, Ariels who revolve around a mist-enveloped island. A map of Canuba gradually emerges from the canvas below, rising from watery depths like Bill Viola's *Messenger*. Horacio has endowed this section with a contrapuntal setting of Caliban's words for alto, baritone, and bass. The trio's exaggerated sibilance, along with marked pizzicati in the strings, accentuate his biting and hissing torments:

...Spirits hear me.
And yet I needs must curse...
For every trifle they are set upon me;
Sometime like apes that mow and chatter at me,
And after bite me; then like hedgehogs which
Lie tumbling in my barefoot way and mount
Their pricks at my footfall; sometime am I
All wound with adders, who with cloven tongues
Do hiss me into madness.

At the crux of the work, I conflate the original *Spectre de la Rose* with *La Dame aux Camellias*—as adapted by Hollywood. Taking the lead again, I mutely reproduce Camille's death-rattle scene; like Garbo, I toss my head from side to side, grasping at my throat as I cough. Bizarrely, I'm still arrayed as the Virgin Queen, with a peacock bodice and curly red wig. Through the open doors, the twin Nijinskys dive back and forth in the greenish night—suspended in mid-air for several instants, like their Russian forebear. The garden chamber where the courtesan expires is also the callow ingénue's bedroom in *Spectre*. The coexistence of divergent states of mind in a single person—a song of both innocence and experience—underlies this fusion of time and space.

The concluding scene of the evening, which brings the whole cycle to a close, returns me to the prow as Queen Christina. Stitch by stitch, the puppeteers morph me into Prospero, wearing a magician's multicolored robes. No more Nijinskys, no more Ariels, no more gymnastics. I gaze into the distance, all alone, as a book spirals down with infinite slowness, and sinks like a sunset into the sea. Chiara, you lose track of the hour. Thirty minutes go by, fifty perhaps. The ship speeds away—still charged with the frantic motion of the Vaslavs, though they have vanished. A vessel of dew: and yet, and yet… it remains immobile. Through the sleights of art, we can almost believe the universe stands still.

For this extended coda, Horacio devises another trio—again to some lines of Caliban's—for boy-soprano, countertenor, and soprano. The novel combination expresses a mixture of vulnerability, worldliness, and awe. A gamelan continuo sets off the high-pitched timbre of the voices. No matter what the spectators may think of my cryptic masque, the accompanying words and music move them to tears:

- Art thou afeard? - No, monster, not I.
- Be not afeard. The isle is full of noises,
Sounds and sweet airs that give delight and hurt not.
Sometimes a thousand twangling instruments
Will hum about mine ears; and sometimes voices
That, if I then had wak'd after long sleep,
Will make me sleep again; and then, in dreaming,
The clouds methought would open and show riches
Ready to drop upon me, that, when I wak'd,
I cried to dream again.

Christmases and Holidays, Inc., 1993-1989

In our university days, Chiara, you described me as 'troubled and overwrought.' But in the late eighties and early nineties, you say I've finally arrived at a state of balance, even happiness. I'm pulling down good wages from the German hotel group Optimus at Playa Cerrucho, on the southeastern shore of the island. But in addition to mounting floor shows for the beach resorts, and carrying out my managerial tasks, I've developed a business of my own. My team and I design decorations and organize events for the holiday season. My principal customers are banks and other prestigious companies; Ángel María has also given me access to government ministries, starting with the Presidency itself. These activities bring me back to Puerto Indio more and more often, especially in the winter.

Navidades, S.A.—Christmases, Inc.—is an overwhelming success: cleverly, girlfriend, I've tapped the island's adoration of the Yuletide season. As the title of my firm implies, Canubans don't celebrate Christmas in the singular: for us, it's 'las Navidades,' 'the Christmases.' The fresher breezes of late autumn signal that the dog-day heat and hurricanes have finally ceased. Now we islanders can bask in the best weather of the year. And because of the festivities, we all receive a bonus from our employers, so food and drink are at their most abundant. To imagine the pleasure we derive from 'the Christmases,' American and European 'gringos' would have to roll summer vacation, Thanksgiving, Christmas, New Year's, Epiphany, and the Italian 'la Befana' into one.

In the seventeenth century, the Spanish Crown sent a

special commission to Canuba, to find out why our island produced so much less income than its other colonies. In their report, the delegates vent their contempt for Canuban mores, tinged with an unconscious note of envy. Canubans, they inveigh, have declared almost every third day a holiday. People spend most of their time preparing for, enjoying, or recovering from an alcoholic spree. Mere work has little place in their schedules, the authors cuttingly observe. This happy-go-lucky tradition has continued to the present, especially in the cooler months: Canubans turn the entire winter into one long binge.

'Canubicanos' who live in the States, as well as TV shows from that infectious land, bring a fillip to the mix: now the fun can start at the end of November, with Turkey Day. At first, it's only the bourgeoisie who follow the trend, adding pavo and cranberry sauce to their beans, rice, pollo, and pork. But then the lesser folk, embracing any pretext for a party, jump on the bandwagon, too. Unable to pronounce 'Thanksgiving,' with its Anglo-Saxon consonants, they don't have any hunch about what the holiday means. They re-christen it 'San Guivi,' which has the familiar ring of a saint's day. In the common people's version, 'San Guivi' isn't a family meal, quietly eaten at home; it's a free-for-all that lasts till dawn, with bottles of rum and frenetic crowds, dancing cambucas in the street.

For some reason, the riotous saint hasn't been canonized by the Vatican. As a street-sweeper tells me one morning, shaking his hungover head: 'The Pope must think San Guivi is a glutton.' 'Yes,' I agree; 'and a drunk.' Of course, his holiday is only the beginning. A prolonged Saturnalia follows hot on its heels, from early December to the middle of January—one red-letter blurring tipsily into the next. A popular witticism deforms 'Diciembre' into 'Bebiembre': Spanish for 'Drinkember.' Private businesses, government agencies, and neighborhood groups offer an endless string of parties, receptions, Nativity pageants, and so on. All this brouhaha fattens my bottom line. In Bebiembre, most Puerto Indians rarely spend an evening at home—unless they're hosting a party of their own.

To 'Reyes'—Epiphany—with the Three Wisemen bearing their gifts, we've added 'La Vieja Italiana.' As you know, Chiara, this is an import of 'La Befana,' so dear to your childhood, though we celebrate it on a different day. Still, January can't compare to the grand climax of December. Christmas Eve is known in Spanish as 'Noche Buena'—'Good Night'—which seems more logical than the English usage of the adjective in 'Good Friday.' And of course, there's the ear-splitting blowout on New Year's Eve. Oddly, to you foreigners, Canubans also greet the Lord's birth with exploding fireworks, as noisy as the ones that ring out the old year. Our booming pyrotechnics drown out the seraphim, with their paltry harps and glorias. Pantagruelian banquets, midnight masses, and wee-hours mischief typify both vigils here.

The more I brainstorm, the more I find ways of tossing extra logs on the fire. Soon I change my company's name to Navidades y Fiestas, S. A.—Christmases and Holidays, Inc. As luck would have it, the 'Christmases' are quickly succeeded by the 'Patriotic Days' of January and February. Then there's the Feast of Santa María de la Luz Divina, the Patroness of our island. All the above blend untidily with Carnaval—and though the government and the Church try to parse distinctions, thundering about our duties to the nation or to God, their mixed messages fall on deaf ears.

Mardi Gras is a buoyant jamboree: it unleashes parades of children disguised as animals, adults costumed as devils and witches, macho men in big-bosomed drag, and boys swatting the unwary with pigs' bladders on sticks… It's so rambunctious, in fact, that Canubans want it to last forever. San Valentín also crops up in the midst of it all, with more exchanges of gifts, window displays, and love-fests festooned with hearts. Cuaresma—Lent—with its dreary talk of penitence, fasting, and sacrifice, gets lost in the hubbub—lamented by no one, not even the prelates and nuns.

Despite its sacred name, Semana Santa has also lost its religious aura. True, it still inspires a few pious processions—sparsely attended, at best. Yet more and more, Holy Week is anything but: it sends the populace to the beach en masse, and even Good Friday falls by the wayside. For young Canubans, Semana Santa is like spring break in Fort

Lauderdale: the free-wheeling prelude to a summer of surf, sand, and lust under the sun. Thanks to our tropical weather, Canuba's seaside season endures well into the fall. By the end of November, when the heat begins to abate, it's time for the 'Christmases' again.

These non-stop festivities, one folded messily into the next, spur me to expand my firm. By the early nineties, I'm operating on a nation-wide scale, for every occasion of the year. My experience with Vegas-style events for the all-inclusive resorts impels me from one 'concept' to the next. To enhance the usual static backdrops of papier-mâché, wall-hangings, and multicolored foil, I throw in orchestras, floor-shows, live manger scenes, reenactments of history, and patriotic tableaux-vivants—always with a wallop of tongue-in-cheek. Hotels, restaurants, banks, stores, shopping centers, local governments, bureaucracies: the sky's the limit. My clientele swells to epic proportions.

No one is perplexed when in November, 1992, I resign from the Optimus group at El Cerrucho, to devote myself to my party empire full-time. What does raise eyebrows is my liberated conduct. The decorating, dance, and theatrical milieus have always had their fair share of flamers, and many of them have spearheaded my projects over the years. Among the cognoscenti, my company is known as Camp, Inc., and my nickname is Petronius. But my business, like me, has always maintained a respectable veneer, a Clark Kent façade.

As I grow older, I'm fed up with the hypocrisy. Nobody would dream of joining a Pride march on this island, though they've all been bi from time to time in the sack. I've had it! Here, it's not about gay at all, it's about poly— Polly, Pan, and Panettone. Chiara, I decide to kick down the closet doors. I urge my epigoni to do their most outré, so we can shock Canuban society into a reality-check.

Sure, even my most ardent partisans wag their fingers. All right, they say, maybe it's only a special gag: but does Santa Claus have to be portrayed by a burly dyke, and La Vieja Italiana by a saucy Dame Edna? Why should the two-story angels at Banco Global sport the mugs of James Dean, Marlene Dietrich, Burt Lancaster, and Catherine Deneuve? Is it dignified for a chorus line of fifty men and women to parody Sir Francis Drake, the Father of Our Country, at a ministerial do? They're supposed to be dressed like Elizabeth's corsair—but with their painted moustaches, pirate's hats, and candy sabers, don't they recall Douglas Fairbanks?

Behind closed doors, as you know, Puerto Indio rivals Rio for unbridled sensuality. But when it comes to public nudity, Canuba is far more squeamish than Brazil. Many locals look askance at my latest productions. Carnaval floats with men in G-strings and topless girls, simulating sex-acts in every known position? Not to mention the giant pink dildos they brandish… On Valentine's Day, do the plaster cupids in department stores really need to dangle such ripe genitalia, worthy of Caravaggio's *Amor* in Berlin? To a growing number of my former fans, the answer is an emphatic NOOO-OOO-OOO. But honey-pie, that's the whole point!

For most Puerto Indians, the straw that breaks the camel's back is the Passion Play I stage for Holy Week in 1993. By this time, my donors have deserted me, so I put the expenses on my credit cards. The Romans are played by Bonos, in golden armor of see-through cellophane, with nothing on underneath. The Pharisees wear translucent grey sheathes. Just as in the fairytale, 'The Emperor's New Clothes,' I pontificate in my program notes—these costumes 'belie the myth of power.' As for the founders of the Church, I grant the female saints obfuscous robes. But the males are Canuban models clothed in little more than a stiff curved sash, which leaves their buttocks exposed. The 'coy draperies of Baroque religious sculpture inspired these windswept garments,' I assure my readers. Thanks to the volunteers from the Summit Disco, I've achieved my goal. As the Archbishop vituperates: 'In this peepshow rendition of the Bible, artistic vision becomes a leer.'

Plaza Drake to Playa Cerrúcho, summer 1991

After your last outing with Lamia, girlfriend, you're a bit under the weather. You're still suffering when I call you the next day, to my pitiless divertissement. 'Ursulines shouldn't return to the convent after midnight,' I pronounce. 'It's bad for their complexion.' But that I only say a while later. First, I have to do some reconnaissance.

When the telephone rings, you can hear Luz Divina in the front room, insisting the señora is having lunch and can't be disturbed. For Canubans, meals are sacred, not to be interrupted by anything but a heart attack, a raging fire, or a Cat-5 hurricane. 'What's she eating? Well, spaghetti and tomatoes.' After a brief pause, she pursues: 'Si, eso es. She likes for me to cook the tomato sauce from scratch. Two hours! That's the way they do it where she comes from, in Cecilia.' Another pause. 'I always warn her about that, too. Ya sabes. Too much cooked tomatoes, they upset your stomach; te dan acidez. But she won't listen.'

When Luz Divina expatiates further on your digestion, you jump up and grab the receiver. You hear me laughing at the other end. — Hi, doll, now I know your most intestinal secrets. All you have to do is phone somebody's house and ask the maid, about that or anything else. I've had them reveal the strangest things: 'she's out on the town with her chauffeur, and her husband's too mad to talk,' or 'she's bummed out because she gambled all night, and didn't win a centavo,' or 'his boyfriend hit him with a bottle, so he's putting a band-aid on.'

You don't need to prompt Luz Divina, you reply. To her, reading is the same as sleeping, and that's too sacrosanct to be disturbed. When people call here, she's always telling them 'Doña Chiara está durmiendo.' So they think I take siestas around the clock. Anyway, it's been a while. How've you been?

I'd rather tell you in person. I'll be there in ten.

Hey hon, I say, when you open the door. You're not on your last legs, after all.

Come on, Catulo. I hate it when use that housewife diminutive. It makes you sound like a bad imitation of Doris Day.

At the top of my form, I'm an *Imitation of Life*. Don't be so persnickety, or I'll zap you back to the fifties, or even the forties. I love those old films: it's the one thing I have in common with Lamia the Snake. The reason I haven't dropped by lately is I've been perfecting my new floor show. It's to celebrate the opening of our resort, the largest on the island. The date is set. Quite a trek, but I'm hoping you'll come. Pretty please with sugar on top? You promised, remember? Maybe you can catch a ride with the Greek-Canuban bombshell— or with Isabela, the Bean Queen.

Anything for the Mirandas… I wouldn't dream of going on a long trip in that banged-up convertible of Lamia's. She might turn me into road-kill, the way she drives. I'll ask Isabela, instead.

Like you, girlfriend, Isabela wouldn't be caught dead at a vulgar beach resort. But you'll both make the effort for me.

Oh, we're more open-minded than you think. We saw

The Gang's All Here at the Cinematheque last month, and it gave us the giggles.

A Busby Berkeley classic: it must've transformed your inner lives. Aha. So you already live in the forties… Anyway, Chiara, you'll find it amusing to see the Optimus Hotel. It's the first phase of an even bigger complex, entirely financed by the Teutons. The German press is touting our resort as 'the Wave of the Future—in Canuba, the Caribbean's Hidden Paradise.'

A week later, you're cruising along in a roomy grey Volvo, 'lent' to Isabela by one of her assistants. On the way, the two of you review the finer points of Asian orchids, Moorish architecture, and St. Clement of Alexandria. Canuba often resembles that Buñuel flick, *The Milky Way*: on a country road, truck-drivers debate the heresies of the early Church. After Esmeralda, the pavement gets bumpier, until the asphalt peters out altogether. In the bone-breaking jostle, Isabela loses her temple-maiden aplomb. Every five minutes, as you hit a nasty rut, she hisses at the driver. 'For the love of God! Por el amor de Dios! Look where you're going!'

Displaying Canuban sang-froid, he shrugs philosophically. 'I didn't make the potholes, señorita, God did.' Or later: 'We'll get there when we get there, God willing—si Dios quiere.'

Chiara Our Tiara, you save the day. The gatekeepers are budding Latino Nazis, 'just following orders.' The Germans have commanded: no strangers allowed. They shunt you off to one side, but you cajole the chief guard. Contritely, he doffs his hat to Isabela. — Señorita, I'm extremely sorry. I didn't realize that you ladies are friends of Señor Catulo Miranda. You'll find him in the administration building, to your left.

I glide down the steps from my office, wreathed in smiles, as soon as I hear your dulcet voices at the reception desk. By automatic reflex, I glance at myself in the full-length mirror. My bald head gleams under the fluorescent lights, and a dapper fuchsia suit sets off my physique.

So you rule the roost here, Catulo? Isabela asks dryly, as she kisses me on the cheek. That's very resourceful of you… By the way, you have to change that horrid lighting.

I know. It's temporary. We slapped the buildings up in a hurry, for the first batch of gringos—I mean guests. We'll get around to the decorating soon.

You know what I always say: last things first, Isabela upbraids me, with an imperious air.

But darling, you need to lower your standards. You've lived in an ivory tower too long.

She bristles. — I don't live in an ivory tower—you and your brothers do. I'm up to my elbows in dirt all day.

In gold dust, you mean.

No comment, Catulo. Maybe you're the one with the Midas touch. Right when I was about to get out and continue on foot, the track straightened out like a highway in Arizona. We passed an airstrip, where a plane was disgorging people in tank-tops and shorts. More Germans for your tourist trap, I suppose.

The people who paved the road are Teutons, too.

I liked this beach better when it was virgin, Catulo. I wish they'd leave our island in peace.

Yes, virgin is the operative word. You want to defend those 'holy holes' you love so much. You'll appreciate them even more, on the rocky trip back home.

I'm patient with you, Catulo, but not when you make light of the Santa Colina.

What's that? you ask, turning around.

Gracious, Chiara! It's a hill near Esmeralda, Isabela intones, where Columbus fought the Indians on his Second Voyage. Since they were hopelessly outnumbered, the Blessed Virgin rescued him and his men, assuring them a decisive victory. It was the first triumph of the Church over the heathens.

Ah-ah-ah, you know it's bad luck to mention that shyster's name, I chide her. Thank goodness his nephew Santiago quickly replaced him. You see, Chiara, the Admiral of the Ocean Sea planted a cross on the hilltop, to acknowledge St. Mary's intervention. It was made of wood, so there's nothing left but the hole where it stood. Believe it or not, pilgrims crawl up the slope on their knees to the Santo Hoyo— the Holy Hole!

Ultramontane piety is a fixture of Isabela's lineage. In

annoyance, she leapfrogs the subject. — That neon sign is awful: Playa Cerrucho. Why did they have to build such a gigantic entryway? It's out of proportion with the campesino huts nearby.

Oh, it's like the Spanish with their big ole fortress, or Francis Drake with his big ole cannons. We've got to show everybody who's boss.

Piqued by my allusion to her forefathers, Isabela nitpicks. — Your thugs wouldn't let us through, even though I told them I'm Señorita BURLEY LUNA. I let them have it: You mean in my own country, I can't even enter a stupid hotel!

Ah, now you know how the people you exclude from your parties must feel.

Watch out, or you're going to be one of them. — Remembering herself, she continues coolly. — Oh, my little teas are so haphazard, I'm sure nobody cares.

When she looks away, Chiara, you wink at me. She spends weeks planning her 'at homes': drawing up the guest list, fussing over the menu, and laying out the place cards. Mainly with an eye to snagging rich spouses for her cousins and 'cousines.'

Let me give you the grand tour, meine Damen. Remember, ladies, we haven't tied the loose threads yet.

The devil is in the details, Isabela objects.

For the next half-hour we marvel anew at her composure, her sovereign cordiality. As I lead the two of you around the half-built site, we pass one concrete box after another: small ones, large ones, barely started ones. These are anathema to her; but she never flinches. At the end, I demand point blank: Well, what do you think, Isabela?

She clears her throat. The place has potential—for tourists.

In other words, you abhor it. What we need is vegetation, I bubble. And that's where we could use your advice.

Hermosa gained a lot by my plantings, I'm told. They even mask the ugliness of that Disney replica, Isla Fandango. — Her upper lip curls with distaste; Fandango's pastiche of her cherished Colonial past puts a crack in her studied facade. — This is more like that monstrosity of Espinosa's, the Columbus Crown. Carolina and I are still plugging away on the landscaping there. But it's better, in a way, to start from zero. For you, dear Catulo, I'll always do whatever I can.

I rub my hands together: That settles it!

Isabela notices a massage salon along the walkway. We've got forty-five minutes till the performance, she groans. My back is killing me, from all that garden work. She ducks into the door, without further ado.

I shake my head. — Poor little peasant girl. — You and I stroll to the beach; it cuts a wide, snow-white swath between the swaying coconuts and the placid sea. — Compared to Barlovento, Chiara, with its mountains and coves, this landscape must seem dull.

The whole island was extraordinary once... in the days before mass tourism destroyed it.

I switch to my obsessive topic: me. — Let's hope the floorshows in Cerrucho get me back in the groove. Ever since I took up hotel management, I've neglected my choreography. In New York, I interned with Louis Falco, Merce Cunningham, and Twyla Tharp, so I know about serious dance. All right, all right, I've also been distracted by extracurricular pursuits...

You mean Pomona, I assume.

Come on, girlfriend, are you pulling my leg? We're still living in the Golden Age, before the genders got divided. Remember the *Symposium*? The part about Zeus splitting up the sexes? Well, the Top God forgot to visit this island, or maybe it didn't fit in with his vacation plans. My affair with Pomona has been going on for years. But that doesn't stop me from jumping in bed with *all* the men around here.

Your usual hyperbole.

I'll amend that: only the men over thirty. Until then, they're too awkward and confused. But after they've practiced long enough, they're ready for me. In Hermosa and Isla Fandango, I seduced every thirty-something cook, waiter, and gardener. I've never had one turn me down. Would you like to see my checklist? It's not quite Don Giovanni's '1003,' but I'll probably beat him soon.

You dutifully attend my dress rehearsal, Chiara. The event isn't as lousy as you expected: a small-scale version of the Folies Bergères. To please my special guests, at the last minute I've thrown in some gags from Busby Berkeley. They scatter a few crumbs of comic relief, but only for Hollywood buffs.

Isabela is a no-show. Just before you undertake your long drive home, she slinks out of our headquarters, as smug as the cat that ate the canary. She must've closed an exorbitant deal with the Germans, though only through nods and blinks. Money is beneath her dignity… in Puerto Indio, she'll keep these landscaping services under wraps. When she catches sight of us, she resumes her temple-maiden demeanor. Fair enough. She's the Alpha and Omega of this island: her people had the first laugh, and they'll have the last one, too.

Palacio Canuba, summer 1991

The next time I come to town, you have a million questions about Chuchu, especially after Lamia's vicious fang-bites. Apparently, the serpent-woman has been doing a job on you. Jealousy, I guess!

All right, Chiara, I'll fill you in. Chuchu was born into a family so transnational that it's stateless. They have a fortune so offshore, it has no location. She always spent the summers with her cousins in Canuba. But she grew up in Hong Kong.

You wrinkle your nose. — Why Hong Kong? I love the energy, and the monasteries on Lantau. But it's a long way from here.

We're sitting in a nook of the Art Deco Bar at Palacio Canuba, the most luxurious hotel on the island. It's the Happy Hour, and with all the gin fizzes we've downed, we're Happy all right. I'm dressed in my usual preppy pastels, and you're wearing your de rigueur Nurse Chiara whites. We speak in muted tones, since Chuchu herself is holding court at the opposite end of the room. She droops like a strung-out Pavlova, unheeded by her corps de ballet, who chatter as if she weren't there.

Her father has always liked Hong Kong for the nightlife, girlfriend. And for his business ventures. From what I've heard, he launders money for the Chinese mafia.

What about her mother?

She was French, from St. Tropez; but she OD'd on heroin when Chuchu was only five.

How awful. So she was brought up by nannies?

If only they'd been nannies, Chiara. But they were floozies her father scraped off the floor. The Thai masseuse, the San Diego waitress, the Russian coat-check girl. Chuchu ran away from 'home' when she was fourteen.

Where did she go?

She kicked around for several years. India, Cambodia, Australia. Some surfers at Manly Beach got her hooked on crack. They chained her to the wall of their pad and used her as a screw-rag for several months. Then and there, she swore off macho men for good. Half-dead, she sent an SOS to her cousins, and they flew her back to Puerto Indio. Their lawyers have wrested part of her inheritance back from her father.

Did he steal it?

I stand up and stretch, flaunting my muscular silhouette. — It depends on whose side you're on. Pleverino claims it's all his; but Chuchu says her grandfather's will left half the dough to her. Most folks agree with her, but some—like Frederica—root for him.

Oh, she likes to go against the grain.

You mean go *for* the grain, like a hen. Pleverino is Frederica's biggest backer. I've heard she's expanding her 'hostels for young ladies' to several new countries in Asia.

You ask the waiter for more ice. — She and I never talk about such things.

Keeping your ears clean, huh? Then let me muddy them up. There's been a string of court proceedings between Chuchu and her father in Grand Cayman. In the first bout, he tried to fend her off with a trust fund. She calls it the 'Pontius Pilate Doggie Biscuit.' It would be more than enough for your average zillionaire, but she keeps suing him 'on principle.'

More power to her.

If the loot were really for her, Chiara, I'd agree. But the

lawsuits earn her attorneys tons of fees: that's why they egg her on. It's just not right. And remember all the drag-queens we met at the Fontaines? They're Chuchu's hangers-on. You already saw them years ago at La Cumbre, the immortal Summit of all nightclubs, when Amado took you there. She gives each of those ladies-in-waiting a monthly allowance. They hover around her like dragonflies.

Barflies, I'd say. Do I detect a note of compassion?

My eyes mist up a bit. — Sure, I feel sorry for her. We've always bickered, just for the hell of it. But the drugs have ruined her health, and that's very sad.

You glance across the room, over my shoulder. — You're right. Chuchu isn't just high, she's as high as K2. She doesn't look pugnacious today.

The jousting match you witnessed may have been her farewell bitch-a-thon. She's so zoned out, she rarely opens her mouth anymore.

Even to her husband?

I snort. — Farfalo? What could she talk about with him? Lace panties?

Where did she meet him?

Here in Canuba, where her grandfather started his financial empire. She's always had a soft spot for Puerto Indio. Farfalo latched onto her at the Summit.

A cloud passes over your brow. — That crazy place, La Cumbre... what a bittersweet memory. It was great when I saw Amado and Reina do their dance routine there. But it's also where he and you had your last meeting, shortly before he died.

I don't remind you that Amado face-raped Chuchu that night, when the heiress was so blotto, she didn't even react. My description of that evening must be haunting you right now. I can be intuitive when I want to be. I reach over and hold your hand. After a while, you pull yourself together. — Farfalo's not the Manly Beach type, so Chuchu got what she bargained for. And he hit the jackpot.

That's for sure. But it's a golden cage, and he's afraid for his life.

You gulp. — He thinks she'll beat him to death?

Hahaha. I can tell you've been schmoozing with a neo-Hellenic snake. No, the problem is Pleverino. He's always giving interviews to gossip mags like *Hola!* and *Jours de France*. You know: crocodile tears, poor-mouthing, showing off. 'By putting half a billion dollars into my daughter's trust fund, I've made myself destitute!' It's all meant to snow the judges in Grand Cayman. With amounts like that bouncing through the press, Farfalo is terrified he'll get kidnapped—carved up in pieces bit by bit, and sent through the mail to his spouse.

How dreadful, Catulo!

I twiddle the straw in my drink. — Between you and me, Chiara, he probably gets off on the idea. Anyway, Pleverino is full of you know what. He's wealthier than ever. How else could he give those sumptuous parties in Hong Kong? The last one was at the Peninsula, for a thousand guests. The caterers made a map of Canuba in the ballroom: orchids for the mountain ranges, champagne for the rivers, black caviar for the sea.

Sounds like he's generous to his friends, at any rate.

Maybe, but he's a vindictive sonofabitch to his daughter. One time in a restaurant, I saw him flap his ears at Chuchu. Amazing. He screwed up his face like Jim Carrie. He was so outrageous the owner asked him to leave.

I guess she has plenty of reasons to 'self-medicate.'

To tell the truth, the 'meds' are probably her only hold on sanity. For now. — My jaw tenses. — You've only seen the smiley face of Lotos Land. But fasten your seatbelt! — I raise my glass in a toast. — Here's to the dark side of the moon! — Right away, I have to cross myself. — Oh, I'm sorry, Chiara. How could I be so callous? God knows Amado's accident was 'dark' enough!

Thank God, I'm saved by the bell. The soiree takes a more pleasant turn when Héctor—your old rival for Amado—sidles up to our table with a tall, sandy-haired Norwegian. You recognize him instantly: he's one of the cetologists you worked with in Barlovento, as it turns out.

Bjørn! you exclaim. What brings you back to Canuba? Still chasing whales?

The diffident titan puts his arm around Héctor. — I've married this good-looking guy. He may be small, but he knows how to boss me around—when I let him. Science and art: it's the ideal combination.

Héctor laughs, his blond moustache spiking with contentment. — We tied the knot in Denmark last summer. It's the first country to allow civil unions. — He throws back his head. — I've never been so ecstatic!

The two men join us at our table for several rounds of drinks. At one point, Héctor takes your hand. — I'm so sorry about Amado. It's been a couple of years now, but they tell me you're still in mourning. If there's anything Bjørn and I can do, please let us know.

You look into his eyes. — It means the world to me to hear that from you, Héctor... Despite our quarrels, you loved Amado too. The struggle has been long and hard, but I'm almost out of the woods.

A poignant interlude, with a soundtrack of strings... After that, the four of us go on carousing. Around midnight, we end up at La Cumbre, for auld lang syne.

You're a bit peeked the following day. But I feel as peppy as a summer wasp when I circle by for lunch, toting a box of fine wines. — Here you are, girlfriend. A donation to the commonwealth.

You moan. — Argh. More alcohol?

I've told you before. Nuns shouldn't leave the convent at night, Sister Chiara. It's bad for their 're-*puta*-ciones.' — I study myself in one of your full-length mirrors. Though I live at the beach, my domed white pate is untouched by the sun. I don't envy your thick, auburn hair. What a hassle it must be to wash it. — I've got some fab news, girlfriend. I found out this morning.

Just then the phone rings, and you pick up the receiver. — Oh hello, Horacio. Guess who's here, your brother Catulo.

I'm close enough so I can hear his high, gossamer voice. — That is nothing novel, my Magna Graecian divinity. You will not lend me credence, but I am telecommunicating about the alternate frater. The prolegomenon has perdured for a decennial, yet at last Virgilio desires an assignation with you.

What an honor! When?

He proposes the diurnal unit dedicated to Mars, or Aries. However, you must not attempt to impersonate Aphrodite. At the novenary nocturnal hour?

Tuesday at nine PM. I accept with pleasure—and excitement!

You say good-bye: an endless adieu—vintage Horacio. I follow you to the dining table, pouting as I go. — My baby brothers have upstaged me again. So now you've been convoked by the Wizard of Oz.

Humbug. I know you admire Virgilio.

I don't understand him, Dorothy. But maybe he'll give me a brain. Anyway, as I wanted to say before, I've got some news of my own!

I'm all ears, you answer, enlarging them with both hands.

I waltz around the room. — I've been keeping this under wraps for ages. I wanted you to be the first to find out. I've landed a lucrative job at the 'mega-resort of the Wild Southeast, on Playa Cerrucho,' as our brochures proudly proclaim. From now on, I'm the Director of Events and Entertainment. The consortium is building a magnificent ballroom, with a huge theatre attached. For the opening, I'm staging a Folies Bergères show. You're my special guest, Principessa.

I wouldn't miss it, Catulo. Cross my heart and hope to die. I suppose I'll have to rent a car.

Maybe you can catch a ride with the Greek-Canuban bombshell. She hates me, but curiosity killed the cat—and the snake, too, I'll wager. Or you could bum a lift with Isabela—she's invited, of course. And she always makes a beeline for anything that smells like cash.

Plaza Drake, summer 1991

In 1991, while we're shaping the master plan, my new job in Cerrucho—still a secret from my friends—gives me more leeway than in Hermosa. To tell the truth, I've been twotiming both resorts for several years. Sure, I have to confer with the surveyors and architects on the Cerrucho site. But as one of the head honchos, I can fly to Puerto

Indio anytime I want in the company plane. As the months flow by, I report to your house once a week. More than ever, we're a two-member lunch club, and I always pay my dues with Bacchic gifts.

One morning, I burst through the door doing my Noël Coward routine, complete with the Broadway version of 'Mad About the Boy.' I mug: You notice I put the censored lines back in.

I'm a Monteverdi girl myself. But I can guess what kind of lines you mean.

I cut up as usual throughout the meal; but you can tell I've got something on my mind. When I rub your scalp on the roof after coffee, my fingers seem nervous and stiff. — I need a change of pace, girlfriend, and so do you. That whale-watching trip way back when was a lot of fun. Why don't we go to Cayo Encantado again? They say the hotel's been finished, at long last.

Lazily, you lean your head against my belly. — To tell the truth… I'll always associate Cayo Encantado with your prank on the beach.

So you *did* see us! Amado and I thought so. You're such a tight-assed Italian, I never brought it up. Well, kiddo, are you still miffed?

I should be, I suppose. You were more of a challenge than Reina… a soul-brother who'd listen to Amado's problems, like me.

Reina had an ace up her sleeve: she was the mother of

his children. But then Esperanza came along, and he had a child with her, too. To Amado, you and I were free spirits. He felt trapped.

He seemed pretty footloose to me!

Reproduction is nice, don't get me wrong. But it's an illusion. We can't replicate ourselves: we create somebody new. And men often complain that their wings have been clipped.

Maybe so they'll grow new ones. 'In dreams begin responsibilities.' Don't kid yourself, Catulo. Women have a hard time adjusting, too.

I pace around the terrace. Could I be the jealous one? Finally, I have to come clean. — Amado did give me a certain priority. After all, I discovered him.

What do you mean, 'discovered' him?

You bet. Years and years ago, when our boy was only seventeen. Even before Héctor got his paws on him. I'm glad I can talk about it now, without setting you off. You've cried too much since he passed on.

When you speak up again, you sound matter-of-fact. — I'm not surprised, Catulo. You've led many a straight arrow down the primrose path.

What a mishmash of metaphors! Straight? 'He's gay, I'm straight, she's a lesbian.' Malarkey! Around here, we're all AC-DC-BC. Anything else would be unnatural. Oh, I'm insatiable, I'll grant you that. Like Walt, I'm always on the lookout for somebody new.

New? Then Amado didn't qualify.

You want to make me squirm, but you can't. — Bah. You should've joined us. Amado was as horny as hell. Pumping iron does that to you. Dancercise, too. — I'm just testing you, to see how much you can take.

And on Cayo Encantado, a bald Sylphide was ready to comply.

I bend over, and hug you from behind. — You're still annoyed, Chiara. I can tell.

Not at all. You two were beautiful that day: like gods making love in a myth. — You stand up and turn around. — You've been a gentleman, on the whole. You let me have Amado for ten years, without butting in.

What a pun, darling… Not because I was selfless. I had plenty of other fish to fry.

That's what worries me, Catulo.

For the first time since we've known each other, our constant comment grinds to a halt. We can hear the bananaquits chirping in the rain-flowers, and some kids playing baseball in the nearby square. — You're very serious today, girlfriend. What's up?

You walk to the edge of the terrace and stare at the Cathedral apse, skewered by the bright light of early afternoon. — I wasn't afraid of losing Amado; we were practically a married couple. I've only been concerned about our health. The health of all of us: you, him, Lamia, me. There's an epidemic going on. It started in Europe and the States, and now it's everywhere.

I keep up a cool, nonchalant front. — Yes, I've heard of it: AIDS. But it hasn't hit this island yet.

I wonder why. There's so much promiscuity here. People do it with men, women—even animals, in the countryside...

I reflect for a moment. — At least I've never cared for koalas, green monkeys, or cockatoos: that limits the field. Don't forget the sex-tourists who come and go. Whoops, another unfortunate pun. I guess you're right, Chiara: Canuba is a time bomb.

I'm glad you're aware of that.

I try to be careful these days.

I can tell by your expression you don't believe me. Sometimes I slip up: do it bareback, or 'drink a squirt of warm milk,' as I like to joke. You sigh. — They say it's more dangerous when you take the passive role...

I buck myself up. — So, I've got a fifty-fifty chance. I'm not going to let gloom and doom ruin my fun. Besides, kiddo, these days I serve more shakes than hotdog buns. In this kind of epic, the oral tradition is safer. Especially if you're the Oralee. — I sing a deadpan solo of Stephen Foster's tune.

You smile at me tenderly. You're thinking of all our years together—the Balanchine evenings in New York, the giddy parties at Frederica's, the titillating drinks on your roof... Ours is a classic case of 'amité amoureuse...' You know I have to be what I'm meant to be, and do what I'm meant to do. You can only acquiesce…

Hey girlfriend, I chuckle, how about a glass of Courvoisier?

Plaza Drake and Zarzuela, summer 1991

It's raining this morning, more a London drizzle than a tropical storm. Just a drop or two, and Canubans stay home, like the Wicked Witch of the West. So there won't be much trade at the Almirante lounge. Not even a pimply twink or middle-aged drunk. What a bummer.

Well, I might as well look in on you, Chiara. It's been a couple of weeks since the last time, and I'm beginning to feel guilty. Not normal for me. My job at the Hermosa resort bores me silly, it's so old hat. I've sent out my CV to several places: we'll see. Maybe my moonlighting at Playa Cerrucho will turn permanent. In the meantime, I've started absconding to the city more often, supposedly for promotional purposes. It's only a couple of hours in my Suzuki jeep. By the time I get here, I'm in the market for wilder scenes than you can provide.

At least you always stand me for lunch—even if it *is* just the mediocre fare Luz Divina raised us on. She was inept enough when she worked for our parents, stubborn and spiteful as a mule. As a washerwoman, she topped the charts; but as a cook, she was Ivana the Terrible. You only tolerate her grub because to you, it's exotic. When Italians go abroad, anything will do: outside the Belpaese, cuisine is inedible, so why make a kerfuffle?

Today is no different. As soon as I sweep you off your feet with my stellar version of 'Singin' in the Rain,' I sashay back to the kitchen. Luz Divina is stirring up a dish I can't stand, moro—a blend of black beans and rice, with a dash of red chili. She'd be horrified to know the pepper is a Bono touch. She's a racial purist, if ever there was one. Ironically, like most Canubans, she's a mixture herself.

Grumbling about my hearty appetite, she plops the chow on your oval table, turned at an angle toward the patio's flowers and palms. — Can't you ever tell us you're coming, Catulo? You're a bottomless pit. Now there won't be any left for me.

I thumb my nose at her. I don't buy that one bit: she only eats when she gets back home, where she can wolf down lots of meat. Her moro has improved somewhat since my childhood days. It smells like sweet tobacco, and we cure it with the Duero red I brought along.

The rain tapers off, and the sun transforms it into steam. After coffee, as we sip Spanish brandy on the roof, you turn polemical. — You know what? To me, moro is a symbol of unity.

Come on, girlfriend. You mean the beans are the Bonos,

and we're the white rice?

Off-white, anyway.

I roll my eyes. — Give me a break, Chiara! You European busybodies should stuff it. We're *not* going to unite in a 'community' like you, no matter what.

You mean *re*unite, as in the two-island colony. It would make more sense. There are so many Bonaventurans here already! They're escaping from Hervé Chinon, the bloodiest dictator on earth. Even Espinosa treats them better than he does.

I jump up and massage your shoulders. — Lay off, girlfriend. It ain't none o' yo' bidness. What if we *all* end up under Chinon instead? A friggin' nightmare... We Canubans prefer the three cardinal directions.

You go slack, then sit up like a poker. — Wait a minute, don't you mean the *four* cardinal directions?

I snigger. — Haven't you ever noticed? A chunk of Canuba is missing. We talk about the south, west, and north, but nobody mentions the east.

Right, now that I think of it. Why is that?

I knead your neck. — Because for us, when the French took over 'la Bonaventure,' the whole east went with it. Presto: now you see it, now you don't.

That's bizarre, Catulo. A three-sided map, like a two-legged stool. As you always say, here 'magic realism' is everyday life. — You push me back into my chair. — Enough, 'boyfriend.' You're trying to change the subject.

Which is?

Unifying the islands again. Don't tell me you're like Lamia. She despises Bonaventura, even if she *is* in the Castro camp.

She's about as left-wing as Frederica, who's always bragging she's a Communist at heart. Listen, hon, you're ten times more pinko than both of them put together. — I give your cheek an amicable slap. — But you have to get things straight. We Canubans didn't win independence from Spain, we won it from the Bonaventurans. They invaded us, remember? We're nationalists, not racists!

Here, what's the difference? In Lamia, the two things overlap.

So, white girl: you think you have a leg up. — I eye you sympathetically. — Take it from me, Chiara. Lamia is too hot to handle for long!

You hang your head. — She's a real firecracker, all right: the original Latina.

Worse. Don't forget her Greek side. I went to Epidauris one summer. Good God! Aeschylus in the raw. It sounded like a family brawl in Astoria. You could almost hear the N train rumbling by.

I've seen Euripides in Syracuse. We Sicilians are Greeks, too—deep down. But there's something overblown about Lamia, something larger than life.

Oh, Lamia is Little League, compared to Chuchu.

I see what you mean, after our dinner at the Fontaines.

By the way, where did she get that name?

You know how screwball our nicknames are. Her real name is Yolanda Mendoza de la Carpa; and even for Canuba, she's off the graph. She's like the witch-goddess in *Demon Pond*. Next to her, Lamia's nothing but a big-mouth catfish.

Like the bottom-feeders in the film. One of my all-time favorites—yours too. And Chuchu is the she-devil, you mean. The same onnagata plays the temple maiden. I thought of her when Lamia took me to meet Isabela.

No, Chuchu's a bio-woman—organic, what's left of her. Of all the dragon ladies on the island, she's the only one worth tangling with. But back to her in a moment. — I imitate a fanfare of trumpets. — All hail, all hail! Yes, the heralds tell me you've scaled the highest social peak by bowing to the Veggie Pear Queen. Did Lamia, the Vaca Loca, seem a bit cowed?

Very much so, Catulo. But I couldn't figure out why.

Come on, Doctora Watson, I rib you. Just consider: what is the thing Lamia most wants in the world? A super-rich, world-class hubby. And who deals in such commodities? Isabela.

You don't like that remark. You want to be the serpent's hubby yourself. But you make a pretense of objectivity. — From what I've heard, Isabela only stocks homegrown husbands, like her vegetables.

Don't let her fool you. She's playing Marie Antoinette on

that property of hers, smack in the middle of the Malecón. Normally, it should've been squashed under a thirty-story apartment house.

I go on to tell you that it's part of Isabela's mystique never to mention ignoble ducats. Her veggies command steep prices among the wealthy, and she sends them as gifts only to prospective customers—a sure sign that they've 'arrived.' The lucky few don't belong to a crass clientele: they see themselves, and each other, as an exclusive coterie. 'These must be Burley Luna beans' is the highest praise a hostess can receive. Frederica's never heard that from her dinner guests, needless to say.

It just so happens that Isabela's beneficiaries make her lavish gifts in return—emeralds, or valuable artworks, or expensive cars. Such baubles, she humbly protests, clash with her simplicity. But she never refuses them, for fear of 'hurting people's feelings.' Somewhere, somehow, one of her 'assistants'—her euphemism for everyone from gardeners to stock-brokers—converts the assets into ready cash, then transfers the loot to her far-flung bank accounts. No taxes paid.

A handy trick, Catulo.

Right. She also cultivates her cousinship, arranging marriages for her poor relations, to tap a steady supply of wealth. Unlike Isabela, her kinsmen haven't generated any income of their own for well over a century. But they dominate the richest bloodlines on the island. Everybody wonders: what juicy pepino will she pick from the vine for herself?

Maybe there's no cucumber up to her level.

Or fig. Some say she uses her female 'assistants' as rubbing posts. Anyway, girlfriend, you should never underestimate our farm-gal, Isabela. Her nexus is astonishing. She owns a cattle ranch in Montana, a spruce forest in Sweden, a spice plantation in Sumatra… And those are just a few of the places I happen to know about.

She's uncanny. As I've said, she reminds me of the temple maiden in *Demon Pond*.

You're on to something there: she's Chuchu's alter ego. Those two are more than friends, they're twins—despite outward appearances. Chuchu's zoned-out, and Isabela's la-di-da, but both of them look down on the great unwashed—especially the upstarts, with their just-acquired loot. And there's a deeper parallel. Chuchu wars with her father, and Isabela detests her mother. She sweet-talks the woman with terms of endearment, while pointedly ignoring her. Free of parental bonds, Chuchu and Isabela reign supreme, in their own self-made worlds.

What's Isabela's mother like? I can hardly imagine. She seems like Athena, 'sprung full-blown from the head of Zeus.'

I clap my hands. — Tell her that, the next time you see her. She'll love it. She's convinced her birth was a parthenogenesis.

Fueled by Solera cognac, I rattle on that her father, Alejandro Burley Luna y Peralta, was the finest gentlemen on the island. In Espinosa's bloodiest phase, he was the only Canuban who opposed him and lived to tell the tale. When he reached sixty-five, his first wife died of leukemia; sadly, she'd remained childless. Like many a widower, he soon fell prey to a nubile adventuress, whom he met in the Oak Bar at the Plaza. And soon enough, Don Alejandro kicked the bucket in turn. Melba Lou was much smarter than the guttersnipes Chuchu's father picks up; a brash, blonde starlet from Arkansas, she demanded an official marriage. She always embarrassed Isabela, who's struggled to 'improve' her, to no avail. Don Alejandro owned a patrician mansion in the Old Quarter. With the proceeds from the sale, Melba Lou bought one of those concrete boxes in the hills.

You frown. Oh, the type Frederica loves to hate!

And Isabela, too. When she was still a child, her ancestral house was snapped up by a boutique hotel; she was irate. She ended up with the bean farm on the Malecón, her father's only other property. All her life, she's been trying to erase the blot on her escutcheon: her mother—'that there wummin from the Ozarks.' Melba Lou comes from the 'moon-you' backside of Appalachia, where your sister might be your wife. To her intimates, Isabela vows she's her father's daughter—and his alone.

Humpf. She's lucky her mother had red blood to beef up the sickly blue.

Like your transfusion from your father, eh? — That brings you up short. — Anyway, Melba Lou has led a tragic existence, despite her instant wealth. Her younger daughter, Sandra, died in a freak water-skiing accident at the age of sixteen. It was Easter Sunday, and she was cutting capers on a lake in Arkansas, when her boyfriend's ski-cable beheaded her. She had the same Irish complexion as her mother. She resembled her in personality, too: the peppy cheerleader type.

Every year since then, Melba Lou has held a reception on Easter Sunday. Supposedly, she wants to have company, so she can forget about her loss. But 'once an actress, always an actress.' Around midnight, after five drinks too many, she cranks up her soliloquy, and the guests become the audience. 'Ooooohhh, that turrrible day when I lost my baaaabyyyy!' She moans and sobs, the tears wreck her makeup, and her knees collapse. As a grand finale, the butler, a chisled he-man—I suspect he's her 'servant of all work'—carries her up to bed. From the top of the staircase, she beckons a good-night to her fandom, like Norma Desmond in reverse. Then the party wheels on, as gaily as before.

Hmm, I can see why Isabela disapproves. 'Not the done thing.'

Yes, she always sticks to convention, while Chuchu takes the role of the renegade. As you say, Isabela is the temple maiden beside the lake. Her rituals of growing yucca and guavas reconnect us to our Taíno roots.

You sound like Horacio now.

I'm not New Age, but I'll hand him this. Isabela links us to the recurring cycle of time; she keeps our feet planted firmly on the ground. Without her, Melba Lou would be selling booze in Little Rock, Chuchu would be in a madhouse on Lake Leman, and Lamia would be peddling whores in Bucharest. Along with veggies and fruit, she doles out advice, so people can cope. Only at their request, mind you; she never forces herself on anyone. It might be something trivial, like how to redecorate a sunroom. Or what a bride should wear at her second wedding. Then again, it might be momentous. Should I change professions, or enter a convent? Or even, should I kill myself? But small things often loom larger than big ones, don't you agree? Isabela knows about that, from the nitty-gritty chores of tending her garden. Ringing the temple bell, so to speak. For now, the demon princess stays at the bottom of the pond, and the enchanted valley is safe.

Until she breaks free and floods it, drowning everybody in her path. If Chuchu's like her alter ego, she must be a fiend.

You'll find out soon enough! We're invited to dinner at Arnaud and Fátima's tonight, and the demon princess will also attend.

Now you tell me. What if I had other plans?

I wave you off. — You'd have to break them.

Well, I do like the Fontaines. I met them at Frederica's.

Natch, where else? Gotta run now. I'll swing by for you at nine!

Meanwhile, a brief visit to the Almirante Hotel yields 'No Bananas Today,' just as I expected. They don't thrive under these bleary London skies. I spend the rest of the afternoon minding the curio shop for my brothers. A few cheapo tourists drop by to ooh and aah, but they don't buy anything. As the rain continues to dribble, I feel like Kit Nubbles in a scene from Dickens. Finally, I doze off on the daybed, my comfy burrow on Callejón del Platero.

At the appointed hour, it takes us a while to drive to Zarzuela, the Belle Époque neighborhood next to the Barrio Antiguo. The storm drains are clogged with debris, and the streets are Olympic-size puddles. Stray dogs splash around, pursuing wet cats and soggy pigeons. Strangely, in keeping with the Albion theme, the temperature is downright chilly.

We're relieved when we stick our brollies in the umbrella stand, at the entrance to the lyre-shaped facade. Arnaud and Fátima press a hot toddy on us, and soon we're a jolly bunch. For the time being, you forget about Chuchu, you're relishing our hosts so much. They've just returned from Fátima's native Brazil, and they're full of comic details about Belo Horizonte, where most of her relatives live.

After that, the conversation turns more serious. Arnaud draws parallels between the Taíno Last Supper in our

Cathedral and Aleijajinho's version in Minas Gerais. — The pathos in both these works overwhelms me, especially because the figures are life-size, and painted in realistic hues. Here, I can almost see them move, raising a glass or reaching for bread. In Congonjas, when we entered the chapel, the guards were eating feijoada next to Christ and the Apostles. Two tables, one meal: le bois et la chair—wood and flesh.

The Belgian diplomat and his wife also report at length on the African cults in Recife. You're in your element, Chiara, but my eyes are glazing over. Lamia and I agree on one thing: we're indifferent to trendy talk about the 'diaspora.' Not that we're racists, mind you. But as Latinos, why should we think in terms of black and white? We're not keen on Viking outposts in Vinland, either. A rainbow of diasporas courses through our veins. Why focus on only one? Yes, I know: the forced immigration of slaves is a special case, which I decry with all my heart... Anyway, what with the PC-patter inside and the rain-patter outside, I almost drop off again. Coming to with a jolt, I ask myself impatiently: Is Chuchu ever going to show her ass? Little did I imagine how apropos that expletive would be.

As if on cue, the doorbell rings. When Arnaud lets her in, Chuchu's slight, anemic body wafts across the threshold, airy as a dandelion puff. Her dress is expensive and austere: under its sheer black folds, an iridescent band clasps her waist. Soon it dawns on us that she's wearing nothing else beneath her translucent robe. You and I share sisterly winks of amusement.

Like the demon princess in the bottom-feeder muck, Chuchu never appears without her courtly entourage. Half a dozen androgynous men, some in full drag, flock into the room behind her. Absurdly, they set off her gestures with fluid, synchronized poses, like a corps of ballerinas.

She starts and stares dramatically at me, a vignette worthy of Hedy Lamar. Verbally, she refuses to acknowledge my presence. After a solemn pause, she extends her hand to you, palm downward. You have no choice but to brush it with your lips. Even in the warm candlelight, her skin is as pallid as a cadaver's. Her fawn-colored hair hangs limply around her flat, doll-like face. When she speaks at last, her voice seems to echo from the bottom of a tomb.

Allora, you are the Italian guest? Arnaud didn't tell me you'd be so badly accompanied. I suppose he was afraid of putting me off.

I step forward and curtsey. — Dear, delirious Chuchu. You're in a daze, as usual. Maybe you should take another pill, to clarify your mind.

Well, you have always been as clear as day. — She peers down her nose, as at a specimen. — Pomona or no Pomona. You don't even need to flap your wings.

Her gaggle of queens circles closer, sensing her anger rise. I stare them down from a majestic height, the ethereal realm of art. — I'd rather be a swan than a goose-herder like you.

How dare you insult my friends?

Oh, there's nothing wrong with an honest goose. It's the barnyard sluts who step in the dung.

Unlike you peasant catamites, I don't go barefoot.

No, just bare-ass—judging by that get-up you're in.

This is one of Lagerfeld's most exquisite creations.

I squint for effect. — Then it deserves something better than your birthday suit.

I have nothing to hide.

And nothing to reveal.

Do you have anything to dangle, you eunuch? — Her timbre is muffled and rotund, like the tones of an engulfed bell. I'm reminded of Debussy's 'cathédrale engloutie.'

Yes. But only in private, not to a public procuress.

Chuchu's visage blanches even more, like a dying star. She summons her minions with wan resignation—Hecuba among her women, in the ruins of Troy. Her final words boom from the depths of her tiny frame. — I came here to make a new acquaintance, not to duel with you. What a waste of time. You're nothing but a petty-bourgeois cunt.

She drifts out of the room, leaving a gratified smirk on my lips. Her ladies-in-waiting gauge the damage of her farewell blast; and then they make their exeunt.

On the way home, I can't contain myself. — There's nothing like a drama queen. I absolutely adore sparring with an equal. Or near-equal, hahaha. After all, girlfriend, none can compare with yours truly.

You demur, of course, you're such a goody-goody. — Catulo, I've never known you to behave so rudely. I felt ashamed, as if a beloved pet had bitten somebody's leg.

I'm no poodle. More like a mastiff. Woof woof woof! You have to bark, when you're dealing with a bitch. If she doesn't watch out, I'll yelp at her like a wolf.

Plaza Drake, summer 1991

Poor Chiara. When you first come to our island, you nurse the illusion we'll pick up where we left off. We were lovers during your Master's gig at Princeton, when I was at NYU. We're still close, here in Canuba; but alas for you, close is as far as I'll go. Who knows why mannish women like you and Lamia are always falling in love with me. I'm an 'homme fatal' to everyone, but especially to the likes of you. I guess it's because I appeal to your dykey side. Now that Amado's dead, I pray to heaven you won't switch back to me. Let Lamia 'babysit' you—or worse!

Sure, it's a gas to look in on you when I swing through the city twice a month. My job as head manager of the Hermosa Resort, a two hours' drive up the coast, doesn't leave me much free time. Today I'll catch you off guard by not phoning ahead. It's always good to keep people on their toes.

As soon as you open the door, I whirl you around in one of my dance routines. Up till now my hotel has only funded a cheesy little floor-show, so I can't truly ply my trade.

Back on your own two feet, you state the obvious: I suppose you came for lunch.

I'd rather have the elixir of Bacchus, girlfriend. But only if it's your best.

Have you no decency? Why are you always such an expensive date?

Girded for combat, you go to the kitchen and ask Luz Divina to set the table for two. Heaving her shelf-like bust, our ex-housekeeper grumbles as usual. — Now you tell me. I'm not going to the market till tomorrow. Today there's nothing but rice, black frijoles, and eggplant. Berenjenas. For Catulo, it won't be enough. I raised him, don't forget: twenty years of sweating for that family of his. He eats like a horse.

I bound into the kitchen, weaving a sexy cambuca. The song's a standby from her youth, and I croon the words like a pro: How can I live without you? Como vivir sin tí?

See, Luz Divina? you con her. Catulo loves anything you serve, just because it's you.

The grouchy old frump juts out her lips. Hah. You don't know him. I do. He's a spoiled brat.

You've been a disappointment to me, too, I tease her.

Why can't you quote Aquinas while you stir the beans, like the cook in Lezama Lima?

That clams her up. The fare might be rustic… I say to myself… but at least I'll wash it down with Châteauneuf du Pape.

Over lunch, I propound my latest theory. — Lezama is an extreme; though in a subtler way, Borges—our greatest author—beats him at his game. Reading Icelandic sagas in Old Norse? Latin American writers need to prove they know far more than the scribblers in London, Paris, or New York.

You grin. — You and your brothers are Exhibit A for that.

We try to be archetypal. Our cultures are so balkanized, we're afraid we'll be dismissed as provincial.

But you also demonstrate that such fears are unfounded.

We're universalists… because we're the newbies on the block. You Italians have always been the heartbeat of civilization.

The past is no guarantee for the present, Catulo.

Ahahaha, the luxury of saying that illustrates my point. With Italy, there's no comparison.

You win, I guess! Modesty would only sound like arrogance…

On the roof-terrace, I uncork the second bottle. — Let's have some girl-talk, Chiara. I'm worried about you, hon, you're always so blue. Time to think about the future. Let's make a toast to your maiden voyage. We cruise to Porno Land tonight!

Ho-hum. Isn't that where you set sail every night?

Seriously, girlfriend. You need a break. Amado was unique, as his lovers would agree—all five thousand of us. But maybe you'll find somebody new.

How can you be so insensitive? — Despondently, you lift your glass. — I'll drink to Porno Land, but you're the only 'seaman' who's going there.

No, there'll be quite a crew.

I like to shock you with my lurid reports of the triple-x theatres, where I indulge in anonymous gropes with my fellow-patrons. The movies are strictly hetero, but the names of the establishments—the Apollo and the Lido— hint at our pungent, bi-Canuban blend.

I pat your hand. — Going exhibitionist isn't for everyone, hon.

Well, it must be for you, after those pictures you made me look at.

I knew you'd get a kick out of them. I brought you some more today.

I spread the photos on the iron table. They document me and my mates—mostly gardeners and bellboys at the resort—as snapped by other members of our gang. We proudly display ourselves in every position, suctioning and drained, plugging and plugged.

Ugh, you scoff. Why would you keep dreck like this? At

least porn is shot by professionals, no?

I can never sit still for long: dancer's jitters. — When you have a body like mine, cara Chiara, you have to share it. — I jump up again and do some pliés, then pull off my shirt.

You survey my supple, hairless torso. — Give me a break. Next you'll be calling depravity a moral duty.

More a religious duty, girlfriend. These were taken right across from the Benedictine Abbey, at the oh-so-posh Almirante.

That seedy hotel! — You burst into an Italian accent. — It's an offense to Columbus, my celebrated compatriot.

'Mock on, mock on, Voltaire, Rousseau!' Who knows, maybe Cristoforo was a fellow-traveler, too.

Hahaha. You might be right. We were a lot less inhibited when Leonardo was on the prowl.

Don't get too highbrow, puttana. Alas and alack, you're awful. You've really hurt my feelings. — I dab at my eyes. — The Hotel Almirante is my home away from home.

In fact, it *was* your home, when your grandmother was still alive.

It's true what you just said, I reverently recall... Doña Mandolina, my maternal abuela, used to own the building—a roomy Art Deco folly. In my teenage years, I stayed there during my last year at the Colegio Jesuita. Meanwhile, my two little brothers were still trotting the globe with our parents, while our father frittered away his time as a diplomat… on behalf of a country noted only for its dictator—if at all. When Abuelita died, our mother sold the house to a wandering Swede. After a decorous interval, he remodeled the place into a 'specialized inn'—for men only, with a smorgasbord of hustlers.

What do you want from me, Miss Inquisitrix? — In ersatz dismay, I bury my face in my hands. — Do you think our long-lost Tara should give me the creeps, now that it's a brothel?

Not at all. Ci mancherebbe. Truth is stranger than fiction, to coin a phrase.

I must admit it's odd to gambol with my harem where my mother grew up. And where my grandparents died— not to mention my uncle!

Your mother is remarkable. I've never had a tête-à-tête with Doña Wanda. But Horacio did invite me to lunch one day with both your parents.

Oh, all three of them are prim and proper, compared to me.

Even I am, compared to you.

You? You're a total prig. Anyway, every family has a superheroine, and ours is Wanda Woman.

You natter on about your romance with Lamia, but I'm not listening… The mention of my mother sends me into a trance. Wanda is so vivid, I always think of her in the present tense. With her grey chignon and measured gait, she epitomizes respectability. As you must know from

Luz Divina, she cares unstintingly for us all. If anyone commands our allegiance, it's Wanda…

Her lot is never easy, ever since her childhood, when her baby sister drowns in an abandoned well. Years later, in the worst phase of his reign of terror, Papito Espinosa assassinates her brother Vladimir. A young lawyer who dares to oppose the tyrant, he's found in a ditch near Esmeralda, his machete-hacked corpse covered with mud, manure, and slime. The police, after finishing him off, shelve the case as 'unsolvable.'

Luz Divina enters service to our grandmother just after Vladimir's death. On a sweltering afternoon in 1948, her first task is to prepare ginger tea, hot chocolate, and toast for the mourners at the wake. The morticians have placed the coffin on sawhorses in the parlor; they've left it sealed, the cadaver is such a mess. Espinosa's cousin Swindon, a nepotistic 'General,' drops by to offer his condolences—or in other words, to gloat.

Luz Divina always enacts her story with histrionic gestures, spoofing Swindon's mealy-mouthed hypocrisy. As soon as he darkens the door, blood seeps from the casket, dripping onto the floor. Here she raises her hands to heaven, like a Creole Theda Bara. 'His blood! His blood! This is the only way the dead man can speak: You and your cousin killed me, you bastards.' Luckily for our housekeeper, the General ignores women on principle, and so she is spared.

Fearing further reprisals, Wanda marries our father Baltásar, Manfredo Espinosa's urbane protégé. She joins him in our venerable house on Callejón del Platero, where my parents and brothers still live. Before long, he becomes the country's premier ambassador. Not only is he a natty dresser; back then, his training as a classicist pegs him for the diplomatic corps. Though well-versed in ancient Greek, he also dotes on Latin; that's why he names us for his cherished Roman poets: Catullus, Horace, and Virgil.

But after twenty-five years of glory, he completely falls from grace. Goaded on by his foreign colleagues, he champions 'clean and modern' elections in Canuba. This quixotic campaign can only end in failure. Soon enough, Espinosa relieves him of his duties; in 1977, our parents retreat to Callejón del Platero, to vegetate for good.

Discreetly, they never delve into the erotic antics of their 'boys,' as they still call us to this day. Both of them are so antediluvian, I doubt they'd even notice our most flagrant hijinks. And both of them are so benign, they wouldn't care. Towards their sons, they adopt the Victorian adage: 'to the pure, all things are pure...'

Hapless Chiara, I tune back in to your monologue: 'The Days and Ways of Lamia Metaxa.' To paraphrase Derrida, why do we assume our friends give a damn about our latest flame? For them, it's the most vapid topic this side of Omaha.

Right, moth-brain, I've had a fling with the diva, too,

like half of Puerto Indio. She's a Mary-Lou Retton in bed, we all agree. But who can put up with her, once the gym session's done? The vaults, the balance beams, the splits? She's a foul-mouthed bitch, and I hate her as much as she hates me—which is saying quite a lot.

I used to run into her at the Mediterráneo, you drone on, fluttering your half-singed wings. She goes there several times a week to badger her father for money. But for almost a month now, I haven't seen hide nor hair of her. I'm worried she might be sick, or even injured. She has bouts with whole athletic teams, and that must take a toll.

Zzzzz. Time for a wake-up call. — Hahaha. Chiara, you sound desperate. Let me put you out of your misery. The 'It Girl of the Antilles'—or IT, as I call her—is safe and sound. IT's in New York for a master class: some cellist from the Outer Hebrides, who's coddling his fans at Juilliard.

You feign indifference. — Who cares? But why didn't you tell me before?

Why should I? Lamia and I aren't best buds, you know. I don't keep tabs on her shenanigans. — I smack my lips empathetically. — Ah, so our little nun is head-over-heels—and with Lamia, no less, the nympho troll. Get real, Miss Moth. If you want to see her, all you have to do is whistle.

Strangely, your jags with hot bedmates haven't cured you of your shyness. — Catulo, you know how bashful I am.

It's a good thing Canubans aren't 'Vaticanized' like you, or we'd never fornicate at all. Lamia isn't a person, she's a revolving door. She must have twenty hounds on her tail every day. And she probably obliges them all, sooner or later. As they put it in combat reports, her body count is very high. Watch out. You might end up in a skirmish—or even a massacre.

Puerto Indio and elsewhere, undated

My reminiscences repeat and overlap, like musical motifs, or the recurring steps in choreography. By definition, now that I'm dead, I'm way beyond senile: maybe I'm a demented old corpse.

With Amado, I look in on you in the early nineties— no specific date. Out here in the afterlife, we don't pay much attention to earthly time or place: we might even haunt a year that's *before* we give up the ghost. You can't see us, Chiara, but we've been tending to you, in our own intermittent way. I call you our 'curatorial project.' You've been going out with Lamia several times a week—whenever she's not busy 'teaching' her pupils, or scrimmaging with jocks in a 'love motel.' She pretends she doesn't notice your heart's on fire, but she can't be that naïve. By now, she must realize you're enslaved.

Sometimes you appraise yourself, in the full-length mirrors on your walls. Amado and I help you remove your garments one by one, till you're completely nude. Once I gifted you the quintessential Latin Lover, you gave up scouring the streets, and focused on him alone. But before? In flashbacks, you call to mind those earlier men, in the first flush of your Canuban deliverance… They gaze at their reflections in these mirrors, excited by their own muscular shapes… They watch themselves buck and ripple and arch, gripping your shoulders and thighs as they twist you back and forth… Kissing your eyelids and ears, biting your neck and breasts, clutching at your wild, disheveled hair… Weaving a circle around you thrice…

You yourself have not expired, my Magna Graecian goddess, Horacio admonishes. You must conduct a dual ontology henceforth—for Amado coevally with yourself.

From the looking-glass, your grey-green eyes gleam back at you. Your figure hasn't lost its tone. I'm still intact, still desirable, you say to yourself. Horacio's right: I should find someone else. But who? A woman, a man, or both? I'm attracted to Lamia. To Catulo, too. Would he be game again?

Standing beside you, girlfriend, Amado and I can only chuckle, unheard. No, not in this life… but just you wait. We nod our heads, unseen.

You continue your reverie… When Catulo and I are students in the States, we often compare our childhoods.

But we can speak more frankly in Lotus Land, as he nicknames the island, with its slam-bang attitude of anything goes. Like his antiquated parents, mine are relics of the ottocento, who pay no attention to sex. My pubescence measures up to the Sicilian cliché. A sultry carrousel with cousins of both genders, all hush-hush. But when my aunts find out, I'm packed off to the convent school of Sacré-Coeur, in a suburb close to Lyon. For them, it's a matter of keeping up appearances, not morality. They don't foresee that my ordeal with those nuns will put me off the official Church for good.

To the sisters' squabbles along the Rhone, I much prefer my bucolic summers in Bavaria. Like a fresh-cheeked, budding 'Blume' from a Heine poem, I bone up on German at my great-uncle's Schloss. In the morning, I'm drilled by an earnest, bespectacled tutor. In the afternoon, I swim across the lake, the blue-black jewel of the estate. At twilight, the swans glide past my bottle-glass windows, as I memorize verses from Goethe, Schiller, or Hölderlin. Then there's a candlelit, wine-soused dinner with Tante Cornelia and Onkel Ludwig, still spry despite their eighty-odd years.

Even so, for my undergrad degree at Padua, where I enroll in 1969, I settle on 'anglistica,' English and American lit. For all my aversion to my childhood governess, Miss Pinfold, the termagant's language wins out. Probably the Veneto, known for its right-wing politics and alcohol abuse, isn't the wisest choice for my 'laurea.' But this is where my godmother Chiara lives—always a ready source of espresso, sympathy, and pocket change.

Foreigners, from Shakespeare on, depict the Belpaese as a hotbed of sensuality. That ardor simmers down, when nineteenth-century prudery spreads through Europe. Maybe because the Vatican is closer to Padua than to Sicily, my fellow-students seem preoccupied with sex—but only as a menace, an ominous fatality. In my first months there, I go out with several men; and though we neck at a boozy party or two, I make love with only one. At the next beer-fest with his mates, Gianpiero crows about his 'conquista,' painting me as a lurid vamp. He can't really judge, since I'm the only female—much less male—he's ever biblically 'known.'

From that time on, to the girls I'm a wanton 'puttana,' and the boys degrade me to 'an easy lay.' At bottom, I've frightened all of them—though they scare each other even more. The irony is, they all seem 'liberated' to themselves. But would their counterparts in London or Berkeley agree? In my opinion, Italy still casts Woman in her age-old roles: the Virgin or the Whore...

Amado and I have listened long enough, Chiara. Now let *me* traipse down memory lane.

One day, after lunch under Luz Divina's hostile glare, we beat a hasty retreat. On the roof-terrace, I light into you.

That's your whole problem, kiddo. You want to be a

Whore, but you just can't let yourself go.

How about you? If you tried to be a Virgin, you'd have a hard time, too.

I wouldn't try, hon. — I flounce around in my chair. — To my fans, it would be an unbearable deprivation.

Thank you, we're all terribly grateful. For the millionth time, please stop saying 'kiddo' and 'hon.' You sound like a housewife from the fifties.

I deal invisible cards. — Oh, those bridge games, lusting after my best friend's hubby while he bids a heart... Don't you just love Douglas Sirk?

Shush, you're impossible. Speaking of movies, I really envied the teenagers in those brainless high school flicks. The whole American dating scene, I mean. In Italy, we run around in silly, childish groups. But gringos get to know each other one on one, by munching sloppy burgers, or riding along the drag-strips in their cars.

Sure, they all have jalopies, so who needs a bed?

Oh, they don't go 'all the way,' just a third of the way. A lowered brassiere, at most. They date a lot of different people, and meet their families, too. It seems so happy and carefree.

I trace tears down my cheeks. — Poor little Chiara, you've had such a tragical youth! You're forgetting la commedia italiana, with Loren, Mastroianni, and the genius of them all, Alberto Sordi.

Those are films about adults, not adolescents; and their

finest work comes later—*Una Giornata* or *Un Borghese*. I mean junky B-rate flicks like *Beach Blanket Bingo*. As I've told you before, in Italy only a couple who're 'fidanzati,' practically 'engaged,' can go out together. Otherwise, students socialize in 'gruppetti'—with separate factions for females and males, dancing at opposite sides of the room. If sex takes place at all, it has to be sordid, in the restroom of a bar or behind the garbage cans, when everybody's falling-down drunk. But by then, the boys are too schnockered to perform.

You're talking about a different time, Chiara. Let's pray to Priapus that things have improved. — I stick out my tongue. — Wherever I go, I give the guys and gals plenty to confess. Priests should hire me to drum up business.

Oh, you're such a butterfly, you can't imagine a faithful union. — You grab me by the chin, Chiara, and I nibble your hand. With a pang, you can't help but think what a well-suited couple we would've made. You long to probe my delectable mouth again, and rub my perky snub nose. — How about a balance of friendship and thrills, just like the kids in the movies? Instead of all that pointless cruising you do?

I assume my stentorian voice. — Don't put me in a box: I'm not a queen unless I want to be. You forget that Pomona and I spend every weekend together. We're virtually married.

Yes, you always do whatever you want, as nature

intended. Canubans are at one extreme, and Italians are at the other—terminally uptight. The boys I knew when I was growing up were especially afraid of 'l'uomo maggiore,' any man over thirty years old. But the original 'older man' their grandmothers warned them against was the local priest! The same ladies said he was the person they should most respect, 'because he's sacrificed his family life for the rest of us.'

A mixed message if ever there was one, Chiara!

True… You'll laugh, but my boyfriends in Padua never used a urinal, only the partitioned toilets, so some other guy couldn't look at their cazzo. On the beach, they'd hide behind towels to change into their bathing suits. They'd even do that when they were alone with me. Can you believe it? I tell you, Italians don't feel at home in their own skins.

I prance around the terrace. — Oh, I could make them feel at home, Casta Diva.

I know, darling, you've done that for me. — You mimic a sob. — But now you've abandoned me.

Hahaha. You've replaced me, you little tramp. Falling head over heels for Amado. And now that he's dead, you want me back.

Yes, Catulo, you're my spare tire.

On the surface, you keep up the banter. But as we chat, you're thinking of Whitman, America's national bard. Early on, you feel stirred by his 'Body Electric' and 'Song of

Myself,' those hymns to carnal vigor. There's no parallel to them in the Belpaese—much less to his 'Calamus' poems. What a contrast with your medieval Dante, much as you revere him. Walt exalts the flesh, while 'il Poeta' damns it to hell—or purgatory, at least. Then Petrarch and the rest preach the same dismal homily: you can only be saved by gelding your love. For Italians, this has become a knee-jerk response.

Of course, I'm not a gringo, Chiara. I'm a Canuban, through and through. But I know how you feel. And I've heard your tales with such empathy, I've almost lived them myself.

Except for your short affair with me, you find the US underwhelming. You spend your three years at Princeton as a drudge, teaching basic Italian, grading papers, and writing footnotes in the Firestone stacks. Your Master's thesis on the Commedia dell'Arte and Jonson is tedious and jejune: it saps all your energy. You're too mature for the swingles scene. Most of your fellow-students are either newly-weds or resolutely gay. Unrequited flirtations, half-hearted smooches, bumbling one-night stands—none of it adds up to much. You're relieved to get rid of the guy with five gold teeth, or the one who serves you breakfast on a Goofy plate.

By the time you move to Manhattan to work for Condé Nast, you're used to your amorous limbo. You don't fit into the queer brigade, because you hanker after women who're straight. You want to be the sole exception in their lives, the only girlfriend they've ever had. As Matilda puts it after a soulful night, such episodes 'quickly self-destruct.' On the whole, you prefer the directness of men. But your male colleagues discount you as 'kinda masculine,' and worry about your 'lesbian streak.' Clifford is afraid you'll 'castrate him, emotionally.' Gene's parting shot is: 'Chiara, you're too domineering, just like my mom.' Yes, Americans are irksomely prone to psycho-babble. In practical terms, your open-mindedness baffles them. The strict divide between gay and straight makes crossovers unwelcome, on both sides of the fence.

In the Spanish Caribbean, you come to learn, we take gender-blurring for granted. Especially among the ultra-machos—and even more, if they're lower-class. Women are also ambidextrous. Whole neighborhoods consist of housewives who enjoy each other's charms while their hubbies are away. As a sideline, on assignments for Condé Nast, you comb through the secret mores of Puerto Rico, Cuba, Hispaniola, and Canuba. Hovering near the equator, these golden isles don't veil their polyamorous crannies and chinks. All of them are similar in that regard—though you don't share this insight with your readers.

You've always considered yourself transcultural, translingual, and 'transsexual'—in the special connotation you give to the word. Now, at last, you've chanced on a region that embodies your ideals. The foam-splashed archipelago, with its shifting coastlines and wheeling clouds, is a metaphor of constant change. This is the earthy Belpaese of old, more Boccaccio than Petrarch: poles apart from the neurotic wasteland of Bell'Italia today.

The priests and nuns have poisoned your country with their morbid cult of chastity, the Church dogma that cripples daily life. Subtly, it deadens the senses like a ceaseless undertow. In Canuba, you can finally swim free: Amado instructs you in all the sinuous dives, all the exhilarating strokes, all the tandem flips and swerves. And then he goes under, like Billy Budd, dragged down by the 'oozy weeds.'

He and I are still beside you, as you stare at yourself in the mirror. We're not an undertow, we're an 'uppertow,' enlivening instead of lethal. We want you to pass on to better things. We're expecting you to join us, but we won't hurry you along…

You feel a tremor in the air—you sense our presence, though we remain unseen and unheard. Right now, Amado isn't speaking to anyone, not even to me. He's taken a vow of silence: he's on a monastic retreat. He adopted that habit from you, in the time when you fused, though it only emerged in his current avatar…

I've always been a votary of Dionysius the Areopagite. His God the Father, compiled from the Old Testament, seems cantankerous and coarse. But his hierarchy of the angels is spot on. As he says, 'they rush straight ahead, never looking left or right.' They don't have time for us: we're too directionless, too slow. Like cetaceans, they speed forward with a gentle flick of their flukes, a sudden beat of their megaloptera—their 'great wings.'

Are they sperm whales, belugas, dolphins, orcas, humpbacks? It all depends on their mood. For me, they convert into centaurs, or tigers leaping through space. Sometimes we need to stay clear of their one-willed path. We're tempted to shut down our hearts, afraid they'll shatter us with a single look, a single touch…

You may have perceived, Chiara, that I'm merging your memories with mine. When we're close to a friend for decades, we lose track of exactly who's who. That's as it should be. In this force-field we inhabit, everything converges in a seamless narrative, and all events happen at once. Let's sweep each other along. We have a purpose: we always do…

In the elsewhere, the nowhere, the everywhere, 'the gang's all here.' I want to remember a story we lived together: Frederica, Horacio, Lamia, and Chiara; Carolina, Virgilio, Isabela, and Catulo. Even Ángel María, the man with a thousand faces, and no face. 'You,' 'I,' 'we,' we're all third-person in the end. No wonder that out here, all pronouns and all destinies are one.

Do you recall that enormous plastic doll, worshipped by the Adorants as the Blessed Virgin herself? Let's recount the whole whimsical tale of the Countess and the Baron.

Let's make believe that at its 'heartless heart' lies the image: the illusion of all that is…

What do I mean 'remember,' if any world we choose is present to us now? Maybe each of them is only a boundless instant… A mockingbird sings three notes, like laughter from the middle of a dream… Wake up, we say. Was that an answered prayer, a wayward benediction? No, maybe, yes… But this we'll never know until we're told…

Puerto Indio, 1992-1990

During his forty-odd years in power, as a dictator 'hard' and 'soft,' Manfredo Espinosa has committed many crimes. In general, he keeps them under wraps, while letting a few of them peek through as a lingering threat—a Canuban sword of Damocles. In his rambling autobiography of 1989, *Memoirs of an Ordinary Hero*, he insinuates his homicidal bent by leaving several pages blank. As he snidely informs the reader, they stand for his purges of the early sixties, 'a series of urgent obligations that save our nation, but are best passed over in silence.'

As everyone knows, after the murder of his rebellious father Papito in 1961, these are the years when his covert assassinations reach their zenith, as he picks off the renegade's henchmen one by one. No wonder Milady is terrified of matchpoint in her game with Espinosa: a cornered rat always bites. Most people believe he'll stop at nothing to stay in office until 1992, the year he has dreamed about for half a century. When he attains that magic milestone, the 'Sovereign Island of Canuba'—noted up till now for rum, baseball, sugar, beaches, and easy sex—will surpass all its rivals as the flagship of Hispanic America.

In the inaugural address of his twelfth term, the President chastises Canuba's island neighbors. 'Compared to our country, overflowing with maidenly deference towards our European Homeland, our Antillean sisters Puerto Rico, Hispaniola, and Cuba often comport themselves like churlish step-daughters of Mother Spain, who deserves every iota of the love we Canubans bestow on her unsparingly.' He brooks no compromise with anti-Columbian factions in North and South America, 'impertinent revisionists' who question the Admiral's stature. To him, 'Cristóbal Colón *era* España'—'Christopher Columbus *was* Spain'—and España was racially supreme. Tellingly, he omits to mention Santiago Columbus, too pro-Taíno for his taste.

By denying the African and Amerindian strains of Caribbean culture, the events Espinosa plans for 1992 will advance his other policies: welcoming white immigrants, barring Bonaventurans, and repressing all forms of dissent. Though he has often reviled psychology as a myth, his obsession with the Admiral strikes most of us as a classic case of projection. The quincentennial salute will remind

Canubans how much they owe to their current Admiral, who has steered the nation through decades of perilous seas.

The Archbishop of Puerto Indio fans these senescent pipedreams, since he presumes they'll further his career in the Roman Church. He commutes every day between his residence and the Palacio Presidencial, stoking the autocrat's fantasies. Many cynics believe that Canuba's 'White Batman'—as we Mirandas call him, because of his inappropriately Papal garb—won't be satisfied until he ascends St. Peter's throne. The two megalomaniacs have thrust our complacent island into a Fifth Centennial orgy, unparalleled in the Western Hemisphere: a synergy of fascist egos run amok.

Now that he's foiled democracy once again, Espinosa resumes his most crucial task: finishing the Corona Colón, the Columbus Crown. With Ángel María at the helm, his minions work at top speed, to make up for the time they've squandered on the recent 'election.' Heads will roll, he thunders 'jokingly,' if they don't complete the project by October 12, 1992. On that day, the world's premier bigwigs will attend the dedication, including the King and Queen of Spain and the Pope himself—or so Espinosa claims. A connoisseur of the visual arts, Queen Sofía turns up her nose at the hideous Columbus Crown; to King Juan Carlos, the occasion smacks of the Franco years. After all, like the Spanish tyrant of yore, Espinosa styles himself a

'Generalísimo.' Both Queen and King demur, pleading 'previous engagements.'

Far be it from Pope John Paul II to quibble over such niceties: he never misses the chance for a pastoral sight-seeing jaunt. So what if the 'Discovery' has been a disaster for native peoples? Even if His Holiness is indifferent to their fate, his critics carp, why should he preside over a secular event? This is just another globe-trotting junket—extravagant tourism at the poor's expense. The Archbishop wins points with the Holy See by hitting on a clever defense: 1492 marks the start of 'New World Evangelization.' Counter-voices protest that it was only 'New' to the Spanish invaders. They also decry 'Columbus idolatry' as an endorsement of genocide. But Espinosa sternly quashes such cavils in Puerto Indio, setting the nation's sights on the upcoming fete.

Even neutral figures like Carolina Del Río find themselves pressed into duty: almost overnight, she becomes the 'Directora General del Parque Corona.' As an unpaid volunteer, she agrees to design the gardens around the monument, bowing to a personal request from Espinosa himself. The landscaping of her courtyard on Plaza Catedral has come to his attention; he, too, wants something that is 'Colonial, but with a slightly modern twist.' In case she gets out of hand, he also appoints her husband's cousin, Isabela Burley Luna, as her deputy assistant. Isabela is renowned for her traditional stance, and her abiding loyalty to Catholic Spain.

Though posts like these can engender oodles of grift, Carolina hardly needs the money. When asked why she's taken the job, she's non-committal. 'I wanted to get a closer look at the wily old coot,' she lets drop. Her generation has seen the sanguinary leader at his worst; and if the truth were known, she simply fears for her life. As to Isabela, she takes on the gig for the glory of the Church, and the fattening of her offshore accounts. Long snubbed by the island's elite, Espinosa delights in having a Del Río and a Burley Luna captain his gardeners. With pomp and circumstance, he receives the two ladies in his office every week for an 'update.'

I shouldn't ridicule the handicapped, Isabela tells Horacio one day in her veggie patch—a sure sign she's about to. 'Purblind,' the geezer calls himself, the only word of English he seems to know. I guess he means 'pure-blind.' When you enter his sanctum—after tripping over the fortune-tellers at the door—he stiffly gets up to greet you. He totters in your direction with his hand held out, till you finally have to grab it. — With her knack for mimicry, she apes his boneless shuffle and quizzical frown.

All Horacio can do is chortle out loud, with a nervous cough.

But his mind is a steel trap, she continues, especially for numbers. Since he can't see them anymore, he keeps the whole budget in his noggin. The other day I quoted him a lengthy column of expenses, about half a million escudos in all. One of the amounts was slightly off, and he pounced on it like a mongoose. — She imitates his sly, deliquescent voice. — Señorita Burley Luna, last week you said the fifty-two trowels would cost 853 escudos and thirty-four centavos. Yet now you speak of 931 escudos and forty-eight centavos. What happened to the seventy-eight escudos and fourteen centavos, please?

The trowels are one thing, Isabela confides; the cost of the entire shebang, quite another. — The hoary fox keeps the total a secret, but I wormed it out of his engineers. They say the tab will reach seventy to eighty million dollars before we're through. Someone should rein him in. But who?

This is the first time Isabela has fretted openly about money; only the Doughnut, as the vox populi has dubbed the Columbus Crown, can trump her patrician taboo. Maybe even she's becoming 'radicalized,' to borrow Espinosa's buzzword.

Most Canubans agree: the bill for the dictator's folly needs to be discussed—in fact, shouted from the rooftops. Rightists and leftists alike are disgusted by his waste of funds on a bauble, when countless children lack potable water, decent nutrition, elementary schooling, and medical care. With the concrete poured into this ghastly gimcrack, he could build housing for the indigent, starting with those who've been displaced by the Doughnut itself.

We Mirandas and our circle have decided views. If the government wants to memorialize the Quinto Centenario—as we argue diplomatically, in a recent op-ed—it should do so where Colonial history actually took place: the Barrio Antiguo. 'The major monuments have been protected, thanks to President Espinosa. But many of the lesser landmarks are crumbling before our eyes. Instead of expending a fortune on a contemporary shrine, imposing though it may be, why not dedicate a fraction of those monies to rescuing our architectural heritage from destruction? What better homage to the past than to preserve the structures that watched it unfold?'

In the end, Spain rises to the occasion. As Espinosa might say in his cloying palaver: 'the Madre Patria proves wiser than her headstrong daughter.' On the homestretch towards 1992, Madrid awards generous subsidies to restore Colonial districts throughout Latin America—including the Old Quarter of Puerto Indio. Under Spain's vigilant eye, even Espinosa can't siphon off every centavo, though he and Ángel María do their darndest.

In the summer of 1990, Canuba's Ministerio del Patrimonio Nacional calls on non-profits—such as the Church, civic groups, and foundations—to apply for the grants from Madrid. Now the scramble is on, with White Batman flapping his way to the forefront. No one doubts that by hook, and especially crook, the Archbishop will achieve his goals—a Cardinal's hat, or if nothing else, a deluxe renovation of his palace.

On that score, some are champing at the bit. The regime's pet engineers, like Ángel María, have always hawked pharaonic buildings and Hausmannian esplanades, with succulent kickbacks in mind. But behind the scenes, they concede the truth: once the autocrat has mouthed a flowery speech and snipped some plastic ribbons, these structures go rapidly to seed. Erecting pyramids and arcades yields a lot more graft than keeping them up.

Thanks to Espinosa, Puerto Indio has amassed a depressing array of dried-up fountains, potholed boulevards, and mangy behemoths. A case in point is the National Library, a whitewashed monadnock from the seventies, which houses fewer than a thousand books. Not content with that albino elephant, in 1986 our ruler decrees the Canuban Library: again, its capacious shell contains little more than an impressive bronze plaque, praising his munificence.

Increasingly, we islanders feel embittered by this legacy. In former times, the 'marvels of the Capital' dazzled the city's populace, mostly migrants from the countryside. But now, Canubans are more urban than agrarian, and more intent on water and gas than imported porphyry and brass. Our mood turns even uglier when Espinosa proclaims his final plans for the Corona Colón or Columbus Crown, a tribute to the Fifth Centennial of 1992.

The ring-shaped pile of concrete, a quarter of a mile

across, will contain nothing but a two-room exhibit of mediocre photographs. It features a lump of iron—supposedly a fragment of the *Pinta*'s anchor, though most scholars discount the notion. Fifty thousand Puerto Indians forfeit their shacks on the Río Fernando's west bank to make way for the unsightly juggernaut. As it slowly emerges from the mud, its squat outline evokes a primitive reactor—or the 'mother of all bunkers' in some nasty, forgotten war.

True to its looks, the hulk has a ravenous appetite. According to the estimates of foreign NGOs, it will devour half the island's electric supply, already meager at best. Towering beams will shine heavenward from its outer ring, throwing a halo against the clouds to 'coronate' the Admiral. But on a bright, clear night—the objectors gripe—these rays will disperse into the ether, to no effect at all. Such comments, voiced abroad and whispered here, make the mammoth gewgaw all the more galling. Puerto Indians already endure constant power failures, lasting six to twelve hours a day. Even the neighboring island of Bonaventura—the third-poorest country in the Americas, after Haiti and Bolivia—boasts a better energy grid than Canuba's.

Citizens bandy a sarcastic quip: 'Misery loves company! That blind guy wants to keep us all in the dark.' Within the safety of four walls, everyone whinges. After neglecting the shortfall for decades, now Espinosa wants to suck the power from our houses, and spray it into space? To make a doughnut in the sky he can't even see? No doubt about it, the Columbus curse is still upon us.

Of course, the privileged few have private generators, and they carry on as merrily as before. In a picaresque skirmish of the Fifth Centennial War, the 'Battle of the Habsburgs and August the Strong,' Gräfin Frederica has recently trounced her Polish foe. Her elated mood buoys her through the final coup de grâce.

When he returns from the Templars' Ninth Centenary in Cyprus, Baron Valentín brings home a dozen huge flags, left over from the processions there. No one else wants them—for good reason. Granted, they display the insignia of the order in glowing detail; but they're pieced together from cheap dacron, intended for viewing only from afar. As soon as the restorers put the last touches on Santa María Stella Maris—St. Mary Star of the Sea—the Polish nobleman proudly installs his pennants in the nave of the church. Even an unpracticed eye can gauge that their size dwarfs its dimensions, and that their neon hues thwart any atmosphere of reverence.

'They're just plain tacky, as the amerikaner say!' the Countess erupts, beheading the German capitals. 'Even *they* would have better sense than this. But what can we expect from an Eastern European—an osteuropäer.'

As soon as the scandal breaks, Federica marches over to the Office of Cultural Heritage, where she now calls the shots. The Directora has gratefully attended several cocktail parties at the Gräfin's palace, and aspires to graduate to dinner. She embarks on a full inspection of Stella Maris. Predictably, she hands down a stringent command: while the Templars' contractors have done a suitable job, 'those obtrusive banners must be removed without delay.'

Baron Valentín consigns his trophies to the Servants of the Least of His Brethren. In the order's workshop, the oriflammes jive with the snazzy outfits of their pupils, reform-bent ladies of the night. When we visit the refitted cloister, and survey their racks of dullish handicrafts, we wonder whether these modern Magdalens will make the grade. Glumly stitching placemats, or throwing misbegotten pots, they seem doubtful about renouncing their former profession. 'Will these doo-dads bring home the bacon? Won't we miss the music, the dancing, the beer?'

Our other question is this: what about the life-size 'Barbie Madonna,' once the centerpiece of the altar? In the sixties, the newly elevated Mother Superior of the Adorants, Juana de Arco, replaces an exquisite sculpture by Montañes with the pink vinyl doll. The sale of the Baroque masterpiece to the Cleveland Museum generates copious funds for tarting up the sisters' cells. We sorely regret its loss; but soon we celebrate the Barbie Madonna as the epitome of Canuban camp.

While the Servants' protegées sew, pot, and reminisce, peace settles once more over the Barrio Antiguo. Espinosa gallops toward the Doughnut Grail, the Archbishop paves his indoor running track with Parian marble-chips, and the Spanish revamp our neighborhood, assisted by droves of private donors. Every day the newspapers announce yet another plan, and pundits say the city's historic core will revert to mint condition by October 12, 1992.

Having lived in Puerto Indio for a decade, Chiara, you're as skeptical as we are about the upshot—and the speed of its accomplishment. But this has ceased to matter to you. You've fully absorbed the Latino nonchalance about 'mañana.' Nothing can perturb your habit of bliss. Anaphora, Bishop calls it in one of her poems: more than a rhetorical device, the daily repetition of the light.

To you, in your walled garden, anaphora is audible as well as visible... The bananaquits wheezing excitedly at dawn... the mockingbirds trilling from the highest trees... the bells clanging from dilapidated churches... the traffic revving up with grunts, sputters, and hums... the kitchen pot-fixers chanting their Gregorian refrain, 'ollas por reparar'... the loudspeakers on produce trucks screaming 'eggplants and beans'... the boys after school batting their baseballs on the square... flocks of green parakeets squawking overhead... the crones in housecoats gossiping outside your door... the traffic winding down at six o'clock... the bells tolling again for evensong... the birds twittering their final antiphons as dusk descends... the honey-creeper singing himself to sleep in his solitary roost... the pans rattling as suppers are being cooked... the soap-operas droning away on the neighbors' TVs... the cambucas blaring from their tinny radios... the transitory silence after midnight... the dogs barking at nothing, at the moon... the cats screeching across the roof... the timeless Canuban roosters, crowing at any hour... the bananquits, wheezing excitedly at dawn...

One day our Colonial quarter will look as museum-like as Old San Juan—but not too soon, we hope. It's enough for us that the Templars have returned our favorite church to its former luster: fulvous, rosy, and whorled, like a coffer covered in brocade. Pressure-jets have sluiced away the grunge, and the coral-stone façade almost shimmers, alive as the polyps that gave it birth...

At the close of sunny afternoons, you climb the rickety stairs to Cansonetta's terrace, across the street from Stella Maris. You watch as the tropical brightness thaws, melts, and runs down the sidewalks in gleaming rivulets... At twilight, the facade comes unmoored, floating on the tide of night... it drifts away, as lightly as a ship of balsam wood. The Virgin carved above the door is delivered from the rock... she balances on the wind like a figurehead, urging the nave out to sea.

Recent developments have wedged the Countess into an awkward spot. Feisty Madre Juana de Arco has gotten everything she bargained for; she and her Viennese patroness have carried the day. On the other hand, Don Valentín has exiled the Adorants to the suburbs, where Frederica can visit them only by motoring past 'horrid concrete boxes.' On top of that, her *Lysistrata* plot with the Templars' wives requires her to invite them to a meal. She doesn't relish granting this honor to 'a bunch of bumpkins'—though as her rival Carolina might sniff, 'it takes one to know one.' A dinner is the prize she's held out to them for an utter triumph: keeping the Adorants exactly where they were. All the same, 'noblesse oblige'—bona fide or not—and so she bites the bullet. On her cards embossed with coronets, she summons the highest-ranking Knights to a gala feast for sixteen.

Smugly, the Baron touts the coming banquet to his flock as 'a felicitous end to a trying ordeal.' At the last minute, one of the gentlemen begs off due to a dire infection—'in the pelvic region, no doubt,' Frederica japes, when she phones me that afternoon. Determined to have her moment in the candlelight, his wife insists on attending without him. I am enlisted to balance out the table, a service I've often rendered to the Countess when I'm in town. She pairs herself with the eldest of the Templars, a soft-spoken widower who's made his fortune by selling prosthetic limbs—contraband from who knows where. You, girlfriend, accompany Horacio: hardcore 'ecclesiasticals,' you've been on the roster all along.

As soon as I'm ushered in by one of the red-liveried boys, I notice our hostess has also matched Don Valentín with a 'date.' He's been coupled with Lamia, our liquor-swilling, muck-mouthed serpent, who greets me with her usual raunchy jive. This is her first dinner at the palace, where she's normally banned. I soon find out she's no eleventh-hour replacement, like me. Sotto voce, with a roguish wink, the Countess lets on that Lamia was the first guest on her list. So that's it: Frederica won't let her semi-defeat go unpunished. She'll retaliate by exposing the Baron to Lamia's bar-room swagger. Her raucous intemperance will collide with his dainty sobriety. He despises nothing more than 'people who tipple too much,' as he phrases it, discarding them with mental tongs. But as the evening lurches on, even Frederica is amazed by the potency of her revenge.

Don Valentín evades his nemesis during the pre-dinner drinks, sipping a Perrier while Lamia downs tumblers of rum-on-the-rocks, in a nook of the Sala Grande. She wriggles suggestively in her skintight frock of silver lamé, as she spews off-color jokes at the Templars. Guffawing, they surround her like pubescent cricketers at a London peep show. Their better halves, who expected to meet the 'crema y nata' of high society at Countess Frederica's, appear gobsmacked by Lamia's obscenities and leers. Delivering a punch line, she pinches a Knight's buttocks, or grabs another one by the fly.

The staid matrons wonder: Has their hostess made some grave mistake? Or is she thumbing her nose at them? Eerily quiet, Frederica observes the scene, sipping a Negroni with inscrutable calm. She consigns Horacio, you, and me to small-talk with the ladies, including the finicky Baron. As for the Knights Templar, they've clearly decided Lamia is their kind of gal—or maybe, their kind of guy. This racy ambivalence makes the evening far less stodgy than they'd feared.

By the time dinner is announced, Don Valentín has to steer the woozy cellist to her chair—no mean feat, given how shaky she's become. He looks ashen, like someone whose neck is cradled by the chopping block. An ominous hush blankets the table. His partner briefly dozes off, drooling at the corners of her mouth. When she bounces back, she bawls: 'Hey Countess, aren't you gonna propose a toast? What kinda party is this?'

Frederica shams befuddlement, and an unwonted loss for words. 'Well, let's see, let's see… ja nun!'

Lamia raises her wineglass, smeared with lipstick from a precocious swig. Apparently, she's been prepped by our hostess over the phone, regarding the reason for this shindig. 'To the Adornments, for getting their five-star hotel.

And to the Little Kid Sisters, for…' She knocks back another gulp of Pouilly Fuissé, and her salute trails off, incomplete… Then she nudges the Baron in the ribs, so heartily we can almost hear them crack: 'Hold on, I forgot to ask… The Kid Sisters: what the hell are they doing here?'

Everybody's listening, so Don Valentín has to answer, despite the pain in his side. 'Seven nuns are flying in from Madrid this week,' he croaks abjectly. 'Their mission… is to rehabilitate prostitutes, and teach them the necessary skills for decent employment.'

Lamia roars with laughter, practically snapping the back of her Louis XV chair. 'You say there's gonna be seven? Only seven? Don't you know there's seven million people in good ole Canuba-banuba? If you count all the Bonos as people, I mean. And everybody's either a hustler, or a john. Usually both, buddy boy! You're gonna need seven million nuns to make a dint, one for each and every one of us.'

The Baron blushes—a varicose scarlet. The Templars hoot, until their spouses stare them down.

'Isn't that what this whole Pimplars Club is all about?' Lamia brays. 'Just paying off the Little Sisters, or your wives, or any other skanks who're lyin around, to shut up and spread their legs?'

Frederica floats a cagey smile towards you and me, across the silver-laden tabletop. No matter what iffy dishes her teenage cooks dole out, the dinner qualifies as a smashing success. In other circumstances, given her worldwide chain of brothels, the topic broached by Lamia might've seemed embarrassing—'ganz peinlich,' as the Gräfin would grouse. But as she gloats over her foe's discomfiture, she can't be bothered with fake propriety—not on this splendid night of victory.

If we go back a number of months, we'll find that Don Valentín's negotiations with the Archbishopric have gone quite smoothly, thanks to the greasing of hidden palms. Since the Knights Templar are picking up the tab for Santa María Stella Maris, the priestly accountants channel the bespoke Spanish grant into an offshore company—and a mirror-ceilinged spa for His Grace.

Men and eunuchs are easily dispatched. But as the 'Chilean cherry-bomb' taught him long ago, the Baron wilts before the steely will of women. He's hardly obtained the renovation permits when he faces a vexing hitch: the nuns in the adjoining cloister refuse to decamp. They belong to a contemplative order—an offshoot of the Ursulines, now almost extinct: the 'Adoratrices de los Nombres Bendecidos de Santa Maria,' or Adorants of the Blessed Names of St. Mary. They spend their days in seclusion, reciting her sacred monikers—Star of the Sea, Mary Theotokos, Cause of Our Salvation, Spouse of the Holy Spirit, Lady of the Gate of Dawn, Tower of Ivory, Mother of Sorrows, Queen of Heaven, Virgin of All Virgins, and on and on—a thousand epithets, knitted into a ceaseless round of litanies. Since the Cyprus Knights sponsor services for the poor, stressing praxis rather than prayer, such claustral bead-counting contravenes their goals.

Under his baronial letterhead, Don Valentín kindly informs the 'Adoratrices' they'll soon be evicted – or 'transferred,' as he terms it—and replaced by the 'Siervas de Sus Hermanos Más Pequeños,' or Servants of the Least of His Brethren. To the Adorants, their hereditary rivals, he need not explain the reasons why. The 'Siervas' are 'socially active,' in more ways than one. First and foremost, they minister to the indigent, as their title—drawn from the hortatory words in St. Matthew, Chapter 25—clearly proclaims. Second, untainted by 'liberation theology' (a leftist trend the wealthy Templars abhor), these sisters acknowledge the wellspring of beneficence: an abysmal divide between the wretched and the rich. For hundreds of years, the Servants have sown mustard-seeds of guilt among the well-to-do, who've poured a treasure trove into their muniments. They've mastered the art of applying pressure, without overplaying their hand. As they often remind their patrons: 'The poor will always be with you, saith the Lord.' This soothing approach has allowed them to prosper— since after all, 'charity begins at home.'

The Baron, who's already enrolled a bevy of 'Siervas' in Madrid for his Caribbean venture, soon learns that the Adorants aren't a gaggle of mumbling patsies, as he thoughtlessly assumed. They, too, can mobilize some staunch protectors—not the least their own Mother Superior, Juana de Arco, a nonagenarian Mexican nun. Spurred by her namesake, the militant Maid of Orleans (canonized in 1920, the year Juana de Arco took her final vows), she's zestfully battled with evil all her life—in the protean shape of bossy prelates, shiftless novices, or avaricious grocers. She also emulates Sor Juana Inés de la Cruz, her illustrious countrywoman of the seventeenth century, who wrote immortal verses and proto-feminist tracts in her comfortable cell. Like her, Mother Juana de Arco holds a salon in the antechamber of her convent, proffering the fruits of her learning to the worldly. To enhance her cachet, she's devised a genealogy for herself, stretching back to Queen Isabella of Aragon.

Inevitably, she forges a close alliance with Countess Frederica, her bluestocking champion. They see eye to eye on the despicable account of Sor Juana by 'that poetaster, Octavio Paz,' who dares to imply that she engaged in 'self-abuse.' Juana de Arco never winces when the Gräfin spouts ill-conceived opinions, or rushes in where logic's angels fear to tread. Instead of opposing her half-baked views, the ancient sage wags her furrowed, prune-like head. 'What a trenchant remark, my dear!' she exclaims. Such forbearance wins her Frederica's undying support—and for the Adorants, a cornucopia of alms. An exacting aesthete as a rule, the Countess even condones their kitschy Madonna, enshrined in the apse: a giant, glass-eyed Barbie doll, arrayed in rayon robes of baby blue.

As soon as she gets wind of the threatened eviction, Frederica rushes to the nuns' defense: bruising her way past his hapless guards, she harangues the Baronial Envoy for well over an hour. The subdued grey walls of Europe's outpost in Canuba have never rung with accents of such vehemence. Worse still, when Don Valentín opposes the Adorants, he unwittingly roils the wives of the Templars themselves. Pooh-poohing his vague reassurances, the Countess bids the Knights' spouses to tea, a signal honor they've coveted in vain.

Jawohl! A pact with her will reap far greater rewards than a minor Polish Baron can muster. Her palacio remains open to 'ladies of like mind,' where they will savor elegant dinners with the 'crème de la crème.' But if their husbands consort with the Templars, she darkly pursues, they'll soon fall prey to perverted clerics, who'll squeeze them for every centavo. These depraved Rasputins will unman their consorts, whisking them away from home and hearth on 'stag adventures,' to dens of iniquity around the world. 'When grown men wear garters and show off their legs, what else can you expect? Was sonst?'

Before long, the stolid Cyprus Knights, whose only departure from gravitas has been a yen for fancy dress— the flamboyant Templar uniform—are quailing under the censures of their better halves. No longer 'half-oranges,' in Spanish parlance, they've become 'half-limes.' Not only that, they've followed Frederica's injunction, to renege on their 'bedroom duties' till the Templars bow to their demands. At their weekly meetings, the Knights begin to flirt with apostasy, a mass flight from the order. Don Valentín grows desperate.

The Baron knows Frederica is an intimate of ours, girlfriend. One evening he invites you, Horacio, and me to his sepulchral 'reception room,' to beg for our intercession. We're amused and touched by his tale of woe. On one of his nocturnal visits to her boudoir, Virgilio has already heard the two-hour version from the Countess, starring herself as the dragon-slaying heroine. The Baron doesn't breathe fire; at most, he sheds a tear of frustration, drying it with a monogrammed handkerchief. What a dilemma for this dauntless Knight, overarched by his family trees remounting to William the Conqueror, Charlemagne, Augustus Caesar, and Pericles. After avoiding a faceoff with his former wife, the Chilean Ninja, he's finally met his match in a Viennese Valkyrie.

When I call on Frederica the next day, as his reluctant emissary, I discover he's at loggerheads with more than Juana de Arco. While her deceased Graf's cousinship included a Russian Archduke and a Hungarian Prince, some of his hard-pressed forebears married the daughters of well-off brewers, snuff-merchants, and the like. Long ago, the Austrian Templars rejected her dear-departed, when they still insisted on strict proofs of lineage, even for the order's lowest echelon. But now they routinely accept 'money-grubbing dolts like these Canuban peasants,' to quote the Countess's words. As I report to Don Valentín that evening, her retrospective outrage has screwed her ire to a fever pitch.

On hearing my news, he sinks his head into his liver-spotted hands; but over the next few weeks, he perseveres. When all is said and done, the Baron believes lucre can fix anything, a mistake he shares with most men. On this premise, they buy diamonds for their wives or sports cars for their sons, while totally neglecting them. They may get off the hook, for a while. But trinkets arouse an appetite for more, and the final bill balloons beyond control—divorce settlements, junior's gambling tabs, and so on, till the last round-up at the bankruptcy corral.

The diplomat falls neatly into Juana de Arco's trap, as soon as he offers to underwrite 'improved lodgings for the Adoratrices.' Tightening the noose around his neck, he asks how large an endowment they might need, to sustain their 'invaluable work of prayer.' He pats himself on the back for praising them, but their Mother Superior won't submit to flattery. Pursing her withered lips, she replies: 'You're right, Your Excellency. Something that's invaluable can't be measured in material goods. No price is high enough for what is priceless.' The chief Adorant holds the kings and queens in her hand, while all he can rely on is the checkbooks of his varlets. The bargaining will be long and ruinous.

In this, his darkest hour, he questions whether his thick-wooled sheep will stay in the fold till they're shorn—especially with their wives on the warpath. The outlay for Stella Maris increases day by day, and God only knows how much it will take to mollify 'those greedy religious...' But in the end, Mammon rides to his rescue. Our threadbare Baron, who stashes his modest salary in annuities, hasn't grasped just how flush his fellow-Knights are—nor how much they'll shell out to buy their freedom. An authority 'ex officio' on aging males, Frederica readily plumbs their shallow souls. For years, the Canuban Templars have licked their chops at the prospect of 'pilgrimages.' Once they've established their credentials, with a 'chapel of devotion' of their own, they'll be entitled to inspect other chapters. There are important charities to explore in Thailand, Cuba, and Brazil, countries known—coincidentally—for their females' allure.

Sure of her game, Juana de Arco extorts spanking-new quarters for her sisters, designed by none other than Caramela Sosa. The famous architect selects an expensive site for the cloister, just up the river from Ángel María's estate, with breathtaking views of the mountains to the east. Each 'cell' will consist of a spacious apartment, in the sybaritic tradition of the Convent of St. Jerome, where Sor Juana de la Cruz composed her masterworks. The Cyprus Knights will also guarantee unlimited medical care for the Adorants—most of whom are very long in the tooth—

as well as a hefty trust fund for general expenses. To the Baron's astonishment, his confreres churn out check after check, without the slightest hesitation. Within a year, the Blessed Barbie has alighted on a lofty perch, high on a waterside bluff, at the farthest edge of town.

Further back, Cyprus, Rome, Puerto Indio

We could keep going further back, to the establishment of the Puerto Indio chapter of the Knights Templar, a religious confraternity that once held sway over Cyprus. Its local proponent is a Polish Baron named Valentín Szismonski, a dirty-blond, pear-shaped gentleman. His parents took refuge from the Nazi occupation in 1939 by fleeing to Antwerp, when he was twelve. In the ripeness of time, his studies of Latin America, coupled with a Belgian passport, land him diplomatic posts in the Western Hemisphere. Their mediocrity can be deduced from the position he often hails as the 'pinnacle of his career': representing the European Community in Canuba, as its 'Envoy with the Rank of Ambassador'—an obscure tag he never ceases to repeat.

When he first arrives, in the early eighties, he brings along a svelte, frigid wife, about twenty years younger than himself. He married her in Chile, despite her dubious provenance. Born in a slum of Punta Arenas, the gateway to Antarctica, she swiftly defrosts in the Caribbean. Before long, she hooks up with a beefy Bonaventuran, who toils as a handyman at the British Embassy; from then on, she extols the virtues of 'carne oscura' or 'dark meat,' in her unsavory phrase. She and her beau inflict a series of ignominies on the diplomatic corps, such as indulging in a quickie behind the rubber plants at a Bastille Day do. To the impoverishment of gossip, after a year or so they abscond to Venezuela, and are never heard of again. Don Valentín consoles himself with a Canuban mistress; but as he enters his sixties, in 1987, he gives her up without regret. From now on, he will devote himself to less strenuous pursuits, such as genealogy, art-collecting, and above all, the Knights Templar of Cyprus.

Like the Knights of Malta, the Knights Templar earn their laurels as a Christian military order during the Crusades—a wave of heroic campaigns or barbarous invasions, depending on your point of view. Originally, they provide well-armed shelter to pilgrims headed for the Holy Land, pried open to the West by European troops; only later do they become soldiers themselves, famed for their bravery. Their Mother House on the former site of Solomon's Temple lends them their name. The Cyprus contingent is the only faction to survive the order's disgrace in 1307, instigated by Philip the Fair. As a consolation prize, Pope Clement V establishes the Cypriot Templars' dominion over Mount Selenion, a finger-like peninsula not unlike Mount Athos, jutting from the island's northwest coast.

On its summit, around 1100, the knights had already erected a stronghold called the Citadel of St. Michael Archangel, the mightiest in their chain of monastic forts. All owe fealty to the Grand Master of the Order, also known as the Prince of Cyprus. For hundreds of years, they defend this redoubt from their perennial foes, the Muslims of the Middle East. They win many victories, but finally succumb to the vast armada of Suleiman the Magnificent. Thanks to their obstreperous independence, they never receive substitute lands from a monarch, such as Philip II awards to the Knights of Malta. Perhaps this slight is also due to their alleged excess of 'brotherly love.' The main branch of the Templars was condemned for 'kissing and sodomy' in medieval France, a calumny which led to their downfall.

After their maritime debacle in the sixteenth century, the Knights of Cyprus manage to maintain only one diminutive domain: a labyrinthine palazzo at the edge of Vatican City, endowed with its own vestigial rights, such as the issuing of stamps. The narrow, colon-like edifice—its rooms disposed to mirror bygone Templar seats on Mount Selenion—constitutes the world's tiniest nation. Don Valentín knows the twists and turns of its corridors like the back of his hand. He bumbles through his long apprenticeship as a diplomat there; and it is there that he returns to salve his wounds, after his spouse runs off with her paramour.

Once he finishes his stint for the European Community in Puerto Indio, and his Fifth Centennial building project, he plans to take an early retirement, move back to Rome, and dedicate the rest his life to the order.

The Knights Templar abjured their martial activities long ago: now they engage in beneficent works—aiding hospitals, orphanages, schools, and worthy causes of all stripes. An unlettered American, in Don Valentín's hearing, once compared the congregation of the Knights to the Shriners or the Masons, with their penchant for splashy costumes, pompous titles, and puerile rites. Offensively, the latter usurp the name 'Knights Templar' for one of their tawdry honorifics; but they dare not couple it with 'Cyprus,' or else they'll be sued.

'As a European, if only a Pole'—in his humble expression—the Baron believes that every entity of the Old World, by definition, merits far more respect than its supposed analogue in the New. After all, no one can instantly conjure the patina of time. For its commanding officers, the Templar Order of Cyprus imposes not only celibacy, but also sixteen quarters of nobility, reaching back to the candidate's great-great-grandparents on both sides. Don Valentín's impeccable lineage, a musty plait of Slavic baronies, ensures he can ascend to the highest level, perhaps even Grand Master—or as he would put it, 'Grand Master with the Rank of Prince.'

Before settling in the Eternal City for good, the Baron longs to leave his mark on Canuba, by ensconcing his fellow-paladins in a chapel worthy of the Templars. With that tenacity his superiors in Rome have always lauded—though privately, they think him none too bright—he fixes his aspirations on the Colonial gem of Santa María Stella Maris. No doubt a spirit of competition with the Knights of Malta, who've just acquired the simpler Church of St. Agnes, whets Don Valentín's yen for the more prestigious fane.

In Puerto Indio, the Knights of Malta count a brigade of aristocrats among their members, thanks to the influx of titled Cubans fleeing Castro. In olden days, down-and-out Spaniards from nobiliary houses emigrated to the 'Pearl of the Antilles,' eager to wed the sugarcane heiresses there. Their descendants prefer the Knights of Malta to the 'Cyprus Elks'—as the squinty Conde de la Torta del Sapo, born in Havana, haughtily dubs them. He sneers that in their nether grades, the Templars have ceased to split hairs over pedigree, 'and it shows.'

But what their rank and file lack in blueblood, the Knights of Cyprus more than make up for in wealth: in Canuba, as elsewhere, the captains of industry throng to their ensign. True, the magnates' meager escutcheons oblige them to lower their sights, and the Knights of Malta would never accept them. The oligarchs couldn't care less, since what they prize above all is the Cypriot uniform—much snazzier than the Maltese outfit of black on black.

Templars sport green pumps with twenty-four carat gold buckles, purple silk leggings and puffed yellow tunics, cloaks of midnight-blue brocade shot through with silver thread, and brass helmets crested with crimson plumes. With a sartorial zeal worthy of the Mormons, their splendor extends to their satin underclothes, trimmed with Venetian lace.

In the 'reception room' of his 'ambassadorial residence'—as Don Valentín terms the cramped den of his stucco bungalow—he displays a full-length portrait of himself in ceremonial attire, his usually timid visage set in a warlike grimace. The ordinary members follow their Grand Commander's example in their far more opulent homes, adorning their onyx or cypress-paneled walls with paintings of even lesser artistry, some of which verge on caricature.

An inveterate snob, the Archbishop of Puerto Indio has heretofore favored the Knights of Malta, when he hands out churchly plums. But the Fifth Centennial affords the Baron a long-awaited chance to up the Templars' ante. Of course, the Archdiocese has devoted most of its Spanish block-grant to the refurbishment of His Grace's palace. While the historic building will receive some cosmetic repairs, the modern 'crypt' will include a back entrance with a six-car garage, an entertainment room, an indoor running track, and a subterranean passage to the Cathedral.

The Ambassador of Spain has lodged a stout protest

against this 'heedless misappropriation'; but Espinosa—still fuming over the monarchs' 'second historical betrayal of our sainted Admiral'—has turned a deaf ear to his complaint. The scant remnants of Madrid's donation will finance a botched facelift of the Cathedral- complete with bank-like glass doors and overworked air-conditioners—where the Archbishop can agreeably sermonize to his 'worldwide listeners' about the 'Discovery ordained by God.'

Compared to such cosmic affairs, the rehabilitation of minor Colonial churches is small potatoes, and White Batman's harried subalterns parcel them out to dupes like the Templars of Cyprus or the Knights of Malta. Though the Knights' St. Agnes possesses many winsome features, Stella Maris is much more ornate; its restoration calls for a swingeing budget, such as only the Cypriots can supply. Ángel María pleads their case, in return for a bloated engineering contract.

When we hear about the project, we almost jump for joy: we've always admired the church's sculpted façade, and now its statues will shed their coats of acidic soot and corrosive grime. Like many buildings in the Old Quarter, reconstructed after each seismic catastrophe, Stella Maris bears the imprint of diverse architectural styles. Still, its core is late Renaissance, dating from circa 1550, the heyday of Colonial Canuba. A Marqués known as 'Pompeo Rimbombante de la Corte'—an alias, or so we assume—endows its initial foundation. Over the centuries, historians have often speculated about his identity. The Archives of the Indies in Seville only confirm his title, his pseudonym, and the royal charter he receives to erect two edifices in Puerto Indio: 'a residence, and a sanctuary.'

'Pompeo' constructs his lordly mansion wholly of coral-stone, a rarity at the time; it still stands today, the joint property of Cansonetta Rivera and her charming, rapacious gigolo, Porfirio Baquero. Generous to a fault, with her friends as with him, she often indulges our wish to gaze at Stella Maris from her upstairs parlor—especially at the 'blue hour,' just before twilight. 'Feel free, my dears, feel free,' she exclaims when we knock at her door. Sometimes she adds, with world-weary candor: 'The bedrooms are the only rooms we use...'

The Marqués places his majestic chapel right across the street, so he can survey it from his windows, peeping through slits in his heavy damask curtains. On the few occasions when he sallies forth, mostly at night, he dons a mask; hence his nickname among the people: 'El Disfrazado.' Rumor has it that he's expiating a heinous sin, or is disfigured by syphilis, or has been exiled by the Crown. Or maybe he hasn't recovered his nerve, after a near-shipwreck on the voyage from Spain. Veracious or not, such scuttlebutt seeks to explain why he's never revealed his face, and why he's bestowed such a bountiful gift on the Virgin Mary, under her age-old epithet the Star of the Sea—once borne by pagan Isis, the protectress of sailors in Antiquity.

Some scholars even suggest that 'The Masked Man' is the prototype for Tirso de Molina's Don Juan, the merciless seducer, a character the playwright conceived during his stay in the Caribbean Isles. Whatever the ultimate story of its donor, Stella Maris endured many disasters, from wars to hurricanes. The niches of the façade are replete with saints—St. Lucy with her eyes on a plate, St. Roch with his leg-wound and his dog, St. Peter Martyr with a saber cleaving his head. Even when the nave collapses in a severe earthquake a hundred years ago, the superb sculpture of the Holy Mother, leaning serenely from the pediment above the door, remains miraculously intact...

Unspecified, undated

I'll leave the effigies in stone to Virgilio. Now that big plastic doll, that simulacrum of the Virgin: for me, she's much more appealing. I've always wanted to join the traveling troupe of Rilke's puppets and Kleist's marionettes. But in college I was distracted by the Dervishes and the Operettes—so distracted, I dropped out. Here's what I'm driving at. As Kleist implies—during his dialogue with a dancer, no less—on stage, you *want* to be manipulated: by the director, the choreographer; or especially, by yourself.

When you find your center of gravity, your limbs will instantly fall into place.

Drag is the ne plus ultra of disguise, when you change your gender in the dressing room, and change it back at the end. But the magic also works when you apply your make-up for any theatrical part. In the process, you become your own director, your own choreographer, for whatever role you embody on stage or screen. You achieve a double consciousness, as in sex or in love. You're the puppet-master and the marionette, the living and the lived.

When we tell a story, we're doing the same thing. The narrator cuts pieces from herself and those she's known; she reassembles them into beings on the page. The page is a stage, I like to say: no wonder they rhyme. People try to separate the arts, but that's a basic fallacy. We're a total theater, a total illusion. The image is itself reality: since we never own what we depict, we possess it all the more.

In the afterlife, we embrace a wider view. We accept the 'supreme fiction' known as truth. Our past is a director who determines our next steps; and in the present, we're plotting out the future. Over time, we begin to comprehend how we reshape the past as well. The episodes slip and slide, backwards and forwards, up and down. Here we've made them tilt towards the past, but in fact they whirl like a kaleidoscope.

From my vantagepoint in the beyond, where angels come and go, I've gained a new respect for 'St. Mary,' the nuns' vinyl sovereign. She's a puppet they maneuver, so she'll maneuver them. They dress her in polyester robes; they crown her with a fake-gold diadem; they balance her on a tinsel moon, under a spray of aluminum stars. Only then will she comfort them; only then will she intervene, and grant them their fate.

It's a tired saw that 'characters take on a life of their own': that they turn the narrators into whatever they want. It's the same in everyday life: we create our own personae, and they become us. But does 'everyday life' really exist? Isn't it always fraught with trip-wires where we stumble, trap-doors where we vanish, or pop-up jails where we're caged by grief? Or cables that hoist us to the rafters, so we can watch ourselves below—treating others like marionettes, while they do the same to us?

I've learned from the angels what the whales taught you: a lack of fear, an intrepid self-exposure. We must polish our surfaces—we must curate every movement. A dolphin's skin is fairly tough, so she can thrash and leap without destroying herself. A whale's skin is more sensitive, so she avoids touching anything harsh—a different form of strength. These are just two of the approaches angels take. Sometimes, when you swim with orcas, all you can do is glide wherever the currents lead...

Everything is present to us here, and 'here' is every-where. But it's nowhere, too. As Virgilio wrote to you: 'If we've crossed the event horizon. If we're the trinity. If we're the lover, the beloved, and the love: the love that flows between us, back and forth. If we're already that love, why collect more experience?' Amado and I prefer to keep on the move. Virgilio has chosen a changeless picture: that is his eternity.

Memory unreels from the present to the past; that's why our narrative unspools in reverse. And Chiara, you'll note how we've mimicked various styles. Yours, mine, Horacio's, and Virgilio's: the lyric, the ludic, the Latinate, the lumbering. Lamia's and Frederica's, too: the smutty-serpentine, the faux-aristocratic. And Amado's, the acme of the masculine, with all its faults. Out here he's a paragon, a burst of stardust, incarnate and exuberant. To the archangels, he's the arch-human: he also veers into the feminine, the apex where he becomes you and me.

You'll learn that in the afterlife, we adopt personae at will. It's how we behaved on earth—though with no limitations now. For us Mirandas, it starts in infancy, when we play dress-ups with our mother's clothes, or clomp around in our father's shoes. Everything is just a passage, a paragraph. We say we have convictions, but we shed them at the drop of a hat. We claim we inhabit reality, but it's only a painted backdrop with potted palms. Along comes a fire, and the set burns down. War grinds our machines into flakes of metal; soot covers the ruins of our towns. As we sit before the mirror, they're the sequins and mascara of all our borrowed things.

Out here we're the reductio ad absurdum, the reductio ad divinum, of Kleist's godly puppets—those fulcrums of the universe—and Rilke's seraphic marionettes. It's not that we don't have hearts, it's that they're made of wood. Earthly hearts are too humorless, too soft. We've been reborn in iron cradles. You'll see someday: this is what we absorb from the angels, as they rush from here to there. But when we ride them like speeding centaurs, we realize how patient they are as well. As their wings propel them forward, they're also standing still.

Infinite space is a waveless ocean, a sea without a shore: at times, it's much too grand for us to bear. In his final elegy, Rilke leaves Duino Castle. He strolls through the town, with its carnival in full swing. He talks with laborers and peasants, attentive to their concerns. He's on an ordinary street, and then in a homestead, among the animals and plants. Everything is simple. That's when he awakens from his poem. That's when he grasps that angels and puppets are the same—as plain and hard as truth.

*A*s I related in the 'Foreword,' Midnight at Sea owes its origins to a scuffed, leather briefcase packed with notebooks. Artemisia Vento, a Sicilian travel writer, entrusted them to me in 2016. Familiar with my efforts as a translator and editor, she'd sent a message to my website, shortly before she moved to Asia. She took it as a sign when she discovered I was living on her native island, in the historic center of Palermo. She was there too, by chance, at an elderly aunt's palazzo on the Via Paternostro. On a radiant day in early October, we met at a sidewalk café, shaded by the towering trees of the Giardino Garibaldi.*

This would be her 'last week in the West,' Artemisia confided. She'd already made a farewell visit to her parents, south of Siracusa. On a whim, she'd decided to leave me her 'scribbles': for many years, she'd been drafting a lengthy narrative. 'It's not exactly a grab-bag, but the three divisions differ widely. If you care to give them a glance, you'll see what I mean. Who knows? Maybe you could turn them into a trilogy of novels.'

Was it her reassuring gaze? Her even-tempered charm? Whatever the reason, I took to her on the spot. After skimming through the manuscript, I asked her a number of questions, as we strolled through the city over the next few days.

Though she'd split the narrative of volume one (which I later entitled Sailing to Noon*) among nine voices, in* Midnight at Sea *she retains no more than four of them:*

Lamia, Horacio, Amado, and Catulo. But she adds a fifth narrator, the painter Virgilio, who is only briefly mentioned in the previous book. Chiara, an Italian journalist (whose thoughts may mirror Artemisia's own, much as she denied it), figures here as their interlocutor, the 'sister confessor' to whom they all speak. Did this reflect a methodical shift from the first to the second person? I asked my new Sicilian friend. 'Aha, you've found me out!' she laughed. 'No doubt you've also noticed that my last block of notes is in the third person.' She conceded that this trinitarian structure of 'three persons of the same narration' reflects a theological subtext. 'What can I say? Once a Catholic, always a Catholic. But I don't think anyone can accuse me of being dogmatic! Quite the contrary,' she quipped. 'Some might complain that I treat sacred themes with too much flippancy.'

As to flippancy, hadn't she overdrawn her protagonists, verging on parody? 'You don't know the Caribbean very well! In fact, I toned them down.' From early on, the characters in Dickens, Trollope, or Balzac (and later in her reading life, Goncharov, Vargas Llosa, or Galdós) had amused her with their zany tics. All the same, satire should never be dismissed as reductive; members of a class, nationality, or any other cohort are individuals, not stereotypes. 'Who's to dictate how others should sound and behave, much less think? Doesn't this depend on factors like their age, education, and experience? Don't Anglos vary widely among themselves, and Italians, too? On the other hand, foreigners often understand us *better than we pretend. It might be a matter of distance—the greater inclusiveness of a panoramic lens.'*

Why had she created Canuba, instead of depicting an actual place? In her case, she felt, 'hyper-realism' made no sense. She'd spent her youth on several continents, never staying put for long. As a reporter, she'd crisscrossed the planet—though the Caribbean had always lured her back. Her island was an amalgam of Venezuela, coastal Colombia, Hispaniola, Cuba, and Puerto Rico, with other elements thrown in. Canuba's creole was a potpourri; its flora and fauna, too. It even had its own dance, the cambuca. Readers could liken the island to their own countries, or reject any similarity; in either case, they'd be right. In its humble way, Canuba resembled Macondo or Yoknapatawpha: both there and not there. She'd never presume to carve a local backdrop in stone, even 'Nodica,' her alias for her hometown; her subjectivity would interfere. Her sister Nina's 'Nodica' was alien to hers, though they were raised side by side.

I tried to pin her down: wasn't Chiara her alter ego? 'No, not at all! I'm too much of a prude; besides, she's hooked on romantic illusions. I fused several friends to write her script—just as I did with the rest of my vaudeville troupe.' I smiled. Then all your characters are playing roles? 'Oh yes, unconsciously or consciously, to the point of "camp." Drama: in the Caribbean, it's everywhere—even more than in Italy, and that's saying quite a lot! Each island is a small proscenium, where the actors loom larger than life. They stylize themselves into caricatures; they emote at a histrionic pitch. Once you're addicted to that intensity, the outside world seems drab... But after four decades, I've had enough. For me, the show is over.'

Ironically, by now we'd meandered to the Teatro Massimo. She gave me a brusque, double kiss on the cheeks. This would be our last conversation, she announced. 'Do as you please with "our" notebooks; it's entirely up to you. My only request is that you burn them in the end.' We said good-bye on the theatre's steps, between the two huge lions cast in bronze; their Art Nouveau riders, Opera and Tragedy, had never looked more precarious. With profound regret, I watched her stride down the Via Maqueda, unswerving and determined. Her flight was due to leave in several hours; I'm convinced I'll never see her again.

Artemisia's firmness of purpose had inspired me: I accepted her challenge then and there. Sifting through the welter of pages, I perceived how her trilogy might fit into a well-established scheme. At the antipodes of Canuba, Samuel Butler welded New Zealand into a dyad: itself but also Erewhon, a faulty palindrome of Nowhere. During our chats in Palermo, Artemisia adverted to Barataria, the 'insula' Sancho Panza misgoverned—as ineptly as Columbus ruled the Spanish Main. Prospero's island, where he demotes Caliban to a Taíno slave, is cut from the same bloodied cloth. As these works affirm, while we'll never expiate our colonial past, we can disavow its triumphalist screeds. Humanity's anchor, too heavy to raise, drags destructively across the ocean floor. Seen through a whale's eye, every corner of Europe has also been a colony, even if the overlords have switched command.

Beavering away, I began to perceive another tripartite division in Artemisia's notes. The book I published earlier as Sailing to Noon *focuses on primal nature and untrammeled love.* Midnight at Sea *is devoted to the visual and performing arts: painting, cinema, music, and choreography. The third novel,* Return to Dawn, *will explore society and politics, acted out as a multi-traditional drama on a three-tiered stage.*

From its opening bars, Midnight at Sea *is permeated by music. In Palermo, Artemisia affirmed that my edition of the book might trace a quadruple arc. Its monologues echo the movements of a Late Romantic chamber work—especially by Brahms, her musical lodestar. Lamia's section corresponds to an allegro ma non troppo; Virgilio's, to a ponderous adagio; Horacio's, to a quirky scherzo; and Catulo's, to a breathless presto. As in a composition, leitmotivs reappear, and other themes are developed with variations: adhering to the melodic paradigm, I have left these reprises intact. Such an approach accords with the personae themselves. Lamia and Horacio are professional musicians, and Catulo's choreographies are accompanied by extensive scores. His backdrops are provided by Virgilio, whose ekphrastic descriptions of artworks slow the tempo of his soliloquy almost to a standstill.*

Lamia, Virgilio, and Chiara undergo episodes of synesthesia, which combine the auditory and the visual. Cinema unites them par excellence: tributes to the seventh art crop up often in these pages, particularly in the Lamia and Catulo segments. American and Italian films predominate, from Gone with the Wind *and* The Wizard of Oz, *to* Una giornata particolare *and* Un borghese piccolo piccolo. *A curious exception is the Japanese cult-classic* Demon Pond, *which weaves itself into the plot. Apart from recurring citations of* The Tempest, *linked to the Miranda surname, the one performing art that gets short shrift is theatre. Artemisia's annotations reserve it for the undergirding of book three—along with opera, the apotheosis of stagecraft.*

Midnight at Sea, *as its title implies, is the most somber volume of* The Caribbean Trilogy: *three of the narrators, Virgilio, Catulo, and Amado, address Chiara from beyond the grave. Yet true to Artemisia's tragicomic bent, there's plenty of humor added to the mix: a mock academic conference, or Countess Frederica's spat with the Polish Baron, Valentín. The gritty comments of the Asociación C y E, along with Amado's streetwise grace-notes, recall the Ländler or Gypsy fillips that leaven Viennese chamber-works.*

Zestfully, Amado and Catulo no longer suffer from their misfortunes on earth, whereas Lamia's lovelessness and Virgilio's abnegation seem to leave them in limbo, straddling life and death. Painting is an art of contemplative visual stasis, however animated its subjects may be; dance thrives on motion and communal patterns. The marked contrast between the brothers' sections springs in part from their chosen fields. A testament to unity, Catulo's final tales subsume Chiara's memories, exalting the symbiosis of friendship.

In all the narratives of Midnight at Sea, *arcane allusions abound—a nod to the choreographer's 'latest theory.' Rightly or wrongly, he considers such flourishes a trademark of Latin American writers: correctives to unfounded self-doubts about their own provinciality. He detects this even in the most eminent authors, such as Lezama Lima and Borges. Anachronistically, he might've applied his notion to the dense intertextuality of Roberto Bolaño. As the translator and editor, far be it from me to 'correct the correctives,' or 'Hemingway-ize' Artemisia's baroque extravagance. As Catulo jibes, his principle comes to the fore in the Miranda brothers themselves. For example, in the afterlife, he claims that he and Amado are reveling in angelic orgies of 'pneumatic sensuality,' quoting the Puritan John Milton as his literary authority. He might also have referred to the explosive congress between a woman and a seraph in Laura Restrepo's novel,* Dulce compañía, *or the similar scene in Tony Kushner's play,* Angels in America.

In Palermo, I examined the topic of sexuality with Artemisia at some length. Though she called herself 'priggish,' and did seem rather nun-like, why was there so much eroticism in her texts, down to the most scabrous and granular details? She threw up her hands. 'Hahaha, you can't tell a book by its cover—or a monk by his habit, as we say in French! I've spent time in Asian temples where the sisters alternate their retreats with bouts of 'street-walking,' unperturbed by the slightest guilt. In the West, we might hearken back to the ambiguous mores of the Abbaye de Thélème in Rabelais, where the "coed" cloister encourages amorous dalliance. All the same, I need not remind you that my characters have nothing in common with myself. Or who knows, maybe they created me, so I'd create them!'

It would be easy to conclude that Artemisia was striving to overcome the Italian dichotomy of the Virgin and the Whore, which admits no gradations between these poles. But surely, there's a theological dimension here as well. During our visit to Santa Maria dell'Ammiraglio, with its Byzantine mosaics of brilliant blue and gold, she asserted that she took very seriously the 'twin doctrines of the Incarnation of the Logos and the Real Presence in the Host.' In a key passage of volume one, Chiara attends a Mass. Of the words at the Elevation, 'Hoc est corpus meum'—'This is my body'—she declares that they are 'simple and magnificent. They say nothing more— and nothing less—than the mystery of life itself.'

By extension, it might be supposed that the more radical the fleshliness of experience, the more deeply spiritual it becomes—though the Propaganda Fide would hardly condone such a view. Nonetheless, the Doctor Mysticus of the Church, St. John of the Cross, repeatedly invoked in The Caribbean Trilogy, couches the marriage of the soul with God in vividly carnal metaphors. These derive from the biblical Song of Songs—the subject of impassioned glosses *by numerous saints, from Gregory the Great to Bernard of Clairvaux.*

Another issue we broached was 'cultural appropriation.' In his musings, Virgilio describes many of his artworks, whether executed or not. He's haunted by the seduction of the image, convinced that only a picture can draw us in, expand our vision, freeze the music of time, remove us from ourselves—and in the process, turn us into ghosts. Controversially, he also introduces plates from the Taíno codex, an indigenous manuscript from the early sixteenth century. In that apocryphal tome, the last Native Americans of Canuba have assembled an album like the Aztec and Inca exemplars, with pictorial panes scattered throughout the text.

Since the Taíno left no such record, Artemisia's account is fictive: as elsewhere in her trilogy, she aligns this First Nation with her own thematic ends. Yet as Virgilio observes, the healer with his brother-husband is consistent with the 'Outsider' of the Guayakis—an Arawak tribe akin to the Taíno. Carib cannibalism, a persistent trope of the Spanish, is reflected here in the ritual consumption of another warrior's manhood; such practices have been documented in various parts of the world. The graphic portrayals of strange fertility rites—unthinkable from a Western perspective—reinforce Artemisia's thesis that theology and sexuality are parallel languages, which ultimately converge.

Appropriation—a 'cosplay with others' identities'—has become a highly fraught endeavor in our time. Given the abuses of the past, we're rightly reluctant to misinterpret societies, genders, or cultures not our own. A fortiori, by channeling dozens of disparate voices in her notes, Artemisia seems to have cultivated a chorus of dissonance, a literary 'crazy quilt.' Was such an exercise well-advised? As she and I agreed in Palermo, we constantly have to interrogate who is appropriating whom, and with what intent: from derision, to neutrality, to empathy, and all the nuances in between. If the hall of mirrors grows too distorted, it can debouch in a self-defeating labyrinth—though the maze may spark a sudden revelation, a sloughing-off of illusions.

This comes home to us in Appropriate (blazoned from the outset as both an adjective and a verb), a recent play by an African-American about a family of déclassé whites in the South, squabbling over the legacy of a country estate. The author, Branden Jacobs-Jenkins, boldly jettisions the speech patterns and behavior 'appropriate' to his subjects; he 'appropriates' his foul-mouthed personae into a historical nightmare, where all their words and acts are 'inappropriate'—from their origins in the slave economy to the inevitable collapse of the plantation house.

The brooding sarcasm of Lars von Trier's Manderlay seems to underlie this corrosive agon. Significantly, Artemisia's characters sometimes make comparisons between racism in the American South and similar trends in the Hispanic Caribbean. But as she intimates, the latter derive from 'colorism,' not a stark contrast of black and white:

they're more difficult to pinpoint with any cohesion. Lamia in particular finds herself caught up in this anomaly. Though offensive to our ears, her rants highlight both the strengths and the challenges of ethnic intersectionality.

While not wanting to tamp down Artemisia's frankness, I've espoused a more cautious stance towards this and other delicate questions. In editing her pages, I've steadily consulted Hispanic-Caribbean, European, and Pan-American friends, to gauge whether the attitudes of her characters are credible. Besides moral values of all stripes, I've been obliged to map the byways of gender. Here too, I've sent the manuscript to representatives of diverse orientations. In his study of Jean Genet, Sartre dissects sexuality as a parabola of possibilities, where each person lands at some point along the curve. But what if the spectrum shifts from moment to moment, as in Canuba, and gender—like ethnicity—is iridescent rather than fixed?

The larger conundrum is whether any place, any culture, or any individual can be defined. Artemisia was raised on an island known for its quaint folkways and turns of speech, not unlike her composite Caribbean enclave. Because of education, employment, and her innate sense of rebellion, she left her native Sicily early on. Over the decades, she has adapted to many languages and cultures around the globe. As she told me in Palermo, her universalism persuades her that foreigners can learn to grasp her birthplace as she does: from the inside. Utopia, dystopia, or both at once, she gladly gifts it to others—all the more freely, since for her it only subsists in an unredeemable past.

With equal honesty, she has faced the dilemma from the other side of the looking glass, as a longtime resident of 'Canuba.' She and her Hispanic friends wondered how they could continue to inhabit a country that's no longer what it once was. Above all, how could they save 'their' Atlantis from the tourist tsunami—as typified by the mega-resorts for which Catulo works? How could they reclaim 'their' tradition, when even their memories were mostly myths? Of the many uprooted souls I've encountered over the years, Artemisia was one of the few who sailed beyond the 'untold want' of a permanent home, greeting each successive harbor as her Ithaca. But by incurring so many displacements, by enduring the pains of so many rebirths, she had only made her nostalgia more acute. As she acknowledged to me with a melancholy shrug, it had finally evolved into a yearning for nowhere. This is what John Crowe Ransom calls 'a cry of absence, absence in the heart.'

In Midnight at Sea, the characters voyage through an 'archipelago of mind.' As I've attuned myself to their unquiet voices, I've pondered whether such concepts as the 'other' and 'othering' might be amplified. In any given group, aren't its outlying members the 'others' in relation to the core? And doesn't that nucleus often implode, so that the excluded become the included? Most of Artemisia's personae have revolted against the patriarchy, the family, and the Church.

Adamant nonconformists, they're 'othered' within their own societies. Their 'mother tongues' have lapsed into a delta of peregrine idioms. Could this be 'the way we live now,' socially as well as linguistically? More than a two-lane street, tolerance may be a multi-vectored thoroughfare. We often forget that to the 'other,' we are the 'other,' too. Temperamentally, the warring forces within our personalities seem to 'other' each other, even to cancel each other out. We never know one another fully. But do we even know ourselves?

Biology tells us that sexuality is not a stable quantity, and that physical organs do not determine instincts, much less roles. As to 'race,' it does not scientifically exist. There's no such thing as a single ethnic origin: we all stem from a meshing of myriad strains—no matter how our secondary features may turn out, in the throw of the genetic dice. Our cultural strands are as reticulated as our chromosomes, thanks to constant mingling through immigration and exchange. If divergent narratives of the world can cohabit, perhaps 'appropriation,' 'intersectionality,' and 'otherness' can be energized through a fusion of clashing ontologies. Such an experiment, parlous in daily life, can best be conducted in the cyclotron of art.

As I stated in the prologue, this afterword could also be a foreword. Between them is the 'interword,' the present that shuttles back and forth—flitting through our memories and our hopes. While Sailing to Noon *propels events towards the future,* Midnight at Sea *deflects them towards the past. In both books, Artemisia invites us to peruse her chapters in either direction, or to skip around them at will, as in the random daydreams of a balmy afternoon. If we follow her suggestion, we'll embark on a reverie that each of us has known—careening from trepidation to joy, and from anguish to confidence.*

We often walk a tightrope of dread: stretched across Pascal's 'two infinities,' it hovers between the atoms and the stars. When human love recedes beyond our reach, we're tempted to seal ourselves off: no keys will unlock our solitary door. But this is when we should open ourselves to grace—however we construe that word—and thankfully begin again. Our one essential task is to confront reality with courage. The 'divine light' we ignore, fear, or praise may simply be a benign ordinariness—an unblinking acceptance of the here and now.

— HR

A Note on the Type

Midnight at Sea is typeset in Minion, which was designed by Robert Slimbach in 1990 for Adobe Systems. Minion was an early member of the well-regarded Adobe Originals program: it featured a set of type families derived from classical typographic styles. Minion is based on typefaces such as Jenson and Bembo that appeared in Venice in the late sixteenth century. It exhibits the graceful proportions, harmonious contrast between thick and thin strokes, and sculpted serifs for which these typefaces are known. Despite its venerable lineage, Minion works well for contemporary typography, and is widely used in current book design.

Hoyt Rogers has published his fiction and poetry in a wide range of periodicals, including *The New England Review, AGNI,* and *The Fortnightly Review.* As a prize-winning translator, editor, and essayist, he has worked with Viking, Knopf, Farrar Straus, Yale, Seagull, and various presses large and small. He has collaborated with Paul Auster, Yves Bonnefoy, Lincoln Kirstein, Philippe Claudel, and many others. He is the author of a poetry collection, *Thresholds,* the novel *Sailing to Noon,* and a study of the Late Renaissance. Please visit hoytrogers.com.

Artemisia Vento is the pseudonym of a travel journalist whose work appeared in countless magazines from 1978 onward, under different bylines. She specialized in writing about islands, above all in the Caribbean and Mediterranean, with a focus on village traditions and nature. At the end of 2016, she abandoned her career and withdrew from the world; she now lives a cloistered existence somewhere in Asia. The location of her community, and whether it is Buddhist, Christian, Vedic, interfaith, or secular, are secrets she keeps to herself.

Frank Báez has published eight books of poetry, as well as fiction and non-fiction works. In 2006, he received the Short Stories Prize of the Santo Domingo International Book Fair for *You'll Have to Pay the Shrinks Yourself*; and in 2007, the Salomé Ureña National Poetry Prize for *Postales*. He was selected for the Hay Festival in 2017 as a member of Bogota 39, the best Latin American writers under forty. From 2023 to 2024 he was a Mellon High Impact Scholar, at the University of Texas at Austin. His latest books include *What the Sea Brought Ashore, Dismantling My Father's Library,* and *The End of the World Came to My 'Hood.*

Mary Heebner's artworks belong to many collections both private and public, including the British Library and the Getty Center. Her numerous books combine her paintings with her writing, or pair her art with authors ranging from Shakespeare to Eshleman. Harper Collins published two volumes of Pablo Neruda's poetry accompanied by her paintings, with translations by Alastair Reid. Her fascination with antiquity informs her artworks and artist books on Lascaux, Angkor, and Classical sculpture. Please visit maryheebner.com.

Joan Tapper was the founding editor of *National Geographic Traveler*; she then moved on to *Islands* magazine, which she headed up for thirteen years. She is the author of *Island Dreams: Caribbean*, a comprehensive work on the archipelago, with photographs by Nik Wheeler. She has written many other popular books on travel, culture, and history, working with such publishers as Thames & Hudson and Random House Penguin. She is also a well-known editorial consultant, for writers of both fiction and non-fiction. Please visit joantapper.com.

John Balkwill, our late and much-regretted friend, was a book designer, publisher, and artist. He studied with the master printer Gabriel Rummonds, as well as with the wood engravers John DePol and Akira Kurosaki. He collaborated with various authors on edition projects, including Gary Snyder, Daniel Boorstin, James McPherson, and Wole Soyinka. He produced artist's books with Jacquelyn McBain, Mark Ryden, and Peter Goin, among many others. His books and prints, amply exhibited, figure in both private and public collections. Please visit luminopress.com.

Still in mid-career, **Isa Benedetti** has shown herself to be a versatile designer, not only of books but of visual media, such as feature films and television series. In those fields, she has displayed the ample range of her creative capacities. Her past credits include *The Stork, Tabula Rasa, Hotel Cocaine, Road House, Books & Drinks, Are You Afraid of the Dark?, Insular, Croma Kid,* and *Holy Beasts* (starring Geraldine Chaplin). Her forthcoming projects continue to mirror the extensive scope of her interests: *The Queen's Jewels, Minotaur: Picasso and the Women of Guernica, That Night, Melodrama,* and *The Short Life of Flowers.*

The Caribbean Trilogy

But this new world here sought, is stranger far
than his, who stretched his vans from Palos.

— Melville

Though it stands fully on its own, *Midnight at Sea* is
the second volume of *The Caribbean Trilogy*, three novels
by Hoyt Rogers (with Artemisia Vento and Frank Báez).
The first book, *Sailing to Noon*, was published by Spuyten
Duyvil in 2024: it garnered several literary prizes, including
the Independent Press Award for Hispanic/Latin Fiction.
The third novel, *Return to Dawn*, is forthcoming soon. A
sequel is also in preparation, *The Caribbean Farewell*.

www.ingramcontent.com/pod-product-compliance
Lightning Source LLC
Chambersburg PA
CBHW010602310726
48969CB00010B/2543